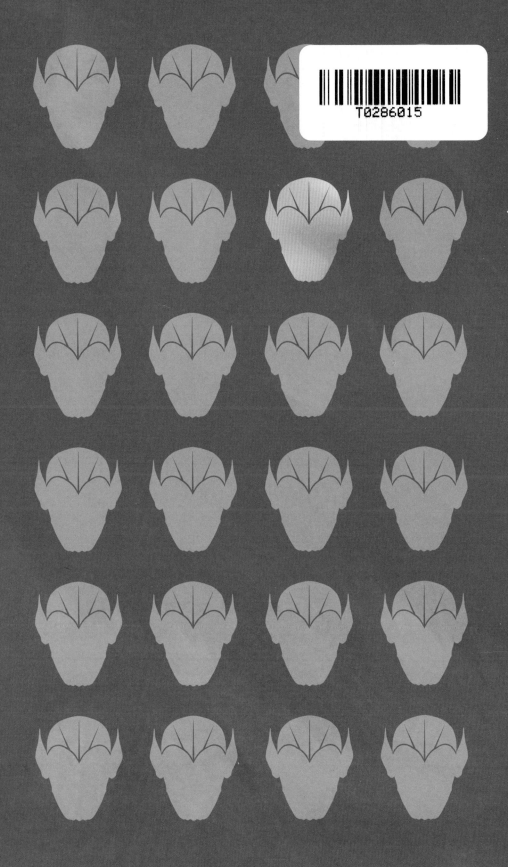

MARVEL

A NOVEL OF THE MARVEL UNIVERSE

NOVELS OF THE MARVEL UNIVERSE BY TITAN BOOKS

Ant-Man: Natural Enemy by Jason Starr

Avengers: Everybody Wants to Rule the World by Dan Abnett

Avengers: Infinity by James A. Moore

Black Panther: Panther's Rage by Sheree Renée Thomas

Black Panther: Tales of Wakanda by Jesse J. Holland

Black Panther: Who is the Black Panther? by Jesse J. Holland

Captain America: Dark Designs by Stefan Petrucha

Captain Marvel: Liberation Run by Tess Sharpe

Captain Marvel: Shadow Code by Gilly Segal

Civil War by Stuart Moore

Deadpool: Paws by Stefan Petrucha

Guardians of the Galaxy: Annihilation by Brendan Deneen

Morbius: The Living Vampire – Blood Ties by Brendan Deneen

Spider-Man: Forever Young by Stefan Petrucha

Spider-Man: Kraven's Last Hunt by Neil Kleid

Spider-Man: The Darkest Hours Omnibus by Jim Butcher, Keith R.A. DeCandido, and Christopher L. Bennett

Spider-Man: The Venom Factor Omnibus by Diane Duane

Thanos: Death Sentence by Stuart Moore

Venom: Lethal Protector by James R. Tuck

Wolverine: Weapon X Omnibus by Marc Cerasini, David Alan Mack, and Hugh Matthews

X-Men: Days of Future Past by Alex Irvine

X-Men: The Dark Phoenix Saga by Stuart Moore

X-Men: The Mutant Empire Omnibus by Christopher Golden

X-Men & The Avengers: The Gamma Quest Omnibus by Greg Cox

ALSO FROM TITAN AND TITAN BOOKS

Marvel Contest of Champions: The Art of the Battlerealm by Paul Davies

Marvel's Guardians of the Galaxy: No Guts, No Glory by M.K. England

Marvel's Midnight Suns: Infernal Rising by S.D. Perry

Marvel's Spider-Man: The Art of the Game by Paul Davies

Obsessed with Marvel by Peter Sanderson and Marc Sumerak

Spider-Man: Into the Spider-Verse – The Art of the Movie by Ramin Zahed

Spider-Man: Hostile Takeover by David Liss

Spider-Man: Miles Morales – Wings of Fury by Brittney Morris

The Art of Iron Man (10th Anniversary Edition) by John Rhett Thomas

The Marvel Vault by Matthew K. Manning, Peter Sanderson, and Roy Thomas

Ant-Man and the Wasp: The Official Movie Special

Avengers: Endgame – The Official Movie Special

Avengers: Infinity War – The Official Movie Special

Black Panther: The Official Movie Companion

Black Panther: The Official Movie Special

Captain Marvel: The Official Movie Special

Marvel Studios: The First 10 Years

Marvel's Avengers – Script to Page

Marvel's Black Panther – Script to Page

Marvel's Black Widow: The Official Movie Special

Marvel's Spider-Man – Script to Page

Spider-Man: Far From Home: The Official Movie Special

Spider-Man: Into the Spider-Verse: Movie Special

Thor: Ragnarok: The Official Movie Special

A NOVEL OF THE MARVEL UNIVERSE

SECRET INVASION

AN ORIGINAL NOVEL BY

PAUL CORNELL

TITAN BOOKS

MARVEL

SECRET INVASION
Print edition ISBN: 9781803362489
E-book edition ISBN: 9781803362502

Published by Titan Books
A division of Titan Publishing Group Ltd
144 Southwark Street, London SE1 0UP
www.titanbooks.com

First edition: September 2023
10 9 8 7 6 5 4 3 2 1

This is a work of fiction. All of the characters, organizations, and events
portrayed in this novel are either products of the author's imagination or are
used fictitiously. Any resemblance to actual persons, living or dead (except for
satirical purposes), is entirely coincidental.

FOR MARVEL PUBLISHING
Jeff Youngquist, VP Production and Special Projects
Sarah Singer, Editor, Special Projects
Jeremy West, Manager, Licensed Publishing
Sven Larsen, VP, Licensed Publishing
David Gabriel, SVP of Sales & Marketing, Publishing
C.B. Cebulski, Editor in Chief

A CIP catalogue record for this title is available from the British Library.

Printed and bound by CPI Group (UK) Ltd, Croydon CR0 4YY

With thanks to the original writers and pencilers:
Brian Michael Bendis & Leinil Francis Yu
and Jason Aaron & Jefte Palo, Roberto Aguirre-Sacasa & Barry Kitson,
Mike Carey & Cary Nord & Terry Dodson, Matt Fraction & Gabrielle Dell'Otto
& Doug Braithwaite, Greg Pak and Fred Van Lente & Rafa Sandoval,
Jim Cheung, Leonard Kirk, Brian Reed, Alex Maleev, Khoi Pham
and John Romita Jr., Michael Gaydos, David Mack and Billy Tan,
Marco Castiello, Adriano Melo, Christopher Yost,
Takeshi Miyazawa, Christos Gage & Fernando Blanco
and to Tade Thompson and Douglas Wolk.

PROLOGUE

TONY STARK

TONY STARK had never felt more alone.

That was saying a lot. He'd felt pretty damn alone on several occasions in the last year or so, never mind during his excuse for a childhood. He'd felt pretty damn alone when he'd been captured in a war zone. At least then he'd ended up imprisoned with a genius who'd designed the first version of what he'd been working on and improving ever since: the powered cutting-edge-tech armor that made him Iron Man, founding member of the Avengers and the one who usually picked up the tab for all their good works. But even during all those years of being a public hero—one who, eventually, the public came to know by name and to trust—he'd still felt pretty damn alone through all that.

But right now... yeah, this was the nadir. He'd kept fighting for what was right, pushing hard to keep the public onside with the super hero community. Since he'd become Director of S.H.I.E.L.D., the global taskforce that was the official liaison between the political world and the super hero community, he'd pushed through the Superhuman Registration Act, which had been an attempt to hold his fellow heroes accountable, to give them official status and training, to make them more than a bunch of distrusted vigilantes. He'd also spearheaded the plan to send the Hulk off into space to live on a peaceful alien world where "smashing" was, hey, probably just saying hello. Both steps had saved countless lives, those of the everyday people super heroes were meant to protect.

But from moment one of all that, Tony's so-called "friends" had jumped on their high horses.

Steve Rogers had actually *led an army* against him. Because, it seemed, Steve Rogers, when push came to shove, cared more about getting to be Captain America than about, you know, *America*. The media had started to call it the Super Hero Civil War. That made it sound much more glamorous than it had been. It had felt more like the end of the world. Tony's side had won, like they were always going to, because getting the public onside with "I want to wear a flag and beat up whoever I like with no consequences" can only get you so far. But it had been such a hollow victory. Even those he'd been onside with now seemed to be holding him at a slight distance. It had been a bitter business, they seemed to think, and that bitterness now felt like it was being directed at him. These days he was basically in charge of super hero culture, and he was absolutely sure the world was now a safer place because of it, but it had left him… yeah, pretty damn alone.

And of course, Steve had gotten himself arrested, and the bad guys had used that opportunity to… to assassinate him. Steve Rogers was dead. Captain America was dead. Tony closed his eyes at the pain of the thought. His job was to anticipate consequences, to follow chains of cause and effect as far as chaos would allow. He should have seen that coming. That thought haunted him night and day. He opened his eyes again. No. He couldn't let himself be drawn back into brooding about that, because… because…

Because now, now with what he'd just discovered… well, it was the worst possible time for him to be isolated, and the worst time for there to be no Steve Rogers to annoy the hell out of him, because it turned out the world was being threatened by something else he hadn't anticipated—and what was coming might be the actual, not metaphorical, end of it.

He sat now, in his Iron Man armor, in a randomly selected empty warehouse belonging to Funtime Inc., a shuttered Stark Enterprises subsidiary. He sat with a body bag at his feet. He sat there waiting to see if anyone would respond to the call he'd sent out.

Energy fluctuation detected, said his armor, *matching Dr. Stephen Strange's projection from the astral plane. Identity confirmed. Occupation: Sorcerer Supreme.*

And there he was, Doctor Strange, cape and all, shimmering before him, not quite there, an angry look on his face. Strange was the guy who'd made it his job, solo, to deal with all the threats to the world that came from the brand of extra-dimensional advanced technology that people like Strange liked to call "magic." He was, justifiably, an arrogant so-and-so, quite akin to Tony himself. They didn't ever seem to see eye-to-eye as a result. And Strange had become a big part of the alternative or rebel faction of super heroes who still sought to oppose what they probably saw as his evil deeds. Whatever. Tony was incredibly heartened to see him now.

"Whose body is that?" Strange said. So, straight past the hellos.

"I didn't think you'd show up."

"Curiosity... got the better of me."

"Well, of part of you."

"I'm on the astral plane. I thought it best if there was a barrier between us. All things considered. Now, who is that?"

Tony found he couldn't help himself. "How is everyone? How are *your* Avengers?" Because that was what they still felt able to call themselves, the team that Strange had committed himself to, the team the public supported now (according to the polls) but would, as soon as they messed up, quickly come to regard as vigilantes with no official sanction.

Strange sighed. "Please do not start your 'why are you doing this?' thing with me—"

"I wasn't going to. I don't care about any of that right now."

His armor beeped to signal an approaching presence. *Blackagar Boltagon*, it said in his ear. *Alias: Black Bolt. Occupation: Monarch of the Inhumans. Identity confirmed.* So, it wasn't going to be just the two of them.

Into the room strode the king of that hidden race of genetically altered people, silent as always. He pointed immediately to the body bag. Strange just shrugged at him, the closest Tony had ever seen the Sorcerer Supreme come to rolling his eyes. Tony had no idea where the Inhumans stood on all he'd achieved. As foreign nationals, the Superhuman Registration Act didn't apply to them, and they'd never seemed to have any special fondness for the Hulk. Were they even super heroes?

His plan not to say anything until a significant number of his peers had deigned to join him in the flesh then paid off. Inside the room appeared Reed Richards, the leader of the group of scientific adventurers known as the Fantastic Four and, beside him, the half-mutant half-Atlantean Namor, King of Atlantis, both of whom had previously been invisible. Much of what applied to Black Bolt also applied to Namor, with a side order of "foolish humans and their petty conflicts." Reed, however, had always stood by Tony, because here was a man who valued rationality above all else. He had even stuck to his principles when his rather more, err, feisty, wife, Susan Storm-Richards, had sided with the rebels. Those two were trying to work it out now, and Tony was being a little lax with the rules to let them do that. Which was, hey, corruption, from a certain point of view, but he was pretty sure that was the only time he'd ever given in to the idea of one law for his people, another for the rebels. And it had been about showing mercy to someone on the other side. The fact that Reed, of all people, should join his frenemy Namor in wanting to arrive here stealthily... well, that was what Tony meant about his friends keeping him at arm's length now. "Tony," said Reed. Namor just folded his arms.

The door opened and in walked... *walked*, okay, because he was usually in a wheelchair, but hey, such transformations happened in their line of work... Professor Charles Xavier. Xavier was the visionary who'd anticipated a future of conflict between *Homo sapiens* and the mutant offshoot of it who called themselves *Homo superior*. Which was just terrible branding. Such people usually had super-powers, and Xavier had wisely made them into a community of super heroes. And thus, many of them had fallen under the purview of the new laws. But a few months ago, in a terrible event that had been nothing to do with Tony, thank god, one of their own—a former Avenger even—had decimated their ranks, removing the powers of 91.4 percent of all Earth's mutants. Many of the remainder, under the aegis of Xavier's "X-Men" project, now lived on an island off San Francisco, which Tony called putting all your eggs in one basket, but hey, whatever suited them. Xavier had always insisted that X-Men live under the local laws, and honestly Tony's issues were the least of his problems, given that he was currently at odds with those living on that island, but neither had he been returning Tony's calls lately. "Good day, everyone," he said now, mild as ever, on the surface.

Tony's armor confirmed the identities of everyone present... as far as it could.

So, they had all finally decided to join him. These were the individuals who'd taken it upon themselves, before the Civil War, to hold summits about the state of the super hero community. The six of them had sometimes saved the world just on their lonesome. They were the great power brokers of their kind, and Tony felt pathetically grateful that he could still bring them together. Perhaps there was now some hope after all.

"Is... is that Captain America?" said Namor, pointing at the body bag, a look on his face that was schoolboy adulation morphing into fury.

"Of course not," said Tony, yet again enormously frustrated with what his colleagues believed him to be capable of. He bent to unzip the bag. "This was brought to me. I thought it was worth getting us together again. To show you this." He stepped back from the bag to let them see what was revealed.

Inside the bag lay the corpse of an alien Skrull, one of a shape-shifting interstellar empire that had occasionally been a thorn in the side of he and his colleagues and, well, Earth. Skrulls could impersonate anyone, really well. And this one, as its costume revealed, had been impersonating Elektra Natchios, the great assassin and occasional right hand of the crimelord known as the Kingpin.

"How the hell did you get that?" said Strange.

Tony had been anticipating that reaction. "Jessica Drew, Spider-Woman, brought it to me. Your 'Avengers' found it in Japan. And you didn't think to tell me?"

Strange had an awkward look on his face. "Given your recent actions, we thought *you* might be a Skrull."

"Because my recent actions aren't, you know, *in character*?"

Strange shrugged. "There is that. Still, I'm surprised at Jessica. I thought she was one of us."

"She still is." Tony refrained from adding "you idiot." In actual fact, Jess was clearly trying to keep her friends in both camps, which Tony honestly thought was admirable, if kind of misguided. "She's just got a sense of responsibility about the bigger picture. From what I've been told, Skrull Elektra was quietly taking control of the Japanese underworld."

"She was undetectable by my magic," said Strange, "by Wolverine's mutant senses and by Spider-Man's superhuman ones. We only realized she was a Skrull when she died and reverted to her natural form."

Richards stood up from checking the body with one of his many scanning devices. He was always fascinated by Skrulls. His team had been the first super heroes to meet them, and had immediately ticked them off. "That's an entirely new development. That's fascinating. We'll need to do an autopsy on it."

"*Yes*," said Tony, relieved. "We need to find a way to detect them while they're still alive."

"Where is the real Elektra?" asked Xavier.

12   "Dead. Gone. I don't know. I got S.H.I.E.L.D. to search.

She's nowhere to be found. I brought this to you because I think this means we're at war. And I think it's our fault."

The looks on their faces told Tony that they got what he meant. Though it had happened years ago, the memory of it was fresh for all of them.

THE SIX of them had journeyed to the Skrull homeworld, immediately after the Avengers—united and mighty back then— had put an end to the Skrulls' devastating war with the militaristic aliens known as the Kree. The six of them had hidden their spacecraft using Strange's magic, and had listened in on the Skrull Emperor delivering the mother of all "it's been a bad year for us and there are going to be layoffs" speeches. The Emperor had spoken of a prophecy, that the Skrull homeworld would be destroyed, but that the Skrulls would find a new home having conquered Earth. Yet, and this had brought a smile to Tony's face back then, they'd just had their asses kicked by one single human being, a civilian at that, whose latent psychic powers had turned the tide of battle in the Kree-Skrull War. A Skrull scientist had stepped forward then and talked of how Earth was home to an unusually high number of such "genetic atrocities," the sort that Skrulls killed at birth.

"We simply cannot expect to conquer the Earth with a frontal attack." That was what the scientist had said. Those words came back to Tony now with particular force.

Now he wished they'd listened a bit further, but that had been the moment when, surfing the drama, Tony and his colleagues had elected to reveal themselves, their images projected into the Emperor's chamber by Strange. "We will not tolerate another invasion attempt on the Earth," Richards had told them. Because it was Richards, who was almost as malleable in form as the Skrulls were, who'd always beaten them from their first encounter, that they feared the most. "This is a warning. Our world is defended. However, if the Emperor were to declare that the Skrulls have no claim on the Earth… then there could be peace between us. And the fruits of mutual exchange."

The Emperor, to give him credit, had taken a moment to think it over. "Every single member of your species will die under my rule," he'd finally said. "And your families will be the first blood I taste."

Richards, always the daddy, had looked more disappointed than angry. "Well, obviously I'm sorry to hear you say that—"

"Black Bolt," Tony had interrupted, because he'd had no more regards to give, "what do *you* have to say?"

And the King of the Inhumans had opened his mouth that day and had allowed himself to utter a single syllable. That was Black Bolt's power and his curse, that his words had literal, gravitational, weight. He had to keep his silence, always, or disaster erupted.

That single syllable, something like a sigh, had blasted the Skrull Emperor's barge into subatomic particles from stem to stern.

They had tried to speed away in the craft that had brought them there, Namor exulting in the deaths of their foes, Richards tutting at him for it, but nemesis had swiftly come for them. The Skrull defense systems closed around them like a fist. They had always known it was going to be tough. They had thought it would be worth it to neutralize a future threat. But Tony had realized, as he floated in space that day, the ship flying to pieces around him, Skrull forces closing in from all sides, that hey, maybe they had shown a little hubris here, just six of them taking on an entire empire.

HIS MEMORIES left him, and he was back in the room with the corpse and his (maybe) friends. "One Skrull dresses up," Namor was saying, pacing and gesturing like he was onstage at the Met, "and you say that means we're at war?"

So Tony was going to have to go there. "After the year we've had? Yes. The Avengers have been torn apart. The mutants are all but gone. Your own undersea nation has been devastated. Nick

Fury, the guy who created S.H.I.E.L.D., got paranoid and seems to be in hiding and Cap... Captain America... is dead. Doesn't it feel like we're being worked over, manipulated from within?"

"A lot of that," said Namor, "was *you*."

"No! I mean, yes, okay! But also no! Everything is upside-down. I can *see* it now. Looming ahead of us. And this body... this is the key!"

He looked around them. If they could have seen his face under his mask—which he wasn't going to remove around his antagonistic former friends with super-powers—they'd have seen how wild he probably looked at this moment. Because Skrulls got to him like they got to all of them. All six of these people had been captured by them, tortured by them...

IN HIS case, the Skrulls had just taken away his armor. Later, he'd heard the awful things they'd done to the others after their capture following the destruction of the Imperial Barge, but in his case they had just realized he had a heart condition, that his armor kept him alive—or at least it had back then—and so they had deprived him of it. They'd put him in a cell, naked, waiting to see what happened.

Or that's what he initially thought they were doing. Because then they had done something else, something that his mind was dragging him back to now. The guards outside his cell had been suddenly cut down by lightning. A magic Viking hammer had blasted the door open. And there had appeared the Avengers of that time, with the Vision and Quicksilver.

"It seems thou art in need of some friendly assistance!" Thor had bellowed.

It had taken Tony a moment, but he'd got there. "Oh, come on! How dumb do you think I am?"

The Skrulls impersonating the Avengers had immediately given it up and started arguing amongst themselves about how this wasn't the way to get information out of him. But one of them had had a brain on them, the one playing Cap, of course. "Wait," they'd said, "this is interesting. He didn't *expect* his teammates to rescue him. No one knows he and the others came here!"

Excited by having gained that tidbit of intel, the Skrulls, laughing, had come closer, Thor giving Tony a little slap just because he could.

Which had been the moment when Tony had seized that devastating technological Skrull weapon in the shape of a hammer from his hand, and, having figured out from across the room how the alien activated it, fried them all.

He'd managed to execute, at high speed, an escape plan, improvised on the fly. He'd freed Strange and Xavier first and they had brought vast destruction down on the Skrulls as they'd freed the others. They'd finally sped off into space with a magical and mental image of Galactus, the Great Devourer, protecting them.

It had all been... so easy.

NOW HE looked back to the others around him, to Namor pointing in his face and again yelling at him. "Tell us plainly what you are trying to say!"

All right then. "We're at war because the first shot has been fired. That shot was Strange and the Avengers not trusting me about this corpse, thinking I might be a Skrull. That distrust is a shot, because it was fired by the Skrulls' main weapon: stealth. None of us could have detected this thing. So we need to find a way to... trust each other again, to build that trust! And if that means I have to—"

"Actually," said Black Bolt, "I have a better idea. I take the body." Everyone turned to stare at that very precise, very English voice that none of them had heard before. That completely impossible voice. That voice that meant— "And your people die," Black Bolt finished, "so that my people may live." And then he took a breath.

Massive energy fluctuation detected! shouted Tony's armor.

16   Everything around them turned to fire.

TONY LAY in the rubble, recovering from the enormous noise, from the shock of his world becoming a blur of motion. His armor had saved him, had taken the blast, and was now desperately trying to recharge as he was desperately trying to raise himself, hoping against hope that his colleagues... his friends... had somehow... somehow...

A shadow fell over him. A Super-Skrull, the enhanced warrior form of their military class. Tony saw, through the smoke, its body morph smoothly from the form of Black Bolt into its natural green, muscular shape, ears spiking backward, eyes full of hate. Except this one, as Super-Skrulls tended to do, wore the colors of one of its foes, the power set of which it was now duplicating, a costume that Namor had once favored. Oh god, did that mean—

Out of the smoke flew Namor, straight at the impostor, bellowing his battle cry. "Imperius Rex!"

Well, that answered that question, at least. But Tony's mind was stacking a whole bunch of others, including whether the Inhumans had been ruled by that Skrull, and for how long, because there was surely a set of decisions that had subtly shaped the world—

The Super-Skrull spoke another syllable with his synthesized Black Bolt powers and Namor went flying.

But then Strange was up, his hands blazing with power. "Conjuring a containment spell. If someone—"

And there was Xavier, his hands to his temples. "You monster!" he shouted at the Skrull, getting its attention.

The Skrull actually laughed. "Monster? I am you."

What did that mean?! Xavier staggered back, shouting in pain. Did this thing have his powers too, or... or was that all for show? Was this even the real Xavier?

Tony got a ping from his armor indicating it was back to full power just as the Skrull leapt toward him at super-speed. He managed to get a gauntlet in the way and blasted it in the face. Then Richards was on the alien, his malleable form wrapped around it, finding its weak points.

"It wants the corpse," he shouted. "Tony, get it and you out of here!"

The Skrull hauled Richards into a ribbon and threw him aside.

"Cyttorak's Crimson Bands!" shouted Strange, and there they were, impossible bonds, the nature of which itched at Tony's rational explanations, wrapping around the beast.

It broke them with a single effort, sending weird energies flying across the room, making them all stagger. Tony saw Strange wink out of existence when the wave hit him, there and then gone.

And then Namor was on the Skrull again, his face that of a soldier. It was a look Tony rarely saw on his colleagues, a look he associated with... with Cap.

Except Namor was no Captain America. "Die, you Skrull bastard!" he bellowed, and spun its neck in his hands as he hauled it off its feet.

"You can't snap the neck of a shape-shifter!" it laughed.

Namor flung the beast by the head. Its body slammed into a spike of jutting metal. It burst up through its chest. The Skrull tried to haul itself up. It roared a final, defiant cry—

And then it died.

"I know," said Namor calmly, "I was distracting you." He spat on the ground.

"You... you killed it?" whispered Tony.

"Excellent observation skills. As you yourself said, this is war."

"I... I mean it had information." Tony saw that Strange had appeared again. "Where the hell did you go?"

Strange looked taken aback. "That was... like nothing I ever—"

Alien life-forms incoming, said Tony's armor.

What was left of the roof exploded and two more Super-Skrulls dropped into the room. Tony felt his heart rate spike and his oxygen levels hit critical. They had barely survived *one* of these things! So... so it was time. Already. To do something he had only thought of as a final, desperate weapon of war. "Charles," he shouted, "you have my consent, see in my thoughts what I'm planning to do! Tell the others telepathically!"

What about you? the voice came back in his head. Tony had felt nothing, the psychic intrusion completely undetectable.

Just do it! he thought.

And he did. Tony saw Strange teleport the rest of them out. As the two enormous creatures rushed at him.

He had what he needed now. His armor had been connecting to the clustered power plants of an entire state, downloading their power at the quantum foam level. This was his last gambit. He'd been brought to the point of using that *now*. At the *start* of this war.

The Skrulls reached him. He let the power seep out from the universe underneath this one at a distance of one nanometer from his armor.

Again, the world around him exploded.

THEY FOUND him, ten minutes later, once again sitting beside the corpse, at the center of a perfect circle of smooth glass. Somewhere in that glass was what was left of the Skrulls. Half of the East Coast would now be without power for a day. He hoped the emergency generators had kicked in. He was pretty sure what he'd just done would have killed at least one innocent bystander. He would have to find out and do what he could to make amends. But he had had no choice.

"I didn't know you could do that," said Richards.

"Just the once. Now they know about it, that's the end of its usefulness. If you're a species with a faster-than-light drive, it's child's play to block it."

"I couldn't read their thoughts," said Xavier. He seemed shaken. It was the first time Tony had ever heard his voice sound like that. "The first one… its surface thoughts were exactly what I would expect of Black Bolt."

"Where is the real Black Bolt?" asked Richards.

"We have to assume the worst," said Tony.

"As you said," said Namor, "they are trying to turn us against each other."

"What have they changed so we can't detect them by any means?" said Richards. "Before... super senses, telepathy, magic: they could all work if you knew where to look."

"When they captured us," said Strange, "they took something."

"'I am you,'" said Tony, realizing what Strange meant. "That's what the first Super-Skrull said."

"Our genetic material," said Richards. "My god. And it's not just us. How many of our community have needed medical treatment over the years, have given blood samples?"

"We need to move fast," said Tony. "Because, yes, we are at war, and maybe we've already lost."

Namor was looking around them all, his expression calculating. "No," he said. "No." And suddenly he was airborne, shouting as he departed. "I can't trust any of you!"

The four of them were left standing there, looking at each other. "He's... right," said Richards. "I... we... I need to be certain of a few things before we can resume..."

"I cannot continue this conversation," said Strange.

"I am... used to sensing thoughts, knowing who... who..." said Xavier, looking agonized.

"Please," said Tony, "wait!"

But within seconds, in their various different ways, they all departed.

Tony Stark had thought earlier that he had never felt more alone. Now he knew he had been lying to himself.

Now he was alone, they were all alone, and they were at war.

And it seemed this would be a war they could not fight together.

ONE

ABIGAIL BRAND

ABIGAIL BRAND was feeling dutiful and yet also a little impatient. She was the Director of S.W.O.R.D., the Sentient World Observation and Response Department, a sister organization to S.H.I.E.L.D. that maintained as its headquarters The Peak, a space station orbiting Earth. That was the vantage point from which Brand tried, a little desperately, to keep track of all the potential alien threats in what was now looking like an extremely packed cosmos. One space station housing one agency was supposed to pay attention to literally the rest of the universe. The priorities of government in a nutshell.

So, Abigail Brand took her lunches while walking and she never needed to check her step count. But while being very busy and really quite seriously motivated by the possibility of missing some world-ending threat, she was also, as a bureaucrat by training, highly aware of morale and protocol and impressing the right people by being seen to participate in organizational tradition. That last part was particularly important to her as a mutant and an outsider appointment, and as someone who the senior members of various security organizations still looked at with sighs on their faces when her naturally green hair appeared on their Zoom calls. All of which was why, when Commander Timothy Aloysius Cadwallader "Dum Dum" Dugan, the longest-serving surviving officer of S.H.I.E.L.D., declared he was coming up for a tour of inspection, she got her department heads, and everyone else who needed a boost, assembled on the shuttle deck to meet him. Dugan had actually served in the Second World War, in Nick Fury's Howling Commandos, and was alive now only as a result of extraordinary robotics, drugs and hey, probably some magic in there too. Or maybe only his jaunty bowler hat kept his head from falling off.

"At ease," he drawled, as he doffed it to the crew, proving her wrong about that part. "This is just a get-together of two world-savin' agencies, nothin' to get the balloons out fer."

Homespun charm: check. Brand found herself satisfied at the grins she saw on the faces of her people. Now they could all damn well get back to work. "Let me show you the—"

Which was when the red alert sounded and the whole deck started flashing and blaring. She ran to the command center, Dugan and several of the department heads beside her. "We got a bogie," said Hadley, hitting sensor controls. "And it's coming in fast."

"Give me details," called Brand as the approaching spaceship swam into view. The cameras had caught it and were now focusing in at speed. It had a sleek shape, designed for atmospheric entry, but it was coming in too fast and at too steep an angle. Which meant it was either damaged or on course for a surprise attack. It was rounded, without hard points, suggesting a cargo vehicle, and it had no obvious weapon ports.

Hadley put out a radio call on all the frequencies regularly used by recognized alien species. "Unidentified alien craft hitting Earth space at vector—"

"That's a Skrull ship," said Brand. "Could be the troop transport variant. Read the damn manual."

"Ma'am."

"*One* Skrull ship?" She shook her head at how odd that was. "Keep looking. Is this an invasion?"

"Nothing, ma'am, scanning whole sky," called another technician.

"It's entered Earth's atmosphere," said Hadley. "And... it's flying. Just about. It slid out of the dive but it's still not looking like it's under proper control."

"What is this?!" Brand looked over her shoulder to see Dugan watching calmly. She was grateful to him for leaving her to it. That's what you got with the real professionals. She looked back to the screens. "Where's it headed?"

"It's... going to crash land... southern hemisphere... very southern, coordinate estimation puts it coming down..." The technician looked up at her, understanding the implication of what he'd just seen. "It'll land in the Savage Land, ma'am."

That was a hell of a place for anyone, particularly insurgent aliens, to land by coincidence. The Savage Land was an anomalous region of the Antarctic that had been created by aliens in prehistoric times. It was full of extraordinary resources: super-powered schemes were always in motion there, along with continuing general weirdness, and, yeah, actual dinosaurs. It was a rich stew already, never mind with added Skrulls. Brand turned to her communications officer. "Get me Tony Stark."

SECRET INVASION

23

TWO

TONY STARK

IT TOOK a week, but the promise of getting to conduct the autopsy on Skrull Elektra had persuaded Reed Richards to once again be in the same room as Tony. Richards had, at the door, told Tony that he had an exit ready, should, presumably, Tony show any signs of growing pointy green ears. He continued to look judgmental as well as nervous. Tony understood the latter feeling all too well. A week ago they'd both met with a Xavier who could walk, a Strange who'd vanished and seemingly returned and a Namor who'd survived the power of "Black Bolt" almost unscathed. Any and all of those things, in previous times, wouldn't have been worth mentioning… well, maybe the walking thing. But Xavier had done exactly that once before without being a Skrull. Tony would have consoled himself with the idea that Namor had killed that Skrull, except that Skrulls were absolutely ruthless enough to do things like that as part of a cover. Even now, he didn't feel he trusted Richards entirely, but he was the one with the expertise here, and Tony had decided he would keep an ear open for the sort of carefully dropped misinformation the Skrulls were so adept at.

Tony had opted to bring another specialist into the circle

today, an Avenger who'd seen his point of view during the Civil War: Henry Pym, the former Ant-Man, Giant-Man, and all sorts of other identities. Pym never could seem to choose one and stick to it. Pym only ever looked judgmental and nervous at Tony when the subject of Pym's ex-wife (and Tony's ex-girlfriend) Janet Van Dyne came up; that probably wasn't going to happen while the three of them were standing around an operating table upon which lay the naked corpse of a green alien woman. Tony brought Pym up to speed, adding that every futurist bone in his body— which was his whole skeleton—was screaming that undetectable Skrulls, undetectable freaking Super-Skrulls, on Earth meant that this now was war.

"Okay," Pym said, puffing out his cheeks in amazement, "you say they're undetectable now. What if they're not? What if it's just a trick?"

"How... could it be a 'trick'?" said Richards. He always treated Pym like he was a promising if slightly too eager pupil.

"Maybe those rebel Avengers are the only Skrulls and they're messing with Tony by setting this up. I mean, they're the only source we've got on them being undetectable, right? Them and Xavier? Maybe that explains why that group weren't onside for putting super heroes under official oversight!"

Oh, wasn't that a tempting thought? It didn't feel quite right, though. "Let's table that for now, and—"

An alarm went off inside Tony's armor. "Director Stark, this is Maria Hill at S.H.I.E.L.D. actual. You asked to be immediately informed of anything about the Skrulls. Word from S.W.O.R.D. is we've got a downed alien craft. It's a Skrull transport ship." His vision flooded with images of the crash site. Oh god, the Savage Land?! There was so much there the Skrulls could use. "Any survivors?"

"We can't tell from the satellite imaging. The Savage Land plays hell with our sensors. We have to send a team in. I can lead it myself."

"No, I'll do it." Tony turned to the others. "I have to go."

"Understandable," said Richards, "but this autopsy is also of the highest—"

"I'll call in for reports."

Henry Pym gave Tony that judgmental and nervous look, which was, it seemed, not entirely reserved for the topic of Janet. He shrugged at Richards. "He'll call in."

Tony raised his hands in frustration, wanting to pause for a moment to explain, but no, he had no time. The roof opened and a moment later he was airborne, the lab shrinking below him. He brought up the priority line to Avengers Tower. "Avengers assemble," he said. For all the good it was going to do.

THREE

DANNY RAND

DANNY RAND watched Luke Cage's posture shift as he took the call. His old friend, the hero formerly known as Power Man, the Hero for Hire, stood in front of the picture window in this empty office block in Manhattan. An empty office block that their team of Avengers—what the press were calling the "Rebel Avengers"—were secretly using as their headquarters. As the result of a racist experiment conducted when he'd been in prison for a crime he hadn't committed, Luke Cage had gained steel-hard skin and considerable added strength. He had served with huge distinction as a member of the official Avengers before Tony Stark had asked him to kowtow to authority, and Luke had been the very first person to tell him where to shove it. Danny had been proud to be at his side when he'd done that, and was proud of all his friend had done since. Luke had been initially relaxed to hear the voice of their friend Jessica Drew. She'd always maintained links with Stark's "official" Avengers—indeed, she'd just returned to their ranks, obviously because that Skrull-Elektra corpse had made her feel she had to tell someone official.

But then Luke had tensed, straightened, ready for a fight.

Danny knew he was going to switch the phone to speaker before he'd done it. Some of this foresight was down to Danny having fought alongside Luke for decades, as Power Man and Iron Fist. Some of it was down to Danny's training as a master of the martial arts. And maybe some of it was because he had the people skills to keep his enormous business empire ticking over even while he was on the run from the law, though it was pretty hard to access much of it right now without tipping off the authorities as to the location of the heroes who wouldn't sign up for official registration.

Jessica's voice rang out across the room. "Guys, I'm sorry, I had to take them that Skrull. I just had to. I knew you'd argue with me about it. Tony agreed I wouldn't have to say a word about how to find you, and we can't be tracked on this phone, and—"

"It's okay," said Luke. "We appreciate you keeping the lines of communication open, and we trust you. How's the other Jess doing?" That was Luke's wife, Jessica Jones, the super-powered P.I. who, following something terrible in her past, had given up on being a super hero. She had been with the rebels for the longest time but when they were attacked at their last safe house, she—with Luke's blessing—put the safety of their baby, Danielle, first, and gave herself up to Tony Stark, signing the Superhero Registration Act. In return, he let her and Danielle live with his Avengers at the Tower. Stark liked to make these grand gestures of reconciliation. Jess had carefully left at a point where she didn't know where the team were headed, but the current location of "the two Jessicas" had made the remaining rebels uneasy. Luke was putting the best possible face on all that. "Just tell us what's happening right now."

"Okay, thank you. Love you guys. I just got the call to assemble, but everyone's scattered, it's going to take a while for us to ship out. A Skrull ship just crashed in the Savage Land."

Danny looked around the room at the expressions on the faces of the others. The man known as Logan, or Wolverine, just grimly nodded. He'd been saying how he expected the Skrulls to make a move sooner rather than later. Logan was a mutant, a member of the X-Men who split his time between working with them and helping out their team. It was just as well being stealthy was one of the two things he claimed to be "the best at"—the other thing being extreme, bloody violence, facilitated by the adamantium skeleton and retractable claws that had been implanted within him against his will as well as by his natural mutant ability to heal just about any wound. That ability made him very long-lived and thus very certain, in an old man way, about what he stood for. He too quickly told Stark where to go.

Clint Barton had closed his eyes. He seemed to take their discovery of Skrull Elektra in Japan personally, his bad year getting exponentially worse. Clint was an Avengers loyalist, a former criminal who'd been saved from that life by Steve Rogers and set up as a super hero, an Avenger. All he'd had then was his skill with a bow—albeit an incredible level of skill—and back then he'd called himself Hawkeye. While he was with the rebels, he wore a different costume, using only the martial arts skills he'd honed throughout his career, calling himself Ronin. He'd declared that he'd be Hawkeye again when the Avengers were united once more. As though he was keeping that name pristine. Also, of course, someone else, with Clint's blessing, was using it now. And maybe he was giving her space with this gesture also.

Maya Lopez, known as Echo, the skilled martial artist who had killed Elektra and thus revealed this whole issue, looked perplexed and angry. Danny realized that, being deaf, she couldn't hear what was being said over the phone. In that moment Clint realized too and brought her up to speed using sign language. He wore a hearing aid to help with his partial deafness and she did not. Danny got the impression those two were together now, at least on and off, but if they were they kept that to themselves. Echo possessed the amazing power of photographic reflexes, meaning that she only had to see a physical movement once, even the most skilled of martial arts sequences, and she could copy it precisely. Danny envied her that and hoped he'd never have to test his own skills against someone so familiar. He doubted the real Elektra would have survived the encounter.

Pacing, his expression unreadable under his mask, but his body language showing the righteous anger that made Danny so continually pleased by him, was the Amazing Spider-Man. He had thoroughly explored both sides in the Civil War, drawn to Stark's concept of order, but finally opting for the freedom to always do the right thing. Because here was the purest super hero of any of them. He'd been doing this since he was a kid, and he did it for the best of reasons. Lately he'd taken to saying that all he was after right now was "a win that felt like a win." Of all the people in the room, if Danny ever needed to trust someone with his life, it'd be whoever was under that mask. Luke was Danny's closest friend, but Danny could say that about Spidey to Luke's face and Luke would just be like, "Mm-hm."

The only irregular member of the group they hadn't been able to locate to summon to this meeting, convened after they'd returned from Japan to talk over the next step, was Doctor Strange. His absence, given that without magic they were basically people who hit things and loosed arrows, was very much felt.

"What do you want a bunch of heroes on the run from the law to do about that?" Luke was saying to Jessica now.

"At this point," Jessica said, her voice over the phone warm and humane as always, "I trust you more than Stark to, you know, not be a Skrull. So I may have picked the wrong team here. But hey, now I've told you this, maybe you could get a head start. Wouldn't you *like* a head start? Oh. Sorry. Gotta go."

Luke ended the call, glanced at them, saw they were ready and willing, and hit another number. "Hey, man," he said, "I need a quick drop. Yeah? Great. Okay." He emailed some details then turned back to the room. "So," he said, "you guys ready to piss off *everyone*?"

DANNY ALMOST felt sorry for Natasha Romanoff as she stood beside the Quinjet on the takeoff ramp atop Avengers Tower. The Black Widow, even when she'd been leading the Avengers, had only ever *associated* with super heroes, rather than understanding the culture. She was, at heart, an intelligence officer, a spy, and she, like Logan, went back a long way. She was practical to the point of horror, and of course she'd seen Stark's point, choosing to stay in his team. Now he saw a moment of horrified reaction on her face as their team literally appeared out of thin air. They'd been teleported through a chilling nothingness by the man Danny only knew as Cloak and appeared on the other side of it at this new location, stepping out of the cloak that gave their helper his name. Cloak was someone who'd demonstrated no interest in either side of the Civil War, and yet was willing to be summoned by Luke Cage to help out. In that second, Natasha got halfway to aiming her wrist blaster with one hand while the other went to an alarm. But a moment later Spider-Man's web plastered her flat against the wall.

"You people are out of your—" she yelled before another web left her unable to do anything more than yell in an entirely muffled way.

"You guys have fun stealing Tony's car," said Cloak in a voice that had the emptiness of the void about it, and vanished.

They all piled into the Avengers Quinjet. "Man, Nat's going to have so much stuff to yell at me about," said Clint.

"You two used to go out, right?" said Luke, taking the controls.

Echo looked sidelong at Clint as they strapped into their seats. "Who haven't you gone out with?"

Clint managed an awkward grin. His answer, if there was one, was lost in the roar of takeoff. Which was probably just as well.

THE SHEER speed of a Quinjet always amazed Danny. They were out over the Atlantic and heading south in seconds. "Uh," said Spider-Man, "just FYI, Tony can control Quinjets from his armor."

"Not anymore," said Logan, holding up a mess of electronics on the end of his claws.

"He can still follow us," said Danny, "he controls the world's satellites."

"He knows where we're headed," said Luke grimly.

"I thought the Savage Land was, you know, made up," said Maya.

"It's real," said Logan. "I spent a lot of time there. Completely different temperature, different ecosystem, prehistoric animals. Great place for a vacation." His Canadian rasp was so dry that Danny never knew when Logan was being sarcastic.

"How do we know this isn't a Skrull trap?" said Spider-Man.

"Oh," said Luke, "I hope it is. I'm so sick of hiding. I'm sick of not trusting each other. Avenger against Avenger. I miss my wife and kid. I want to put this right. I want things to go back to normal."

"Amen to that," said Clint.

"When were things ever normal?" said Maya.

"Relatively speaking," said Luke, flashing her a grin. "Hey, if it takes me punching a Skrull to get us on the path back to that, I'm going to stand right there and do that. When Tony Stark arrives, he can damn well join in."

THE JOURNEY took eight hours. They talked about Japan, about how Skrull Elektra had been in political control of the organization of ninja assassins known as the Hand, about how the Hand had exercised their own mystical form of mind control over Maya. She had fought back through sheer willpower and killed her tormentor, Elektra, only to find another nightmare beneath. The idea of a Skrull being at the apex of that pyramid of dominance scared all of them. Danny spent some time sleeping and meditating, readying himself for what was to come.

With five minutes or so of their journey left, the expanse of the Antarctic ice caps beneath them, Clint, in the co-pilot's seat, reported that their pursuers were in sensor range: four flying figures and another Quinjet. The sheer firepower Stark's Avengers had compared to theirs had always made Danny hope they'd never get into a direct confrontation.

Well, maybe Luke was right about the Skrulls being something they could unite around. Ahead, clouds were rushing closer, surrounding an unlikely mass of green and brown far below. Luke set the Quinjet into a dive through the cloudbanks. They were going to have less than an hour on the ground before the other team got here. An hour in which to find the crashed Skrull ship. They'd beaten longer odds, but—

The clouds broke ahead of them. Rearing up at them was an enormous—

—mouth full of teeth?!

The dinosaur—or whatever it was—lashed out. Suddenly the forward ports were dark and all their motion had become a sickening spiral.

They burst out into the light again and a canopy of trees came up far too fast. The Quinjet plowed into the thick foliage, millions of small impacts slowing them as they slewed to a stop and finally, almost gently, crashed into a tree trunk.

They hung there, jungle suddenly outside, creepers and vines hanging past the window, the cabin visibly crumpled around them. "Thank you for choosing Avenger Airways," said Maya.

Luke unclipped his harness, fell from his seat, managed to crawl arm over arm on what had been the ceiling to get to the hatch, found it warped shut and sent it flying with a steel-hard fist.

One by one, helping each other, conscious of the minutes ticking past, they slowly made their way down Spider-Man's weblines to the forest floor. It was freakishly hot out here, and yet one could still smell in the air bitter cold, as if the odd breeze penetrated from the tundra.

Logan declared that, even if whatever new process the Skrulls were using to stay hidden meant he wasn't sure if he could sniff one out anymore, he could still smell the burning vegetation where the alien ship had crashed. He led the way at speed through the jungle, his claws ripping apart anything in the way. It took them in a straight line to a clearing that had been created by the long furrow of a spaceship crash. At the end of the trough, still steaming, lay the stubby, awkward shape of the alien ship. All that could be heard above the shrieking of the local wildlife, was the ticking of cooling metal. "Do we open it?" asked Danny.

"Whatever we do," said Logan, looking up, "we do it now, 'cuz we ain't alone anymore."

From above, Stark descended at speed in his Iron Man armor. Beside him was Carol Danvers—Ms. Marvel, as she was back to calling herself now—the most professional of them all. Carol had been career military for decades, and seemed to view her acquisition of super-powers as a continuation of that. Besides that, Stark was her sponsor in recovery from alcohol addiction. Of all Stark's allies, Carol was the one whose attitude made the most sense to those who disagreed. She was the compassionate voice of order and she had never acted toward them like they were the actual bad guys. That made her politically dangerous, but at least she wasn't going to cave your head in with her super-strength or energy blasts. Also in the air was Simon Williams, Wonder Man, a moderately successful actor and long-time Avenger who, despite the fact that he was literally made of ionic energy, had never seemed to enjoy the costume or mindset of super hero culture. He came to these affairs dressed for outdoor pursuits, not in spandex. Whenever they'd talked in the past Danny had found him distant, kind enough, but just without much in the way of commitment to everyday life. Maybe that was how actors were; maybe that was how ionic beings were. Either way, when Stark made him the offer he'd probably just shrugged and regarded it as job security. Wonder Man wasn't Danny's biggest concern, though, because beside him was the most worryingly powerful individual he'd ever encountered.

Bob Reynolds called himself the Sentry. The others were former friends, and Carol especially would not come in swinging, but Danny had never understood what the hell Bob's deal was. Everything he heard from him felt like the proclamation of someone who was in the midst of an untreated mental health crisis, and Stark fielding him in an active team seemed like incredibly risky cruelty.

"Step away from the ship!" bellowed Stark's amplified voice. "You're under arrest!"

At the same moment a Quinjet landed behind them. Out of it leapt a glaring Natasha, and beside her Jessica Drew in her Spider-Woman costume. Like so many of them, Jess was a result of genetic experimentation. She could glide, zap people, and, err, influence those of the right persuasion around to her point of view through pheromones, though she insisted she never did that with friends. Right now, she led the charge, doing her part to maintain the illusion that she was all-in for Stark. Also exiting the jet was Ares, the actual Greek God of War, who'd seemed to pick Stark's side because it was where he'd get more war and less skulking around, already laughing his head off and swinging an impossibly large ax. How the hell could Stark justify him as an appropriate hire for a peacekeeping organization? Beside him flew Janet Van Dyne, already shrunk down to her fluttering form as the Wasp. Janet staying with Stark's team had been the biggest blow of all. A founder member of the Avengers, and then Chair so many times, she'd been the one they'd all looked to in moments of crisis. Back in the day, she'd been seen as happy-go-lucky, the heiress adventurer. But then her husband and co-adventurer had turned out to be not the best guy, and everyone had seen the steel of Janet Van Dyne. Janet staying with Stark made sense. Not only had they been lovers, here was someone who knew what happened when super hero teams fell apart, who would always opt for order over chaos. Whenever the rebels encountered the official Avengers, Danny had watched his teammates have problems fighting Jan, because of her skill and energy blasts, but also because they didn't want to fight her while she would do whatever it took to get the job done. If she'd been leading the other side instead of Stark, that would have troubled a lot more consciences in the rebel faction. But Janet had been standing back from leadership for the longest time. "Is this where you all finally see sense?" she called out now. "Come on, we've got Skrulls landing on Earth!"

Of all of them, Danny was only sure that Jessica, who'd done so much to try to keep super hero culture together, wasn't a Skrull. With a lot of them, being Skrulls would make so much sense.

Luke walked up to Stark as he landed and got right in his face. "You figure you got jurisdiction in the Antarctic?"

"I figure we're fighting a war and you rushed out here to meet a Skrull warship. Plus, you took my stuff."

Carol looked between them, obviously frustrated. "But there could clearly be several reasons for that. Luke, come on, look at the odds here. Seriously, stand down. Let us handle this."

Luke adopted that look of sheer bloody-mindedness that Danny loved. "Nah," he said, "I'm openin' that spaceship." And he marched away from Iron Man to do just that. Everyone's gaze followed him.

Stark actually raised his glove, the center of his palm glowing, his repulsor blast powering up. "Luke, don't make me do this."

Luke had got to what looked like a hatch on the side of the craft. "That suit of yours can't hurt me. The real Tony Stark would know that."

And he heaved the hatchway open.

FOUR

ABIGAIL BRAND

BRAND HAD finally managed to get her satellites to pierce through the interference of the Savage Land. Now she, her technicians and Dugan were staring at screens upon which it looked like the two different flavors of Avengers were about to start fighting each other rather than do anything about the Skrull ship other than let Luke Cage rip it open.

"What the hell?" she said, listening to the microphone coverage hacked out of Stark's armor. "What did Cage mean 'the real Tony Stark'?"

"He thinks Stark's a Skrull," said Dugan. "Both teams think the others are Skrulls."

"Oh no," said Brand, amazed that that development had happened within super hero culture and that was the first she'd heard about it, "that's just—" She stopped mid-oath as she saw Dugan taking his hat off, his expression turning to solemnity. "What's this now?"

He held the hat to his chest and suddenly she saw his eyes turn into featureless green orbs. "He loves you," he said, quite gently, in a voice not at all his own.

He pressed a button on his glove.

○————————○

ABIGAIL BRAND found herself flying through the air. The air itself congealed around her and her staff as gelatinous survival capsules burst from every wall and engulfed them. *Catastrophic hull breach* was all she could think in that second as every monitor in a command deck that was disintegrating around her showed nothing but flame. And then that flame burst from below to engulf the still, calm figure of... so Dugan had been a Skrull?! This was all about Skrulls now?! When had that happened?!

She had missed it! It had finally happened, the awful thing she hadn't been able to see coming!

She saw some of the capsules that had formed around her staff being caught in the flame, exploding, fire piercing them, bodies engulfed in fire, screaming. Everyone else burst out into empty vacuum, as the Peak... the Peak was in pieces, every piece exploding, the modules cascading down toward re-entry!

She was in space. Oh god. Oh god. She was floating in space!

The gelatinous capsules were doing their job—for now—floating away from the wreck that was expanding behind them, the deaths of hundreds of people taking place just over there as they bobbed over here, helpless.

No, not helpless! She refused to be helpless! She grabbed the comms stud on her collar and called S.H.I.E.L.D., on the enormous blue green globe she was looking straight at now. "Helicarrier, please come in!" No answer. Why was there no answer?! "This is Brand, the Peak is gone, we have massive casualties! My people are stuck out here in low Earth orbit and we only have ten minutes of air! We... we need a super hero with space capabilities or a S.H.I.E.L.D. launch to orbit craft in the air *now*! Can anyone—"

She broke off, even in desperation, as her gaze chanced away from Earth. Sheer horror took hold of her gut. She could not believe that she had heard not a single whisper of what she was now seeing. Her nightmare had come true.

Shimmering into visibility right in front of her was an enormous Skrull war fleet. And they were heading for Earth.

FIVE

TONY STARK

TONY ALWAYS hated that these self-righteous former friends he was facing right now seemed to think he went about opposing them with glee, rather than, as was always the case, sadness and frustration. He wished his helmet's facial features could show how little he wanted to raise his palm and send Luke Cage flying away from the spaceship hatch with a repulsor blast—which he was pretty sure he could do, whether or not it hurt Cage—but here was a twist. Surely the real Luke would know Tony would be aiming to do that, rather than futilely attempting to harm him?

"He loves you," said a voice in his ear, coming from the comms link in his armor. It took him a moment to realize who it was. Edwin Jarvis, the Avengers' butler, who at this moment should be back in Avengers Tower looking after the systems. Tony wondered for a moment what sort of fan fiction Jarvis had been reading in his free time, but, okay, yeah, maybe that was a good, if weirdly phrased, reminder from this man who'd been father figure to them all; even when he and Cage had been brothers in arms, and that actually at heart the super hero community did still care about—

Alien virus detected, said his armor.

The pain hit him like a truck.

It rushed into his veins, into his head, spasming every muscle in his body. It was entering him through the connection to his armor, he realized in his agony, at a subatomic level. Whatever had got into the armor had, in the same instant, got inside him too. He was dimly aware of falling to his knees, screaming in pain.

"Every system has malfunctioned!" What was that voice?! He recognized it. It was Maria Hill, his deputy at S.H.I.E.L.D. "Abandon the Helicarrier! All hands! Abandon ship!" He could see it now, his suit switching to an emergency camera feed from one of the fighters that was scrambling to fly—no. To fall, to fall like a toy from the deck. The camera spun: He glimpsed the enormous bulk of S.H.I.E.L.D.'s flying headquarters rolling over in mid-air, its antigravity engines failing over New York as it desperately tried to get itself away from all those people—

"Hill?!" he managed to shout. "Hill?!" But there was only raging static in reply and the fire in his own blood.

His internal screens flashed from one emergency call to the next, across so many of his facilities, *alien virus detected* blaring out from all of them, running figures in Queens and Westchester and Long Island, explosions and screams. He could feel his body stumbling, his limbs reeling. But all his attention now was on his camera feeds from around the world.

He saw, his hands rending the air in helpless dread, the guards at The Raft, his maximum security prison for super villains, backing away in fear as security systems dropped out and all the cell doors opened. There was… oh god, which criminal was that? Was his name Shockwave? The one who didn't have a face! And he'd been let loose! And what was he doing to those guards?! It was all failing, his technology, his systems, everything he'd built, all falling apart at once!

Tony curled up around himself, oblivious to everything but physical and emotional pain, forced to watch, helpless, as his world was being very precisely torn apart.

SIX

NORMAN OSBORN

NORMAN OSBORN should have been sitting pretty at this enormous desk of his. He had respectability now. He had done that most modern of things: He'd gone into therapy and sought forgiveness. He had done it in public, entirely putting his past as the Green Goblin behind him, to the extent that Tony Stark had shaken his hand as a fellow billionaire, whispered, "Set a thief to catch a thief," winked at him and put him in charge of the Thunderbolts program.

Norman was pretty sure that thief bit had just been a joke. But he really didn't appreciate it. The Green Goblin side of his personality had murdered cops, civilians, anyone who was in the way of a series of frankly petty schemes to rob banks and rule the underworld. He had put on a ridiculous green mask, adopted a voice, and turned all Osborn's amazing patents into a gothic funhouse ride.

The therapy had been real. The seeking forgiveness part… maybe not so much. The Goblin was part of him now, no more a separate personality than anyone else's "devil on my shoulder." The job Stark had given him had presented the ideal career ladder to *actually* rule the underworld, and he no longer needed to rob banks. If he ever had. And all without having to compromise his dignity.

The position of Thunderbolts Director gave him an Actual Mountain Base to play with, here in Colorado. His job was to take charge of and reform super villains who'd been captured and opted for this instead of jail. Some of them were naively serious about the whole reform thing. Those he encouraged because they gave him no trouble. Some of them certainly shared his point of view, never expressed, that here was an opportunity to hack the system and gain real power. They went in the front row on training missions against major league super villain opposition. Or sometimes, when his team was used for political ends, against small countries within whose borders the U.S. government wanted to do off-the-books things.

The only problem with this setup was something he'd forgotten since committing to a civilized lifestyle: how annoying super villains could be. Today his charges had sent to him a "delegation," with the noble aim of, it turned out, asking about some of them going on chat shows and whatnot, to gleam before the public.

He had looked at "Songbird" and "Moonstone" and "Swordsman" in their ridiculous, personality-crutches of costumes and had begun his reply with due official politeness. "All the public need to know about you—"

"It is merely damage control before the fact," began Moonstone in that snooty academic's voice, interrupting him, "an attempt to get ahead of any sightings or encounters with civilians, where—"

Sure enough, he couldn't help himself, his voice rising to a bellow. "—is that you're a bunch of idiot criminals who are now no threat to them because *you work for me*!"

They looked taken aback by the change in him. Great. Always good to show them that. He felt it, a moment later, the mocking laughter in the back of his head. *But they don't understand who you really are. If they did, you wouldn't have to raise your voice.* The Goblin. That was fine. He knew he was always there. And if it helped keep these fools in line there was no harm in letting him out to play. He was about to take a breath and tell them to go get a coffee or something—

The picture window in his office burst into shards with an explosion of energy that sent them all flying. Norman looked up to realize that, fortunately, he'd been shielded by Swordsman's armor. Indeed, all three of his charges were hauling themselves to their feet as alarms screamed, indicating this impossible breach of their electronic security, as into the room flew... oh, what the hell was this now?

Hovering there, impossibly, was a terrifying figure. It was a man from the earliest days of Norman's career as the Goblin, an incredibly powerful alien on the side of the law, the platonic ideal of the noble adventurer who, the whole community had been told, had many years ago died of illness rather than violence. He wore a red and blue costume with a yellow star on the chest, golden rings on his wrists and ankles, and a mask that revealed a slash of silver blond hair. His fists glowed with the power that had just blown out the window.

In the remains of the window stood the Kree warrior Mar-Vell.

Captain Marvel was back from the dead.

SEVEN

JOHNNY STORM

JOHNNY STORM, known as the Human Torch, had hated the Super Hero Civil War. He had, obviously, sided with the "rebels" who hadn't wanted to have all their details logged on some government computer. That, despite the fact that his family, the Fantastic Four, or just the FF, were the epitome of the sort of "super heroes" that the public, and, okay, the government, already knew everything about. If they *were* super heroes. Johnny saw himself first and foremost as a celebrity and influencer, the charm in front of Reed Richards' scientific detachment, the one who waved from the red carpet and chatted on social media with his good friend, the pop superstar Dazzler, about his team defeating planet-ending threats like Galactus and exploring other dimensions like the Negative Zone so they could bring back cool stuff to help everyday folk. His own ability to safely emit and control flame was most satisfying for him when he was snuffing out a fire in a housing block with a click of his fingers, rather than when he was fighting any of those idiots who called themselves super villains.

But hey, he knew how tough the life of someone like Spider-Man was. It was a privilege for Johnny and his family to be able to live without masks, to afford the sort of defenses this midtown Manhattan home of theirs, the Baxter Building, provided. Johnny's sister Sue, the Invisible Woman, had the power to project invisible forcefields and walk in anywhere without being detected. With that incredibly practical brain of hers and those powers she could probably have ruled the world. But no, she felt the same way he did: the guys in masks were, by and large, doing the right thing.

So, it had come as a huge frigging shock when Reed, Sue's husband, and the supposed leader of this team, the genius of all geniuses, had said of course he thought Tony Stark had the right idea. Why on Earth would anyone think differently?

Ka-boom.

There had been the mother of all shouting matches. Reed and Sue had immediately taken it away from their kids, Franklin and Valeria: Johnny and Ben Grimm, the Thing, had found themselves doing the first stint of what was about to become a lot of Uncle Time. Ben had been particularly gentle with the children, a look on his face that said someone should give those two idiots a good talking to. Because Ben, despite having been, decades ago, transformed into a monster made of rocks, or maybe *because* of that, was the most caring of them, the most deeply affected.

Sue had actually walked out for a while, taking the kids with her. Ben, who'd refused to take sides in the "war," took to yelling at every single member of the super hero community he met that this was decadent crap and they needed to stop before they hurt someone other than themselves, eventually brought them back together. He'd knocked all their heads together, kind of literally. Reed had done some under-the-table deal with Tony Stark, and then they were all back together again... well, kind of. Reed and Sue still spent a lot of time away, sometimes together, trying to work it out, sometimes not. Right now, Reed had sequestered himself away working for Stark while Sue was... well, she was coming and going about something, probably one of her charity things.

So Ben was over to keep Johnny company and play with the kids, and the two of them had tussled a little, throwing barbs and smoke rings—and okay, just one chair—back and forth, making Franklin and Valeria laugh at how silly they were. And this time they didn't even set off the smoke detectors, which, thanks to Johnny, Reed was always having to adjust. Now they'd settled down to playing some virtual reality golf, which Ben had turned into a festival of him stumbling about, missing the ball and pretending to think he'd hit it.

The doorbell to the living area at the top of the Baxter Building rang, indicating someone had satisfied all the myriad security systems downstairs. Johnny and Ben pulled their VR masks off to see Sue, in her FF uniform, obviously on a mission, given the purposeful look on her face. "Hey, sis—" Johnny began.

But Sue walked straight through the lounge area and out the other side. "Mommy?" asked Valeria, plaintively.

"Mom needs quiet time," said Franklin, looking like this was the serious, grown-up thing to say.

Ben looked stormy at that. "Nah," he said. "You want to give her a call, matchstick? I don't think she realized we was in here."

Johnny did his best to keep the smile on his face, but he went to the videocall screen and activated it to track which room Sue was in, intending to very gently tell her that he knew how she was feeling, but maybe just get out of your head for a sec and say hi to the kids. The system quickly found Sue in… that was weird, the Negative Zone chamber? This was where Johnny had experienced, with his family beside him, some of the worst moments in his life. The chamber contained a portal to another dimension that was home to horrors that mostly looked like giant bugs. Access to the Negative Zone had to be carefully controlled. At the right setting you could just walk in. At the wrong setting, it was like a black hole trying to haul everything in this universe into that one. Johnny activated the camera feed and saw Sue standing at the controls, tapping away. Presumably some urgent upkeep Reed had sent her to do. But why wasn't Reed doing it himself? "Hey, sis?" he called again, knowing the phone in the chamber would let her hear.

Sue turned to look at the camera. She still had that absent expression on her face. And was something weird going on with her eyes? "He loves you," she said.

She hit a key.

Johnny yelled as the door to the Negative Zone dropped away behind her. "Negative Zone breach!" shouted the building alarm system. "Danger! Danger!"

"What the *what*?!" yelled Ben from across the room.

A maelstrom burst through the chamber, hauling everything in it, Sue included, into the pulsing green heart of the Negative Zone. It was only a floor above them! Johnny realized he only had seconds. He lunged for Franklin and Valeria, intending to ignite the rest of his body and blast his way out of the window with them. But he saw Ben, in the same second, grab them into his arms, intending to shield them from whatever happened next.

But even as Johnny's fingers reached all three of them, the green whirlpool blasted through the roof of the lounge area and grabbed him, grabbed Ben and the kids, grabbed everything and everyone around him—

And hauled them all off into imploding, roaring nothingness.

EIGHT

DANNY RAND

BOTH AVENGERS teams gathered around Tony's screaming, writhing form. He'd managed to haul his helmet off, but his eyes weren't focused on them: they were staring wildly into space.

"He's having a seizure," said Carol.

"I'm taking him back to New York," said the Sentry. "If I go sub-orbital—"

Danny stepped in. "That might kill him! Is anyone here a doctor? Has anyone seen Strange?"

"He's trying to distract us!" said Luke, running back over with the hatch cover from the ship in his hand. "People, I am hearing movement inside that thing!"

"It's not a trick," said Spider-Man. "I think he's been infected by something. Him and the suit."

"Get the armor off him," said Natasha. "Ares, grab the boots."

They tried, but the armor's own defenses prevented them, electric shocks sending them stumbling back and biomechanical tendrils hauling the armor plating back into place. Stark kept yelling in pain. Danny suddenly became aware that some of the group had turned away from Tony to look across to the ship.

Logan's nostrils were flaring and the expression on his face was one of sheer astonishment. What the hell could he smell?

Danny turned to look and found himself as astonished as Logan was. Emerging from the crashed Skrull ship in a cloud of smoke behind them was... another Spider-Man?!

So... that had to be a Skrull, right?

And there was Emma Frost, the White Queen of the X-Men, Jean Grey beside her, in her Phoenix costume...

But Emma Frost was meant to be on the island home of the X-Men, off the coast of San Francisco. And Jean Grey was dead, and her many deaths and resurrections were so cosmic in nature it was hard to believe that a duplicate might have accomplished them.

So those must be Skrulls, right?

And there was Sue Richards of the Fantastic Four. But, come on, there was no way a Skrull could have been living in the Baxter Building, right under Reed's nose.

She had to be a Skrull too.

Out of the smoke behind her stepped the original Vision, of the Avengers, an android who'd been ripped apart in combat over a year ago. All they'd need to do to see whether he was a Skrull would be to open him up, right? Beside him, arm in arm with him, because it looked like they were... still together as a couple, which they hadn't been in years... was the Scarlet Witch, the mutant who'd gone rogue and decimated the numbers of her people across the world.

Danny heard Logan growl at the sight of her.

Another version of Wonder Man stepped out next. And oh god, the hits kept coming, because there was another Logan, in one of his earliest costumes; Carol, in her first costume; Stark himself, if that was him, in the early Iron Man armor...

So he must be a Skrull, right? Because otherwise why would the Skrulls attack one of their own who was screaming at their feet?

If one of these guys in the ship was a Skrull, didn't that mean they were all Skrulls?

And there was the mutant known as the Beast, Dr. Henry

McCoy, in an earlier form of his… ever-changing… body, because now he looked quite different.

Danny found himself thinking that if the one they'd all worked with in the last couple of years was a Skrull, that had been an easy assignment.

But no, no, because these all must be Skrulls, right?

Now here was Thor! Thor, who'd long since shut himself away in Asgard, disgusted by the mortals fighting themselves. He'd… died or something, along with all his people, in that mythological Ragnarok thing, and then come back different and…

Oh, another easy assignment.

But no, no, because these guys here, they must be the Skrulls! Right?!

"Oh no," said Luke, beside him.

From out of the smoke stepped Luke's wife, Jessica Jones. Still wearing the super hero costume she'd showed Danny pictures of, back when she'd called herself Jewel. "Wouldn't Killgrave, the Purple Man, when he was controlling Jess, wouldn't he have found out she was a Skrull?" said Danny. "I guess only if he'd asked. Or maybe the Skrull wouldn't have actually been controlled, but would have used it to establish—"

Luke grabbed him and forced him look him in the eye. "No," he said, "because this is a lie. That isn't Jessica. That's a Skrull."

"And… I guess that is too," said Danny.

Because out of the ship was stepping, in his earliest Power Man costume, the look of which had been influenced by all the Blaxploitation movies he'd watched in prison, Luke Cage himself.

"Yeah," said Luke, "that's a Skrull."

"Anyone know where we are?" called a voice from the ship, a voice that made all of them standing here in the clearing stop staring and look at each other in amazement.

And sure enough, slowly making his way through the crowd to the bottom of the gangplank was—

"That's not Cap," said Clint Barton, sounding personally affronted by the idea.

Except it looked and sounded exactly like Steve Rogers. And… why would the Skrulls even try to fool them with a duplicate of someone they knew to be dead.

"This is a psy-op," said Natasha, beside them. "Every one of those Skrulls has been picked for maximum impact in one community or another, the messages their existence convey are a bunch of contradictions that—"

"Oh no," said Clint.

Danny looked to see who it could be now. The last two out, at the back of the crowd, were holding hands. It was another Clint, in his Hawkeye costume, and beside him… oh no.

It was Clint's dead wife, Bobbi Morse, the Mockingbird.

"That," said Maya, immediately joining them, "is a Skrull."

"Right!" said Danny. "Right?"

"Oh my stars and garters!" exclaimed this version of the Beast.

"Sweet Christmas!" agreed the impostor Luke, staring at the heroes gathered in front of them in the clearing. Luke had always euphemized his speech patterns around his rich clients back in the day, and now around his family.

"Is this it?" asked the new—or old—Carol from the spaceship, seemingly a genuine inquiry to the heroes standing in front of her. "Did we make it back to Earth?"

"Yeah," said this new Logan, "I was just about to say that, 'cuz I'm seein' some familiar costumes here… and some familiar faces… but I don't think we're talking legacy heroes, 'cuz I'm smelling some familiar scents too." With the sound of adamantium slicing through his own flesh, he popped his claws. "I know who I am," he yelled. "I've spent the last few years fightin' Skrulls for that. And maybe I ain't stopped yet, because who the hell are you all supposed to be?!"

NINE

REED RICHARDS

REED WAS glad that he'd kept working all night in Tony's laboratory, Henry Pym beside him, and he was especially glad that they'd switched off all distractions... even if he couldn't now find his damn phone... because he was pretty sure they'd finally got it. He went through the biology again on his tablet, running the test results from the Skrull-Elektra corpse a third time, just to be sure, and then he finally felt ready to say it out loud to Henry, who'd been such an enormous help. "We did it," he said. "I know exactly how the Skrulls made themselves undetectable to all our systems, to Logan's and Spider-Man's senses, and even to magic and psychic powers. It is indeed based on our DNA. It's incredibly clever."

"Thank you," said Henry, producing an alien gun from inside his jacket and pointing it at Reed, quite calmly.

"Oh no," Reed managed to say. "Not you too." He sent a thin tendril of himself snapping out from his back toward the alarm button. "Listen, I've known Skrulls, I've worked alongside Skrulls, we don't have to—"

The Skrull who was Henry Pym fired.

Reed felt his body explode, every part of him stretching to its fullest extent, his eyes and fingers and skin and uniform and hair expanding in a moment to splatter all over the wall and furniture of the lab. At least that was how he consciously understood it, a moment later, as he lay there in pieces, the pain fighting with the complete impotence of having no control at all of the liquid that was him. He wanted to sob but he had no throat to do so. His mental processes felt spread out, dreamlike… he was helpless.

He had not reached the alarm.

The person he'd foolishly taken to be Henry Pym, who clearly had the memories of Henry Pym stretching back years, who had passed every test for an impostor that Reed had slipped into conversation, stood over him for a moment, admiring his handiwork. His face contorted, morphed into the green, stern visage of a Skrull. This Skrull was oddly lacking in triumphalism, his expression—because all the humanoid races of the galaxy shared body language, due to a common ancestor—that of someone who'd just done the job he had to do. "He even loves *you*," he said.

TEN

DANNY RAND

"I'M PICKING up some surface thoughts here, darlings," said the newly arrived "Emma Frost" in an accent that was every bit the mutant telepath's haughty *Masterpiece Theater* Bostonian, "and you're not going to believe this, but these people actually think *we're* Skrulls."

The newly arrived "Logan" just growled in return, taking one step further out of the spaceship, claws still bared.

"After what we've been through," said their "Spider-Man," "I don't care what they want us to think they think."

"But we're on Earth, right?" asked "Luke Cage."

"Either they got here first, or, while we've been away, they've taken over the world," said "Captain America," half to his own team, half to the watching groups of Avengers, exactly the way Steve Rogers did, always aware of who his audience was.

Danny shared the silent, horrified astonishment of his friends and foes on this side of the clearing. Luke took a step forward and raised his fist toward them. "Oh, will you all just cut the—"

"He smells like me," said the Logan who stood beside him, pointing at the other version of himself.

"Right back at'cha," said the other Wolverine.

"Could… could this be a time travel thing?" asked Echo, looking between the groups.

"How would that work?!" said Jessica Drew. "From the look of these guys, we're the ones from later. We'd remember this!"

Echo puffed out her cheeks. "You people get up to some crazy stuff with time, that's all I'm saying." Her eyes kept straying to Bobbi Morse, and how she was holding onto her Clint Barton.

Danny found himself actually engaging with the idea that what he was looking at was real. These guys sounded so like themselves; so like the versions he'd grown up around. There was a nostalgic gravity to them. This would explain so much, wouldn't it? Hadn't Spider-Man moved from one side to the other during the Civil War, as if he was trying to create as much chaos as possible? Danny had thought that experience had resulted in a certain weight settling on that young guy's shoulders, but what if that had just been a Skrull not quite getting Spidey's amazing sense of humor? Cap had died in really suspicious circumstances, the body immediately shuffled offstage: maybe because some Skrulls in positions of power didn't want it examined? Sue Richards had put the FF into chaos mode when she'd walked out on Reed. Jean and Emma, when Jean was alive, had always been the two opposing poles of the mutant community, the figures about whom the whole culture orbited. And Wanda, the Scarlet Witch, had seemingly fallen victim to mental illness and had actually attacked both the mutant community and the Avengers, delivering the terrible blow that had begun the spiral of events of the last year or so. Also, nobody knew where the supposedly "real" version of her was right now. Which spoke of an agent who'd done their job then went undercover. If Danny had sat down and thought about who in their community, in the last few months, was secretly a Skrull, Wanda would have been top of that list.

There was another troubling possibility that had already occurred to Danny, which the presence of these familiar faces was doing a lot to underline: What if some of the Skrull substitutes didn't know they were Skrulls? Danny knew himself really well. Intensive martial arts training did that to you. He didn't know of any gaps in his memory, and he had no idea how a Skrull might go about duplicating the power he possessed—that of the Iron Fist—and yet... and yet how could he be sure that he himself was the genuine article?

He could not, he decided. All he could do was to accept the possibility, to watch for anomalies in his own thoughts, and to re-center himself around that uncertainty, so that, if the worst did turn out to be the case, then he would at least have a chance of still doing the right thing.

He took a single breath and was again at one with himself.

"Your faces say you are starting to think these are your fellow mortals!" bellowed Ares. "They are not! Why would they be?! Idiots! Do not trust the shape-shifters!"

And yet a great number of Danny's... side... oh, were they all on the same side now? A great number of them stepped forward, angrily confronting their opposite numbers, as if they could argue their way to owning their real identity. The two Lukes were immediately in each other's faces, each yelling that *this* was what the Skrulls thought they looked like?! The two Logans had squared up even more so, circling and sniffing each other in a feral dance of domination, seemingly both astonished at what they were smelling. Spider-Man walked calmly up to the other version of himself, indicating his own head with his finger. "Hi, so, my Spider-Sense isn't even tingling, which makes me think maybe you guys aren't a threat—"

"Oh yeah?" his opposite number replied. "Mine's doing the hustle."

"Wow. I just about got that reference. So... you left Earth before you were born?"

And yet Danny had heard Spider-Man make all sorts of references to media across the ages. That sounded like their Spider-Man grasping at straws. Oh no. What could he do? What could any of them do?

"Do not trust them!" Ares kept on bellowing.

Virus detected, all systems failing, Stark's armor repeated. Carol looked desperately up from where she was doing her best to help him, hoping something would sort out the almighty mess everything around her was becoming.

"My sensors indicate they are human," said the Vision, indicating Danny and his friends, "and yet—"

Danny's Clint hadn't taken off his Ronin mask. He was just staring and staring past his other self at Bobbi Morse, who was now looking back, a look of recognition on her face.

"Don't trust them," said Maya, putting a hand on his arm. "This is too good to be true. This is bait."

"I know you Skrulls are looking to start some," said their own Luke. "I know you're waiting for us to start it, so some of us might start to wonder about who they've been fighting alongside. But I know who I am. And I know *that* isn't my Jessica." He pointed to Jewel, who looked back at him shocked.

"*Your* Jessica?!" she called back. "Wow, you're one Skrull who hasn't done their homework!"

Luke ignored her and looked back to his duplicate. "And I know in the end this comes down to somethin' very simple. You need your asses kicking!"

And he slammed a steel-hard haymaker into the jaw of his other self.

The clearing erupted into chaos, the rebel Avengers following their leader by leaping into action, many of the others reacting to that by jumping in to attack them in return. Everyone else found themselves defending or fleeing or diving for cover.

The two versions of Simon Williams collided with a sound like thunder right in front of Danny, sending him tumbling.

He righted himself in a second to find the Vision narrowly missing his shoulder, the Sentry on his tail.

He spun just in time to raise what could in a second become his blazing Iron Fist against... a Spider-Man who held up his hands and stepped back. How could he tell which one this was?

A moment later the other Spider-Man, whichever that was, fell on the first, and webs were flying around two figures as they leapt and spun, each missing the other at tremendous speed. "I know I hate myself," said one of them, "but this is ridiculous."

"Please tell me I'm not this annoying," said the other.

"You are."

"I know."

And the webbing kept flying.

Danny turned, looking for an opponent he could be sure of. Did the Skrulls have telepathy? There was Emma Frost, her hands in the air, as if manipulating someone's mind, but Danny couldn't see her target. Did they have mutant-hex-magic-whatever it was? Because there was the Scarlet Witch, also gesturing, flickering light around her hands suggesting that either the Skrulls had the special effects worked out or this was the real thing.

Then Cap was on him, and Danny had no more time to think.

Oh, god, he was fast! Danny's own martial arts skills were stretched to the limit as more than six decades of combat experience and an invulnerable shield went for his head, feinted, went for his legs, then tried to put him down. Danny jumped, dodged, rolled aside, and realized he was unwilling to land a blow. He'd sparred with Steve Rogers: this felt like Steve Rogers. He didn't want to fight Captain America!

As he dodged, he saw Carol—their Carol—take off like a rocket, carrying Stark. That was for the best, he had a moment to realize, before Cap was on him again. How was he going to—

"Have at thee!" roared Ares, one blow from his sword against Cap's shield sending Danny's opponent flying. The deity glanced at Danny for a moment. "Mortal fools," he said, then ran after Cap, who was already back on his feet.

Danny spun around to see Hawkeye aiming at him, at almost point-blank range. He was going to get only a moment to snatch the arrow from the air.

Echo clobbered Hawkeye from behind with her billy club, right across a pressure point that should leave the victim unconscious...

if they were human. Had Danny ever seen Skrulls knocked out like that too? Sometime? Maybe? At any rate, this guy was on the ground.

"Like I haven't been through enough this year." Ronin, Clint, grabbed the bow and quiver from the unconscious Hawkeye and looked up at Danny. "I didn't want to pick one of these up again but here we are. Do you think the Skrulls can replicate what I can do with this?"

"I—"

"Whatever. Follow me or don't. I reckon I can prove a few things from cover." Clint and Maya ran for the treeline.

Danny considered for only a second, then followed.

Ronin found cover in seconds, ever the experienced sniper, and Danny and Maya dropped into the undergrowth beside him. "Okay," he said. "First target: Emma Frost." He rose, aimed in a moment and loosed an arrow. Danny watched it fly across the clearing full of fighting figures and land in Emma's leg. She staggered, and her opponent, Natasha, started landing blow after blow.

"She... didn't see that coming," said Danny.

"So that's evidence," said Maya. "They're all Skrulls."

"Next: Cap."

Another arrow flew across the clearing, to where Cap was sidestepping every ferocious attack of the God of War, a display of matching mythological grandeur.

Without looking, he swung his shield into the path of the arrow and blocked it.

"Damn," said Clint. "Maybe... maybe?!"

"Maybe!" said Danny, sharing his discomfort. "But... but if one of these is the real thing, then wouldn't they all be—"

Danny and Clint turned to look at each other. "Oh, come on," Clint began. "Why would I show you?"

"To convince me about that Cap."

"Stop it!" said Maya. "We're real. They aren't. The end."

Danny was about to say something about the need for some way to tell friend from foe when suddenly an enormous roar rent the air of the clearing.

From out of the forest canopy burst, its tiny eyes gleaming to match its rancid teeth, an enormous, rampaging Tyrannosaurus rex.

It ran at the fighting mass of heroes, screeching in infrasound, maddened by the noise, seeking only blood.

ELEVEN

BOB REYNOLDS

BOB REYNOLDS had been keeping it together well—at least, until the dinosaur arrived. As the Sentry, he wielded enormous powers of flight and strength and power beams, but they were dangerous powers. Powers that scared him. He wanted to use them in the service of everyday people, but every time he tried to do so... oh, there was such horror.

He had never wanted to fight other heroes. He was meant to be the epitome of what they all stood for. He hated this, yet when Tony had finally reached out like nobody ever had before, offering him a home, a way to start dealing with the mental illness that had been written into him by decades of... of authorities and villains and magic and mutants messing with his mind... how could he say no to that? He had been on Tony's side in the Civil War, because didn't these guys know that without rules, without order, all their power meant nothing?

But look what that had resulted in—as with, it seemed, every decision he took. For god's sake, Captain America was dead! Didn't that say something about what unleashing chaos resulted in? Why did they all have to fight all the time? Where were the bad guys?

They were inside his own head. That was the reply that always came. He kept putting it aside, but it was always there.

The central thing about Bob was that everyone had forgotten him. That was the gravity he could never seem to escape. The memory of his existence had been erased from the minds of everyone good, everyone kind, and everyone else. The only thing that remembered him was the monster inside his own mind. He was always playing catch-up, always desperate to make other people keep remembering him now.

The moment before the dinosaur arrived, he had been struggling with the Vision, his own grip matching the strength of what was either the android Bob remembered from his career as one of the world's earliest super heroes or the Skrull impersonating him.

"Listen," he said, "Vision, if that's the real you, hey, you may not remember me. But that means you can't think I'm a duplicate, right? I mean, why would they duplicate me? Okay, okay. It's complicated. The world was made to forget me, *I* was made to forget, because that was the only way to save everyone from… from… something I think is… part of me. Something I call the Void. But I'm an Avenger now. I remember you. I remember how hard you fought for your own identity, for your right to be treated as a person. I respected that. Please, we don't have to fight now, we could take this somewhere else and work out all the facts and—"

"This is what you wanted, Bob," said the Vision.

"What?" Bob found himself freezing inside. The sound of that voice… It had been very like the cold, distant tones he'd always heard from the android hero, but also…

"You did this, Bob," said the Vision, quite calmly. His features were changing now, morphing into the dark red demonic face of…

Bob was looking into a mirror.

"This is all you. I am the Void. I brought this to you. Because you were right. I *am* you."

Bob knew it was true.

He knew in his heart it was true, because he didn't really

deserve to be the hero. He'd killed his own wife, hadn't he? The Void had killed her. Or was she not even dead at all? It was all being overwritten, all the time, glitch after glitch, all the retroactive continuity that made up his life. And he was now grappling with the thing, the being, the part of himself, whatever it was, that kept breaking his reality, kept tormenting him with everything the super hero life could have been for him and yet was not.

He cried out like a helpless child, and flung the Vision, the Void, away.

The being floated in the air in front of him, mocking him with his own voice. "You made all this happen. The Civil War, this so-called invasion, all of it. I'm here because you couldn't bear the world and asked for a way to make it burn. And it's working. Everything is coming together, just like you planned. You're making *them* feel what doubt is like. You're making *them* suffer losing their identities. This is what they get for forgetting you when you most needed them."

Bob didn't know what was true and what wasn't. He looked down and saw his friends, his colleagues, fighting that damned dinosaur. Even that was his fault: He had engineered this whole situation. He had done so much harm. To intervene in what was happening below would only cause further harm in the end, because he was incapable of controlling himself.

But he could still save them. He could still do the right thing and save the day. By not being here to cause any more harm.

Bob pointed his fingers upward and flew straight up, hard and fast, leaving it all behind him. The Vision-Void he left behind laughed as he went. Bob kept flying until he could no longer hear that laughter.

TWELVE

TONY STARK

TONY DESPERATELY tried to focus, to cut through the pain and communicate with Carol. His mask had fallen open as his armor malfunctioned; the bite of the wind on his uncovered face as she took them up through the cloud layer was actually helping. She couldn't be thinking of flying him all the way back to New York, but there were bases nearby, weren't there? She was Carol Danvers. She was the most practical person on Earth, she'd have memorized the locations of medical facilities on the way over.

He couldn't let her take him there. "Carol," he managed to croak into her ear. "Stop. Stop. Listen to me. We need to go down. Down there. Back." And he gestured vaguely to the north of where the battle was raging, close to the site of the spaceship crash. Or at least he hoped that's where he was gesturing.

"What?"

"I know… what I'm doing. Plan. Please."

She looked at him, sized him up, and then they were hurtling back down again. He managed to guide her by hand gesture, relying on memory alone to find the location, because he couldn't rely on the damn suit anymore. They hit the warmth of the local atmosphere again, and there, in an older clearing, a crater formed by violence, was the ruin he was seeking. "What is that?" she asked.

"The Mutate Citadel. It... belongs to the indigenous people of the Savage Land. Belonged to. I don't know. Magneto experimented on some of the locals, created his own race of mutants. Back when he... used to do stuff like... anyway, he... he had a laboratory here. Only... lab in..." He couldn't finish, but she got the idea. She descended through the remains of the roof, setting him down amongst smashed machinery and—oh— some very old corpses. There must be something about this place that stopped the local predators from taking them. So that'd be a weird feature. He didn't have the margins left to deal. He leaned heavily on a console and started hitting controls. Yeah, there was some power left in this thing.

"Carol, listen to me, you... you fly back to the mainland, right now. I've been infected, my armor, body, brain... with what I... it's got to be an alien virus," he said. "Probably a Skrull virus. At least some of those guys in the spaceship, they've got to be Skrulls."

"I'm taking you with me, at least," Carol replied.

"They've hacked all my tech—at S.H.I.E.L.D., at S.W.O.R.D., at the Avengers. I have to... rebuild. From scratch."

"But, the others, our team, they're—"

"The entire world... in danger. Go. Find out what's going on. There have to be some of the local teams of heroes left, the ones I put together in the Initiative. Them or the rebels. I don't care. Any. All. Get everyone who's left..."

"What are you going to do?"

He already had a console open and was grabbing at a bunch of useful parts. Maybe he could find something here to create a body/brain block for the armor that'd stop some of the pain. He realized after a moment that she'd asked a question. "I built my first armor from less than this. I'm going to use the one thing the Skrulls can't imitate: my brain."

THIRTEEN

CLINT BARTON

WHAT THE hell was this now?!

Clint Barton ran through the jungle, head low, sprinting around the perimeter of what was now not just a super hero battle zone but the site of a freaking dinosaur attack, with his current girlfriend beside him and his dead wife apparently in the middle of it all. The battle had veered away from the crash site, following the course of the dinosaur, which, it seemed, had scattered the engagement into a whole bunch of skirmishes, some of them involving said dinosaur, some not. The dinosaur itself seemed to have continued on its way, maybe not having found the mouthfuls of easy snacks it had been anticipating.

Clint deliberately circled around the whole damn thing, aiming to stealthily get back to the crash site and see if he could get a look inside that ship. Maya would not let him out of her sight, and was indeed running in the same manner as him, having copied his actions. Maybe there'd be something in that ship that'd tell him if, for instance, that the Danny Rand they'd just been talking to before they got separated was the real thing. He'd certainly seemed like it, but that's what Skrulls did. They took people you loved and made them into scarecrows of themselves, walking and talking as if they were alive again and yet also still dead, and right now he wanted to put an arrow through every damn one of them.

He wanted to put an arrow through their Bobbi.

Their Mockingbird. Mocking him. Only they knew, they knew, he would never be able to make himself do that.

It felt weird even to hold a bow again. Weird and wrong. As Ronin he'd used everything but. Deliberately. To escape from that identity. He wanted desperately to get back to New York, get someplace where he could get word to his protégé, Kate Bishop, who these days was the only Hawkeye in town. He needed to know she was okay.

He heard movement nearby and slowed down, raising a hand to let Maya know what was going on. There was Logan—the version of Logan he'd been on the same team with, judging by the more modern costume—upwind of him, thank god, just getting to the other side of the clearing where the spaceship had crashed. He marched through the jungle, ripping through foliage in his way, looking like he was on a mission. Maybe the same one Clint was.

From the other side of the clearing stepped Luke Cage, the one Clint had served alongside. As ever, Luke, with his indestructible body and will, wasn't one for hiding. "Hey," Luke called out to Logan, as if testing the water. Or were these two undercover agents wondering if they could break their cover now they were alone?

Clint slipped into hiding and watched, ready to string an arrow. Maya, looking annoyed at his doubt, hesitated a moment, then followed suit.

"I don't care who you look like or who you smell like," said Logan, sniffing the air, "ya come near me and I'll gut ya."

"Except you can't. Unbreakable skin."

"Unbreakable claws."

So at least one of these two was the real thing. Or did they know Clint was watching?

"Oh," said Luke suddenly. "Look at this." He went over to

some undergrowth from which a blue and red boot was sticking and pulled out from it a corpse.

Clint could see what it was even from cover. It was Spider-Man. Except it was also a Skrull. The red and blue outfit had been ripped open to expose a green-skinned corpse with pointed ears.

"Damn," said Wolverine. "The T. rex did that to him."

"This means they were all Skrulls," said Luke. "This means it was all just a damn trick and—"

"Don't mean nothin'. Everyone scattered. Spider-Man kept the same costume. So we don't know which spider this was."

Luke paced in a circle. "I don't get it. What's the Skrulls' plan?"

"Huh. They got us all stuck down here fighting for our lives, fighting each other, fighting a war where we can't trust the soldier next to us. I'd call that a plan."

"I mean, they hate us so much, why don't they just send Ego the Living Planet in our direction or drop Brood eggs every other mile or somethin'?"

That sounded exactly like the real Luke. Both sounded like themselves, come to think of it. But Clint knew better than to trust his senses about this. All he knew was that now, when he met another Spider-Man, that was someone he *could* trust. Unless him thinking that was the whole idea.

"Yeah," said Logan, "I been thinking about this. I think they need the planet intact, with us not on it. Especially *us*. They hate us, ever since they first met Richards and realized super heroes were kind of like them, with powers and all. So they're getting us to do the torture, they're getting us to kill each other. And we—"

"We fell for it. I didn't see the scope of it. I didn't see them taking Stark out."

"If that was even him. I think these Skrulls right here, they're a suicide squad. They're committed to the bit and they're gonna play it to the end 'cuz they don't care what happens to—"

Logan's nostrils flared and he spun, popping his claws.

Clint heard the sound from the undergrowth too. He reflexively grabbed an arrow and drew before he saw what it was emerging from the bushes across the clearing.

Oh god, it was Bobbi. It was Bobbi, and she was dragging the corpse of another Skrull out of cover. The Skrull Hawkeye.

Clint had to breathe for a moment, to push down deep inside him the anger that the sight of this pretense made him feel.

Maya put a hand on his arm. They made eye contact and she shook her head, willing him not to believe.

But then, he looked back, she would, wouldn't she?

Bobbi was talking to Luke and Logan as if she offhandedly trusted them. "I was pretty sure we had a Skrull or two in our group before we crashed, but… oh god, oh god…"

There were tears on her face, Clint realized.

"Me and this thing… I mean, we were *together*. In the camps. We never had a chance to be… intimate, thank god, but… but I have *kissed* this!" It was her voice, her attitude, her way of moving. It was her. No, no, it wasn't her, it couldn't be her. Clint felt his hands shaking and quickly lowered his bow. He had to breathe. He had to deal. Bobbi, this thing that looked like Bobbi, was now staring questioningly at Luke and Logan, who still seemed not to know what to do. "Does this mean there's a Clint Barton here on Earth still? Is my Clint still alive?"

Her Clint. Oh. Oh god. Yes, he wanted to shout. Yes. Only… only…

Maya slapped him gently on the shoulder to make him look at her. She shook her head again. And now the look in her eyes was pleading.

Logan stepped forward slowly, claws raised. "Drop the act."

"You think I'm a Skrull? You're the Wolverine, right? I know you from S.H.I.E.L.D. files. Can't you smell who I am or something?"

"They can fool our senses now," said Luke, following Logan, looking more conciliatory. "So, Bobbi. Patsy Walker told me she went to the afterlife and saw you there."

"Which afterlife would that be?"

"Well, Hell, but you know, I didn't like to say."

"Then I would say that would involve demons, and in my experience, demons lie."

"And hey, your boyfriend from before Clint is going to be around here someplace, right?"

"Okay, you're really testing me, good," said Bobbi, brushing away her tears. "If you mean Ka-Zar, the Lord of the Savage Land, he'll be holding back somewhere wondering what this is, and he was not my boyfriend. And you can call me Dr. Morse. I got my degree at Georgia Tech, and I think you and I met at... you and Danny held some sort of rooftop party in San Diego to attract clients? A bunch of us West Coast Avengers came along to support you two. I have been stuck in Skrull prison ships and camps for, I don't know, maybe a year, and—"

"Nah," said Logan, grabbing her by the throat and throwing back his arm to slice her. "Nice legend, kid. Too perfect."

Clint saw the sudden terror in her eyes. He couldn't stop himself. He drew and loosed.

Maya leapt to her feet beside him, furious.

Logan yelled as the arrow hit his shoulder, spinning him away from his target. Bobbi instantly rolled over and leapt into a fighting stance, ready if he came at her again. "Clint?!" she called, looking round with a pretty great grasp of where the arrow might have come from. "My god, is that you?!"

"Get away from her!" Clint shouted to Logan and Luke, standing up and out of cover and making sure they saw he had another shaft nocked. These two should know he could shoot fast enough to keep Logan's healing factor from getting him back up; that he would, if pushed, see if Luke had steel-hard eyeballs. They would take him— of course they would—but did they really want to do this?

But never mind them, never mind them, he could settle this. He marched toward Bobbi. Maya kept pace with him. Bobbi was staring at him in disappointment, anger even. Oh, she recognized the quiver, but not him, not in this costume with the mask. "Where... where did you get that?" she said. "Who are you?"

He was now aiming at her. It kept her rooted to the spot and it kept the other two from moving on him. "Tell me something about October twelfth," he said.

"Clint?" She was sobbing again. She knew it was him.

"I know who I am. These guys do too, now they've seen that Skrull on the ground. October twelfth."

Bobbi sat down on the ground. She looked away. When she replied, her voice was a whisper. "When we were Avengers together, a couple of years ago… I… I had a miscarriage. We didn't tell anyone. We figured his or her birthday would have been October twelfth." She looked up at him. "October twelfth. That would have been a nice day." She took a deep breath and wiped away her tears again. "Oh, I should have tested Clint the Skrull with that one."

Clint dropped his bow. He found himself pulling off his mask as Luke and Logan looked warily at him. Bobbi stared at him.

Maya stepped between them. "No," she said. "Clint, how did Bobbi die?"

"Mephisto disintegrated her. So… so that could have been—"

"No!"

"But nobody else could know this!"

"No!"

"Maya—" began Luke.

Maya grabbed Clint and made him look at her. "Even if that is the real her, and I don't think it is, what you and I have between us, this relationship or whatever it is we've just started out on—"

"Oh no," said Bobbi. "Oh, I'm so sorry."

"—is that just done now?! Shutter comes down? Oh hey, your blond partner is back, the brown woman can pack up her things?"

"You gotta admit," said Logan, "this is kind of a unique situation."

"So you've accepted this now?!" She looked angrily between all of them. "Then live with the consequences. I wish you luck, Clint. With your Skrull bride." And she was off at high speed into the undergrowth.

"Maya!" Clint called helplessly after her.

"I… I don't expect things to go right back to— You thought I died? You saw Mephisto—?"

"I'm sorry," said Clint. "I should have known."

"I can give you space. I'll talk to her. I don't want to—"

"No," said Clint. "No." He couldn't stop himself any longer. He grabbed her and kissed her. She kissed him back. She was his wife, his Bobbi, and she was really back. Her hair smelled right, her mouth tasted right, she was exactly right in his arms.

After a long moment they parted again. "Hey," she said, breaking into a grin. "You slept with a Skrull."

"I… I guess I… we need to talk about when you were taken."

Luke and Logan stepped forward. It seemed as though they were cautiously going with this. "Barton…" began Logan.

"There's no way they would know what she just said. Nobody knows that."

"Unless *you're* a Skrull."

"Well, there's that."

"Damn it," said Luke, "I'm just going to trust somebody. All you three. And Maya deserves your respect about this, right? You are not just going to walk out on her."

"No," said Clint. "I… may have kissed Bobbi just then, but that is not the end of that conversation."

"Agreed," said Bobbi. "Very much."

"So, you know what I'm gonna ask, right?"

"About Jess," said Clint.

"What about Jess?" said Bobbi.

"My wife," said Luke. "Jessica Jones."

"Jessica Jones is your wife?" said Bobbi. Her face fell. "But— Oh. Oh, I'm so sorry."

Luke looked grim. "Yeah. Tell me about it. So, how likely is it that I've been living a lie? That somehow I *had a baby* with that lie? Because I was listening to you making jokes about sleeping with a Skrull, and—"

"That… does make me wonder," said Bobbi. "I know the

Skrulls have experimented with cross-breeding, I met some of the results. But also I now figure the Skrulls maybe let us escape, to mess with your minds and to plant some of their people in with us. Like my Clint. So your Jess might be the real one. Except I got to know… no, I can't know, not after my Clint."

"*I'm* your Clint," said Clint.

"*Now* you are. Maybe. After you talk to Maya."

"So," said Luke, "maybe that's Jess, maybe not. Is that really Cap?"

"Oh," said Bobbi. "Even if they used us to smuggle in some Skrulls, he blew up so many of them to get us here. That's the real Captain America for sure."

FOURTEEN

TEDDY ALTMAN

THEODORE ALTMAN, the King of Space as his boyfriend often called him, stood in Times Square, staring at the Baxter Building in terror. He and his friends, who were often called the Young Avengers, had ventured out from hiding in disguise just to get a hot dog and spend some time doing everyday stuff in New York City. The post-Civil War security situation seemed to be easing up a little, but they were still all wanted fugitives for refusing to sign up to that moronic Superhuman Registration Act. Teddy's codename was still Hulkling, because in his natural form he was big and green, but these days he knew he was actually nothing to do with any of the various kinds of Hulk. His ability to shape-shift and change his skin color made it easy for him to walk through the crowds undercover, but his friends had largely resorted to hoodies and scarves and moving slowly away from the NYPD. In the past, Teddy had looked up at the Baxter Building as a sign of stability and hope, because in there lived a family of famous, accepted, public heroes: that was all he wanted to be, truth be told, though not enough to become a government stooge. These days, however, the Baxter Building was a sign of complexity, and even—though he hated to think it—corruption, because there lived a bunch of people who had taken different sides in the conflict, who were somehow back together because they were, wow, exceptions to the law.

Still, he and his friends hadn't wanted anything bad to happen to the FF or their home. They had all kind of thought that one day Reed Richards might well, in his Centrist Dad way, say something in public about how he'd been wrong, his wife had been right and, well, maybe this whole Civil War thing had been a bit of an unfortunate mistake, and perhaps his friend Tony should do something about that. But right now, Teddy and his friends put thoughts like that aside because, along with a frightened crowd of innocent bystanders, they were watching the top of the Baxter Building warp and weft out of reality, awash with green light, a sphere of it wrestling with the everyday matter inside.

Tom Shepherd, the mutant known as Speed, flicked out his phone to start taking pictures, just like many in the crowd were doing, his hands a blur. He flashed Teddy a grin from under his shock of white hair, enjoying the spectacle with that slightly amoral air of his. But Teddy could see something else going on as he looked around. Some people were walking away quickly. Some people had already started to run. A hot dog vendor was packing up. There were stress reactions, and people shouting things, and asking each other where the Avengers were.

New Yorkers *remembered*.

And now of course there were sirens, coming in from every direction.

"Guys, it's the FF, we gotta do something," said Elijah Bradley, codename Patriot. He was the team member Teddy most admired: someone with no powers except willpower, who'd trained himself to the peak of physical prowess, part of a family lineage that took the racist experiments the U.S. government had conducted in the 1950s to make another Captain America and threw them back in their faces. No team with Elijah in it could ever work for Tony Stark. And yet here he was, immediately saying they had to help Reed Richards.

"They might not welcome us doing something," said Billy Kaplan, Wiccan, Teddy's significant other. "We go up there, we might get ourselves arrested." Like his boyfriend, Billy had originally gone by a misleading codename. He used to be called "Asgardian" but now he was trying out "Wiccan," which neither of them felt quite did the job either, because the magical skills he'd finally admitted to the team he was using instead of Asgardian powers weren't entirely Wiccan in origin. And because if they ever stopped having to live off the grid, they'd get in a load of trouble for it on Insta. Billy and Tom Shepherd were siblings, seemingly somehow the children of the Scarlet Witch, though right now they didn't like to talk about that, and they both had a much stronger connection to their... birth parents, including the mothers who had actually given birth to them. Wow, did any of the other super hero teams have lives as weird as theirs?

"Nope," said Kate Bishop, Hawkeye, the team leader. Kate was an expert archer and martial artist who'd managed to impress Clint Barton enough that, when he'd gone into hiding, he'd allowed her to inherit his codename. She'd got past some awful crap in her past to become a great leader, and she and Patriot were managing to very successfully alternate leadership duties while the Young Avengers were effectively on the run. "I agree with Eli, we can't think like that. We should call Clint, see what *his* Avengers are doing, offer help." She hit a button on her phone and sighed a second later. "And of course it's gone to voicemail."

"What's the logical course of action?" said the Vision, an android who had only the other day chosen the name "Jonas" for himself because of a band he liked, and had started experimenting with contractions in his speech. His structure—mental and physical—had been formed out of the original Vision, who had been with the Avengers, but he had an entirely different personality. He had gone, a couple of weeks back, to secretly visit Cassie Lang, the one person in their team who'd signed the Superhuman Registration Act. He hadn't told them until after, because he knew they'd object. And they had. Because she had burned so many bridges when she'd walked, seemingly unable to comprehend why anyone would think differently to her. But none of them felt they could trust Jonas any less as a result. Especially after he'd said, rather charmingly, that he'd gone to see her because he was "into her" and then blushed, which must have been deliberate. "What's the ethical thing to do?" he said now. "And what's the balance?"

"I can't get used to you using contractions," said Billy. "Could you just do that... better?"

"I am... sorry?"

But Teddy caught something in the sky flying past the Baxter Building, something that had suddenly made him feel even more concerned.

Something swam into view, revealing itself. A Skrull KV-6 Armored Cruiser, the green light of its engine pulsing. Teddy knew what it was because he had been making a study of everything humans knew about the Skrulls, poring over the Avengers files because, within the last few months, he had learned he was half-Skrull himself. Indeed, he was actually part of the royal line, son of Princess Anelle, grandson of Dorrek VII, Emperor of all the Skrulls when the Skrull Empire had been a thing, legally making him Dorrek VIII. Hence the "King of Space" bit. Not that it had counted for anything on Earth, and especially not with his teammates.

To see this here, now, obviously somehow connected with whatever was happening to the Baxter Building... this was the worst. This was the return of the bad old family stuff that had killed the woman he had regarded as his mother. "No," he whispered. "No. We have to—"

The ship opened fire.

Bolts of energy impacted at street level a second later, sending chunks of pavement and people flying. The crowds scattered, screaming, pushing past each other, hurting each other in the insane scramble. Smoke and the smell of death hung in the air. There were corpses now, lying in the street. Teddy stared, feeling adrenaline rush through him, his heart racing. He breathed, controlling it, letting it motivate rather than dominate him. They saw themselves as Avengers. They had to live up to that.

"Everyone bring a costume?" asked Kate calmly, undoing her belt.

Patriot was already pulling his mask over his head. "Here for that," he said.

Sure enough, the Vision had already transformed into his real self, Wiccan was waving a hand to reveal his magical garb, and Speed was… in his hypersmooth costume in an instant.

Teddy let his own form morph, changing his exterior appearance in seconds from street clothes to a costume that gave him freedom of movement in combat. In the same instant, he let his face slide into its natural green hotness. Though if the Skrulls were attacking, maybe that wasn't such a great idea… and they were still fugitives… No. If he was going to do this, he'd do it as himself.

He felt Billy's hand on his arm and grabbed it, just for a second. But he was still looking in the direction of where the volley of beams had hit, because he thought he'd recognized the type of energy. He suspected they weren't just force weapons, but…

Yeah. There were figures moving in the smoke. "We're gonna need more than costumes," he said. "Those were concussive teleport beams. They soften up ground forces and deliver spearhead shock troops at the same time."

Kate swore under her breath.

From the smoke stepped a Super-Skrull.

Then another.

And another.

There were at least twenty of them: more than Teddy could count. They had already transformed into their fighting shapes, showing off the powers they'd copied from the heroes of Earth. And like every Super-Skrull Teddy had ever heard of, each displayed more than one power set. There was one that had Wolverine's claws, gigantic in this version, but also Cyclops' visor; one wearing Doctor Strange's cloak with Iron Man's glowing reactor embedded in his chest; one with Ben Grimm's fists and the tentacles of Doctor

Octopus. And in the sky, descending toward them under their own power… there was somehow even one manifesting the enormous energies of the Phoenix.

Teddy looked desperately at his friends who stared, horrified, at what was before them: an actual invasion force. Here in Manhattan. And the Young Avengers were the only ones in the way. The only super heroes at the scene, fugitives from authority, the only line of defense for the vulnerable civilians who were running and screaming all around them.

"Avengers assemble!" yelled Kate, grabbing for an arrow.

The Super-Skrulls ran at them.

FIFTEEN

BALKAMAR

IT HAD been the unfortunate duty of the Skrull covert operations specialist called Balkamar to assume the shape and persona of a particularly vulnerable and thus, he'd initially thought, loathsome human being known as Edwin Jarvis. A mere servant. Balkamar had not viewed the assignment with joy. Still, he had done his duty. The real Jarvis had been hoisted out of a New York sidestreet with a bag full of fruit from a farmer's market and up into a Skrull stealth craft, and Balkamar had dropped onto the sidewalk in his place, moments before another human turned the corner. Balkamar, who'd arrived in time to stop a dropped tangerine from rolling away, had doffed his hat as he passed the human, taking a deep breath and feeling his way into the role.

He had swiftly discovered that being Edwin Jarvis was actually a pleasure. All of the government-appointed Avengers trusted this man they employed as their "butler," and they would regularly share not just vital intelligence with him but their annoyances, their romantic feelings and their emotional connections. All he had to do to solicit further data was to raise an eyebrow, incline his head slightly, or say "sir" with a slight edge of any emotion to his voice.

In the role of an English butler, Balkamar swiftly discovered, less was most definitely more.

Despite having access to all of Jarvis's memories, he discovered he barely needed them. None of these people ever asked how Jarvis was doing. The closest he came had been when Tony Stark finished a sentence with "you know?" and left a pause, suggesting a response was required.

"Indeed, sir," Balkamar replied, and that had been all that was required.

A few hours before, his had been the duty, and the joy, of connecting the data module with the Techno-Organic virus in it to the Avengers' main computer, watching it immediately spread to every Stark system across this world. That had been the level of system security that the Avengers had been happy with their butler having access to. Now he had another joyous task. It had fallen to him to fly a Quinjet from Avengers Tower all the way to the area of ocean that humans, for wonderfully ridiculous reasons, referred to as "the Bermuda Triangle." That had been where the S.H.I.E.L.D. Helicarrier's emergency teleport system had been set up to deliver it when, stricken by the virus he had unleashed, it had been about to crash into Manhattan. Balkamar could only imagine that setting must have been the result of some technician's sense of humor.

The Helicarrier floated on the surface of the ocean as he came into land, entirely capable of sustaining itself as an actual ship. It looked rather more at home in that role, if one were being honest. He stepped out onto the flight deck, enjoying the roiling sea all around, and sniffed the air. It was indeed bracing. Just the spot for his second major action of this invasion. Gracious, this assignment had turned out to be anything but an unfortunate duty! He rather wished he'd brought a packed lunch. He wandered up to the central tower of the vessel, looked up into a security camera and cleared his throat.

"I say?" he called. "Anyone at home?"

After a few moments a door slid open and out onto the deck stepped Maria Hill, the Deputy Director of S.H.I.E.L.D. She had with her a full security detail, armed to the teeth. They were all looking at him like they didn't quite know what this was. "Jarvis?" she said. "We're kind of busy right now. Did... Tony send his *butler* to—"

"Oh, dear me, no," chuckled Balkamar. "I'm terribly sorry to disturb you, Deputy Director, but I was just wondering, if you don't mind awfully, would you be so kind as to offer us your organization's full and immediate surrender?"

"Us?" she said.

"I do so apologize. By 'us,' I of course mean the Skrull Empire, of which I am the merest functionary."

To give her credit, she did take a few moments to consider. "Jarvis," she said finally, "if I may call you Jarvis?"

"Oh, you may. Charmed, I'm sure."

"Could I ask how long you've been a Skrull agent?"

"Please, Deputy Director, a Skrull *officer*. I am not some sort of *turncoat*."

"It's just, you do still seem very Jarvis. When you don't have to be."

"Well, I have intimate access to his memories, and the persona of one's guise can sometimes overcome one, and I must say, in this particular case, I'm enjoying it immensely."

"I'm sorry. This has kind of taken me by surprise, as I'm sure you appreciate."

"Of course. And, I'm terribly sorry, but I'm afraid I won't be answering any more of your questions, because you have rather strayed into playing for time. I would, however, appreciate an answer to my own inquiry. We arranged for you to rise to your current position in S.H.I.E.L.D. for a reason."

"That's... that's incredibly patronizing."

"Please, don't be dismayed, you are of course eminently capable and deserving. However, the important quality we saw in you was that we feel you to be eminently capable of cooperating with whoever happens to be in charge, whatever your personal feelings concerning them may be."

"Still not flattered."

"If I may resume the matter in hand, it is rather *time* for the human race to surrender. You're the internationally recognized deputy director of a global security agency. Were you to publicly announce that surrender, it would save your people a great deal of suffering and make any governments that attempt to hold out seem, well, terribly selfish. In return, we will spare your life and offer you a place in the transition. Which will, I promise you, be to a better world."

Hill looked around, not unreasonably, at the S.H.I.E.L.D. officers all pointing guns toward Balkamar. "You're pretty brave, coming alone to do this on *my* ship."

"Oh dear. To my utter chagrin, Deputy Director, I fear I am not nearly as brave as you assume." He gave a nod and the officers surrounding him all transformed into their natural Skrull selves and turned their weapons at Hill. "Now, please, could we conclude this unfortunate business? And then perhaps we could have some tea?"

SIXTEEN

NORMAN OSBORN

NORMAN NEEDED all his experience as a super villain to dodge the energy blasts that Captain Marvel was throwing around in what remained of his office. To their credit, his Thunderbolts team had rushed in at the sound of the intruder alert, only for the impossible figure facing them to punch, hurl and blast them in every direction. A moment ago, the alien known as Mar-Vell had sent Moonstone flying out through the hole he'd made in the wall of the mountain complex. Now, as the stunned and astonished team of enforcers lay scattered in the blazing ruins, Captain Marvel raised a glowing hand over the unconscious form of Dr. Chen Lu, the Radioactive Man, seemingly intending to make blowing his head off his first execution. Osborn, from his hiding place, stared at that noble visage, the flowing locks of the white-skinned Kree, the proud costume that bore that race's flag, and wondered if this was an assault by Kree forces who'd somehow resurrected… a warrior who'd continually rebelled against their cause? No, that couldn't be it.

Then he noticed something else. A single tear ran from under this man's mask. And he was hesitating, Norman realized. He couldn't make himself deliver the killing blow.

Norman stood slowly, hands raised. "You can't do it, can you?" The figure turned to face him, the energy around his hand increasing in intensity. Norman knew that right now he had to make sure he seemed even less of a threat than the unconscious Chen Lu. But maybe that wasn't that hard in a crumpled business suit. "I don't think you're who you've come dressed as, are you? My name's Norman Osborn. This is my office you've trashed. These are my people you've smacked around. But I notice an intact liquor cabinet over there. Would you maybe like to have a drink and talk to me about all this? I get the feeling you have quite the story."

Captain Marvel didn't reply. But he lowered his glowing hand. Just a little. He looked profoundly surprised. That was what Norman was best at: disruption. Both of markets and of the composure of super heroes.

Norman clicked his fingers to indicate to those of his defeated troops that were still conscious that they should get up, and, rubbing his hands together, strode over to find the whiskey.

SEVENTEEN

CASSIE LANG

CASSIE LANG was the daughter of a criminal. Her dad, Scott, had most recently been in jail for a crime he didn't commit, but before that he'd committed a lot of real crimes, and had then done his time and resolved to do better. He'd raised her, with the grit and truth of someone who didn't want his kid to grow up like he did, to believe in the law. He'd also often been given the benefit of the doubt by a genuinely ethical employer in the form of Tony Stark. Mr. Stark had even helped out when Cassie had helped herself to some of her dad's growth and shrinking gasses, and started her own super hero career as the occasionally giant Stature. Then Dad had… got killed. When the Scarlet Witch, out of her damned mind, had attacked the Avengers. Cassie tried not to think of it as murder, because that wasn't right, but in her darker moments she was really tempted to. Dad had died serving Earth as an official hero, a law-abiding man of honor right to the end.

So, when Mr. Stark had pitched a new law about super heroes registering with the government, well, it had been pretty clear which way she was going to go about that. It had actually come as a shock to her—though it shouldn't have—that her former teammates in the Young Avengers opted to instead go on the run as wanted criminals and pretty much *instantly* started to call her a fascist for trying to explain to them her point of view. She suspected that she understood their motives a hell of a lot better than they understood hers. She was doing exactly what her dad would have done, and she hadn't doubted for a moment that he'd have been proud of her for standing up for what she believed. In those darker moments of hers she'd even wondered if her former friends would have stood with her about her dad's death, considering two of them were, somehow, the children of the Scarlet Witch.

Having lost all her friends, Cassie felt she might as well make use of the benefits of registration and join the hero training program at Camp Hammond, part of Mr. Stark's Fifty State Initiative program, where every U.S. state got a team of heroes to call their own. The camp was run by Dr. Henry Pym, who often stopped by to talk about his shared history with her dad. The first time, he hadn't seemed to realize she would have mixed feelings about hearing other people's memories of him while she was still grieving. But he'd swiftly understood when she'd seemed awkward, and had sat down with her and told her how proud Scott would have been to see her continuing his super hero legacy. She told him then that she'd love to hear more about Dad's life, and also if Dr. Pym was open to chatting about any new possibilities concerning the whole "shrinking and growing heroes" thing, she'd be interested in taking anything he had for a test run. He'd laughed and said he would; while nothing concrete had been forthcoming so far, he kept sending encouraging messages and telling her to keep at her training.

Her tutor at Camp Hammond, however, wasn't so friendly. His codename was Gauntlet, a drill instructor type with a giant cybernetic arm, who required them all to use hero codenames with him and with each other at all times. The discipline of the camp made Cassie roll her eyes pretty often, but she appreciated how well she and the other heroes had started to fight in sync with each other in combat simulations, owing to the extensive training they'd had.

Now, however, she and all the other students found themselves running out into the courtyard between the dorms, because, suddenly, power to the whole camp had just gone down. Somewhere, a hand-cranked siren started to wail. Hardball, Komodo, Cloud 9, Ultra Girl and the 3-D Man; all friends Cassie recognized amongst the many young heroes in training from the various dorms, all looking at each other with a mixture of puzzlement, anticipation and, honestly, fear. They all started asking each other questions they didn't know the answers to, but then Gauntlet came jogging over. He raised a hand and there was quiet. "This isn't a drill. Power is out. All Stark technology is out. We can't get S.H.I.E.L.D., Stark, the Avengers or anyone else on the horn. Right now, you are all to return to barracks until—"

"Wait," said a voice at his shoulder. Cassie glimpsed a tiny figure there: then, growing to full size, there was Dr. Pym, in his Yellowjacket costume. He looked strung out and desperate, his uniform scarred and seared. "Listen, all of you! New York is under attack. Alien ships of some kind. The Avengers... the Avengers are missing. S.H.I.E.L.D. is down. Everything is—"

"Who's attacking?" said the other tutor, running to join them, a highly experienced man in a skull mask and hood: Taskmaster. He possessed a rare genetic trait allowing him to see any action performed once and copy it immediately, making him one of the most skilled martial artists the world had ever known. He had a past training stooges for super villains, but like the Thunderbolts, he'd been given some leeway in order to return to the straight and narrow—something Cassie appreciated.

"Aliens I said! I don't know, I don't know which! I only just got away. I... I can't find anyone!" Cassie had never heard Dr. Pym so lost and uncertain.

But Gauntlet wasn't uncertain in response. He raised his voice and turned to address the assembled heroes. "Everyone who's not suited up, get suited up. It's time."

"Yep," the Taskmaster agreed. "Get your gear. We're up."

Cassie found herself speaking for all her classmates. She felt anxious as hell, but part of her welcomed this. She'd been trained to. She would get to demonstrate her new skills and experience and save people. "We're going in?"

Gauntlet and Taskmaster seemed to realize they should look to Dr. Pym for the order. They did, but in doing so, Gauntlet put his enormous metal combat hand on the man's shoulder. It looked half like comfort, half like an instruction to compose himself.

"Yeah," said Dr. Pym, gathering his wits. "Yes. This is it. This is what you've trained for. We're going in."

THEY WENT by Chinook, those who could fly forming up ahead and alongside. The greenery of upstate New York swiftly gave way to urban sprawl beneath them, but nobody was looking at that. They were all staring at what was ahead: the smoke and flashes between the skyscrapers, and the enormous figures striding between them. Whoever this was had access to the same growth tech as she did. So that was going to be her part in this: to take on whatever those were, one-on-one.

Bring it, she thought.

"It's the Skrulls," said Diamondback, the former criminal who'd once winked at Cassie and said she used to be Captain America's girlfriend. Since they'd heard about Steve Rogers' death, she had borne a grief that indicated, to Cassie's surprise, that that was probably true. She supposed Steve had also shared her appreciation for reformed characters. Diamondback was one of a handful of mature students at the Initiative: people who'd already been around the business of heroes and villains and were only there because they were new to the idea of taking orders. Now she stared out of the side door of the chopper shaking her head. "So we… we shouldn't trust that anyone is who they say they are." She ducked back into the cabin and gave a sudden grin. "Present company excepted, of course."

"You… really don't have many powers," Cassie began, feeling awkward.

"Oh, I'm gonna die throwing precious stones with some precision," said Diamondback. "But I'm gonna die doing my duty."

Which got a shout of approval and a lot of high fives from the students around them.

"Touchdown in ten," called Gauntlet. "I don't want to hear any more talk about dying. You follow your training and you'll be fine. You all stay on me. I pick your targets. Keep your comrades alongside you, we clear?"

"Sir, yes sir!" they yelled back.

Beside him, Taskmaster made a little gesture that said *yeah, that.*

Cassie closed her eyes and took a deep breath.

THEY TELEPORTED into Times Square, which seemed to be the epicenter of the battle. Cassie had wondered who the Skrulls were fighting, and now she opened her mouth in wonder at what she immediately saw: Kate Bishop leaping between the scattered remains of cars, loosing explosive arrows, shouting orders. Nearby stood Billy Kaplan—Wiccan—his hands rending the air as he spoke into life spell after spell, doing the heavy lifting of keeping the… oh god, the enormous Super-Skrulls that were swooping in at her… friends… keeping them back, so Patriot and Speed could run back and forth to rescue civilian after civilian. Teddy was picking up cars and throwing them at the invaders, then shape-shifting out of the way of their energy blasts, keeping their attention on him.

The Young Avengers were holding the line. She felt almost on the edge of weeping to see it. "Are we going to join them, sir?" she asked.

"Initiative: move to support those vigilantes," shouted Gauntlet, "we're all on the same damn side here."

They ran in toward where Kate was shooting. Cassie decided

she wouldn't go giant-sized until she was right in the face of a Skrull, otherwise she'd just be a bigger target. Even so, she was dodging energy blasts immediately. She and Diamondback dropped into cover beside Kate and Teddy, behind an overturned police car.

"Oh, hey," said Kate, looking not entirely pleased to see her. "You here to arrest us?"

"I'm here to fight alongside my friends," said Cassie, "to stop an alien invasion. Look over your shoulder, I brought the cavalry."

"Hi," said Diamondback, "I'm Diamondback."

Teddy looked back to see Cassie's Initiative colleagues join the line with the rest of the Young Avengers. It gave the last few civilians the moment they needed to break and run from the square, aided by Speed and now Taskmaster and his shield covering for them. "You brought the super-cops, you mean."

"Are you going to be like that, or are we going to do this together?" said Cassie.

Kate reached out and touched her shoulder. "We're going to do this together," she said. "And thanks. We couldn't have held them much longer."

"Yeah, you could," said Cassie.

"Okay," said Teddy, "you see that Super-Skrull right there, the one with the Iron Man chest? I'm going to try something."

And suddenly he stepped out of cover, his own chest inflating to abnormal size, which puzzled Cassie for a second until she realized he was going to try to shout over the noise of battle. "Brother of the Empire!" he bellowed like a foghorn. "I order you to stand down!" That got the attention not just of that one Super-Skrull, but of several others nearby also. "I am the son of Princess Anelle," continued Teddy, "and rightful heir to the throne!"

The Super-Skrulls looked at each other as if they didn't have orders to cover this.

Cassie, Kate and Diamondback exchanged worried glances. Cassie had read a lot of history and a lot more trashy fantasy. She knew from both that the one thing a royal house always did when it assumed power was—

Kate and she both yelled as Teddy was hit by power bolts from several directions at once, several other Super-Skrulls actually turning away from the heroes that had swept in to engage them to target him instead. He was blown backward into the debris.

"Teddy!" shouted Billy, breaking off from his spells and rushing forward.

A Super-Skrull suddenly erupted to giant size and punched him off the ground, sending him flying across the square to smash into an advertising hoarding on the other side.

Cassie leapt up to giant size herself as the Initiative rushed in behind her—just as they'd been trained to do when sealing a breach in the ranks.

"Fastball Special!" yelled Gauntlet, swinging himself up her costume into her hand. She knew exactly the move he was after. She threw him at the face of the giant Skrull.

His cybernetic arm hit the beast in the middle of its brow, breaking its face. It started to sway on its feet, and then to topple. Gauntlet rode it down and sent a power blast into its skull as it crashed to Earth, and as the young heroes all around them cheered, Cassie scooped him up again and pulled him back to a line of upended cars, which were being thrown into place as a proper barricade by a combo of tanks and speedsters.

Gauntlet and Kate Bishop glared at each other for a moment, then both nodded in acknowledgment. "Teams of three!" Gauntlet shouted to the Initiative. "Like we trained for!"

"End each engagement fast!" shouted Taskmaster from across the square. "Hold the line until some real super heroes get here, you grunts! Or aren't you hero enough for that?!"

"Good cop/bad cop, huh?" said Kate.

"It works for us," Gauntlet responded.

Cassie couldn't help but wonder, given the state super hero culture was in, where the hell the Avengers might be, if they weren't here already.

But if it was just them, it was just them. She would do her duty.

"We need to find Billy and Teddy," said Kate. "Cassie, next time you go giant, see if you can get to them."

"You don't give orders to my people," said Gauntlet.

"Cassie's my people," said Kate.

Cassie would have said something, but a moment later another enormous Super-Skrull was upon them, and her next few minutes were devoted to pure survival.

EIGHTEEN

VERANKE

SHE WAS Jessica Drew, the Spider-Woman. She often thought of her mental processes as swimming just under the surface of something, the real her just every now and then poking out. This ocean of self was the personality of someone whose life had been artificially influenced from very early on in her life, who had a very strong sense of self because so many people had tried to take it away from her.

She was Jessica Drew. And yet she was also very much something else.

Right now, she was sneaking through the jungle of the Savage Land, trying to find Tony Stark. She had an idea of where he might be, judging from what she knew of the geography of this area, and the angle at which her best friend Carol—perhaps now former best friend, depending on how much she'd seen of who Jessica had been zapping just now—had taken off. She'd just reached the edge of the clearing where the Mutate Citadel was when she heard a noise from above. She looked up and saw Echo, one of Luke's rebel Avengers, standing on a tree branch, looking the other way, and thus possibly unaware of her.

Jessica summoned to her hand the bio-electricity that, in her Spider-Woman guise, manifested itself in what were called "venom blasts." She flicked it upward and it blasted the branch away from under Echo.

She landed safely, of course, on three points, despite being caught by surprise. "It's me, Echo!" she shouted. "Jessica, I'm not a Skrull!"

Jessica considered for a moment. She was certain there was nobody else in the vicinity. Her every sense felt nothing but the jungle itself, for a mile or so all around.

All right then.

"I know," she said, perhaps a little sadly. She closed to where the woman could read her lips. "What are you doing way out here?"

"I… I had to leave some of the others behind. I think they've been taken in by a Skrull. I'm starting to notice these tiny differences in body language, you know? I copied the way that 'Bobbi Morse' moves, and it's not quite—"

Perhaps Jessica telegraphed what she was going to do. At any rate, Maya managed to leap aside from her first venom blast and dodge the second, and was in the act of yelling and coming at her with some sort of martial arts kick when "Jessica Drew" used all of her extraordinary strength and speed to jump forward, grab her by the throat and send a surge of energy through her nervous system.

Maya looked almost disappointed in her. In life. In the hand she'd been dealt. Then all the life was gone from her face.

Jessica threw the body into the undergrowth.

The ocean she was swimming in was Jessica Drew. But what lay under the surface, and occasionally looked out, was a Skrull named Veranke.

She extended her senses once again until she was sure the combat hadn't been overheard. Then, smoothing out the body of Jessica Drew until she was certain it was entirely correct, she headed once more toward the cracked dome of the Citadel.

As she approached, she could hear from within sounds of soldering and muttering and electronic speech. Here indeed was

Tony Stark, his armor still on him but in pieces, equipment laid out in every direction, the corpses of old conflicts—probably remains from one of Karl Lykos's or the High Evolutionary's exploits down here—decaying all around. He seemed oblivious to their presence.

"We… we need to disconnect my bioware," he said to the A.I. in his armor. "The tech virus is hitting my body like pneumonia. I have a fever of at least a hundred and two." He looked it, too. Veranke had become very intimate with the different states human bodies could experience, and Tony was indeed suffering the extremes of the Techno-Organic virus she herself had had a hand in designing. His skin was pale, he was sweating and shivering, and his eyes were wide—as if the reality he was experiencing was slightly askew from anything consensual.

Perfect.

"How are you feeling, Tony?" she called, sauntering in.

He looked up, startled, then relaxed again, just a notch. Veranke's carefully planned course of action as the Spider-Woman resulted in her being the one person that just about everyone across super hero culture trusted. Still, he was being careful. "Not to be impolite," he said, continuing with his work, "but I'd as soon not talk to anyone until we figure all this out."

Veranke sighed. "You can relax now. It's just us. You did it."

Slowly, he turned to look at her. Something in her tone had alerted that futurist part of his brain. He was jumping to exactly the right conclusion.

She straightened up and addressed him as a soldier. "Your work on Earth is done."

"My… work?"

"You will go down in our people's history as the greatest soldier the armada has ever had. All you've done across these last few years, the destruction you've unleashed upon our enemies, turning them against each other, making yourself the most important person in their world, all from the deepest of covers: a cover that I'm sure convinced even you. That's one of the many things the virus is designed to undo. It should be allowing you access now, to your own memories, your own personality. Is it working?"

"Stop!" He looked away, anguished, uncertain.

She walked right up to him, delighted that he was this lost, already. "You will always and forever have my undying love. The love of Veranke, your Queen."

And she took his face in her hands and kissed him. She allowed the pheromones of Jessica Drew, that woman's way of influencing men, to flow into Tony as pure pleasure, pure reassurance, pure healing.

After a moment, he broke away and staggered back. "I'm not a Skrull!"

"I know that's what you think."

"Stop!"

"You served so selflessly. As I said to you on the day you volunteered: I am so sorry it had to be this way. But if not for you, my brave warrior, this day would never have come. I praise you and love you, and give to you your real name, which is Kr'ali Kl'riki Dulu. This is your day, and it is well earned."

He stared at her. She was sure she saw, deep in that gaze, a previously calm surface that was starting to crack.

NINETEEN

CASSIE LANG

GIANT-SIZE CASSIE had been grabbing, punching and using martial arts on Skrulls. When she tried to stamp on them they would squirm aside, or enlarge, or a flying one would grab the one she was on, pulling them away at the last second. She found herself being beaten back by a giant that stood between skyscrapers, sending blow after blow into her face, so she staggered and had been afraid of falling, her head swimming and lost.

She heard Gauntlet shouting and now she shrank, hearing his order, her head ringing. She stumbled as she hit normal size, smoke all around her, the screams of the dying and the roars of the enemy echoing all around. She was aware she was bleeding from her nose; she couldn't see out of one eye. Spinning on the spot, she tried to find the enemy, to send herself rushing back at them, feeling more and more rage as they were... Her friends and comrades were losing. They couldn't hold the line!

She just had time to see a group of Super-Skrulls, all marching together, firing as one, energy from their hands sending the assembled, attacking ranks of the Initiative flying, screaming, their bodies spasming, disintegrating.

The smell of electric death hit her on the wind, and she retched and stumbled again. She wasn't quite sure of her surroundings for a few moments, then she burst through some cars and found herself a hundred yards away from Jonas, the Vision, standing alone at the center of a group of Skrulls, who were all aiming at him. "This will not stand," he said, calmly. "Others will stop you. You will not win."

Cassie screamed as she saw an energy blast catch him straight through the back of the head, shattering his ceramic face into cracked fragments that sprayed the cars in front of her, hit her, like hail. She cried out, falling back, swatting the air, the pieces of her friend fizzing on her, burning through her costume. She was aware that she was sobbing. She staggered, so vulnerable now, aware of that beam right behind her—she had to find cover! Where were the rest of the Young Avengers? Where was Kate? Oh god, where was Kate?!

"Daddy," she whispered, "Daddy, I'm sorry." But she kept moving, kept forcing herself, step by step, to stagger toward the slight shelter of the overturned cars.

The world around her suddenly vibrated with energy, and she was sure the beam had hit her. A moment later, though, she realized that whatever this was, it wasn't harming her. She looked over her shoulder and saw to her horror that three Super-Skrulls had indeed come after her, but... no, now they were staggering, uniquely hurt by this beam or whatever it was, looking at each other, at their own hands as they started to vibrate, faster and faster—

Suddenly they exploded into bloody shards.

Cassie ducked as the remains splattered around her, feeling only hatred, only fury at what these things had done. The vibration cut out, the air clear again, and from all the distant parts of Times Square she heard hopeful shouts, though they were an instant later drowned out by the roars, once again, of the Skrulls.

But there was also another sound. Cassie stumbled to a vantage point in the wreckage, to see where it was coming from. It was an odd sound, but it was definitely human.

What she was hearing was... howling?

Through the gap in the twisted heap of cars and hoardings where, a few moments before, an entire squad of Super-Skrulls had been conducting a massacre, she saw a small group of humans. Most of them wearing something very much like S.H.I.E.L.D. uniforms. In their midst, holding the biggest, weirdest gun Cassie had ever seen there was... Nick Fury! The original superspy, the man who'd created S.H.I.E.L.D.! His head thrown back in the final bellow of a howl that all the others were joining in with.

The Howling Commandos!

That howl had been what defined Fury's unit at the height of the Second World War. Deep behind enemy lines, Nick Fury had taken on Nazi terror and he found something that had made those monsters scared. A loud, proud, defiant call that had sounded through the forests of occupied Europe and had made those who heard it rally or run. Now here he was, right now, howling that same defiance against the Skrulls.

"Okay, Commandos!" Fury shouted, resuming his firing stance. "Let's turn this thing around!"

TWENTY

CAROL DANVERS

CAROL DANVERS decided that desperate times called for desperate measures. After obeying Tony's order and leaving him in the Savage Land, she had flown at maximum speed not back toward the Americas, but pretty much straight up, attempting a sub-orbital hop, and, deep breath, moving a hell of a lot faster when she didn't have atmosphere in the way.

Already just about exhausted, she plunged down toward what she could see, even from this far up… oh god, New York City was on fire!

Something approached from below and she braced herself to fend off a missile. But no, hearteningly, it was a flailing Skrull, flung upward, screaming.

Well, putting the fire and the flying Skrull together told her just about everything she needed to know.

As she got closer to the ground, however, she couldn't help noticing how few humans she could see below, and how many Skrulls. And what was this now?!

Three flying Skrulls, another larger one leaping… No, wait, Super-Skrulls, displaying the shapes of human heroes, rushing up to meet her. She had a second to prepare a power bolt, but then they were on her, flame and energy and magic of some kind, all at once. Not quite enough to hurt her, but enough to send her flying out of control, spinning through something that might have been a newsstand, then right into a wall.

She lay there a moment, managing to breathe, her costume still hot from re-entry. Then she leapt to her feet. From her position she could see... Nick Fury?! Her heart exulted to see he was back, and of course he'd come prepared. He was firing the biggest gun she'd ever seen, bolt after bolt of something explosive, taking down Skrull after Skrull, some bare-chested kid beside him laughing, grabbing smaller Skrulls and throwing them at the bigger ones. A speedster of some kind flashed around the square, collecting civilians and downed heroes, dodging energy blasts. Another woman, or girl, because, god, these were just kids, was making the ground roll under the feet of the Super-Skrulls, keeping them off-balance and calling shots to Fury. A spellcaster in a hood was throwing incantations at the enemy, another kid lashing at them with a flaming chain, and... a boy, a boy less than ten years old walked calmly into the fray, eyes blazing, making Skrulls turn away and flee from his every step. He had about him the detachment of one of the Asgardian or Olympian deities. Carol had never seen any of these people before, but clearly this was why Fury had been in hiding for so long. The old spymaster had seen this coming. Through the smoke, on the other side of the square, she saw their objective: a besieged knot of other heroes—the Young Avengers? And some of Henry Pym's Initiative. "Okay, you punks!" shouted Fury. "Let's wrap it up! I got things to do!" In return he got a howl from these secret warriors of his. Carol raised her voice and joined in. Fury heard and turned to give her nod and a grim smile. "Go get 'em, Major!"

Carol returned the gesture, took a breath, powered up and fired herself across the square like a rocket, turning it into a punch that knocked a Super-Skrull flat into the ground. "You sure you brought enough Skrulls?!" she shouted to another as it swung to grab her.

"The Avengers are here!" shouted someone from the ranks of the Initiative.

"The Avengers were already here!" Carol yelled back, pointing toward Kate Bishop, because, dear god, that girl needed to know right now that they were all in this together.

"Just what I was going to say," called Kate. "But the more the merrier, Ms. Marvel!"

Suddenly Carol was caught from behind by the hand of a Super-Skrull around her throat, and then out of nowhere two more of them were on her. She glimpsed the Howlers cutting past her and understood that Fury had used her as a diversion. Fair enough. She blasted one Skrull at point-blank range, twisted another around and threw it, and then kicked the third into the path of an energy bolt that cut it in two.

When she looked up again, she saw Fury and his people reaching whoever was holed up at the other side of the square. Catching a gap in the fighting, she sped through it to join them. Fury's team were grabbing unconscious forms and hauling up the others, dazed and stumbling, obviously ready to bug out. "What's the plan, Nick?" she called.

"It's called Operation Only Trust Our Own," said Fury.

He dropped the muzzle of that enormous gun and fired it right at her.

Carol flew back across the square, right into the midst of some more Skrulls.

As she struggled to her feet, their blows already slamming down on her, she bellowed in anger at what Fury must have just assumed about her. The ground shook and the air vibrated. The Skrulls around her staggered and Fury and his team, and those they'd rescued, vanished in a swirl of magic.

Then the Skrulls were back on her again, blow after blow, impacts sending her reeling back and forth between them. Carol found herself unable to find her feet, her head ringing from the thunder and the playground ache of the betrayal. Even here. Even now. They had lost all trust between one another, and these things had rushed into that weakness like an infection.

She saw the tiny figure of Henry Pym moving into the space between the Skrull limbs that thrashed at her, his Yellowjacket wings fluttering. She dared to hope for a moment that here was a rescue, that in a moment they'd both have shrunk to microscopic size and be rushing away to regroup.

Then she saw he was smiling.

TWENTY-ONE

NATASHA ROMANOFF

IT HAD always been one of the Black Widow's rules that, when a dinosaur arrives, it's time to leave the party. She had quietly applied that rule, using the distraction of the prehistoric carnivore's intervention in order to slip into the cover of the jungle. From there she observed the way the scattered engagements had proceeded, made some calculated decisions about who was a Skrull and who wasn't, and then, when Carol had grabbed Tony and flown off, used her onboard tech to track her. She had followed them to what the map—which she'd memorized in the Quinjet—told her was a laboratory. She had not, of course, walked straight in, but rather had gone to observe, from the jungle, what he was doing inside that lab.

Natasha, under her birth name of Natalia, had been trained to be an intelligence officer in Moscow's Red Room during the darkest days of the Second World War. She had pursued that career, alongside sometimes being a super hero, ever since. She had used her stealth and insurgence skills against the Nazis, the West, the Russians themselves, Hydra, A.I.M., and literally a hundred other organizations and countries. She liked to think, therefore, that she knew a little bit about human nature. And she felt that she really shouldn't need scientific help to sniff out who was or was not a Skrull.

In the last few minutes, she had become pretty certain that what Tony was doing, alone in that lab, only made sense if he was not a Skrull, or at least did not believe himself to be one.

Natasha had thus been about to step out from the shadows when toward that same building had marched what seemed to be Jessica Drew.

So, Natasha had stepped back into hiding and, using her directional mic, overheard a fascinating conversation in which a Skrull called Veranke had attempted to persuade Tony that he too was a Skrull.

"They'll scramble back together," Veranke was saying to him now, "they'll come to you for leadership, only to discover that you're one of us."

She was really touching him a lot, using Jessica's powers on him. She wouldn't need to do that if he was really a Skrull, would she?

"I know today is a hard day for you. I know you don't remember. But this is what you wanted. For yourself. For the Empire. I promised you I would be here at this moment to help you through it. We will rehabilitate you. We will gradually bring you back to your true form, Kr'ali Kl'riki, greatest warrior of the Skrulls."

Natasha leaned out to chance a glance through the doorway. Tony stared into space, as though he was actually starting to believe it.

Okay, time to end this nonsense.

Natasha drew her automatic and took careful aim at Veranke's head. She would put two in there, she decided, two in the body, one in each leg, then keep shooting what was left until it stopped moving. That tended to solve most problems.

Suddenly she heard a noise behind her. Out of the jungle nearby stepped what looked like Henry McCoy, the Beast, and the mutant telepath Jean Grey, in her Phoenix costume. "Hey," said Jean, turning toward where Natasha was hiding, pointing, "is that—"

Oh, forget this for a game of soldiers.

Natasha puffed out her cheeks, drew a small submachine gun from her pack, swung in their direction, and, firing from the hip, mowed them down.

She watched "Jean" briefly transform into her Dark Phoenix look before enough bullets filled the two of them to make them collapse into bubbling green corpses on the ground.

Natasha let out a sigh of relief that her hunch had been correct. As if the real versions of either of those two could ever sneak up on her! She turned quickly back to the lab.

Tony stumbled out of the doorway, staring at her in horror. Of Veranke there was no sign. "Which way did she go?!" Natasha yelled.

He could only groan at her, staggering, about to fall. She ran and caught him, just in time. "Jess..." he began.

"Tony, it's Natasha Romanoff, Natalia, the Black Widow. Can you hear me?" He just about managed to nod. "That Skrull did a number on you, didn't she? Listen to me: you're not a Skrull. I've seen conditioning at work, and that's what she was starting to do to you." She scrabbled in her pack and found the syringe she was after. "I'm going to hit you with a shot of adrenaline plus some other stuff. It'll hurt like hell, but it'll get you on your feet for about an hour. Let's hope, anyway." She removed a plate from his armor, plunged the needle into his thigh and pushed down.

He gasped and hauled himself away from her. He landed on the ground and rolled over to look up at her, understanding swiftly returning to his features. "You say I'm not a Skrull—and yeah, they poisoned me, but they didn't kill me..."

"They're working you. There are five people on the planet that can stop them and you're one of them. Given your history— the histories of all you super-people—they probably think if they do actually kill you you'll just resurrect like this is, I don't know, a video game. Besides, killing you isn't the point. They want you to feel it, they want to do to you what you did to them."

"I... don't know if I can trust—"

She slapped him across the face. Just slightly. She smiled at his sudden anger. "Kill them or kill me. Decide now."

"… them."

"Cool. Let us go with that feeling then, and worry about the rest later."

"Making some noise here," came a familiar voice from behind them. "I got some news and I'm comin' in."

"Perhaps," said Natasha, turning and firing at the newcomer in one movement.

The bullets from her automatic sent Logan staggering back against the wall, his torso ripped up. "Son of a—" he yelled. "Damn it, Tasha!"

"Give me the word," she said, aiming at him once again.

"Carrot sticks." He growled in the back of his throat, and Natasha saw the bullet holes start to mend and the still smoking rounds pop out of his flesh to fall back onto the floor.

She holstered her weapon. They had come up with that codeword between them in the ruins of Berlin in the spring of 1945. Well, codeword, safe word, it had served for both on that long weekend. "Human Logan, this is human Tony."

"Listen, I got some more human friends, right behind me—"

"Then we will greet them as humans, though we may not take your word for that. But for now, Logan, once you are free of bullets, get out of here and go hunt Jessica Drew. If you see her, kill her."

Logan nodded and grinned, looking like he appreciated the certainty. "Copy that." He gave another little grunt, a final round fell to the ground, and he sloped out, his shoulders hunched, about to hunt.

Natasha turned back to Tony. "Where did Carol go?"

"I sent her back to New York. They'll be going after our people there."

"Okay. So. Rebuild the armor, reboot, form up the people we trust, win this battle, take the war back home."

Tony shook his head. "There's someone I need to talk to first: Reed Richards."

TWENTY-TWO

ABIGAIL BRAND

ABIGAIL BRAND, as she'd been trained to, used her escape bubble to make her way through space. The surface of the bubble was designed to evaporate, at the quantum foam level, on the surface away from where one pushed. So, if one pushed toward one of the Skrull spaceships, as she was doing now, then the other side of the bubble would exert a small force, enough to propel you in the direction you were instinctively trying to move. She had designed the specs herself, based entirely on how stupid human beings were about freefall. Now she very much appreciated her own knowledge of the margins vulnerable flesh bodies needed to do anything in space.

She was heading for one of the Skrull ships; literally the only place left to go. Her employees were somewhere behind her, failing to keep up, making their own escape attempts, or being blasted by Skrulls. She thumped onto the fuselage of the ship: her gloves, talking intelligently to the material of the bubble, attached themselves to the surface through the film. She managed to move herself across the surface, hand over hand, heading for what looked like a viewing port. A thinner material, certainly. She reached into her belt pouch, found a small explosive charge, and told the bubble to let it through. She attached it to the viewing port, set a timer, then went back five handholds, hand over hand. That was as far as she could let herself go if she wanted to get in there fast. A calculated risk, then.

The viewport silently blew open, the atmosphere inside taking the force of the blast mostly upward, as Brand had surmised. She went as fast as possible back to the hole and swung herself into it without worrying about what might be on the other side.

Depressurized empty corridor. Flashing alarms. In green, of course. But hey, she liked green. She should have that on the next space station she built: green alert. She saw another hatch on the roof, bounced the bubble up there, ducked inside and kept moving until she found an air lock. She could read enough Skrull to get her through it, and into the pressurized section of the ship. Skrulls didn't seem to go in for security cameras. That was an interesting little tic, she thought. Maybe caused by the fact that they were used to seeing their own forces looking exactly like the enemy. What would the sight of the enemy on board even mean? She was sure, however, that other systems would, by now, have noticed her progress.

She deactivated the bubble and ran, grateful once again that, due to whatever common ancestor most of the humanoid species of the galaxy shared—probably something to do with the great universal progenitors called the Celestials—they all breathed broadly the same sort of atmospheres.

She found her way to a control room of some kind, and, having taken due care with the sneaking, found it deserted, most of the ship's crew probably either committed on Earth or searching for whatever had caused the hull breach. Inside was an array of monitor screens, using, from what she could work out, everything from hacks into local security cameras to Skrull surveillance tech to display a really pretty excellent overview of...

Oh god, here was the invasion. All of it. Here was Earth, that she had worked so long and hard to defend, being overwhelmed on so many fronts, everything happening at once. She could see scattered groups of the Avengers, both kinds, fighting amongst themselves or getting lost in the Savage Land. She could see an energy bubble warping out the top floors of the Baxter Building. She could see London and various military bases nearby being hit hard by Super-Skrulls, just as hard as New York. Damn it, that must be about magic, right? They were knocking out the UK's defenses, then they'd be heading north to take Avalon. The MI-13 chief Pete Wisdom—the only other mutant with rank in the world's security services, in his case tasked with all the weird stuff—would be on the ground there, though. If she'd realized that, so would he. And sure enough, there was Captain Britain, the UK's magic-powered and really rather complicated national hero, taking down Skrull after Skrull. Those monsters wouldn't find the UK an easy target. On another screen, in some other part of space, she saw Hercules, who claimed to be the half-human son of Zeus but whose adventures on Earth seemed mostly to be about drinking everything in the Avengers' cellar and sleeping with everything humanoid. He was with some of the other immensely powerful beings that called themselves gods battling what looked like some enormous and very anomalous Skrulls... oh, seriously, could those be Skrull gods?! They were all on the deck of some sort of... sailing ship? Behind them, a strange sort of other-dimensional void, scattered with what looked almost liked pictures of stars rather than the real thing. This invasion was being conducted across every aspect of the universe, even extending to higher planes of existence. Hercules was roaring his defiance, and the sight of that gave Brand heart. On another screen, she saw camera views trying to pierce the fog of what looked like San Francisco, where Skrull dropships were landing waves of troops. They were encountering immediate resistance, however, from, oh no, the SFPD, trying to defend themselves with small arms from behind the remains of cars. The Skrulls were firing particle weapons at them, completely ruthless. They would be pretty sure there wasn't much in the way of super hero culture on the West Coast, but the question was, did the Skrulls believe that those who lived on a nearby island would care enough for their human neighbors to—

A blast of ruby-colored energy cut through the fog and several Skrulls, and suddenly there was Henry McCoy, the Beast, which brought a surge of relief because he and Brand were seeing each other, maybe. He was raking a Skrull with his talons, and beside him Kurt Wagner, the demonic-looking German mutant Nightcrawler, was grabbing the surviving cops and teleporting them to safety. Brand herself passed with *Homo sapiens* because all they saw of her mutant nature was her pretty green hair; while she had her issues with how mutant sovereignty was run on Earth, damn it right now she was proud to call them her people.

On some of the other screens, though, Brand saw terrible things: Skrulls walking captured civilians up to ditches in what the scrolling Skrull information feed indicated were places like Wellington in New Zealand, Goma in the Democratic Republic of the Congo, Aniana in Symkaria, simply shooting them at the edge, then kicking each body into the pit. That was clearly not some local outrage, but a standing order, a war crime. Other screens showed cities completely aflame, populations within them gasping for air, individuals combusting into ashes on the spot. Judging from what she'd already seen, the Skrulls seemed to want the world basically intact, but they clearly didn't want *all* of it. Human losses must already be in the millions.

She took a breath and put that all aside into some locked place in her mind. Looking around the screens, hoping to find some sign of human survival, she found what she was after: an energy dome around Latveria and an image of the tyrant super villain Doctor Doom within it, his arms folded, his head thrown back with laughter as the Skrull forces failed to breach his defenses with beam after beam, missile after missile. But Doom surviving all this wasn't the best outcome for the world either. Where was... ah, there was hope.

There was Wakanda.

The royal palace of Wakanda, spears on its battlements, and on every spear the head of a Skrull. Whatever camera this was remained fixed on that image, as if staring at it in horror. Then the viewpoint started to fizz with static until it blanked out, and another came online. This one gave a different view: Skrull ships lying on the ground, without power, in the night-time fields of Wakanda. In the distance stood a single figure, and the camera zoomed in on it.

King T'Challa himself, the monarch and Avenger known as the Black Panther, stood alone in front of his palace. A sword in one hand and a Wakandan tribal shield in the other. He looked entirely vulnerable, but Brand bet that was exactly how he wanted the Skrulls to see him. He had some super-powers as part of his heritage as the ruler of an African country that had never been colonized, which was one of the most technologically advanced countries in the world, and that form-fitting suit he wore was actually armor on a par with Stark's, but his main super-power was preparation. T'Challa would have been planning for a Skrull invasion of his homeland from the moment when he first learned about the Skrulls. Armies slowly marched from the ships, Skrull after Skrull, until they filled the frame. They were organizing into units and heading toward the Panther in good order. The viewpoint was no longer useful for whoever was guiding the cameras, and it switched to an overhead shot, as vast numbers of Skrulls rushed toward that lone figure from all directions, their fascistic culture insisting that his stance was an affront, an insult to their numbers.

Brand saw it a moment before they did: bunkers opened up in the ground immediately in front of them, letting the first wave of Skrulls fall into the embrace of Wakandan warriors. Skrulls being Skrulls, the next wave warped and leapt and flew over that slaughter, but now warriors also burst from behind the King, surging forward. Battle was joined.

Brand found herself inwardly exulting again. If the Skrulls could conquer Wakanda the Unconquerable, they could conquer all. They knew it.

But the Black Panther knew it too.

She realized that she was crying. Well, that was damn well fair enough. She shook her head to clear it. Something on another screen had caught her eye, something shocking.

Reed Richards. He was stretched into a nearly unrecognizable mass of plastic flesh, attached at hundreds of points to the devices of some cruel Skrull lab that was either examining him, dissecting him, or both.

Brand could see his mouth moving. Reed Richards was screaming.

So that was her immediate mission: find wherever the hell that was and rescue Richards.

She turned to head out and try to find some sort of security center when she heard voices at the door. Two Skrulls, looking utterly relaxed and complacent, wandered in and stared at her.

One of them grabbed for a gun and aimed at her.

Abigail Brand realized they had caught her completely in the open, completely unarmed. The tears still on her face might as well be for her.

TWENTY-THREE

PARKER ROBBINS

PARKER ROBBINS sometimes thought he was the only super villain with a brain. That was his special power. When he'd been just a punk kid, some sort of demon in a hooded cloak and boots that looked kind of "Ren Faire" had leapt out and tried to get the drop on him. The young Parker had kicked its ass, taken its stuff, and shot it until it had dissolved into goo. It had been good to know that stuff worked even with demons.

The stuff he'd taken had turned out to be a magic coat and boots, which had looked good on him. He'd started to call himself the Hood, and he'd made some money for himself and his family. He'd completed heist after heist in complete safety, and got quite the reputation, but always he'd found that it had actually been his brain, not his magic costume, that got him free and clear. The real operators in town, those who called themselves super villains and those who weren't that stupid, started to notice.

So when the super heroes had started fighting each other, he'd seen a big opportunity. He'd taken out some of their outliers, and some of the gang bosses, until the mainstream operators of super-powered crime started to see him as someone who, as well as being a useful soldier, would always put together a good operation. He got what he was increasingly seeing as "his people" into where they needed to be, then he got them out. He didn't stage set-piece battles with capes for the hell of it. Twice, some sort of Avengers had come after him. The second time, having made sure he could do it safely, he took revenge on them, actually took out Doctor Strange for a while, busted up his house.

From then on, he'd had all the respect he needed. He had money too. But then some weird stuff had started to happen within his operation. He'd discovered aliens trying to kidnap his business partner Whitney Frost and replace her with some sort of duplicate. He and Whitney had kept that to themselves, but from that point on Robbins had been on the lookout for these "Skrull" things.

Then he'd found one around his own table.

Ulysses Lugman, who'd called himself the Slug, turned out not to be who he claimed to be. In fact, Robbins had never met the real Slug. Robbins spread the brains of the Skrull impostor across the wall of that meeting chamber.

He held parleys, talked about it with a few of the other big bosses, actually tipped off Wilson Fisk, the Kingpin, in jail, leading, he'd heard, to the death of a Skrull in prison fatigues. Some of the bosses had come to feel that the Skrulls were trying to take over organized crime in America. Robbins replied, and he had allowed himself an eye roll, that what they'd get out of that would be less than their budget to get to Earth.

All that had happened without the capes hearing about it. Robbins thought to tell them, but for a while he'd thought this might just be the crime world's problem, that maybe the Skrulls were acting as undercover interstellar cops or something.

Then, in the last couple of days, a few little things had added up, and it had become clear that what the Skrulls had really been looking for within the wiseguys was their points of entry to the world of the capes, their intelligence on their enemies, their secret ways in.

He'd felt almost insulted. But that realization made him ready to act, though he didn't know quite what to do next. He had slept on it.

Now here he was, standing at the window of one of his penthouses in Brooklyn, watching fighter jets speeding to New York, once again burdened by having been entirely correct and nobody else having worked it out as quickly as he had. A few of the guys were sitting with him: Whitney, already in her Madame Masque outfit; Dr. Eliot Franklin, or Thunderball as he liked to be called, because his favorite crime was, it seemed, copyright theft, carrying his enormous wrecking ball on a chain; Bentley Wittman, the incredibly irritating Wizard, who clearly thought he was the brains of this outfit, and Gh'ree, who called himself the Blood Brother, bald and golden-skinned and incredibly tough and spoke only to tell people he'd once worked for someone called Thanos, who was maybe someone big in the Greek mobs. Robbins always felt he was supposed to feel slighted by that reference, but Gh'ree having the speech habits of a punch-drunk hoodlum kind of took the edge off it.

"Whadda we gonna do, Hood?" he asked now, halfway down a bottle of kiwi fruit juice, which was how this guy got intoxicated.

Robbins turned from the window. "Get everyone," he said. "Get everyone we can get."

"It's not our fight!" scoffed Wittman. "Let the 'heroes' and the aliens all kill each other!"

Robbins considered him for a moment. He took a step toward Wittman, and pulled his hood over his head, so his features were lost in shadow. It was what he did before he worked his major mojos, and it freaked the hell out of the small fry. "There being no more planet Earth," he said gently, "would be pretty bad for business, yes?"

Wittman looked around the room, obviously expecting to find support. When he got none, he looked awkwardly back to Robbins. "Well... that's a good way of putting it..."

Yeah. The only super villain with a brain. Robbins lowered his voice even further, making it clear to everyone that this was an order. "Get everyone. We're going in."

TWENTY-FOUR

NORMAN OSBORN

NORMAN HAD slowly risen to his feet at the same time as this "Captain Marvel" had. He had not at any point broken eye contact. "I know something about having voices in your head," he said, "voices pulling you in different directions." He was aware, in his peripheral vision, of his Thunderbolts slowly recovering. He hoped they were sensible enough not to get in the way of this. "And this might sound strange, it *is* strange, but I also know something about not being sure if you're really pink... or green." Because that had to be it, didn't it? The real Captain Marvel had, as well as fighting his own fascist government, also spent his life fighting Skrulls. The Skrulls were known to have shape-changing abilities that included convincing the subject that they really were their cover identity. It was great to have access to the government files that told you about this stuff. This guy showing up, looking like one thing, conflicted about who he actually was... yeah, Norman was pretty sure what he was speaking to.

"Green?" said "Marvel," as if it was an extraordinary revelation.

"And I can tell you this..." Now was the moment to add touch to this approach, so Norman did, putting a hand carefully on the warrior's hard shoulder. "Only one person can decide who you are, inside and out. That person is you. You were sent here to kill us, right? But you don't want to do that. You can feel it's wrong, can't you? May I ask, this form you're in, did you pick it yourself, or was it picked for you by the... Skrull Empire?"

"It was... picked for me."

"Did you know who you really were all along?"

"No!" He shook his head violently.

"Yes, yes, I thought that was the case. What a terrible thing they've done to you. You thought you were the Kree warrior Mar-Vell—"

"Yes!"

"You liked being him. It felt good to be him, to be respectable and respected."

"Yes!"

"And then some remote order was given, and something changed inside you, and you found yourself under what felt like a compulsion, the desires of a previous self of which you were entirely unaware, to come here, to attack us?"

"Yes!"

"But now you think, just because your inner self, what you think of as your real self, is... green... you can't be Captain Marvel anymore. But listen, listen! You can just decide to be him. You can be the man of honor. You can be Earth's protector. You can save us all." He took his hand away from the warrior's shoulder and took a step back, raised his hands, leaving it up to him. "You decide."

The Skrull looked around the room at the destruction he'd caused, but now it seemed like he'd made his decision. He didn't appear guilty about what he'd done anymore. Instead, he looked... motivated.

With a yell of determination, he leapt for the hole in the wall and flew away.

Norman took a long breath and adjusted his tie. He allowed himself a grin. Great work, old man.

120   Security ran in then, of course they did. All around him, the

Thunderbolts were getting to their feet. "Director Osborn," called the leader of the armored grunts who were meant to protect this place, "what happened?!"

"We're at war." Norman turned to address the Thunderbolts. "Get the Alpha team up and on their feet. Get anyone who's off campus back here. Get transport up and ready in five. If anyone does anything out of character… kill them."

"That's going to cause havoc," said Songbird, now back at his side.

"Havoc is all around us now," said Norman. "We have to ride it."

TWENTY-FIVE

NICK FURY

GENERAL NICHOLAS Joseph Fury was, according to his birth certificate, one hundred and nineteen years old. That gave him the right, he had been feeling for several damn decades now, to address anyone short of Asgardians, the Widow and the Wolverine as "kid." He still looked to be in his early forties because of an experimental serum he'd been given during World War II. His prolonged youth, he sometimes thought, was why he did what he did to protect the world. People figured it was a sense of duty, but, actually, it was a sense of obligation. He was an ordinary joe who'd been given a chance nobody else had, and that meant he had perspective nobody else had, so he had to give something back.

He'd spent his decades leading and, when he'd had to, being apart from, various security organizations, notably S.H.I.E.L.D., and he'd spent all his downtime preparing the world in secret for every contingency he could think of. "Shape-shifting alien invasion" had been pretty high up on that list. Hence the building in which he, his new Howlers and the kids they'd rescued were now standing. A lost facility of the fascist cartel known as Hydra, wiped from their records and relocated to deep under upstate New York through impossible science. His new people had fitted it out with everything a headquarters needed, shielding it from surveillance. This was his last redoubt, the place from which humanity could always fight back. Right now, he stood beside a young lady named Daisy Johnson, who he'd found and recruited in Minnesota, whose powers had resulted in him giving her the codename Quake. She sat at the communications desk, trying to find anyone transmitting anything from anywhere. "Not even CNN?" he asked.

"Nothing. Everything is down."

"They cut *all* global transmissions. Even back in the day I could never have done that."

"Do you think we should cut power? If the Skrulls can do this, they might be able to penetrate our shields."

"Nope. Within the next few minutes, I figure they're going to tell us how it's going to be. You keep monitoring."

He heard from behind him the clearing of a throat and turned to see that those they'd rescued had got their act together and come to check in with him. "Excuse me, Colonel Fury?" That was Cassie Lang.

"General," corrected Johnson, without turning to look.

"What's going on? Why did you save just us, from a bunch of places across Times Square, but not everyone else? Why didn't you want Carol Danvers? Is she a Skrull?"

"It must have looked like we ran," said Kate Bishop. She sounded furious with him, but she was keeping it in check.

Fury took a moment to look out over the young heroes he'd brought here. They were looking beat up, all right, but they still had their wits about them. The confidence of youth. A couple of them, like Bishop and Patriot, even had the relative calm of those who'd served a tour or so. It helped that he'd had Phobos to tend to them. That kid could pull the fear right out of you with a look. Fury had decided he might use that move in the field, if it ever came down to having to send these kids into a last-ditch battle. If it ever came to having to lose a few of them to get something done. He would do everything in his power to make sure it didn't come to that, but he'd had a terrible feeling lately that his power wasn't going to be anywhere near enough. He'd prepared for hours like these. But so had the Skrulls.

"That was as close to a win as we could get," he said. "The civilians that could get out did. The rest of the heroes were seen to retreat in good order, as were we. I went back for a moment there to tell a coupla cameras that we'd bloodied the Skrulls' noses."

"You know what they're saying?" Johnson turned to look at the kids. "That 'the Battle of Times Square' ended in stalemate, that three human forces arrived in turn to defend New York, that the Initiative sustained huge losses and showed huge bravery and the Howling Commandos really made the Skrulls suffer at the end there... but that the Young Avengers fought from the start and stayed and saved countless lives and held the damn line. That New York owes everything to you fugitives. That's what they're saying. I think that's what made the Skrulls switch off all the media."

Fury watched Bishop's face get very serious for a moment, as though she was on the edge of tears, but she didn't shed a single one. Finally, she just nodded. Elijah Bradley made eye contact with Fury and held the same expression. Good.

"As to why I didn't take Major Danvers, well, I'm pretty sure that was the real Ms. Marvel, but 'pretty sure' don't cut it in this job. She got taken down by the Super-Skrulls, but some of the Initiative moved in and managed to pull her out, get her to hospital. Word is she's unconscious but recovering. As to why I took you, I have excellent chains of surveillance for all of you. I'd bet my life—I am betting my life—on none of you being Skrulls, because I've done the homework. I took you away because today saved some of our forces, raised morale and bought us some time. But nothing we could do there could win us this war. Now, I'm done explainin' to ya. Stand straight and face front!" He waited until they obeyed the order, a few of them still slightly incredulous, but sure, they were kids. "All right, you yahoos! As of now, you're all part of my unit. You're Howling Commandos, and you howl when I say you howl.

Anyone not comfortable with that, I got a teleport out of here, but you gotta choose in the next thirty seconds, or you're in. As to where 'here' is, that's classified. We're Earth's last redoubt. We're gonna assemble our forces, put together a strategy, win this thing. Any other questions?"

There was silence.

"That is thirty seconds," said a cold, calm voice from the other side of the chamber.

The kids all looked over to the doorway through which the Vision had just entered.

"Oh my god," said Cassie. The android's face was still a patchwork of cracked shards, and he was walking with a limp, but yeah, Fury was pleased at their reaction to how his techs here had been able to piece the synthezoid back together. It had been easy enough, they'd told him, because the body had familiar human anatomy and the pieces slotted together like building blocks. And the hardened consciousness of this guy, the sheer number of hidden memory dumps and downloads... Fury felt kind of a kinship with someone who had so many safeguards concerning his location and identity. Here was one super hero who... well, if *that* was a Skrull, the aliens damn well deserved to conquer the world. The kids all ran to embrace the Vision, and he copied them awkwardly, a frown on his face.

"You're welcome," said Fury. "And thanks for the countdown, Vision."

"You're also welcome," said the Vision.

"Now listen, ya goldbricks," he called, and they came to order again, not as quickly as he'd have liked, but he'd let that pass for now. "I don't expect you to call me 'sir,' and as an elite unit we will not be standing on ceremony. I do, however, expect you to follow orders, immediately and without question. Am I understood?"

There were nods and voiced agreement. Some of them actually did say "sir." Fury knew he'd get to the point where they all would. This was not a bad place to start from.

"Sir," said Johnson, "it's started."

The world's media had returned. The graphics on the enormous monitor screen that Johnson activated on one side of the chamber indicated there was only one broadcast channel for each geographical location. From here they could see them all. On the screens appeared dozens of familiar faces, along with many Fury didn't recognize. They all started talking at once, but the intelligent listening systems of the base managed to sort out what was being said into one coherent narrative. "We're not here to hurt you," said a former President, or rather, a Skrull that looked like one. "We're here to save you. So please forgive us for assuming these familiar forms in order that we may impart our message of peace to you without causing you even more fear."

"We've traveled across the universe," said a movie star, "basically to save your world from what you're doing to it. Hey, did I get the voice right?"

"You have so much potential," said Reed Richards, "but you're on the brink of ecological disaster."

"You have created," said Charles Xavier, "a system of inequality, where material wealth is continually funneled to those who are already rich, at the expense of those who are poor."

"What most disturbs us," said a famous climate activist, "is that you're fully aware of the situation, and though your scientists have told you exactly what you need to do to solve it, still you do nothing."

"Right now," said another former President, "we're just fighting your planet's super-powered community, okay? We're trying not to hurt civilians."

"Unfortunately, we can't always manage that," said a puppet from a children's show. "But please believe us, we don't want to hurt anyone who isn't trying to hurt us."

"You've seen some of our ships," said rock star Lila Cheney. "Join our Empire, and you all get access to technology way in advance of anything you've got now. You get to use all the tech the super heroes have been hoarding."

"They've been fighting each other, getting more and more authoritarian," said a Sixties icon, "when they should have been helping you, helping out the world, right? Instead, they're part of the problem, standing in the way of progress."

"This is day one of Earth as a proud member of the Skrull Empire," said a more modern pop star and social activist. "In a very short time, you'll see the benefits. Come onside now, let our forces through, let them know where our super-powered enemy is, and you'll get our protection as soon as possible. That's a promise."

"We apologize for the inconvenience of depriving you of your communications tools," said that guy who played the drums. "You'll get them all back, okay?"

"Your lives," said one of the British Royal Family, "will go on as before. You will keep your homes, your culture, your family, your jobs. Everything will return to normal."

"We're not here to *take* anything," said the star of a Sixties space series, "only to add things. We're trying not to fight your armed forces, only the super-powered fascists. If individual members of those armed forces stand down, they should be completely safe. They won't be attacked."

"We want all hostilities to cease," said a TV star of the Seventies. "We're here to end wars, not start new ones. We have new energy sources for you, prosperity for everyone."

"We have this saying," said a chat show host, "and this might chime with those of you who have a faith. You'll come to learn what ours is, just as we look forward to learning from you. We say 'He loves you.'"

"Yeah, yeah, yeah," said the Sixties icon, with a wry look.

"Your days of poverty, hardship, inequality, and disease are over," said some senior Catholic.

"Accept change, embrace it," said another movie star, "and this change will make you all you ever wanted to be."

"He loves you so much," said a different British royal.

"And so do we," said a former First Lady. "You'll find out."

And on the screens all around, unselected by the systems, that narrative was being repeated by faces ranging from Magneto to some ayatollah to someone North Korean to someone who looked to be an Indian sports star, to Namor to a Nigerian President to a Japanese film director, to a Brazilian footballer to a South Korean boy band to Doctor Doom to… they had sure done their research, because Fury could see famous Belgians and Bollywood stars and Chinese actors in there, or at least that's what the systems were telling him. He felt a heaviness in his heart. "Switch that damn thing off," he said. "I seen it all before. Bunch of lies and half-truths and a few truths thrown in there so the world's smart guys can say the new overlords made some good points and stroke their beards and betray their neighbors to the space Nazis." He turned and looked at his kids. "Any of you feel yourselves moved by that rousing slice of horse hockey?"

"No, sir," a few of them said, and they were all looking angry.

"Horse hockey?" said the Vision.

Fury cracked a grin. "Okay," he said, "you all get some sleep, the ones that need it, six hours downtime for the rest. When I call you together again, we start fighting back against what you just saw. Dismissed."

He went to Johnson and shared a private look of worry with her. That broadcast was going to win a lot of human hearts and minds. He wished he felt a quarter as certain as he sounded.

TWENTY-SIX

ABIGAIL BRAND

BRAND WIPED away her tears and looked puzzled at the two Skrulls who were pointing guns at her. "What do you mean by this outrage?!" she said in Skrull Imperial Tongue. "How dare you?!"

They actually hesitated. Brand was relieved and frankly surprised to discover these guys didn't seem to have a protocol in place to tell who was a Skrull and who wasn't. The tech of transformation must have moved so fast, with implanted memories and the like, that their culture hadn't kept up. So, their ability to resemble the enemy was a double-edged sword. Brand knew literally dozens of alien languages. She couldn't even remember where she'd picked up Imperial.

"Why are you crying?" asked the smaller Skrull, one of their small drone workers whose first forays to Earth were the origin of the 1950s idea of "Little Green Men."

"I am moved by the speed and size of our victories," said Brand, "and this form expresses that sensation through human emotional responses."

"Who are you?" asked the larger Skrull, keeping his weapon

aimed at her, obviously less convinced than his little pal. "What are you doing in here? Identify yourself!"

"Cease this impudence. I am part of the Queen's delegation—"

"Which delegation?"

"—and you will not point that weapon at me. Here, let me take that." She reached out, taking the gun from the small one's shaking hand.

"I repeat—" said the big one.

Brand blew his head off, and then blew the head off the little one too.

The sound of the energy blasts echoed around the chamber as the bodies fell to the floor. She would have only seconds before security came running. She looked back to the monitors, hit a control to display a schematic of the ship, and found the chamber where Richards was.

And then she was running.

BRAND HAD two guns and, on the way to Richards' cell, while ducking between corridors and inter-wall ducts, she had to use them several times. She popped up in one control room and let loose, mowing down Skrulls and equipment together, before grabbing the single remote control device she'd come for, then dropping down a chute into the level below. A lot of these connectors were designed for a people that could slide and slither and that made it easy to let artificial gravity take her where it would. She took a breath. Killing Skrulls felt good, and that was bad news. Every single decision she had to make now had to be motivated by logic, not by anger. She composed herself on that basis and ran on.

Within ten minutes she had the whole ship on alert, with what little of its complement that had remained on board rushing back and forth, doubtless calling in security from other vessels.

Sliding down into the hallway outside Richards' cell, she found half a dozen Skrulls rushing to meet her, some looking like proper soldiers, armed to the teeth, some like servants who'd just grabbed spanners and the like.

She killed the soldiers first, letting the servants run if they wanted. Then she blew the door and found Richards, stretched between those cruel probes. His cries abated when he saw her, one eye stretched out like a psychedelic splash across the wall. Could a big poster eye look doubtful? This one did.

She ran to a console, managing to read enough to release him. He fell to the floor, a groaning, shivering mass. She activated the emergency blast door, and it slammed down in front of what remained of the seal she'd blown out, just in time to get in the way of more Skrulls running to join in the party. They'd probably have cutting gear. She still had only seconds.

Attaching the remote console she'd taken from that control room to the main board here, she paused to admire how its ports latched on and adapted themselves. Skrull tech had some morphing capability of its own. Then she redirected all systems to this point, using the security clearance this board had had left on it by some lazy Skrull officer, and hit "vent" on every single air lock on the ship.

She heard a reassuring "boom" ringing out down the entire length of the vessel. There would also be screams, lots of screams, for, oh, thirty seconds or so. It wouldn't get rid of all the Skrulls on board, but it would leave those that were left with more problems than she had, just about.

She went back to Richards, and saw that, very slowly, he was starting to re-form his body into something that looked more like his usual human form. "Dr. Richards," she said, putting a hand to his chest, "my name is Abigail Brand, I'm Director of S.W.O.R.D. We met once at a party in Tel Aviv. We're at war with the Skrull Empire and I need you to—"

He suddenly came together and, in one incredibly swift movement, grabbed her weapon and wrapped his coils around her throat. "I am going to get back to my wife and children!" he bellowed, a terrifying note of irrationality in his voice. "Even if I have to kill every last one of you!"

"Not… a…" she managed to begin. But she was only going to be conscious for a couple more seconds. He was trying to crush her neck. She felt good that she'd done her duty, that freeing Richards had been the best possible move she could have made.

Maybe the guilt of killing her would motivate him enough to save Earth.

TWENTY-SEVEN

BALKAMAR

MARIA HILL had been surprisingly cooperative. It helped that
Balkamar's Skrull colleagues composed the entire remaining
complement of the Helicarrier crew—those being the ones who
chose to remain, staying on mission to learn what they could from
Hill, when the order had been given to head for the escape rafts.
Hill had, as much the pragmatic prisoner of war as they'd expected
her to be, just given Balkamar a tour of all the ship's major systems.
She had offered them her own personal surrender, though since
Director Stark remained alive, she didn't feel that her surrender on
behalf of S.H.I.E.L.D. would mean anything to the governments
of Earth's nation states. And after a little research, that checked out.
Balkamar had felt slightly annoyed that, once again, the martial
fervor of his people had blinded them to the finnicky bureaucracy
of these locals. Hill had also awkwardly explained that only Tony
Stark had the codes to some of the ship's security systems, though
she tried on a couple of occasions to access them, even going so
far as to crawl into a narrow, coffin-like alcove that allowed access
to security panels. She had emerged looking fearful that she had
nothing to offer her captors.

Balkamar reassured her that, since she had surrendered and offered them her full cooperation, no harm would come to her. She told him she appreciated that.

They had, eventually, found some tea.

Hill had tried it, said she much preferred coffee, but that she supposed she would have to get used to it, and they had both laughed. He and his fellows finally walked with her back to the main deck, from where they would take a transport aircraft to the nearest Skrull ship. A full debriefing awaited Hill, but Balkamar was confident this would be a civilized affair. She would be very helpful in the transition of S.H.I.E.L.D. into a tool of the Empire. For that they would also need the potent symbol of the Helicarrier, so it was already scheduled to be salvaged and refitted.

"Oh," she said now, stopping as they were halfway to the aircraft. "There is one more thing left for me to do."

"Please, if there is a matter to which you must attend—"

"It's just a small thing. A note to self. When this is all over, I'm going to order a t-shirt online, you know, one of the ones where you choose your own slogan."

"I am sure," said Balkamar, puzzled, "that the Empire will relatively soon allow such businesses to once more flourish, although, dear me, the matter of currency is a whole can of worms that—"

"I've never done that before. But now I definitely will. This is about a bet, you see. You know, a wager? Can you guess what that t-shirt will say?"

Balkamar smiled at his fellow Skrulls. This was clearly an example of that human need to impose narrative on the unfolding events of reality. Hill obviously needed to end this phase of her life with a clever line. "Please, do tell me this charming story."

Hill smiled kindly at him. "Several months ago, a man who I very much respect came to see me. He told me that S.H.I.E.L.D. makes this very cool... I guess you'd call it a type of robot? An android, really. The Life Model Decoy."

"Indeed, my dear, we have read of such things." This sounded like it was going to be good.

"They're normally used in undercover ops. But he told me to start using them in everyday matters of command, to always know where I had one stashed away. In a cupboard or alcove. He told me that doing that wasn't cheating or a cop-out, just a smart strategic policy. So, here's what I'm getting at: When I'm done here, I'm going to order a t-shirt that says—"

Balkamar had suddenly been seized by a terrible certainty. What had she just said about an alcove? "Execute her!" he shouted. "Now!"

He leapt back as his comrades obeyed the order, blasting Hill apart with energy bolts.

But what dropped to the ground wasn't Hill.

It was a thing of gears and ceramics, its face cracked like a statue.

She had done what she had just told them about. She had swapped herself for one of these... abominations! But why, in all honesty? What game was there possibly left here for her to play? Presumably she was on her way already to some safe house, but they now had the Helicarrier and she'd probably been lying about those security codes, so—

"It'll say," finished the Life Model Decoy, turning its broken face to look at him, "*Nick Fury was right.*"

From the control tower high above them, something fell to the deck. It took Balkamar a second to realize that it was a bagful of explosives.

He was slightly further away from the blast than his comrades. Their bodies took the brunt of the explosion.

He lay on the deck, the remains of his friends plastered all around, and on him, glorious in their sacrifice. He took a long breath, rejoicing that he was alive, but otherwise really dashed annoyed. They had been having such a nice time, after all. This felt like a distinct lack of hospitality. He looked up and saw, up on the control tower, a tiny figure taking to the air on a S.H.I.E.L.D. jetpack.

So that had been it. That had been the entirety of her petty revenge: killing a few more of those that had come to save her world.

And after they had had such a jolly chat. It was really terribly rude of her.

He got to his feet, brushed himself down, and took a spyglass from his vest pocket. He activated the zoom and managed to follow the glow of her engine and find her in the sky. Had he at hand a weapon with sufficient range, he would jolly well have had a pot shot at her. He was that cross.

He saw her look back over her shoulder. Her thumb closed on a button on the control of the jetpack.

Balkamar had a moment of terrible realization as he heard, from deep beneath him, the first rumblings of some massive detonations.

"Oh, that is simply… not on," he opined.

And then the deck beneath him exploded.

TWENTY-EIGHT

ABIGAIL BRAND

BRAND SLOWLY awoke, and realized, very swiftly that, one: she was alive and that two: there was no longer anything around her throat. She opened her eyes.

Reed Richards worked at high speed, his fingers an array of fronds fluttering across the alien console. "I don't think you're a Skrull," he said, not even looking over his shoulder. "It makes no sense, biological or tactical. So. Moving on. Oh, and," he finally glanced back at her, "sorry."

"No," she said, climbing to her feet and joining him, "it's understandable." She felt a tremor run through the deck. "Why is the ship vibrating?"

"We're being attacked by the rest of the Skrull fleet. When I sent the remaining crew out into space by turning their security systems against them, the rest of the fleet realized something had happened and turned on us. I'm thinking their anti-missile and anti-beam shields will only last about eight point three more minutes, and I'm working on finding some alternative. I can't get our own weapons to work. I suspect they're jamming them. Longer term, I also need to get the stealth back up. The drive is fully functional and if there's a sufficient gap in their ranks I'm aiming to speed through it and head back to Earth. They used my brain to start this war. I'm going to use my brain to end it."

Brand blinked. "What do you mean 'they used your brain'?"

"Long story. Can you fly this ship? Sit there if you can and start doing so."

Brand did. She hit the scanners and saw the fleet were stationed very carefully in a firing pattern around them, the bombardment continuing. The screen flared every second, in time to the vibrations of energy hitting the hull. There was no gap to speed out of. "Ready to punch it when you find a way out."

"Plot in a course to New York."

"Not New York."

"My family is in New York!"

Brand was about to argue, but the screen in front of her suddenly flared from a new direction. She hit a control and the scene ahead of them flicked up to be visible on the bulkhead. Through the Skrull fleet, right through two of their ships, just in that instant—there was speeding a single figure, leaving explosions in their wake, firing power blasts from their hands now, reducing ships of the line to scattered, expanding blooms of wreckage.

Brand zoomed in on the figure and she and Reed gasped at the same moment. "Captain Marvel!" she said. Because sure enough, somehow, maybe through some time travel thing, or maybe this was some legacy hero, but it very much looked like here was the Kree warrior Mar-Vell, back in action, fighting as hard as she'd heard he'd fought. "Okay, finally some good news!" And here was some more, because Mar-Vell's actions had provided them with just the opening they needed.

Brand hit the proverbial pedal and the ship rushed forward as Skrull ships exploded around them. In a second they were clear, in free space, the Earth looming ahead of them. "Brand!" began Richards, sounding desperate.

"We will get to New York," she shouted back. "But if we're going to save the Earth, we need to pick up a couple of people first!"

TWENTY-NINE

CLINT BARTON

CLINT, BOBBI and Luke followed Logan toward a building he'd referred to as "the lab" only to hear, after he'd gone ahead to make sure it was safe to enter, gunfire. They'd been running to join him when he'd come sprinting back the other way, bullets popping out of his chest, yelling something about hunting Jessica Drew, and that Tony and Tasha were human. On that basis they cautiously entered the lab to find Tony still looking as sick as he had back at the crash site, Natasha standing guard. When she asked them what Logan had said to them, and when they'd told her, she'd holstered her weapon. "We are all human," she'd said. "Probably."

Tony replied by quite spectacularly hurling all over a computer console. What landed there was green and sizzling.

Logan came back in. "Carrot sticks," he said.

"Carrot sticks?" asked Clint. He had one arm still around Bobbi. He didn't yet feel able to let her go.

"Coming from you," said Natasha to him, her eyebrow raised, "that just sounds weird."

"I'd like to know what that's about," said Bobbi.

"You and me both," said Luke.

Clint just shrugged, then looked at Bobbi's expression and spread his arms to say he had no idea.

"No sign of Jessica," said Logan. "The trail just stopped. Like she'd turned into somethin' else and flown."

"Copy that," said Natasha. Suddenly, she drew again, swinging around to face the doorway, and in the same moment, Logan spun and popped his claws. "Company," she said.

And there was. At the doorway stood, spears in their hands, Ka-Zar, formerly Kevin Plunder, the man known as the Lord of the Savage Land, and his wife Shanna O'Hara, who in these parts liked to be known as the She-Devil. They were both dressed in the briefest of furs, which, given the temperature, seemed to Clint to be a lot more sensible than the outfits they were all wearing. Bobbi saw where he was looking and nudged him in the ribs. He nudged her right back.

"You need to tell us what's going on," said Shanna.

"Yeah, you can't have super hero battles here," said Ka-Zar, as if they were children who'd been fighting in his yard. These two were a U.S. zoologist and English nobility respectively, and if any humans could be said to be in charge of this place, they were. As far as Clint had seen, they ruled with, as their backgrounds suggested, a combination of ecological concern and strutting around like one owned the place. If Clint was being honest, they made him uncomfortable, and that went doubly so now they might be Skrulls.

"Err, I think they're real," said Spider-Man, sticking his head around the top corner of the door. "I mean, not one hundred percent, but they remember the last time we met and stuff."

"So do the Skrulls," said Logan. "Us in here, we're the ones we trust. So, you guys can all back off."

"We saw a dead Skrull Spider-Man," said Luke.

"One of them could have changed into another one," said Logan.

"What?" Spider-Man looked chagrined even through his face mask. His body language was always heightened, Clint realized, because he needed to communicate through that all-concealing body stocking, like he was always reaching out to the world, trying to persuade it he was harmless. Would a Skrull be able to mimic that very human thing? "The most wonderful thing about Spideys is that I'm the only one. In this universe. Sometimes. I'm going to go out and come back in again."

"Or don't," said Natasha.

"Skrulls?" said Ka-Zar.

"Hey, Kevin," said Bobbi.

"Bobbi," said Ka-Zar. Shanna looked sidelong at him.

Tony hurled again.

Natasha leveled her pistol at Shanna and Ka-Zar. "Out of the doorway. Now."

Shanna glowered at her. "Point it somewhere else, red."

"I'll point it up your—"

A low rumbling roar came from outside the door. Ambling up to join Ka-Zar came Zabu, the pair's pet saber-toothed tiger. Although "pet" really didn't do that damn thing justice. So, okay, was that a Skrull pretending to be a sabertooth? Or could Skrulls pretend to be his masters well enough to convince a sabertooth's senses?

"Great," sighed Luke, "more tension."

Behind the two Savage Land "nobles" and their carnivore, more people arrived—all of them grim and committed, like the battle was going to continue right here. There was Danny, looking weirdly uncertain toward Luke, the old-timey versions of Thor, Ms. Marvel, Simon Williams and, oh god, again with the Jessica Jones, all descended from the sky. From the bushes stepped the imperious figure of Emma Frost, and near her, Sue from the Fantastic Four. Ares stepped out from yet another angle, looking like he was having a hell of a day at the office. And there was Maya, rubbing her head. "Spider-Woman is a Skrull," she said, and pointed at Bobbi. "So, what about her?"

Clint made awkward eye contact with her and shook his head. *Later for that. Please?* Maya glowered at him. He looked to Luke, whose expression, as he stared at this former version of his wife, still in the garb from when she was trying to be a super hero, was stormy. "Hey," said Clint, "there's no point in having another big battle here, okay?"

"There will be no battle," said Ka-Zar.

"We can help with sorting out who's who," said Clint. "And anyone who's not a Skrull needs to help protect Tony."

"I figure everyone in that ship was a Skrull," said Luke.

"Hey," said Bobbi, "I'm right here."

"Except you."

"Really?" said Maya.

"And Cap."

"And if the two of them aren't—" said Logan.

"We are not doing this again!" said Clint.

"I know exactly which of you are Skrulls and which are not," said an imperious voice. They all turned to look at Emma Frost, who had her fingers to her temples. "I don't know who all of you are, but I am the White Queen of the Hellfire Club. I can read your minds."

"Not good enough," said Tony. "Skrulls can copy that." And he threw up again.

"I don't care," said Emma. "I think I know who's who. I was stuck in that spaceship for god knows how long and now I'm going to make all of you Skrull creatures pay for what you've done." She pointed. "I'm talking to you, Mr. 'Spider-Man'! I know exactly what you are."

Spider-Man actually pointed at himself then looked over his shoulder, presumably to check there wasn't another Spider-Man right behind him. Would a Skrull have taken the time to do a bit? Then he turned back to Emma and returned the gesture. "Now I know *you're* a Skrull."

"They're tryin' to get us killin' each other again," said Luke.

"Yes, tell them!" said Spider-Man. "Unless you're a Skrull, because then, I don't know, maybe start hitting yourself?"

"I did try to tell you," said Ares. "And yet here we are. Mixed up."

142

"I think I know who's acting and who's not," said Simon, his tone slightly accusing.

Bobbi put a slight pressure on Clint's arm. "If we don't know who's who," she whispered, so only he could hear it, "maybe we get out of here, hole up until we find a way to be sure?"

"No one leaves!" shouted Sue. Which was also what Maya's expression was very much saying in that moment.

Clint looked awkward at Bobbi. "Too late. Force fields."

"If she can do them."

Jessica Jones stepped forward, her arms raised, trying to make peace. Clint was amazed at how her body language was exactly what he'd expect of a Jess who hadn't had the traumatic life experiences Luke's wife had had. Luke must be thinking similar thoughts. "Iron Man, Thor..." she looked between the two groups gathered here. "Lead us. Tell us how we're going to get out of this."

"Yeah," said Ms. Marvel, who Clint found it especially hard to believe in, given that their Carol Danvers had brought Tony here. "Can't we sort this out? What's the plan here?"

"I have a plan!" said Thor, his eyebrows bristling. He strode forward and raised his hammer. "I will call upon my father in Asgard, Odin! He is the word and the way! He will see the truth here in a moment! His lightning will rain down on thee and thy fell villainy shall be exposed unto the world!"

Tony managed a slow nod. "Okay," he said. "You do that." Because as far as Clint knew, and this was just from what he'd heard on the super hero grapevine, Odin didn't exist anymore. What they were being asked to believe was that the rest of the Asgardians wouldn't realize that the Thor currently holed up in his palace, angry at mortals fighting each other, was actually a Skrull. Yeah, he was right on the edge of feeling able to put an arrow through this guy.

Thor raised his hammer and made some sort of enormous musical bellow toward the sky, his arms spread wide. He was really going to take this play as far as it could go.

From above there came an answering sound of thunder.

Clint shared with Tony and the others he was pretty sure weren't Skrulls a look of astonishment.

"That..." said Ares, looking absolutely astonished, "is a bit surprising."

They all slowly stepped out into the jungle to see enormous lights overhead piercing the cloud cover.

"Okay," said Spider-Man, "Odin. Fine. Let a god sort it out. It works in Greek theater."

"Those writers," sighed Ares, "always wanted to add their own lines."

Suddenly, from the clouds erupted a blast of blue energy. Before any of them could move it enveloped them all, the glare saturating the clearing, covering them all in its radiance. It certainly felt like what a god would do to find out the truth. Clint stumbled back and fell, like a lot of the others were doing. It was interfering with his head, like it was running through the deepest parts of him. And yet there was no pain. It was like a numbing, glowing blue anesthetic for the soul.

Then it switched off and he lay there on the floor of the jungle, staring at his hands.

They were pink. If he hadn't really full-on known he was human before, not in the rational part of his mind that knew the Skrulls could do the deep cover thing... well, he did now. He whooped. He looked up.

From out of the clouds dropped an enormous Skrull spacecraft. But... but why would the Skrulls do... whatever they had just—

Then he saw that a hatch in the side of the spacecraft was open, and in it stood Reed Richards, brandishing an enormous glowing gizmo, a look on his face like someone dear to him had died.

Clint looked around the clearing.

There was a Skrull in the costume of Thor, his long green ears pushing at the edges of that winged helmet. He looked as shocked as anyone else.

There were Ka-Zar and Shanna, lots of tanned pink flesh still

144

on display. There were Danny, Luke, Maya, Natasha and Tony, all human, though Tony looked kind of naturally green right now anyway. Spider-Man was looking left and right, as if wondering why everyone was staring at him. He realized it was because he was still masked, and pulled off a glove to wiggle a white hand.

There was Ares, cheeks as red as ever, shrugging as if these foolish mortals really should have known it was him.

There was Skrull Carol, and Emma, and Simon, all looking like they'd always known the truth and were just pissed now that their cover had been blown.

And there was Jess, oh god, Jess, green and sinking to her knees in her horror, staring at her own hands. She *hadn't* known. They… they couldn't just treat her as another Skrull enemy, could they? He found Luke again, and saw a lost expression on his face too.

There was a sudden roar, and Ka-Zar was making a gesture of command, and Zabu was suddenly on the Skrull Jessica, ripping at her throat.

"No!" shouted Clint.

Luke just closed his eyes and turned away.

It was the last thing Clint saw clearly before the chaos of battle erupted all around him again. He rolled to grab his quiver from where it had fell and put a flurry of arrows into Skrull Simon as he ran at him, putting him down.

He heard the Skrull Thor bellowing, still sounding like the god he was meant to be, "Hark unto me! This is but another trick! All-Father, please!"

The war ax of Ares connected with the back of his head and took his skull off his shoulders.

Gunfire was everywhere now, as the Widow found targets in all directions. Clint found himself dodging bits of Skrull as well as flying bodies.

He suddenly ran headlong into—Maya.

Who was a Skrull. And he could see the real Maya right behind her.

He stared at her. She went for his throat.

Nat spun and shot her six times through the head and she landed dead at his feet.

Clint looked around desperately. Bobbi, where was Bobbi?!

She'd been right beside him when the beam had hit. Like all of them, she'd staggered away, she must have fallen, so where—

He almost ran right into her.

She stood stock-still on the battlefield, staring into his eyes, terrified.

Her skin was bright green.

She had ridges in her chin and pointed ears. And yet still the blue eyes he'd loved. "What?" she said. "Clint? What's going on? Why are you looking at me like—"

And then she obviously realized her acting wasn't working. Because she broke character and morphed her hands into blades and swung one back—

He put the first shaft through her left eye and the second through her neck.

She fell to the ground, dead.

Clint fell with her. He sat down on the ground, unable to look at the body, feeling every inch of his grief all over again. Maya walked over and didn't say anything, just put a hand on his shoulder. He was dimly aware of what was happening around him. Reed had descended to join them and was shouting at the Skrull Susan about his children as she tried to grab for his eyes. Ares finished that with another blow of his ax. Tasha was assuring Tony that he couldn't be a Skrull.

"Ladies and gentlemen and all others whose loyalties are to Earth," called a woman's voice he wasn't familiar with, amplified from the spaceship above, "New York City is under siege and the planet has been claimed by the Skrull Empire. Anyone wants to help out with that, get on board our stolen spacecraft."

He remained where he was.

"There's still Skrulls out there in the jungle," Logan was saying.

"The Savage Land will unite to hunt them," said Shanna.

"And when that's done, we'll come to help in New York," said Ka-Zar.

They seemed to actually be a good couple. These two who had adventures together in the culture of super heroes. Like he and Bobbi had. He had judged them. And his wife had died again. These things were not connected. It felt oddly like he and Bobbi were somehow still going to do the things he'd started to think about them doing. He'd had in the back of his head a half-formed thought about introducing her to the rebel Avengers, about how annoyed she would be that the Avengers were divided by anything other than a continent, that maybe her return was a sign to do something about...

She had not returned.

He forced himself to look at the body.

It was obscene. He had killed it in a moment of obscenity too. He was a hero. He did not want to be in a war. And yet he was. He wasn't going to be able to help what he did now.

With Maya's help, he managed to get to his feet and saw the others. Remnants of both teams all climbing, together, up a ramp into the floating spaceship. He turned to them, trying to raise his voice. When it came out, though, it sounded too loud, too out of control. He couldn't help it. "Listen to me!" They turned to do that, some of them not yet entirely aware of all that had happened with him, some of them shocked as they understood the meaning of that particular corpse, lying near a building that contained so many corpses from what their culture had previously done here, and so many they'd added today. He pulled his mask from his head. "This doesn't end until every last one of them dies! You hear me?! Every last one of them!"

Maya put an arm around his waist and led him toward the ramp, and then he wasn't aware of much more until they were a long way out over the ocean.

THIRTY

NOH-VARR

NOH-VARR WAS a young member of the alien race known as the Kree, one of the elite warrior caste. However, he was not of the same Kree race that were known and feared in this universe. He had come here from a different reality. A better reality. Or he couldn't help but think of it as better, given how badly he'd been treated by just about everyone since landing on this weird planet called Earth. What he most longed for was to return to his own universe, where he understood the rules. Since arriving in this timeline through sheer astrophysical accident, he'd found himself constantly battling against a human organization called S.H.I.E.L.D., who'd pursued him, dogged his steps, and finally managed, after an enormous battle, to incarcerate him. They clearly thought of him as some enormous threat. For no good reason. They'd tried and failed to get Noh-Varr interested in fighting on the side of the authorities in this planet's ridiculous "Civil War." They'd showed him a costume and told him they'd like his codename to be "Marvel Boy." He'd replied that he didn't take fashion advice from the barely sentient. Why they felt the need to plaster branding on him he had no idea. He had found that some humans reacted to his superior silver-haired beauty in peculiar ways.

He'd decided then that he really needed to put some work into making the life in the prison better, for himself and all the others incarcerated there. Initially, he'd settled on learning everything he could about the two major factions involved in super-powered culture on this world, the authorities and the rebels, but of course his fellow inmates had a rather skewed view of that situation. Then he'd reached out to Tony Stark, Henry Pym and Norman Osborn, who'd all reacted by asking him how he'd managed to appear on their primitive video communication devices. Within minutes, they'd all made him an offer of some kind, trading relative amounts of freedom for his services. What none of them could straightforwardly tell him was who was in the right, where law and order really lay. Oh, they all thought they had an angle on that. Stark said it lay with him, Pym agreed, and Osborn... well, Osborn seemed to see the question as the start of a long conversation. But none of them managed to convince him, none of them had offered reasons he should believe anything said by those displaying such conflicted, contradictory and self-hating body language. And none of them had offered anything like Noh-Varr just being free to go home. He'd told them all he'd think about it and then decided they were all just stupid corporate stooges, none of whom showed the right qualities of imperial leadership. Although Osborn, maybe Osborn had been holding something back...

Mulling it over, he'd finally decided that perhaps he should take over the prison and use that as a staging post for either escaping from Earth to get back to his own universe or conquering the planet, setting up a system of truly lawful government, then escaping it to get back to his own universe. Then, earlier today, all the security systems had gone down, and the techs had started shouting about an alien virus in their systems. Noh-Varr had sniffed the air and realized that the virus was Skrull in origin. He'd realized, a little while back, that they had Skrulls in this reality too, and it seemed they were just as bad as in his own universe. He'd decided that it was probably not a good idea to be around for whatever happened next, wandered to a transport lock, and quietly left the building.

Now he was riding one of the prison's sky cycles, heading for New York, where most of this world's "super hero" community seemed to be based. The only thought in his extraordinary head was, if the Skrulls were attacking, he might be able to use the chaos as cover to find a way back to his own universe.

It was from such thoughts that he looked up just in time to see a burning Skrull transport heading straight down at him.

His superior reflexes allowed him to turn the sky cycle out of the way a second before the behemoth struck him. He felt the disturbance in the air slide past his skin as it fell, fire blooming from it, into the empty parking lot of some kind of... he had no idea what these big human buildings were about. The ship wrecked itself across a mass of cars, sending them tumbling and blazing until it finally settled at the end of a long trench, explosions still wracking its surface.

He took the cycle around the perimeter of the blaze, in case any Skrulls stepped from the wreck. If they did, he would eliminate them. Because, hey, he had a few moments before getting back to the business of escaping this universe.

But he saw a different sort of figure stepping from the fire.

Of course, a Skrull could look like anything, but as this figure walked, he kept firing bolts of energy behind him, taking down screaming Skrulls that burst from the wreckage behind him as they tried to aim energy weapons, tried to throw blades or themselves at him. He dispatched them all, even as he began to stagger, with great grace and dignity.

He was dressed as a great Kree warrior, one, Noh-Varr knew, who was as famous in this universe as he'd been in Noh-Varr's own. That hero's sole visit to Noh-Varr's own reality had been a great adventure that was still sung of.

Was this really Mar-Vell? Was this really the hero... oh, the hero the humans had wanted to name him after! He so got that now!

That had made no sense when Noh-Varr had thought this man dead, but if he was still alive, then obviously the humans would want to link Noh-Varr to the glamour of this tremendous figure. They were, after all, the only two Kree the humans had really got to know.

He quickly landed the cycle and ran to where Mar-Vell was supporting himself on a blazing car, apparently waiting to see if any more Skrulls were about to come after him. This close, Noh-Varr could see that Mar-Vell was badly wounded.

"Are... are you Mar-Vell?" Noh-Varr asked gently. "Are you he?"

It took the man a moment to gather the strength to reply. "Kree... soldier? What's your name?"

Noh-Varr started to give his full list of titles, but Mar-Vell hushed him, putting an urgent hand on his arm. He was beyond wounded, Noh-Varr realized: he was dying. His own medical sensors were yelling at him that there was no way to help him. Oh! That he should be present at the death of such a warrior! "My apologies. What can I do?"

"The Skrull Empire. Taking Earth. You can't let... have to stop..."

Noh-Varr shook his head. He'd heard that Mar-Vell was fond of the humans, but this wasn't his own calling at all. Not after what they'd done to him. "This is not my world—"

"Listen to me! Skrulls do not... understand honor. They lie to their own. Plant... memories in their own... they don't care. They have no honor. They don't understand Kree honor. Or... the honor humans are capable of."

"Well, I'm not sure about that part—"

"I've fought so many Skrulls today. I've saved so many humans. I've learned so much in these last few weeks from being... being..."

His features started to blur.

Noh-Varr stepped back in horror from what he was seeing. This "Captain Marvel" was actually a Skrull! Which meant this had to be a trick, that the Skrulls had sacrificed their own people to convince him of... of... and yet this man really was dying...

He paused, his hand on the gun he'd retrieved from the prison's lockers. "Go on."

"You doubt. You hesitate. Good. I've learned the good side of the Kree. The good side of the humans. I am… Skrull with a Kree… in here. I am dying. Noble enemy? Great warrior? What does your belief system say to you, Kree soldier? Are you two things also? Could you be more than you are?"

Noh-Varr stared. His belief system, which he had not attended to the detail of in far too long, told him that all things happened for a reason. That there was one great war poem being written. And there was something in a specific poem he'd read a lot when he was very young that talked of the conflicted souls of a dying warrior only finding resolution when he passed his charge on to another, one who'd initially… denied an attempt to name him after that warrior. Noh-Varr shivered. "This… feels like I'm being… watched, being read as lines in…"

"You are here now in coincidence for a reason." Noh-Varr found himself reacting in numinous awe at the words. "I am here to pass this on to you for a reason. You cannot let this invasion happen. You must… you must…" He took Noh-Varr's hand and placed it on the symbol on his own chest.

He kept his gaze locked on Noh-Varr's eyes as he saw death approaching him. Then the shadow passed over him. He seemed to greet someone for a moment, just a little smile of recognition, that some old action had been repeated.

And then he was gone.

Noh-Varr stared. He lowered the body gently to the ground.

Slowly, he stood, changed.

"Marvel Boy," he said out loud.

Now it sounded far less ridiculous. And actually rather grand.

THIRTY-ONE

OM'NOLL

WHAT THE human project known as the Fifty State Initiative had designated "Camp Hammond" had always been known to the Skrull Imperial Command as Invasion Base One. Now many Skrulls stood there, looking at each other in triumph and, if they were being honest, relief. Om'Noll walked among them, sharing human gestures like pats on the back and high fives. Om'Noll was a general in the Imperial Planetary Assault Force, and for over an Earth year now he'd been undercover as the human scientist, technocrat and sometime super hero Henry Pym. Pym's shrinking and growing technology had been reasonably easy for the Skrulls to duplicate, plus Pym had a history of erratic behavior and shifts in character. He'd also been on the side of Tony Stark's establishment during the Civil War and had risen to a place of trust within Stark's organization, so he'd been the absolute top target on the Skrulls' list for abduction and replacement. They'd used a stealth ship to take him from his car one night, when he'd made the mistake of driving alone up to a cliff on the California shoreline during a vacation. Om'Noll had dropped into the front seat of the car, enjoyed the rush of using his new vehicle-driving skills, put Pym's depressive personality to one side and grinned all the way to work on Monday morning.

Now he conferred, in person, which felt like a luxury, with the assembling generals of the many small task forces deployed in this early phase of the invasion in the United States of America. They were mostly arriving by teleport, the nature of which varied between scientific, mutant and magical, depending on whether the arrivals were using their own equipment or utilizing their Super-Skrull powers. The Queen had decreed that, as per tradition, they gather in conference the first moment it was safe to do so. She, however, had not yet arrived. This had so far gone unremarked, but Om'Noll could feel the underlying nervousness in the air.

"Okay," he said, seeing that reasonable numbers had now arrived to get a general feeling for the campaign that went beyond what was being shared on their net, "how do we think this is going?"

"S.H.I.E.L.D. is down," summed up Bortha, who was a bit too much of a zealot for Om'Noll's taste, but wildly efficient. "S.W.O.R.D. is gone, Thunderbolts Mountain is in ruins. The Baxter Building is in the Negative Zone, Avengers Tower is locked down, Stark technology is compromised beyond repair."

"But," said Klakalar, who had much more in the way of proper military doubt, "six Earth hours ago, the armada was attacked."

"Yes," said Om, "I was on point for that, being the handler for the sleeper agents in this part of the planet. The Mar-Vell duplicate had some sort of breakdown. I think perhaps creating an agent with a set of memories from someone we know to be dead, who has to process a dead stop at the end of the memory track... let's just say lessons have been learned. His communications immediately before the attack were extremely disturbing."

"We created a powerful enemy," said Klak.

"But our sensors say he's now dead," said Om. He was trying to put a brave face on this, because he knew responsibility for the failure might land on his head at any moment. He was pretty sure he'd be able to blame it on the scientists responsible for the duplication process. He had also failed, on the battlefield, to kill or capture the great human warrior Carol Danvers, though she had been felled at his feet. He wasn't sure, though, if, in the fog of battle, Imperial Command even knew about his proximity to that debacle. Apart from those two things, his own role in the invasion had been glorious, so he was reasonably confident he wasn't about to be hauled off-world in shackles. "In the end, he did less damage than we'd allowed for in terms of losses to human forces in the initial attack phase."

"But most importantly," said Bortha, who, thankfully, had something else on his list of obsessions today, "we haven't heard from the Savage Land."

"The Queen," said Klak. "Yes. The silence worries me."

"She chose her part in this," said Bortha, always willing to skirt the edges of mutinous speech in pursuit of his one true doctrine. "We should wipe that region from this planet. It is home to nothing but mutation and irregularity. We are the Shifting People. We are called upon not to allow that power to take root in enemy cultures. It speaks to me of... Richards."

"Well, that's not on the agenda right now," said Om, taking a little too much pleasure in getting to say that. "Perhaps you could raise it after we've secured our objectives."

"If any of the Avengers in the Savage Land remain alive, they'll be heading here," said Klak.

"Damn right they will. And we'll kick their butts and accept their submission," said Bortha with a grin.

They wandered into the base's control center, where engineers were swiftly swapping out the human tech for Skrull replacements. Much of this process was made easier by Om's foresight in creating modular systems for this compound, with slots designed to accommodate the invader tech. They'd expected at least some of the human Initiative heroes to try to return here, but it seemed they'd been hit the hardest at the Battle of Times Square; some of the survivors seemed to have vanished, the rest perhaps hearing through their media (before it had been switched off) that this location was now occupied territory and lacked the forces to attempt to retake it. This was all great news.

"They will not submit," chuckled Klak, enjoying this just as much as he was, but in distinctly his own way, "and you know it."

"Then we'll destroy them. We have the numbers now."

"But the Savage Land contains so many of their heavy hitters—"

Om realized what he was edging toward. "No. Come on. You always did this in training. No tactical re-invention where none is needed. We stick to the plan. It's working. Just about every world the Empire has liberated has fallen in exactly this way."

"That's very true," came the voice of a female human. The three Skrulls turned to look at the manifestation of a teleport nexus as through it stepped Queen Veranke, still in the guise of the human Jessica Drew. "Thank you for your faith, General Om'Noll."

Om allowed himself a smile.

Everyone took a knee, including Bortha, though he couldn't conceal an annoyed look. "My Queen," he said, finding a more obsequious sound for his voice, "how goes the campaign in the Savage Land?"

"Imperfectly," she replied, taking a screen and a drink from a servant and checking the reports before throwing back a long libation. "The enemy have been severely beaten and were fighting amongst themselves, but their spirits are not broken, and they have not been defeated."

"Indeed," said Klak, sounding smug.

"As you said before I arrived, General, they are doubtless heading here. Richards has rallied them."

Those words caused a reaction throughout the command staff, precisely what the Queen intended. The dual revelation that she had been listening to their early conversation, plus the news about Richards, had sent a shiver of fear through the room.

"Richards escaped his interrogation?!" yelled Bortha.

"For the last time," said the Queen, stepping up to look him in the eye. If this was going to be the moment Bortha declared that the Queen's eccentricities, her desire to lead in the field, made her less than she should have been, she was ready for him. She had been ready for him, she had already announced, before she entered the room.

He looked aside. He knew it. "All I'm saying is, my Queen, this could be a disaster."

Om couldn't let this moment pass without profiting from it. "Did you *see* the Baxter Building?" he said. "I think as soon as he becomes aware of that, Richards' focus will be extremely divided."

"It is a thing of beauty," said Queen Veranke, smiling at him. "You've done amazing work here, Om'Noll."

Om allowed himself a moment of satisfaction. It seemed he was correct that his lack of oversight in the Mar-Vell case was going to be brushed under the carpet. "Is Janet Van Dyne still with them?" he asked. "The Wasp?" He tried not to mention her often, despite her being at the center of his plans, because the name set off a cascade of awfulness in the mind of his cover character, everything from frustrated love to comfortable fondness to snarling resentment. But right now, to feel the sting of all that was worth it—worth it for the satisfaction of reminding his Queen that it was he who had put in place the mechanism for their greatest coup.

"Yes," said Veranke. "She survived the Battle of the Savage Land."

Om spread his arms wide. "Then, whatever happens, in the end we win."

THIRTY-TWO

TONY STARK

TONY FELT sick as a dog, in body and mind. In a corner of the spaceship cabin he'd started to tinker with a plate from his armor, attempting to access a backup server in one of his labs while Brand flew them sub-orbitally back toward the United States. He didn't want to make eye contact with anyone, though Janet Van Dyne kept looking at him as if she wanted to talk, to reassure, to comfort.

He didn't want any of that. He didn't deserve it. Even now, because of what he'd done, one set of Avengers was sitting along one wall of this ship, while another was sitting opposite. Very few words were being exchanged. Clint Barton stared into space, an expression of grim determination locking his jaw because otherwise, Tony felt, the weight of all that man had suffered in the last few years might prove too much.

Damn it. Here he was feeling sorry for a man upon whose head he'd put a bounty. That was what having a common enemy did to you. Historically, though, such healing between factions only lasted as long as the common enemy did. At least they'd all come together now to face it. But had that happened too late?

"Oh, hey," said Spider-Man, "anyone in the mood to hit a Denny's on the way home?"

"Jokes?" said Maya Lopez. "Really?"

"Well, very nearly," said Spidey. "Doing my best here. I don't like silences, okay? Silences say, 'we think the other guy is a Skrull' when right now we absolutely, positively, know everyone in this ship isn't one, right?"

"Right," said Simon Williams. "But the silences might also say 'we think the other guy is the guy who disrupted my entire body at a microscopic level while trying to escape lawful arrest for a crime they *actually committed*,' so—"

"Oh, you want some?!" shouted Luke. "You want to try to arrest my ass right now?!"

"Silence!" bellowed Ares. Shocked, everyone turned to look at him. "We are shipmates," he said. "We are comrades in arms. We carry with us the body of one of our glorious dead. Some more of us will die for each other. Well, some of *you* will. I am immortal. But my point is—"

"His point is a good one," said Janet. And she walked into the middle of the deck and looked around them all. "I'm going to say two words and I want you all to say them back to me. These are two words I think you're all going to want to say, though I know it'll be difficult for some of you."

Tony looked up from his work, feeling admiration for this woman he'd once loved, and with that a horrible taste of hope.

"Oh, oh, I think I know what she's going to say!" said Spider-Man.

"Don't spoil it," said Luke, now looking a lot happier.

"I wasn't going to."

"Avengers assemble," said Janet, very quietly.

They nodded, they muttered it. Some of them looked like they didn't know if they were allowed to say it. Tony said it carefully and out loud.

"Avengers assemble!" said Janet, more loudly. There might have been a time when that would have been returned to her as a shout.

But now, yet again, there was only a mutter. "Damn it," she said, and raised her hands, looking like she wondered what it was going to take to make any of them see sense.

More than that, thought Tony. *I'm sorry, Jan.*

"I just want to know that after I've fought alongside you guys," said Danny, "if we win, you're not then going to try to arrest us."

Tony realized everyone in the chamber had their eyes on him. "I think we... have obviously suspended..." The whole room groaned. "Well, what do you want me to say?!"

"'Sorry,' for a start," said Luke. "'Suspended,' my ass!"

Tony found that he really wanted to say it. But he stopped himself. More was riding on this than just his needs, and he didn't want to be a hypocrite about it. "I get that," he said.

Luke swore at him.

"But in combat—" began Janet.

"We're all on the same side," said Luke. "*I* get *that*."

"Hey," said Rand, "anyone else worried that while we're all caring and sharing, the Skrulls might be following us or about to blow us out of the sky?"

"The ship is cloaked, Mr. Rand," said Reed, who sounded like any moment he was going to tell them all if they didn't stop fighting, he'd turn this spaceship around.

"But it's their cloak," said Cage.

"A cloak is a cloak, Luke."

"Depends on the movie. But point taken. Okay, so now we're at least talking about stuff... the elephant in the room: Jessica Drew."

"Yeah," said Maya.

"The real Jess would love being called that," said Spider-Man.

"She was a Skrull,' said Tony, getting there before the rest of them did, "and I brought her onto my team."

"Because you were running out of anyone in a costume to be on your side," said Rand. "And because you wanted someone to come over from ours."

"And they knew that," admitted Tony, "and they played me

using it. They've been playing all of us all the while during the Civil War. And way before."

"I was enjoyin' that until he got to 'all of us,'" said Logan. "I want to know *how* long she was a duplicate."

"He wants to know," said Spider-Man, "for, you know, reasons."

Logan glowered at him.

"And, most importantly," said Tony, trying really hard not to behave like he was the leader here, but not doing so well, honestly, "where is the real Jessica? And is she okay? And who else did they get?" He looked up at the others, hoping they saw how deep his sickness went. "This is all my fault. I know it."

"There was nothing you could have done," said Janet, landing on his shoulder at Wasp size, which was always what she did when she wanted to talk intimately. "It would have been whoever was in charge."

There was a loud clamor of disagreement about that. Tony again tried to say it first. "Nick Fury saw this coming."

Jan seemed as though she was about to argue, but Spider-Man spoke before she could. "Jan," he said, "this guilt of Tony's is a good thing. Not just for all these guys," he gestured to the room, "but for Tony too, okay? Let him have this."

Jan glared at him like she was getting deeply frustrated that she could no longer unite these people. But that was because nobody could. Not now.

"I know him," said Barton, suddenly looking up from his sullen anger and pointing at Tony. "I fought him often enough. Back in the day. When *I* was a villain and *he* was a hero." Ouch. "He's getting his second wind. Right?"

Tony realized, to his own surprise, that he was kind of right. "Oh, we're going to fight back," he said. "Of course we are. All I need to do is… okay, hack this server, beat the virus, map the Skrull attacks and—" He stopped. "And the rest will be up to all of us. All of you."

Cage made eye contact for just about the first time and gave him a nod. "They came here," he said, turning to the others, "they came all the way here, they threw everything they had at us, with one hell of a plan. And look. We're still here. And we're comin' to get 'em."

There were nods and calls of "yeah" and heroes thumping surfaces. Tony couldn't quite imagine how their community was going to be afterward, but maybe... maybe the healing started here? Jan joined in, but with a look on her face that was asking why they couldn't have heard this from her.

Because you chose the wrong side, kid. Not that you ever seemed to have wholeheartedly made that choice. Sorry.

"Guys," said Brand from the flight deck. "You'd better see this."

They all moved forward. Through the forward screens they could see New York City in the distance. Dozens of Skrull ships floated in the sky above it.

And beneath them, the City of Super Heroes was on fire.

THIRTY-THREE

ALICE CREASY

ALICE CREASY had stopped seeing the difference between "heroes" and "villains" a long time ago. She was nineteen, and where she worked, at a twenty-four-hour drug store, the young staff would listen to Sullivan, the proprietor, talking in his boomer way about how some mystery hero had saved his life in the 1970s, about the latest Avengers gossip, who was in and who was out, who was dating who… and they would look at each other, baffled. It was like hearing someone excitedly talk about romances in the NYPD or the government. It didn't help that Sullivan had told them all the story of him being rescued at one time or another, but he couldn't seem to keep straight in his memory which super hero had saved him. The only constant was that it was one of the ones who'd been around "before they'd started poppin' outta the woodwork." Alice suspected the story might not actually be true, that Sullivan had started telling it to make himself sound more important by association or whatever, and now believed it had actually happened to him.

"Captain America is dead, dude," one of her fellow employees had once said to Sullivan, "get over it." He had quickly found himself on the zombie shift.

But that had just been the truth, said out loud. Captain America was dead and super hero culture was a toxic mess that nobody in her generation cared about. Ever since Alice could remember, whenever a super hero was in the news it was because they were literally destroying some building in New York, having their weekly battle with Terrible Man or whoever it was, not caring if innocent bystanders got hit by the wreckage. That was what had happened to Alice's Gran Creasy. She hadn't been the same since She-Hulk had demolished a wall, sending one brick randomly flying precisely at the center of Gran's forehead. Now Gran sometimes bled from the nose, and had episodes of forgetfulness, but every time Alice said to her that here was a class action suit waiting to happen, Gran looked at her with horror and said that She-Hulk was both an Avenger and had been one of that lovely Reed Richards' people and so she would *never*... blah, blah, blah.

It was like the USA had invented a monarchy for themselves.

The Super Hero Civil War had been, to Alice and her friends and millions like them online, just the latest idiocy these hugely privileged morons had perpetrated against the everyday people of New York. I mean, great, now they didn't even need villains, they were picking sides and fighting each other. Had one side been better than the other? Well, given that Tony Stark was an out-and-out fascist who'd finally shown his true colors, and that Captain America... well, even Alice had to admit that there was one guy who'd never crossed the line, who even the most radical of her friends always gave a pass to, so, yeah, maybe the "rebels" had been better than the "official Avengers." But even so. It was still just grown people with too much money and too much power fighting over trivial differences of opinion while climate change was a thing, and the so-called "heroes" were doing nothing to stop it. The idea that super hero culture should be accountable was absolutely right. What was wrong was that the "accounting" was being done by those complicit in the problems.

Because a "super hero" never seemed to be able to stand up to the big companies and say "actually, the Mighty Thor is going to spend Tuesday sending every oil well in the world off to Asgard" or "Dr. Strange is going to say a spell to end cancer" or "Reed Richards is going to take some of his amazing tech and use it to create proper transport infrastructure" or even just "actually, I think transgender people have a right to live their lives in peace." Because these ridiculously powerful twits thought that staying on the fence was the way to keep the public onside, instead of, say, *never allowing a member of the public to come to harm.* Or how about *let's not have Captain America arrested and get him killed*? The only member of that culture Alice had ever truly liked was Magneto, and so of course he was often portrayed in the media as a "villain."

Watching older generations being invested in the "ethics" of these monsters was like watching them get involved with pro wrestling. Nothing about "super heroes" was real. Memories got rewritten. Reality got rewritten too. There were so many convincing social media posts about how ordinary people's memories had been messed with by magic and powers and whatever, time after time.

And being under it all, in the shadow of it all, oppressed by it all, made living in New York especially, but in any of the big cities since the Initiative, like being an ant in a garden where giants trod wherever they liked. Every part of that sentence had, at one time or another, ceased to even be a metaphor for some ordinary person somewhere. Even the "ant" part. Her generation especially, those not brainwashed by the wonder of these heroes first appearing at a time when, okay, perhaps they had genuinely just helped people, they were the ones who suffered the most.

So, when the Skrulls had made their broadcast, okay, obviously some of it was intended for those who couldn't read media as well as Alice and her friends could. Because some of it was obviously not true. And using those familiar faces, that was creepy as hell, but hey, they were dealing with an extraterrestrial culture here, who probably thought that would have played better than it had. But some of the messages, some of the exact plans the Skrulls had put out on social media immediately after the broadcast... that was good stuff. The idea that the world's great cities would be designated as safe zones, where all acts of violence would be prohibited by Skrull tech… that would come as a blessed relief. The idea that there would be trials for super heroes guilty of breaking everyday human laws, that U.S. law would be enforced equally for U.S. citizens by unbiased Skrull judges who saw all humans as equal… that was pleasing too. Truth and reconciliation commissions to sort out the grievances of all those hurt by super hero culture, sanctuaries for all those persecuted by Earth governments and international laws that would apply to all, immediate action to halt global warming and put in place clean fusion energy… wow. No wonder the heroes had wanted to keep Earth out of interstellar politics. The Skrulls weren't on the fence. They were radicals. They were going to put in place all the changes that Earth had needed for so long.

Alice and her friends weren't idiots. They knew the Skrulls were doing this to gain allies amongst humans. It was so obviously a "hearts and minds" strategy. But that didn't mean it wasn't true.

Lots of her friends, it turned out, felt the same way. Some just felt that anything was better than what they had now, but a lot of others, like Alice, felt that the Skrulls actually had a point. Besides, all the online fascists had immediately swung onside with the official Avengers, yelling that all Skrulls must die, uploading pictures of themselves with guns ready to defend their neighborhoods under the Stars and Stripes and… no. Just no.

Even the Skrull religion, what little of it had been revealed, seemed okay. All they talked about was love, even to their enemies. Wasn't that meant to be the point of Christianity, before a ton of people had started to use it as an instrument of oppression?

So, Alice had decided, this afternoon as the Skrull ships hung in the sky over the city, that she was going to do something brave in response to their broadcast. She would show them that their message had been heard. She got in touch with those of her friends who lived in the same neighborhood, bringing them together to quickly make some signs. Then they stepped out onto the street together and made their way downtown as best they could, driving some of the way and walking the rest after they had to abandon the cars. Sure, the fires and the destruction were scary, but the fighting seemed to be over, and, good as their word, the Skrulls seemed only to be attacking those who attacked them. The media had said, before it was shut down—again, yay—that there'd been a battle in Times Square. If there had, the Skrulls seemed to have won it. Because there were now no super heroes to be seen anywhere.

They received mixed reactions to their placards. Some older people called them traitors. One ranting, wandering religious guy, who appeared to be hurt and was covered in brick dust, told them they were a sign of the end times. A reporter walked beside them for a while, taking quotes and making notes, a sad look on his face.

Their signs said "Welcome, Skrulls" and "Fix the World For Us" and "Peace Across the Galaxy" and "Embrace Change." As they walked, a handful of people came out of their houses, rushing to join them, a wild, proud expression on their faces. "It's the revolution," said one old lady, "finally. I actually thought it would be us doing it, back in the old days. But no. Of course. It needs a higher power."

Alice thought that old lady sounded kind of weird, honestly, but hey, the more the merrier. They'd got to where the major destruction started, in midtown, and found some of the older buildings crumbling. The sight didn't feel odd to Alice. It felt like Tuesday. She, like all her generation, was used to random super hero destruction. "Where *are* they?" asked Maddy, who'd come all the way from Brooklyn for this.

"Look up," said Kels, who was kind of annoying in person, in that what had come over as righteous anger online was just whiny in real life. He kept earnestly telling them things they already knew.

"Yeah, I *know*, the spaceships, but where are they so we can greet them and make them see some humans are on their side?"

Ahead of them a cop car was stopped at the corner, and two NYPD morons were actually… oh, come on, they were arresting a looter! During the transformation of all human society! It was so perfect, it was a summation of everything that was wrong. They were literally failing to see anything above their little world!

Alice got out her phone and took a picture. "Pigs!" she shouted. "You have no power here! The Skrulls are the law now!"

The cops turned to look at them, uncomprehending. "What the hell?" one of them said. "You get back—"

"Back in the box where you want to keep us?!" yelled Kels. "No! No!"

The others took up the chant. "We are here to welcome them!" yelled Maddy.

"Welcome who?!" said the other cop, taking a step toward them, obviously unprepared for this moment and still living in the wrong decade.

"They have come here to save *us*," called Kels.

"Are you out of your minds?!" The first cop threw the looter in the back of the car and marched over. "We're being invaded! The Fantastic Four are dead!"

"Good!" bellowed Kels. "Death to the super fascists!"

"You're just worried because you're out of a job," said Alice, getting in the cop's face. "Utopia means you don't get to use that big stick of yours."

The cop looked to his partner, a tired look on his face. "My big stick'd be wasted on the likes of you. You gotta get to safety before—"

"Mike," called his partner, pointing and then drawing his gun.

They all turned to look.

They were approaching through the smoke that was billowing down a sidestreet. They were walking casually, calmly, as if the world already belonged to them. There was one of the big ones who wore the super hero garb of their enemies, with an X on his chest, while the other two, smaller than him but still bigger than most humans, were in their military uniforms. Altogether, they were the strangest and most liberating things Alice had ever seen.

"They're beautiful," said Kels. "They're so different, so above the flesh. Look at the way their skin glistens."

Alice couldn't help but agree. She was amazed that she could read their body language, understand the confident expressions on their faces. They looked like proper soldiers, how a liberating force should look. "We should talk to them," she said. "Come on."

"Oh no," said the cop beside them. He added a few choice oaths about their stupidity and he and his partner stepped forward, their weapons raised. "You freaks better run," he shouted, and Alice actually couldn't tell if he was talking to the Skrulls or to them.

The Skrulls turned abruptly in their direction, as if they'd just sensed their presence.

The cops, unprovoked, opened fire.

Alice's comrades started yelling, half in anger, half in fear.

Sure enough, the bullets just bounced off something invisible in mid-air. The big Skrull was holding up his hand, saving himself and his colleagues.

"Stop," shouted Alice, "leave it there, we can all talk now—"

The Skrull closed his hand in a fist and the cops screamed. Their guns flew from their hands, their bodies spasmed, and they fell to the ground, blood gushing from their heads.

That had been some sort of magnetic power, Alice thought, somewhere in the back of her head. Just like Magneto. She had never seen anyone die before.

"We're your friends!" shouted Kels, stepping forward, hands in the air. "We welcome you!" The others pointed to his sign, which said just that.

Alice took a deep breath and stepped forward. Maddy did too. The others followed. "You must have a way to understand human speech," she called. "English. They were your enemies. We are not."

"Embrace change," said Maddy, quoting their slogans back to them. "That's what we're doing. We embrace change."

"We need it!" yelled the old lady.

"We just wanted to say… thank you for invading us," said Alice.

The big Skrull seemed to have been listening to them. Now it took some decisive steps forward. It didn't walk like a human somehow; there were different muscles in there. Alice's brain kept looking for the special effects, for the imperceptible signs of this being something from a screen, but no, no. She could smell this extraterrestrial being now. It smelled like… hazelnuts and lime, somehow put together. Those fragrances had so little in the way of associations for her. The Skrull from another solar system had put her in mind only of a coffee shop. It began to speak, raising a finger at them. The words sounded like groans and barks at the same time.

"We can't understand you," said Kels, interrupting it. "English, man."

The Skrull curled its finger and Kels flew up into the air, screaming, blood starting to fly from his spasming body.

"No!" screamed Maddy. "No, you've got it wrong! We're not the enemy!"

"They're just like all the rest," whispered the old lady beside Alice, an expression of utter collapse on her face. "Just more soldiers."

"No," said Alice, "no, I refuse to let this… this lack of understanding between—"

From somewhere behind them came the sound of… howling?

The Skrulls in front of them all looked past them at once.

Alice turned to see what was coming. From the street behind them a number of costumed and uniformed people were rushing. One of them, a giant of course, knocking bricks from the sides of the street as she ran. In front of them, holding a ridiculously big gun was… oh god, was that Nick Fury?! And there was the Vision of the Young Avengers, with his face all messed up, and someone who looked like a gorilla, and someone who was using magic, and they had an actual child soldier in there, and maybe a Skrull traitor, and there were also some of those fascist stooges from the Initiative training program and—

Alice screamed as Maddy pulled her down to the ground. The first energy bolts narrowly missed the top of her head, hitting the Skrulls beside them.

"No," said the old lady, on the ground beside them. She started to crawl away. "It goes on. It just goes on."

170   Alice was so angry now. And yet, as she and her friends huddled,

the battle raging over their heads, it was clear there was nothing they could do right now to stop it or moderate it or try to make anyone listen. Here were "super heroes" and their superspy allies in the establishment, back from the dead, as always, because life and death were yet more things that was a problem only for the little people. These idiots were turning it into a war, getting in the way of transformation, of salvation, yet again!

One of them was suddenly above them, a woman in uniform, trying to grab them. "Take my hand," she said, "I'll get you—"

"No!" shouted Alice, swatting her hand away. "Get off me!"

But then there was a blur and something rushed by her head, making her scream and when she could see again… she was lying on a sidewalk, on a completely different street, maybe miles away, and seconds later… her comrades were all around her.

But not the old lady. And not Kels.

And then suddenly that group of "heroes" were there too, stepping out of a magical portal of some kind. They were covered in grime and small wounds and some were helping others but… they had a smugness about them that said they'd "won."

Nick Fury stepped over to Alice's people as they got to their feet. "You kids get back to your dorm or wherever you're from," he said.

"Why don't you get back to the decade you're from?" said Alice. "Did you kill all the Skrulls, then? Are you satisfied?"

"Yep," said Fury. "For now."

"Three down, eight thousand more to go," said the magic guy in the hood, who had a stupid beard.

"They're here to change the world!" yelled Alice. "What are you here for?!"

Fury hardly even bothered to look tired at her. He seemed to think for a moment about concocting a reply, then just swatted the air and turned back to his people. "Okay, Howlers, let's get out of here before—"

The whole sky flashed.

A second later there was a sound of enormous thunder.

Everyone had ducked, that fear that was so ingrained in them triggered yet again. Yet again. They were being oppressed from above yet again.

"Is that... lightning?" said the formerly giant young woman, now shrinking down to normal size.

"It... it hit in Central Park," said Fury, sounding like he took this to be a hopeful sign. And yeah, there was something, in super hero culture, that lightning had used to mean, wasn't there? There had been a sound in that thunder, a particular sort of sound that Alice remembered from children's TV shows that idolized super heroes.

The flash came again. The sound came again.

And this time, even to her, it sounded like a summons. "Is that—" said the former giant.

"On me," shouted Fury to his colleagues. "Move out. Stay close and stay together. Anything in our way we cut through, but keep movin'!"

And they just ran off toward Central Park, leaving Alice and her friends lying there.

They hadn't even heard her. Not really. Her words had been meaningless to them.

After all that had happened, in the middle of all this, the super heroes had learned *nothing*.

THIRTY-FOUR

MATTHEW CHAVINSKY

HIS STUDENTS called him "Mr. Chavinsky" or "Mr. C." when he allowed it. He had been accompanying a party of his teachers and students from the fourth and fifth grades on a school outing to Central Park, intending to get them to spot different sorts of trees and then finishing with a storytelling session sitting on the grass. They had come in from Brooklyn by bus. They had all been excited, of course, at the possibility of seeing a super hero, and had all been gazing up at Avengers Tower and the Baxter Building, but Mrs. Bolaji had already told them that they shouldn't expect to see these people on a regular basis. And if they did, that often meant trouble, and in those circumstances especially, they should not get too carried away, because that was when they most had to pay attention to their teachers.

And then alien death had descended from the skies.

The school Matthew was principal of had procedures in place for this sort of thing, of course. They had lived through so much in the way of monsters and villains and, indeed, aliens. But, as the other teachers immediately followed their training and gathered the children up into a line, calling a head count, ready to march them

straight back to the bus along the route they'd already planned…
he couldn't help but look in every direction around the park, at
where giant figures were moving, some of them suddenly as tall as
skyscrapers, striding amongst the tall buildings. He could feel the
excitement of the kids turning to fear. Here were the special effects
from the movies they watched, but now they were in their world.

"All right, everyone," he called, forcing himself to sound calm.
"When we're ready, we're going to walk together, holding hands—"
He stopped. Suddenly, people were running toward them from
the gate he was aiming for. He paused, waiting to see what these
people were running from, and indeed, here they came, two of
those giant monsters, dressed in weird representations of super
hero costumes, like they were going out trick or treating. The kids
behind him screamed, and he called authoritatively for them to
shush. He was about to say they would all turn around and walk
the other way when one of the monsters pointed, right at him, and
said something, in what he took to be an alien language. It sounded
like a genuine question.

"We surrender," he said, raising his hands. "We are unarmed.
These are children."

They seemed to grow angry at that, yelling and gesticulating,
power building in their hands. What did they want them to do?
There were screams all around him and the sound of immediate,
panicked sobbing. Any second now, one of the children or teachers
would break and run, and what would the monsters do then?

Mr. Chavinsky decided without ever really consciously making
a decision. This was his job.

"When I step out, take them and run," he whispered to Mrs.
Bolaji, who, to her credit, just nodded back. He turned back to the
monsters and took a step toward them. "Hey!" he called, waving his
arms. "I don't know what you want! Talk to me! I'm the leader!" He
was aware that tears of regret and grief were rolling down his face as
he couldn't help but think of what losing him would do to Alison
and Ben. Ben was autistic, he wouldn't know how to deal with loss.
But this was his duty, this was what he had to do now. "I'm the

leader of all the humans! You talk to me!" He could now hear the class running away behind him, thank god, the teachers calling to them not to look over their shoulders. He was now close enough to feel the heat of the energy these things were gathering. He could only hope it would be quick.

Then there was a flash of light, somewhere in the sky above, and a moment later he heard a sound. It was a sound he had only heard before in family movies about super heroes.

It was the sound of a very specific sort of thunder.

The sound made the monsters in front of him halt, and look up.

Floating in the sky above the park was the silhouette of a cloaked figure, swinging something around his head so fast the arc was a blur.

It looked like a hammer.

The monsters started to bellow, to aim their weapons upward, completely ignoring Mr. Chavinsky.

The lightning took them with a blast that sent the teacher tumbling to the ground. A moment later, though, he found that he could stand and the monsters could not. His ears were ringing. His suit displayed the very slightest charring. The monsters were now piles of ash.

He looked up at the sound of something flying away, and with a sweep of his cape the flying man was gone, like a bullet up through the cloud layer.

He stumbled back to where Mrs. Bolaji was still standing with the children. "It was Thor!" he said. "He's come back! He—" He realized what he was about to say in front of the children. "He… teleported all the monsters back to Asgard."

Mrs. Bolaji gave him a look of enormous fraternal love. "So you're the leader of all the humans now, are you, Mr. Chavinsky?" Oh, he was going to be hearing that at PTA dinners from now on.

He was going to get to go to more PTA dinners. To lots of other sorts of dinners. With his wife and child.

"I am grateful," he said, helping to hustle the class away, "that my term in office was so short."

ON THE way back to the buses, Mr. Chavinsky had a little time to consider the implications of what he'd just seen. Thor—who the media had always asserted was not really an organized-religion-challenging actual Norse god, but merely an incredibly powerful other-dimensional being who'd been around since Viking times, around whom the myths were based—Thor had been away a long time. Mr. Chavinsky had enough interest in the subject to have followed the online speculation that Ragnarok, the cyclic death and revival of all the gods, had actually happened. But recently there had been reports that Thor was back in Asgard, the home of his people, which was now, for reasons Mr. Chavinsky had never worked out, hovering above a town in Oklahoma. He had, people said, become disgusted with the peoples of Earth, with heroes who fought amongst themselves, and especially with his former friend Tony Stark.

The figure they had seen had certainly looked and acted like Thor, and… well, perhaps he couldn't help but save people when they needed help, but still wanted to keep his distance. Several of the children also claimed to have seen Captain America, watching from the trees. But Mr. Chavinsky suspected that was just the business of legends being created. Captain America was dead. And he'd been just a person, not the sort of being that returned in cyclic mythological cycles.

He took one last look as he got onto the bus and prayed he'd get home safely. To have Cap come back… he didn't think the human race could be that lucky.

THIRTY-FIVE

OM'NOLL

OM'NOLL TELEPORTED with the Queen back to New York, to that battleground he'd been hopping back and forth from all day. Walking out into a sidestreet where a guard of honor was waiting for them, they joined a muster at an intersection as Skrulls reported in. Apart from a single teleport assault by Nick Fury's troops, resistance in the city now seemed to be confined to small pockets of military, civil forces like the NYPD, and civilians. The super hero threat seemed to have largely abated. "They've just fallen back," he said. "Fury is a real problem."

"We're getting sightings," Veranke replied, looking at her tablet. "They seem to be engaging in hit and run attacks, hopping across the city in what looks to be a pattern. The analysts think they're heading for—"

That was when they saw the flash and heard the thunder.

The "boom" resounded down the streets and rattled the window frames. It sent the dust of destruction puffing into the air once more. It was, in its way, gentle. It spoke of distant havoc. It was kind to civilians. It came again, and again, now starting to become a regular beat.

Om and his Queen knew the sound well, from their briefings and from experience. It was both a summons and a challenge. "Is that—" began one of the elite guard beside them.

"It's him," said the Queen.

Om looked around to see every Skrull nearby gazing toward Central Park. The look on their faces wasn't exactly one of fear, but it did speak of wariness. "Did you think," he called to them, "that we would succeed in this invasion without confronting him?! I have *awaited* this moment!"

Veranke stepped in front of him and he was silent. "We did not expect our assault on Asgard to prevent this moment. The goal was only ever to delay it, and delay it we have. Indeed, to prevent this moment would be blasphemy, because this too was written! I look at your faces now! To invade and conquer worlds which pose no threat to the invasion forces, this is not the Skrull way! Is *that* what you came here for? Am I surrounded by *Kree*?!"

Shouts of "no!" and "I came for this!" sounded in reply from the streets all around. Om felt pleased that his own limited oratory had only been deployed as a prelude to the greater poetry of his Queen. Never mind what the hardcore said about her, *this* was why he had stayed at her side. Veranke had a genuine feeling for the will of god and had kept her eyes on the path for so long to bring them to this moment. She had walked the path as well as indicating where that path lay. That was fitting for a leader in war. That was fitting for a monarch who hoped one day to have an Empire and be Empress.

"Gather the ground troops," she said now. "All of them. We march to the crucial battle."

THIRTY-SIX

THOR ODINSON

LISTEN!

That was the word that worthy Thor, the King of Asgard, said with his lightning and his thumping hammer, and with that hammer he brought the thunder.

Thor had been angry with the humans, for a time that felt sore long and awful.

Not time in the way his legend lived it. His youth had been before the humans had first evolved. His old age would be after the end of all their human lifetimes.

And yet here he was, caught in a moment. A long involvement, an entangling, of his own life with human heroes. His thoughts had slowed, and he'd allowed them into his heart and let them know him.

And so that heart had oft been broken.

To death he was no foolish stranger. He had returned from it most recently, consumed inside the Midgard Serpent, rushed into the ruin of Ragnarok. And thus, to the fields of fair Valhalla. But as would happen once and future, Asgard lived again and he had clambered, aching, back to his lifetime, heavy hearted and without

Odin, who seemed to have cast his crown asunder. And so it had fallen onto Thor's head. And he felt the weight of wonder.

Not just gods now knew such changes. Heroes had such cycles to them, did for them a spinning doorway, no strangers to the breath of Hela, death weaved in and out their pathways. Thor had wondered if they'd learned that from his kin and felt belittled that he was now just hero. Now he vowed he would a King be, and a god and hove to his people, and leave the heroes to their issues.

Thor of Asgard knew of folly, in himself so often, and in others, more than often. He now was taxed by mortal folly, harming their own world and others, but free will was not a privilege, but their right that he had sworn to, and he would not fix their problems.

Then Tony Stark, friend of the furnace, admixture of fire and of folly, fooled himself that he was wiser, and he had divided comrades.

Thor turned his back on mortal nonsense. Stayed within his risen homeland, floating now above fair Broxton. Oklahoma, plains of pleasing. He and his would-be good neighbors. Nothing more, but nothing lesser. Stark's supplicants had come knocking, with papers for him to write on, he had slammed the doors upon them and made it known that laws for mortals did not apply to gods of Asgard.

They had not sought to press him on it.

And that had been the situation.

But then, oh woe, a few days past now, a friend had fallen, sorely screaming, into Asgard, presaging battle.

"Beta Ray Bill" his name on human tongues had sounded, the syllables in their mouths lacking the wit to render all his grace and heart and goodness. Alien to Earth, he was, alien to Asgard too. A Korbinite, his face unto a horse's muzzle, his body propped by cybernetics. When he, years past, had held Thor's hammer, he had been seen as worthy, and had taken, upon himself, the thunder's mantle, serving as Thor with glory. Odin had seen the magical mishap, and had seen how worthy Bill had walked and had made him his own hammer, the magic weapon called Stormbreaker.

Thor himself regained Mjolnir. As it was, so it would be. But he had rejoiced that there was someone else who understood this. He and Bill fought as comrades, true in all the fields of battle.

Now Bill had lain and bled in Asgard, his hammer taken by trickery, his armor and enhancements missing, naked, tortured, injured, shamed. He had whispered to them the message he'd been told to bring them. They were to take all Asgard, and from Earth and its fields depart, or invaders would be on them shortly. Asgardians offended the invaders. They were not proper parts of prophecy. They were owners sitting idly on an Earth that had been promised to others from the starry vault of heaven's pastures.

"Owners?!" had laughed brave old Balder as he'd lifted Bill and helped him. "They do not understand our presence."

Thor had called the gods of healing, who rushed to take brave Bill from Balder. "And yet I understand their error."

"Too late it is though to correct it," brave Bill had in departing whispered.

"Aye," said Thor, "we will instead correct those that have so misapprehended."

They had made Bill smile, just a little.

As he was healed, he had told them of the Skrulls, their plans and prophets. Thor asked what of Bill's hammer. Taken for their warriors. A great dishonor. Thor told him that was nonsense. He'd left him to the healers' handling and flown hence to address his people from his palace. Across the universe all had heard him, his words upon the wings of ravens. Invaders had been heard approaching, strong enough to test their godhood.

"Doubtless," he said, "the Skrulls see the distance there is now between myself and those warriors I did call friends. Doubtless they see that Asgard has been away. That we have been lost. That Odin is still lost. Doubtless they therefore feel their threat might succeed, that we might step aside and allow them their victory. And yet I look down from this rock upon which our land stands, and I see below us a diner, and a bar, and a veterinarian, and all the small matters of those that we have all befriended. And I think of the Skrulls feeling that we might allow those beneath us to be crushed. That we might squander all honor for our mere *survival*. And *I say thee nay!*"

And the thunder had been heard then, across all Asgard, and to Broxton. And with it there had come the cheering of the massed ranks of Asgardians. That thunder had brought with it stormclouds, massed ranks of cover, full of lightning. The inhabitants of Broxton, whirlwind wise, tornado wary, awayed into their deepest shelters, which was where good Thor had wanted them.

Then Thor sought out his brother. He went to find the Trickster, Loki. Loki who was always scheming. Loki had already plotted; he had begun to spread a rumor that since they all knew Skrulls could shape-shift, surely this Bill must be suspect. Thor had expected such sardonics. He had marched to Bill's bedchamber, a mob of witnesses beside him, and in Bill's hand had placed Mjolnir, his magic hammer, blessed weapon. The alien had raised the hammer, let it fall and so transformed him, into healed and hearty warrior. The Thor he had been, back in glory. And beside him stood the Odinson, now reduced to mortal guise. He stood there as Don Blake, the doctor.

Blake was an idea of Odin, a way to teach the young Thor humility. A "secret identity," made to bind him to the humans, to their heroes and that culture. Thor did not now often use it. But now he saw that Bill's recovery depended on Thor's borrowed power. He intended this to only show the others of Bill's honesty, but now he saw the shape of legend unfolding, weaved by fates around him. "Bill will stay here, fight for Asgard. I'll go to Earth and aid the mortals."

As he'd descended to the ground of little Broxton, he heard the laughter of his brother Loki, and saw how wise this move was. Loki would claim the plot for evil, and yet it had been the best of outcomes. Bill would fight with youthful vigor, not the broken heart of Odinson, and Odinson would do his duty healing and receiving healing to his heart from dint of service. Such was ever Loki's wisdom, twisted like a maze inside him.

Loki would fight hard for Asgard.

The invaders arrived an hour after he had made his decision. Thor's two ravens, Hugin and Munin, flew back and forth, the quantum ripples of their passing sending whispers, granting news to the hard-pressed doctor, who found himself tending to a woman trapped in heavy labor as above them, Thor's own people, were assaulted by the enemy.

The Skrulls had sent some transformed warriors, warped by magic, armored and made awesome by alien incantation. They were called "Godkillers" by those who give such monsters names. Their leader stood there, Super-Skrull, Godkiller, massed might of stolen powers, her mutations proudly plundered.

Bill and Balder swiftly organized the Aesir, the ranks to protect their land all gleaming, while Lady Sif rose to meet the monster in single combat, which well did suit her.

She had fallen, finally, valiantly, violently, her feet not having given a single inch, but dropping bloodied, having bloodied her the monster, in turn on turn of righteous violence. That made the Odinson grow vengeful, in his heart as he did the work of healing, but he stayed with his promise, waited to hear more from Asgard.

Bill took on the front rank of the foe then, as they smashed against the wall of Asgard and rebounded as a tide did. He and the monster fought hand to hand, fire to fire, one knowing every inch of the other, the other knowing not what he had in hand.

The monster had, to the shock of Thor and Bill both, pulled from her scabbard the hammer Stormbreaker.

It had been Bill's and he had not hoped to see it again. Hope was brought him as he saw it. Yet he was sore sad also to see it now. She hit Bill full hard with it across the maw and he fell, for a moment.

Thor looked up from where he had in his hands, in the storm shelter, a newborn baby, mewling, vulnerable.

He heard the monster sniff and heard her whisper "new life" horribly.

He felt her register his weakness, there below her. She jumped from the edge of Asgard, landing on the Earth with a slam that set the humans screaming even in their deepest redoubts.

She had seen the King in exile, had known she could swift kill him, hurt the hearts of all Asgardians.

Bill, Thor saw through eyes of ravens, had pulled himself to the edge, had fallen more than flew, had landed not long behind. But when he had landed, he had lost his wits again and lay, his fingers full five inches from his hammer. Mjolnir, that had been Thor Odinson's, lying useless so close to him.

Thor heard, as Don the doctor, the sound of the monster approaching. Now it approached the doorway of this small local facility. Around him, a fire crew gathered around the bed as the dread of the tread spoke into them of the battle they had begun to be aware of, a battle that was no tornado, now they knew.

They rallied. They were ready to face they knew not what to protect their smallest innocent.

Each one of them worth ten of Tony, a hundred heroes there right with him, their hearts as big as all of Asgard. And inside Don, the Odinson found hope.

Don left the shelter, sealed behind him. Then he stood outside the entrance, the monster's shadow looming, his home above on fire, small against the mighty warrior.

"You aren't getting in," he said.

The monster blinked at him. This had not been as expected. Her mind was made for ready battle. His form was far too frail and mortal for this to be noble. She had no wish for execution. She had sensed him down here, thought him protecting something precious. Indeed he was, but he was no warrior.

Don braced for battle, stout and sure in heart. He would, he'd thought, prove a distraction, giving Bill time to rally. And yet Bill lay, lacking, lost, unmoving, changing back to injured alien, his fingers still short of that hammer.

At that moment, high above, came a rousing, merry, rotund shout. The shout increased in volume as though from someone falling. The monster looked up as the sound was on them. A form impossible to humans had hit them like a warrior boulder.

The giant god of feasts and flummery had foxed the foe in one great falling.

"The Mighty Volstagg is here to save you!" shouted the Asgardian, garbed in purple, helm so tiny, heart so huge. He rolled from that he'd flattened but she leapt to life immediately. Catching his chin, she began choking him.

Don began running even as his friend fell. He reached the hammer lying yonder. Into his hand it had leapt upon calling, Mjolnir to its proper master. His tactic might have been folly, but this folly might become a feint.

He struck the hammer on the land of Broxton. Felt the lightning proper take him. He had achieved again his armor. He stood and met the monster, who let go of Volstagg. He heard behind him Bill awoken. He regretted his absenting. He had learned what he had sought and set his heart again to action. He would not absent himself again from action. He would not hide from human heroes. He would instead upbraid their actions, let them know he would have words. He heard Bill whisper goodly utterance. "Make the monster drop *my* hammer."

He stepped forward as the beast had, certain, rushed him. He swung Mjolnir, in experience born of battle.

In a stroke he smote her.

He moved in and smote her more, hammer meeting hammer, fire meeting fire, lightning illuminating Broxton, giving light to newborn's mewlings. All were safe while he was here. Responsibility had been retaken.

Fire on fire. Heat against heat. Two hammers near unforged and molten, face to face in fierce infighting.

Volstagg's friends, fair Fandral and grim Hogun, fell to ground beside the monster. As it staggered, Fandral stabbed. His good Asgardian sword pierced her. Thor threw back his hammer. He hit the hilt with hunger. The blade bit into the monster. She fell, dropped before them.

But as they'd stood there, panting, hoping, she pulled the blade from in her, cosmic fire birthing wonder, strength resuming in her innards. She leapt up, swung the hammer, Stormbreaker spinning swiftly.

The hurricane hit Thor and also took the others. They staggered. Fell.

And then, surprising them, she released it. The hammer flew straight up. Sky high it went, past Asgard, directly upward. "The beast has thrown away her weapon!" said Volstagg, not the wisest.

"No," Thor said. "She has thrown it at Broxton."

He ordered the others to hold her. He leapt into the air, let Mjolnir launch him. He sped in flight right after. The hammer, blazing, headed upward. And yet it curved, keeping, below it, the town that had been set as target.

Thor had in his mind all the times the humans of the town had helped them. The firefighters arriving to aid the gods from Asgard. Deliveries of food to Volstagg. Tours of children, eyes aglow. They had, he hoped, been equal neighbors.

He was so angry with the humans. For what they did just to each other. When they had such joy and greatness in the tiny things of mortals.

He counted these folk fellow victims of the rift that brought the danger, of division and responsibility gone missing. This was neighbor for neighbor now.

He saw the hammer turn at last. It had held itself at flight's own apex. The moment sat in time so slow. Cosmic time and human lives, woven together at this instant.

It plummeted.

He put himself before it.

He took all the impact. The sky lit up over Broxton.

He managed to hold his own hurling, halting, mind of melting madness in that instant, as he spiraled, floundered, fell so fast.

He hit the ground on fire.

He stepped from out the crater. Saw the monster winning, returned again to wrestle Volstagg. But now he stood there with two hammers. "Villain," he named her, "bane of innocents, seeker of easy success, yield to the better warrior. This is my last word to you."

She broke away from the others, running toward him, screaming. The power in her hands equal again now. She would always have his match, he realized, raging.

He thought again of Loki, thought about the God of Stories. He had put a tale in motion with his ruse of Bill's becoming. A moment in a tale was needed, a turn to turn the tables.

He shouted to his comrade. Threw Bill his hammer. Stormbreaker sang, back to blessed hand, grip gained giving godhead once again. The lightning took him.

Two Thors met the rushing monster.

And yet, to gasps of wonder, from both gods and emerging humans, they stepped aside and let her through. She stumbled, halting, turning, knew not the nature of the knot in which her life had now been caught. She stood outside the town, stood amongst the bristling desert, a shadow on her speaking in silence.

Thor put his hand on Bill's good shoulder and whispered, "Make it fall." The alien looked upward. He looked in horror and yet he trusted in his brother-in-arms.

Together they pulled the storm from the sky, pulled the gravity from the Earth, pulled the magic from Asgard's flight.

They made the rock of Asgard fall straight down.

It hit the Skrull full on, the rock of the city meeting its shadow, meeting the ground, the impact spared from everyone around. The thunder had been kind for humans. The thunder had disintegrated matter. The force reduced the monster. The energy and sentience left her. The Skrull that would have killed the innocent had been in turn dispatched by Asgard.

But now the city tottered, the rock swaying. The humans ran and started screaming.

Thor and Thor had not renounced them. They would not allow collateral. They flew and grabbed the city. Holding and pushing and settling it, their mighty shoulders supporting safely. The ravens crowed, "It is done, city safe and people too, town and

Asgard both made one, battle won as Skrulls broke and flew. Their champion dead, their folly clear, their wisdom lacking, they did not win here."

The Asgardians helped their neighbors. Once the day had been saved in smallness, then Thor turned his gaze to Bill. He told him to heal wholly. He had his own task to fulfill.

Against all his own advisings, he had responsibilities this day, that he would take up even given that others had let theirs slip away. He had made sure Asgard was defended, the people below like those above. He left Sif recovering.

He left them all with love.

He flew east with anger. Forced to join this fight.

He came to New York. He summoned. Hoping heroes would hie to him. He hoped Stark would show his Hel-spawned head.

His anger stood. His anger doubled since he'd seen what doubt and division had allowed abroad.

And here now was a human hero, first to his summons. Thor stared at his uniform. Anger upon anger. Offense upon offense. Here was the smallest example of all that was wrong within heroes.

Who was this stranger standing before him who wore colors of Captain America? Was he a Skrull? Or, worse, a human, stealing the banners of fallen honor? Steve Rogers, he had proven to the God of Thunder, there was valor in these humans, valor now almost departed. Thor asked him in the voice of thunder who he was meant to resemble.

"Who do I look like?"

"A great warrior. But you are not he. Again, I ask you—"

"Weren't you dead too?"

"Ah. You have returned thus. With your eyes a different color."

He laughed. "I'm not Steve Rogers. As to whether or not I'm Cap… that's for others to decide. And you can decide if I'm with you or not when you see me killing Skrulls."

Thor looked around and saw that, from all directions, heroes, or what now passed for that description, were running into the park around them. He did not want to give voice to an agreement with this impostor standing before him. Instead, he turned to find that Spider-Man, thank Odin, had now landed beside him.

"Thor?! I mean, you're the real Thor, right?"

"It's him." Reed Richards, running up now, some human artifice in hand singing its signal. "What are you doing here, Thor?"

Thor raised his hammer once again and again he brought it down, the sound of the thunder adding grandeur. "Summoning here," he said, "away from innocents, the battle."

"Yeah," said Parker, "I, uh, think they got the message."

From the east of the park came a large force, small ground troops first making their way through the trees, then larger foes beginning to bend and snap them, before finally casting them aside. Their numbers slowly swelled until they filled much of this human space. Skrull upon Skrull upon Skrull, a horde of monsters, giants standing out among them and winged ones flying high above them. It was a vision from Thor's childhood, brought here to Earth, such mythic numbers. So many of the horde displayed the colors of their declared enemy, mixed up parts of uniforms, all meaning ripped apart and splattered randomly on the host of battle. Thor glanced at this new Captain America. He wore a slight variation on the uniform of Steve Rogers and incredibly, he carried a gun, another offense against the Captain of Thor's memory. And yet the uniform upon him fit. And the expression on his face was appraising, the proper look of a stern warrior when facing an army large and powerful.

Thor squared his shoulders and made his gaze meet that of the leader of the horde, who now stepped forward from it. She looked, ridiculously, like Jessica Drew, the Spider-Woman. Beside her was a fellow alien with the face of Henry Pym; beside them also was a green-faced Skrull who wore what Thor himself had worn in battle during his first years on Earth a hero. Thor smiled at that one. He was wiser now and much, much older and had died, and these would die in turn for their defilement and slaughter.

From his own ranks stepped forward Reed Richards. "You… you killed my family!" he shouted. "You say you're here to 'save us,' but not one thing you have done has spoken to that."

Thor understood the wisdom of the man's words, though they sounded lost in anger. He was sowing doubt in any Skrulls who had believed their blarings. Or Thor hoped that was what he did now. Richards' voice had sounded maybe a touch too passionate for such calculated tactics. "You're here to… to punish us!"

"Well," replied the alien queen, proud and parrying, playing to her party, "maybe you should have thought about what might happen all those years ago when you took the first party of Skrulls you met and turned them into farm animals!"

Thor saw movement over his shoulder, and turned to see that two new groups were assembling on their side of the parkland. The dishonorable villain called Norman Osborn led beside him a group whose ranks included some Thor recognized as valorous, but some he did not note with honor. Beside them, as if they had now chosen to reveal themselves for Osborn, came also an army of declared villains, including many Thor himself had faced in combat, led by some hooded churl. These unworthy foes had taken advantage of innocence and weakness, and were doubtless only here because the end of all things meant the end of their own profits. Better, though, they stand at the last than flee the conflict. Some might prove themselves of slight worth. Perhaps he would raise a flagon with those that gave their all in battle.

Perhaps he'd raise it in New York, or perhaps he'd raise it in Valhalla.

Tony Stark had stepped forward to stand beside his comrade Richards. Thor found his heart was full of anger at the sight of such a spokesman. It was not well that he felt this, yet there it was. He could not help it. There had been a time when he, Rogers and Stark had been the axis about which spun the world of heroes. And now he could not bring himself to stand beside the man, and this "Captain" at his side had not the way to so step forward. All was still lost here in hearts, that could not be won in this battle.

"Leave now!" shouted Stark to the Skrull Queen, pointing, his finger shaking as his voice did. "Last warning!"

"Interesting!" the Skrull responded. "And no!" There was enormous laughter from the ranks of gathered aliens, a wave of it catching and heartening them for miles in all directions.

Stark lowered his hand, looking sick and lost and desperate.

"I don't mean to poop on the parade," said a fair maid, her hair as green as vegetation, "but we still don't know who we can trust here."

"Yes, we do," said Reed Richards, wise in words. "I figured out what they did. They used our harvested DNA to build individual biostructures, even including genetic memory and neurons, that mimicked every trait we looked for with our scanners and special senses. They took the knowledge they needed to make that technology directly from my brain. They hacked us. But it *was* a hack. And hacks can be traced, their paths reconstructed." He took another device from his belt. "This is a beam that will at least show us the natural form of whoever it's pointed at, that'll reveal who's a Skrull. I've thrown together as many as I could make in the time. I'll start handing them out in a second." His voice stood stark against Stark's weakness, full of focused anger. "They have worked on this with considerable skill and tenacity. Their only mistake was failing to kill *me*."

"Of course, *you* figured us out!" called the Queen, indicating in that moment that she could hear their conversations. "You, all of you, you invented everything it took to bring humanity to its knees!"

"What does that mean?" said Luke Cage, stepping up to join them.

"Who cares?" sighed Logan. The Wolverine weight was in his words.

"Exactly," said Janet Van Dyne, her Wasp wings already beating a blur.

"What you're facing here is a product of your own hubris," called the Queen. "The hate and judgment you face is what you have inflicted on others, you and all humanity. You addressed us earlier, Richards, as if we were hypocrites, as if we had no intention of saving your race. Wouldn't that make things easier for you? But no. We *are* here to save you. We are here to change you. Those humans left under our rule will be happier and they will know their every action is always for the greater good. They will be told what those actions must be. We will all, together, actually save this world you have neglected to save. We will *have* to save it, because it will be our new home. Those humans that remain will finally be safe here. We will do all that despite what you have done to our Empire, because He loves you."

"Uh, he who?" asked the Spider-Man, exact as ever, meaning in mocking.

"God," said the Queen.

From the bushes beside Thor stepped Nicholas Fury, and with him there came the giant Cassie Lang, Kate Bishop, the Vision, the youthful Avengers and others Thor did not know the name of, including a child who seemed Olympian. From their own ranks Ares jogged now and stared in wonder at this arrival. "My son," he whispered. "I… did not know you."

"I am going to fight this battle, Daddy," said the boy, calm and measured.

"Oh, of course," nodded rough Ares, "you absolutely should. Talk later, all right? We'll catch up. If we survive." He slapped the boy heartily on the shoulder, shuddering it, and jogged back, cheerful.

Thor saw on the boy his true expression and for a moment he was angry at gods as well as these fool mortals.

"You say 'God' wants you to do this?" called Fury, stepping forward to point at the alien Queen, all angered. "Well, you can go stick yer god where the sun don't shine." He turned and nodded toward Thor, a stalwart. "Because our god has a hammer."

Thor found in his heart a smile then, for the valorous veteran, made in pain, forged in fury unto his own name. He had decided he would be drawn, as a hero back to humans, just to save them and to tell them of the folly of their actions. And yet to fight in human folly, this would lead to no good ending.

Still. There was a battle. The words of Skrulls bore no weight for him. He had seen them with a baby.

He raised on high his godhood's hammer. He raised it so his foes could see it. He raised it so he might bind friendship, in this slight moment of divided allies who could not weave their fates in folded hands together.

From their ranks came howls and shouts. It had always been thus before battle.

Clint Barton walked up to Kate Bishop, gave her a bear hug, and her weapons. "These are yours now," he said to her.

From the sky dropped Carol Danvers, battered around head and body, her gaze alighting upon Fury. "You were wrong," she said to him curtly. "I woke up ten minutes ago. A woman called Diamondback saved me from the Skrulls in Times Square. She threw this tiny stone at just the right moment. The Super-Skrull pounding me looked up and the Initiative piled in on him. They got me away. They lost three of their number. Diamondback lost her right arm."

Fury looked at Richards' scanner. "Yep, looks like I was wrong," he returned in all good humor and raised his thumb, reckless to her wrath. "Go get 'em, Major."

"That's what you said last time."

"That's me," said Fury, his smile unfaltering, "reliable."

"And hey," Carol pointed across the field toward where the Skrulls were massing, "Henry Pym's a Skrull."

"Thanks for the intel," returned Fury.

"My guys are gone," said Gauntlet, gathering, "except a few who're on their way here."

"What he said," said Taskmaster, beside him.

"Who's gonna say it?" said Kate Bishop, stepping back from her reunion with Clint and looking between Thor, Stark, Luke Cage and this new Captain America.

"You are, kid," said Fury, certain.

Kate Bishop took to her a deep breath, wiped some of the grime from bloodied visage and raised her voice. "Avengers... Assemble!"

And humans rushed to human battle, the God of Thunder right beside them, with hammer high and heart not nearly for all that he stood alongside.

The battle joined. The ranks collided. The legend wrote itself in bloodshed.

From this moment all stories sundered.

THIRTY-SEVEN

JANET VAN DYNE

OKAY, SO Janet Van Dyne was *very* ticked off.

Right now, she was buzzing at Wasp size through the battle, picking her targets, blasting Skrulls in the eyes and ears wherever they reared up before her. *Idiots*, she kept thinking, *they had all been such idiots!* She had been an idiot in the last year or so to prioritize the arguments of her former partner, Tony Stark, over the heroic aspirations of Steve Rogers. She had been an idiot to think that the schism that had resulted had been because the culture of super heroes had ceased to be enough about the law. She had, instead, like the heiress she was, fallen into stereotype and prioritized mere order. And she'd known she'd misstepped as she'd done it, and she'd still gone right ahead and done it. And so had they all!

She had been such a young woman when Henry had experimented on her as well as himself, giving her the power to shrink, the power to grow wings and actually fly—an amazing fairy dream of flying under one's own power. That power fit entirely with her love of fashion too, her love of the glamour that her money had bought. She'd been a founder member of the Avengers, damn it, when it had just been her, Thor, Tony, Henry and, err, the Hulk.

Talk about shattered alliances. *She'd* been the one, after they'd accidentally got together to fight Loki, who'd suggested their *name*. It had been such a ridiculous moment. She'd said hey, this group of what were only just starting to be called "super heroes," who'd found themselves fighting alongside each other and wanted to stay together should have a name that was something colorful and dramatic, like The Avengers, *or*—

And at that moment Henry, her ex-husband, who'd just been someone at that time that she'd admired from afar, had leapt up and down and pointed at her and had said yes, that's it, that's what they should be called, and Tony Stark, Thor and the Hulk had all joined in, and, wow, her contribution was being acknowledged by all these huge guys, by a Norse god! She hadn't really liked the name that much. It had sounded *too* dramatic. She'd only meant they should be called something *like* it. But that reaction had pleased her so much she hadn't argued.

But now it felt kind of like she'd even *founded* them wrongly. That damn name. The wrong foundation. And yet, you heard Kate Bishop shout it, and suddenly there it was again, so, no, no, that was just how her mind had been eating at her over the last few months. It had *become* a fine name.

That first group changed so quickly. She couldn't really look down at this battlefield and lament the changes that had led the Avengers to weakness, because change was part of their DNA. Hey, literally in her case. But what she could lament were specific choices that had brought them to this moment—hers most of all. Historians would look for the one moment where the culture of super heroes had started to crumble and led to alien invasion. They'd probably pick Tony coming up with the Superhuman Registration Act, but right now, as her thoughts were taking flight alongside her body, and she was motoring along entirely on her training and vast experience, Janet had started to believe that maybe it was way earlier.

Maybe it had been the moment her then-husband, Henry, had slapped her across the face.

Because from that point it became crystal clear that she and the guys weren't going to be a schoolyard gang of friends who always caught up with each other, always came together again. From that moment on it had been utterly obvious that, like everyone else, they were just a bunch of vulnerable human beings—and vulnerable, you know, deities—who could fall apart like anyone else. Divorce, breakdowns, psychoses, recriminations, bitterness... not all for one and one for all. Though Henry kept trying for that, had wrecked himself on the rocks of that, time after time.

And here was an awful, wicked hope inside her: What if... that hadn't been Henry? What if he'd been replaced by a Skrull before that? She desperately wanted the real Henry to be alive somewhere, of course she did, no matter what he'd done. But there was also that awful idea that maybe the Henry they could find in a spaceship cell somewhere was the real one, the good one, the one who would never have laid a finger on her because he was a super hero, damn it.

That was almost certainly not true. That was to believe in an Avengers that were mythologically perfect, like nothing was, neither the Knights of the Round Table nor the Gods of Asgard—and hey, the Avengers had had the chance to directly compare themselves to both.

But that was the sort of Avengers that she'd always kept wishing for, that she'd always held in her heart.

That thought, of their own humanity, their own flawed natures, kept dragging on her as she flew in combat mode, hitting and running, adding additional force to the right-side dozens of times a minute, her form a blur.

She blamed herself, of course she did. It was what she did. She had been the Chair of the Avengers so many times, had been the one Cap, especially, looked to for orders, and that had been a hell of a thing when he'd first done that, entirely deliberately, to underline her credentials. But since she'd sided with Tony in the "Civil War," she found she'd been hanging back, completely uncertain, feeling the ache of both sides. So why hadn't she done what Ben Grimm had, and stayed apart from both sides? So many times she'd wanted to call Luke Cage. But that would be literally treachery, and an heiress just couldn't do that sort of thing, could she? Even just now, with some sort of substitute Cap suddenly appearing and being willing to pitch in to this fight—which was just as damn well, or she'd have kicked his ass for wearing that costume—even now she had not stepped forward to join that rough leadership group of Tony, Luke and Thor. They had not looked to her. They had not looked to Natasha either, and she'd led the Avengers for over a year, back in the day. Of course they hadn't. Women. Small. Very small in her case. Didn't get looked to. Had to speak up. Hadn't.

If she'd been determining their strategy for this battle she'd have told Thor to get into the air and bring the lightning down, at moment one. Before moment one. But that Skrull Queen had pretty much immediately closed with her enemies, seemed for a moment like she might parley, and had started to exchange taunts, digging into the egos of Tony and the like. Within minutes the other army had been too close for that obvious first play.

Damn it. Damn it.

At least they now had Carol as well as Thor and Simon and Ares, so that was some heavy tanks in the field. And they had Reed's gadget, so they'd finally be able to know what they were hitting. But this was still going to be a hell of a fight, and it could go either way. Even if they won this, that would be just them freeing New York. Then there'd just be the rest of the entire world to liberate.

Zap, zap, zap she went. Fluttering at supersonic speed. She should have said something. She should have said something. On so many occasions.

There were so many of them. She dodged through an endless super-powered horde. There was Daredevil, of all people, who usually fought ninjas in Hell's Kitchen, only his wits and a couple of sticks to defend himself, living up to his name in the thick of it, having joined the battle without any particular loyalty to anything here except his city and the human race in general. The blue light of Reed's Skrull detectors kept flaring across the battlefield and illuminating Skrulls in their true form, but that didn't stop them using their copied power sets.

They were getting kind of overwhelmed here, from what she could see. The Skrulls kept arriving from all sides, in numbers. Damn it, Thor had called this battle here, because he thought a pitched battle was their best hope and because it was away from civilians, but the Skrulls had clearly been hoping for a set-piece battle too. Her side wasn't going to win this.

No. No. *Put that out of your head, Jan. You've been in worse. When?*

"Get to the Queen!" Reed, bruised and bloody, shouted at anyone around him who would listen. "Get to the Skrull Queen Jessica Drew. Take out the leader!"

"Everyone with a Skrull detector," Tony was shouting, only a few feet from him, "keep it covering the field!"

"Simon, Ares, stand with me!" Thor shouted. "We shall take down their front line if we stand together!"

"Keep the battle moving forward!" Ares was shouting. "Do not yield them the advantage!"

"They could get more advantage?!" cried out Simon Williams, his beloved leather jacket in tatters, his passing guise of an everyday human looking even more out of place than it did on the street. His rosy glasses had been shattered, energy flaring behind them. He was becoming more Wonder Man and less his own special creation every second. He'd spent the last few months hanging back like she had, undecided like she'd been, yet always certain when he spoke, playing the part of a loyalist, decided, a bystander. And now he was paying for it like she was, like they all were.

All these men bellowed in different directions, ignoring each other. Maybe only she, throwing herself from target to target, bio-electricity flaring from her hands every millisecond, could hear them all.

"The words have been spoken!" bellowed a Super-Skrull right in front of her, catching sight of her and trying to swat her with a blazing hand. "We shall prevail!"

The blow missed. She shot him in the eye, and was away as he shouted and one of the Howling Commandos grabbed him.

She flew between Nick Fury and Norman Osborn—the latter of whom she was surprised to see here, honestly, but good for him, the sniveling weasel. They were fighting back-to-back, firing enormous guns, yelling at each other.

"You should be in jail!"

"So should you!"

She resisted the urge to swear into Osborn's ear and flew on.

"I'm sorry!" Tony shouted, suddenly accelerating past her and into the air. "My armor's shot, I'm useless, I'll get back as soon as I can!"

Janet started to shout that they'd hold the line.

But then she saw *him*.

There he was, in the thick of it. He was firing green bio-electricity, or what only looked like it. Making exactly the same attempt at a heroic stance that the real human would have tried for.

Her husband. Her abuser. Henry Pym.

She went straight for him. She couldn't help it. She was fighting for him and fighting against him, and both impulses left her diving at him with every ounce of power her wings gave her.

His head turned at the last second, and with a reaction speed born of the same brew that had changed her own biochemistry, or a Skrull version of it, he flung out a hand.

He slapped her aside.

She spun through the air, her wings catching her and spinning her, an energy blast flashing past close enough for her to feel the heat, tumbling and using every bit of her willpower to right herself.

He'd slapped her *again*.

It wasn't him. It wasn't him. But this Skrull *knew*, damn it. It knew *everything*.

She found herself facing him again and sped off, plowing energy into her hands. "You!" she bellowed. She found all her energy, putting more and more into her hands, ready to turn him into a crater. And then she would yell into his face as he died: *Where was the real Henry, was he the real Henry, which was it who'd destroyed all their lives?!*

He shot up to giant size.

She spun in the air, landing on three points. She saw Skrull warriors start to react, turning to try to aim at her, then shot up to giant size herself and kicked them aside.

The two of them stood facing each other, panting as the battle raged around them, combatants staggered back from them, their giant shadows falling over everything. "Hi, honey!" he called, grinning. "I mean, I was going to save you for last, but if you're going to turn it into a thing—"

She punched him, but he ducked it. She was aware friendly forces were somewhere near her feet. But everything about him was getting to her: that costume he was wearing, that voice, the mock jaunty style he'd adopted when he'd tried to be the hero Yellowjacket, testing yet another new identity, trying to be the laid-back hero like Spider-Man was, and always, always, Janet had been there to go along with it, to pick up the slack, to support all the extremes and suffer through it. "Where is he?!" she yelled.

"You're wondering when we swapped out, right?"

"Damn right I am."

"Well, Jan honey, I'm afraid it was after that little unpleasantness when you pushed me too far that night."

"You're lying!"

"Why should I lie, when the truth gets to you so much more? You know this is true, right? Yeah, I can see. I know you. And while you're fixated on that, I'm in charge of this situation." He ducked another blow from her, his expression never letting up from gloating. She realized, too late, that one of his hands was glowing. Suddenly, it was right in her face, his other hand around her neck. Oh god, they'd practiced this, in case a villain did it. He would shrink or grow with her. He'd got her. He'd finally got her. "The problem with you is, you always—"

His head suddenly flew aside, his goggles shattering, his hands letting go of her as he fell.

Cassie Lang stood there, also giant-sized, glaring at him as he landed on a whole bunch of Skrulls. "Enough with the lectures!" she said. "You're not Mr. Pym. You're a bad cartoon of him."

And that was true, wasn't it? As the Skrull lay groaning at her feet, Jan knew it had been telling the truth, because she'd always known. And yet, she still wanted to find and free the real Henry. Because that was what heroes did. "Love you," said Jan.

"Back at you, boss," said Cassie. "Avengers fricking assemble."

But the giant Skrull was struggling back to his feet, his hands powering up. He bellowed in rage. "I am Criti Om'Noll, and I do the work of God and my Queen! And I am the memories of Henry Pym, and I am going to finally end you, you—"

Janet noted that there were still Skrulls all around him and knocked him flying with a right hook across the jaw.

He staggered back, his every step crushing his own kind, who ran screaming.

Janet realized the only way this could end would be if she killed him. She had never consciously done that before. She had always played by the rules. But what else could she do in this moment? They were fighting a war. Super heroes were killing Skrulls all around her. Cassie Lang was beside her, ready for the two of them to hit him together. But knocking him out, tying him up, they weren't appropriate solutions for war. Was her wanting them to be perfect and hanging back because of it going to doom them all again?

Suddenly, something dropped from out of the sky, moving at high speed. Janet, her eyes accustomed to picking out small, fast-moving objects, realized at the last second that it was a drone of some kind, maybe something used by a news organization.

It hit Henry—Om'Noll—right in the eye and burst out the other side of his head.

Janet yelled.

She'd both lost him and freed herself of him in the same instant. And it had felt awful, deeply, deeply, disgusting. He collapsed onto the Skrulls as they screamed, his shadow hitting the ground, his body sending dozens of them flying and sprawling and crushed underneath him. And there he lay, dead.

Cassie and Janet both swore together.

"You're welcome," said a voice at their feet.

Janet looked down to see Bullseye, the assassin who never missed, the worst sort of super-powered criminal, a smoking hunting rifle in his grasp. "You shouldn't have," she said.

She would never really know if she'd meant it literally... or as if she'd just accepted a gift.

THIRTY-EIGHT

PETER PARKER

WOAH! PETER Parker, the Amazing Spider-Man, always felt kind of out of his depth when it came to really big, deity-sized heroes and villains duking it out, and right now he was dodging power blasts from those guys at an average of one every ten seconds or so. Plus, he was in Central Park, the only flat part of New York City, so, rather than swinging in the air, where he was the master of his own space, he was awkwardly running, jumping, occasionally getting a webline onto a giant and flinging himself away from immediate danger, but basically out of his element and rushing along yelling in panic, getting the odd kick or punch in against any Skrulls who were fast enough to get a bead on him.

Where was he going? No idea! What was the plan here? Nope! He just needed a win that felt like a win, and, actually, no, he increasingly felt he wasn't going to get it here, because he kept seeing the big guys like Gauntlet getting smashed down and being hauled away at the last second, and there didn't seem to be anything like a, you know, a battle plan?! Hey, there was that bench where he used to come sit with Mary Jane, and there was a Skrull hurtling backward into the bench and breaking it in two. Thanks for messing up that nice memory, alien invasion.

He blundered right into Reed Richards being attacked by, oh god, a dozen copies of Reed's wife Sue, who were all shouting "Hi, sweetie!" as they pummeled him with invisible forcefields even as his anti-deception gizmo displayed their Skrull credentials like they were being x-rayed. Reed's elastic limbs were getting spaghettified and the whole thing was just an explosion of blue cloth and domestic violence.

Peter took a deep breath and punched a Sue in the face, which felt bad, but wow, Skrulls who'd taken on the memories and personalities of whoever they'd duplicated were such sickos, which said a lot about—woah!—now they were on him, giving Reed a mo to squiggle out of there as Peter dodged for his life. The forcefields might be invisible, but his Spider-Sense could keep him a second ahead of them if he just switched off his chattering head and let it fly him.

"Susans!" he shouted. "Stormzies! Calm down and start a book club!"

And suddenly they were all past him, apart from the couple who he'd webbed up, and they were off into the melee after Reed again. Skrulls were always going to go for Reed Richards, he was like their catnip. Anti-catnip. Whatever. "All you have is tricks!" Reed shouted as they were on him again. "You're not even like my wife!"

"Let's not get all TMI!" shouted Peter, once more leaping in to help him. But right now, it looked like it might not be enough. The Susans started to focus their forcefields on Reed's body, contorting his torso, making him scream. Peter suddenly realized he couldn't move, that the forcefields had seized him too around his waist and chest. They'd grabbed him in that second of concern, and he couldn't get free, and they were about to kill Reed—

Which was when a bunch of howling kids in uniforms hit the Susans like a tidal wave.

"Hi, Dr. Richards!" shouted a big bald guy who'd grabbed and thrown two of them aside. "Big fan!"

"Not the time, big guy, you'll see him at the afterparty!" yelled a speedster, dopplering past them. Peter shook his head to clear his vision. Not only was he free of attackers, but Reed had been whizzed away to safety somewhere.

"The Queen!" Skrull voices shouted over his shoulder. "Protect the Queen!"

Peter saluted the Howling Commandos, used the big guy as a launch pad, leaping into the air, running across the shoulders of friend and foe alike, to where, in an area rapidly clearing of anyone else... oh, wow, the Wolverine was getting busy.

Peter had seen this a couple of times before. Logan, when he let himself go, when the noble, gentle guy who had all his rules and standards and occasionally olde-world speech habits was out the door and the beast was in... seeing that was not something you forgot.

Now he was going one-on-one with the Skrull Queen, who still looked and moved like Jessica Drew. He was absorbing blast after blast of her electrical powers, screaming even as he advanced, the flesh burning from his chest and revealing the adamantium skeleton below. His claws were out and his eyes flashed with berserker fury.

The Skrulls surrounding them circled, trying to find a moment to fire when they'd be certain of not harming their queen. Peter dove in, just as Danny Rand and Simon Williams arrived to join him, running interference, getting in the way, pulling weapons off them, kicking them hard, knocking them down. But not, he hoped, killing them.

Because there was a line he would not cross. He'd seen a lot of his friends cross that line today. But no, never. He'd rather die. Literally. He'd quietly decided that on the way in. But hey, not soon, right?!

He had a moment to turn and catch a glimpse of fight again. Logan closed on her, taking a hefty Skrull-powered right hook across the jaw. In return, he slashed sidelong with his claws, ripping into her shoulder. She stuck her fingers in his face, blasting him point blank, burning away his eyes. Logan, screaming, rammed his claws in, blow after blow. Her body started to bloom out of the way of the blows, her flesh grabbing his wrists and ripping at them. Neither of them had given an inch of the ground they had now. The Skrulls all around were alternatively cheering and screaming.

Peter realized that he wanted to yell something like "rip her apart!"

He hated that. He wouldn't do that. He closed his mouth again, turned and saw Danny Rand, about to be flattened by a big guy from behind.

The big guy got his arms and face full of webbing, and fell, out of the battle hopefully for a couple of hours. That was the gift Peter could give here, though he was being very careful about rationing the use of his web-shooters.

Danny fell behind the trunk of a tree, panting, and Peter went to join him for a sec. "You okay?"

"Yeah."

A hopeful thought had struck Peter, and he was pleased that it had come to him in the second he'd turned away from the slaughter. "Hey. Hey, I just thought, this can't be so bad, all things considered."

"You don't think this is bad?" Danny surely had an eyebrow raised under that ripped-up mask.

"I've been in a few of these. The big battles. There's a sign for when you really have to worry that this is end-of-the-world stuff, and it hasn't happened."

"A sign? What?"

"The Watcher! The big bald alien guy in charge of watching what happens when the really bad stuff goes down. Who can only watch the universe and never interfere. He's not here, so that must mean we're going to be okay, and—"

As the words left his mouth, Peter realized what he was seeing materialize, just a few feet ahead of him, in the middle of the battlefield. Because yeah, there he was, Uatu the Watcher, in his robes, intangible but visible, watching it all go down as the heroes and villains of Earth were fighting Skrulls all around him. The look on his face was anxious and deeply sad.

"Oh *come on*," said Peter Parker. "Really?"

THIRTY-NINE

JESSICA JONES

JESSICA JONES wasn't a super hero. Not anymore. Not since that time she didn't like to think about. She still lived around super heroes, still lived with a super hero, Luke Cage, when he was able to be with her. When Tony Stark ripped their community apart with his Superhuman Registration Act, she reacted as strongly as anyone else, walking out alongside her husband. The two of them chose to hide her and their baby, Danielle, in what seemed to be the safest possible place, Doctor Strange's Sanctum Sanctorum. Because, hey, the Doctor had just sighed at this little bit of local difficulty they were calling the Civil War, because he was always fighting evil tentacle gods in other dimensions, and told them nothing got into his house that he didn't want in there, unless it was, you know, enormous universe-destroying demon-sized evil tentacle gods who still had to get pretty lucky to be able to do that. And even then, one of those would only be interested in him, not his house guests, and there were all sorts of well-designed spaces to hide.

So, Luke had felt able to head off and form his rebel Avengers and begin his running battle against Stark and his often-kind-of-reluctant Lawful Good allies.

Which was when the Sanctum Sanctorum had been raided by Parker Robbins and his bunch of really pretty-down-to-Earth basic murderers and sadists, and Jessica had to punch a couple of them through walls before running out into the street clutching her baby. She decided the only thing she could do was to… she still hated thinking about this moment, but she was good at processing the stuff she hated to think about… she marched to Avengers Tower, hit the button to get automatic amnesty papers printed out, and had signed the Superhuman Registration Act before anyone had arrived to arrest her.

Stark himself appeared in the foyer a moment later, astonished. He asked, looking horribly hopeful, if this meant Luke had "decided to see sense."

Jessica called him a lot of choice names, explained the situation, and told Stark she would not say a damn word to him about where Luke was and what he'd decided to do, and that she didn't know much anyway, because that was the way she and Luke had planned it. If Stark would allow her that, she wouldn't do anything to help Luke and his team while she was… she was seeking sanctuary in Avengers Tower, okay? Because right now, the world out there had never been more dangerous for heroes and their families. He could make propaganda out of that if he wanted to. She wouldn't spy. He had her word.

Stark accepted that, looking frustrated but also very sad. "I hope when this is all over—"

"How is it ever going to be over?" she interrupted, marching to the elevators, carrying Danielle.

She kept her word. Stark hadn't actually mentioned her presence to the media. Which was… yeah, that had been genuinely kind of him. She knew monsters and he wasn't one. But that was all she'd allow him. He was still a dangerous idiot. If Luke found out, she'd always thought, she hoped he understood. No, she *knew* he would.

Just because she wasn't going to pass on what she found out, however, didn't mean she didn't have the curiosity that befitted her career as a detective. Every day she'd been here she had explored the rooms of Avengers Tower, wondering at the playground Stark had built for those who toed the line.

And then, still just hours ago really, she'd heard alarms and reports that Luke and his team were on the roof, and she'd cheered as she'd gone to a monitor and watched them steal a Quinjet. "That's your daddy," she said to Danielle. "Yes it is." Then everyone in the building headed out after Luke and his team.

And then, while there were no Avengers of any kind around, and, it seemed, nobody else at all in the Tower either, suddenly alien spaceships had dropped into the sky above the city!

Shortly after that all hell broke loose, and there had still been nobody here, and so, carrying Danielle, she had once more gone exploring the depths of the Tower, this time hoping to find maybe a safe with "do not open, amazingly big guns inside" or a panic room or something. Because in the back of her head now, and it had never really gone away since that bad time with Killgrave, but it was underlined now, was the thought that *they*, whoever they were, could burst in here any second, and then having lots of those big guns or better still somewhere they couldn't get to her baby might be a great idea.

That was when she found the cell.

It was a security chamber that, for some reason, wasn't listed on the security manifest. That's why she'd found it. A quick bit of checking had led to the discovery that it had been recently *erased* from those records. God, Jessica thought, had Stark actually disappeared someone and left them to rot? Whoever it was might have super-powers and an interest in saving the planet. Or if they had the opposite, well, she could swiftly slam the door shut again.

So, she had opened the cell, and in it she had found Jarvis, the Avengers' butler, who... oh no, who had been around as always until just... yesterday, maybe?

He looked up at her with his usual dignity, got to his feet, adjusted his vest, and apologized for his appearance. "I believe it was the Skrulls, madam. I was assaulted, at any rate, by someone who resembled me entirely, though I cannot take credit for his extraordinary lack of manners. Tell me, does your presence here now indicate they have begun some bigger assault?"

"You could say that, Edwin," Jessica had said. "And thanks for telling me who those spaceships belong to. Now let's get you to the medical bay, okay?"

He fussed that away, saying he was fine, and urgently asked about the health of the other Avengers, both official and otherwise, as he always did with her. There was little to tell him. He'd only been in the cell for a couple of days, so the Skrulls' penetration of the Tower had been something they'd only achieved recently. And she had actually met the Skrull Jarvis, who had seemed like the real thing in every respect. That sent a shiver through her. Luke and his team had been extremely concerned about the Skrull presence on Earth since before she'd fled the Sanctum Sanctorum, but she always said could they deal with Tony Stark being in their faces first. It seemed Luke had been right about that, damn it.

And now she and Jarvis stood in front of the big screens, baby Danielle in her arms, watching the media coverage of what was already being called the Battle of Central Park. There were drones in the air covering the whole conflict, zooming in from moment to moment on individual combat, the commentators chattering excitedly like this was wrestling rather than, you know, life or death for the planet Earth. She saw Luke going one-on-one with some huge Super-Skrull, letting it throw fire against his skin, taking blow after blow and giving as good as he got, shouting defiantly in its face all the while. And then they cut away, because Logan and the Skrull Queen—who looked like Jess (?!), the other Jessica, Jessica Drew, one of her closest friends… oh, no, come on, had that Jess been a Skrull? And now, oh dear god!—they were ripping each other to shreds, and that was obviously better TV, and hey, at least she wasn't going to see the father of her child killed onscreen, but now she couldn't see what was happening to him, and, and…

She made herself breathe slowly and deeply. She had nearly been lost in her memories then, nearly been back in that time with Killgrave. But this was different. Every time since had been different.

She felt powerless when she *was not powerless.*

She'd told herself she would never be made to feel powerless again. She had chosen not to be a super hero ever since Killgrave controlled her mind while she was in that damn costume. But now she needed to push all that down in her mind and pick a different path. And she could choose to do that. "Edwin," she said, "there's something I need to do."

"Do I take it, madam, that this concerns the battle?"

"Yes. You see, I need to go help. I... *have* to go help."

He nodded. "Indeed, madam."

"So..." She looked at Danielle, asleep in her arms. She smelled her head. "I... I need you to look after her."

"Of course, madam."

"You... you understand what I'm asking?" She realized she was crying. Already, damn it. "I might not come back. None of us might. If that happens, or if they come here—"

"Then I shall do my duty, madam." His expression reassuringly like something out of some old movie about fighting them on the beaches. "Whatever that requires. She will be safe with me."

She took a deep breath and kissed her baby on the forehead. "Baby, Mommy has to go do the right thing for once in her life. I'm going to go help your daddy, and you're going to stay with Uncle Edwin, okay?" Danielle just gurgled. Jessica quickly handed her to Jarvis and stepped away before she couldn't.

She found her old hero costume where she'd seen it, with a little moment of shock that she'd quickly contained, weeks ago, in the enormous storehouse of super hero outfits Stark kept here, which included some very optimistic guesses as to who might one day want a new costume from him. She threw off her clothes and put them in a locker and tried the costume on.

It fit only thanks to it being made of Reed's wonderful unstable molecules. Make that *two* reasons why Sue Storm stuck with him. Why the hell did all the people she and Luke knew do what they did in costume? She hated being in costume, ever since... ever since Killgrave the Purple Man had taken over her mind and made her take it off and had bent her to his will for months after. Yeah, she kept coming back to that.

But this was the *opposite* of that. This was her *choosing* to put it back on.

Just for today. Just to show the Skrulls, and show her own people, exactly who she stood with. She made herself look in the mirror and see the costume as her will, not her burden.

Running to the nearest window that opened, which was most of them, because of course it was, and, not even pausing to think that she hadn't done this for a decade, she... threw herself out of it.

She yelled as she actually fell for a couple stories, but then she got it again soaring upward, and just for a moment that was *amazing*. And then the memories came back again. So she held them in again.

Then she set course for Central Park. It was hard to miss, given all the smoke and power blasts sending shadows flickering between the towers of the city and lightning flashing everywhere.

OF COURSE, as she got close the chaos increased. She dodged a couple of Skrull fliers on the way in, forcing her to land in a tree awkwardly, feeling ridiculously exposed in her costume, embarrassed to be here, but now she had a good view of the battlefield. She could find Luke—oh god, she hoped he was still alive—dive in beside him and there wouldn't even be a moment of them having been split up by the law, not a moment of distrust, she would fight alongside him as a super hero. Just this once. And... and even though the enemy forces seemed overwhelming from up here, even though that they seemed to have pinned down the good guys somewhere on the other side of the park, they would find a way to win, damn it, and—

Suddenly, an enormous blast of energy hit the park in front of her, blinding her for a moment and sending her grabbing for the branches of the tree to stop herself from falling. There were cries from whatever media spectators had been in the streets on this side of the park, and from the huge volume of Skrulls in front of her... oh god, she blinked as she realized her eyesight was returning... those were alien screams.

There, in the middle of a smoking crater at the heart of the Skrull ranks, she could see what from this distance looked like a tiny figure, Skrulls running away from them in all directions, dozens of their bodies surrounding him in a circle of impact, forming a green splatter up the sides of the crater. He turned to address the fleeing hordes, and he shouted, his voice *enormous*. "My name is Noh-Varr!" he bellowed. "I am a warrior of the Kree! In the name of Captain Marvel, in the name of the Kree Empire, I am here to order the Skrull army on Earth to surrender!"

Well, great! Mind you, they paid him no attention, and he'd directed his call to surrender to like, the front row of grunts who were running to rally someone bigger, and she doubted they were going to pass the message on, but still!

Jessica flung herself into the air and used the confusion in the Skrull ranks to fly toward the other end of the park, dodging a couple more fliers on the way.

There was Luke!

Oh, thank god, there was Luke. He stood in tatters, his steel-hard skin still unbroken, calling for the Avengers and anyone else to gather to him, about to deal with another enormous rush from Skrulls down this side who hadn't yet realized they now had a second front to deal with way back there.

She landed right beside him.

He spun, staring at her in horror. "Jess, no, you didn't have to—where's—"

"She's safe. And yeah, I did."

"This is the last place I expected to see you again."

"I am an enigma wrapped in a riddle. Oh, and hey, I may not be picking up on some subtle clues here, but I think you might have been right about the Skrull thing."

"She admitted I was right. Best day of my life." He was so charming when he smiled like that.

"Hey, I need you to say it out loud. That it's all okay. That we were never really apart?"

"We were always together. Always." And he took a moment to gather her into his arms, and they had time for one kiss before the next wave of Skrulls was on them and they turned to meet it.

Together.

FORTY

CLINT BARTON

"HAVE AT thee!" Thor bellowed right in Clint's ear, loud enough to make his hearing aid squeal.

"Hit 'em high and low, Howlers!" shouted Fury.

"Thunderbolts," yelled Osborn, "you will be in the front line, or I will know why!"

Such noise, all around him. Shorting out both his earpieces. Which would be kind of welcome, apart from, you know, knowing what to pay attention to in the battle that raged all around him. Somewhere in the distance, Logan and the Skrull Queen were still hacking chunks out of each other. Clint and Kate had teamed up together, each on one side of Luke Cage, who, now with Jessica Jones beside him, yelled to all these would-be leaders of the Avengers left on the field to stay close on him. The two marksmen provided covering fire—Ronin and Hawkeye, drawing and letting loose throwing stars, staves and arrows at the Skrulls who broke through Osborn and Fury's big guys on the front lines, who'd just been joined by Thor, who was literally sending Skrull bodies flying in all directions. Spider-Man and Maya and that new Cap ran interference, saving him and Kate ammo.

This could not last. He kept having to look around wildly. He could only see green flesh converging from all directions. It felt like there were isolated pockets of heroes now, everywhere on the field, of which theirs was the biggest. Any second a power blast was going to get through and—

Kate screamed as what his experience had told him was going to happen actually did. She staggered back, her chest armor on fire, collapsing in front of him.

He located the Skrull who'd done it, weapon still in its hand, aimed and threw a throwing star in a single thought, a single moment, nailing the monster in the eye. A second later they were down under the new Cap's shield.

But there was Kate, lying on the ground, eyes closed, unmoving. He threw himself on her to snuff out the flames, and was about to start CPR because she didn't seem to be breathing, damn it, his girl didn't seem alive, come on Kate, come on—

Powerful hands hauled him to his feet. There stood the Vision, his broken face hanging off in pieces, one eye missing. "I will transport her to safety," he said.

Clint barely had time to nod.

He grabbed her and flew straight up like a rocket and Clint could only stare after them for a second.

But there were sounds all around. Horrifying sounds.

Kate might be dead. Bobbi had been dead, then alive again, bringing his grief back to life, then she'd died again. There was no comfort for him now.

He saw Kate's bow and quiver lying on the ground. Her own bow, not the Skrull one, which she must have discarded as soon as he'd given it to her. He grabbed it, and doing this felt just as weird and bad as it had in the Savage Land, but now... now...

He looked up and took down a Skrull warrior right in front of him with an arrow through the eye. He turned and loosed at every Skrull who was aiming up at the departing Vision, *one two three*! They all fell, spinning, arrows in their ears, throats and eyes.

218   He ran through the ranks of them, breaking past Thor, Spidey

and Cap—even Osborn and Fury's grunts—in clear space now, just running and shooting, letting his experience carry him, running through all the little vortices of fighting on the battlefield. The others probably shouted after him. He didn't hear.

He realized what he was heading for as he ran, what the fury in his heart was rushing him toward.

There, ahead, was the Skrull Queen, a mass of continually transforming flesh, wounds folding themselves up and refilling as blow after blow landed on her; her own attacks ripping Logan apart, his flesh regrowing on metal, the two of them locked in combat, a bundle of meaningless fury.

No. You do not take my girl and live to keep fighting. He caught a flash of something white moving inside the Queen's head. A skull? A brain? "You're going to hear her name!" he shouted. "This is for Hawkeye!"

She swiveled an eye in his direction.

He loosed.

The arrow went straight through her head, brains flying out the other side. Caught at just the right angle, she spun from Logan's grasp.

She hit the ground.

Was she dead?!

The Skrull ranks all cried out at once.

Logan swayed on his feet, staring as his face re-formed around his eyes. He looked almost sad that he hadn't delivered the final blow.

Clint stood there too, swaying on his feet, aware it was just him and Logan, their own ranks far behind them and furious Skrulls surrounding them.

He slowly turned to face them. So, he would go down fighting. He had done what he came to do in her name. If he could just get over there to check the body, he had to make sure...

From behind them, but getting increasingly closer, Skrulls were shouting, power blasts echoing. "He is coming!" they screamed. "The Kree is here!"

The Skrulls didn't know where to look. Some stared in disbelief at their Queen on the ground, waiting and waiting for her to rise, but others glared at the human forces with renewed anger and strength born of revenge. A scant few were looking behind them, to where whatever this was, blasting through their ranks, bodies flying into the air.

Logan started to run toward Clint, perhaps hoping to protect him, as the Wolverine's body pulled itself together out of thin air.

But Clint had seen something, some serious-looking guards rushing to protect a Skrull combat engineer, or whatever it was who had pulled some kind of device from a backpack and was assembling it, a few ranks back. "Logan, go after whatever that is!" shouted Clint, and aimed and loosed in the same second, but one of the guards threw themselves in the way and took the shot. It staggered back, but others started to leap into the space, all of them obviously aware of the power of whatever this was going to be.

Logan turned and began hacking into them, but they were shouting "He loves you!" now and throwing themselves between their technician and anyone who might have an angle to fire on him. Clint took them down shot after shot, and Logan threw them aside as he hacked, but they also had to deal with furious Skrulls leaping at them, trying to claw at them or pull them back, and within seconds a hum of power rose, and suddenly there was a gurgling noise of some sort of signal being sent. Whatever that thing was, that Skrull had activated it.

Logan and Clint turned together at the sound of a gigantic scream.

"Oh god," said Clint, "is that Jan?!"

FORTY-ONE

JANET VAN DYNE

JANET HAD continued her hit and run raids, getting more and more frustrated. So many different voices issuing commands, when they should have agreed on some sort of command structure as the first damn thing when they'd met at the edge of the park, before the Skrull Queen had dragged them into combat. They could have even done it in the Quinjet, and now they were being split up into separate clusters: some heroes fighting alone, exactly what the Skrulls wanted. She'd glimpsed what looked like a Kree soldier using very sophisticated weaponry, and the Skrulls didn't seem to have planned for him. He was causing havoc, but one Kree couldn't turn the tide. She needed to find some way to pull all their guys back together again on the field and, and—

She was suddenly seized by a deeply weird feeling that made her rush back to the center of Luke's small group, safely through the blaze of Reed's detector, and halt for a second, fluttering in mid-air. She felt like she had when her body first shrank, she realized, when she'd first felt her wings sprout from her back. There was something happening deep within her body, something beyond the everyday. Back then it had been wonderful, a fairy-tale transformation, but now, now it felt... wrong... dark...

And then she realized. She was starting to grow, but she hadn't willed it. Lately she'd been avoiding using that ability too often because she hadn't trained with it. And now it was happening.

She rushed upward, everyone on the ground growing smaller, her wings vanishing into her back, becoming another enormous target beside Cassie Lang, who looked over to her in shock. "Jan?!" Jessica Jones called to her from beside Luke Cage. "Jan, is something wrong?!"

Then the pain hit her. Enormous pain. System-wracking, complete blackout pain. But she could not afford that now. She had to stay on her feet, because her falling, her even moving too fast, could kill those she loved. "Cassie!" she tried to shout, but it came out as an enormous scream. Her vision fluttered with blood, but she could see Cassie stepping as best she could toward her.

She'd be here in a second. She had to stay upright until Cassie could help. But the pain, the pain!

And then she remembered.

"It's an anniversary present," he'd said.

Henry had said. Oh god.

○────────○

THIS HAD been just a few weeks ago. He'd called her over to Camp Hammond and met with her in his office, placing a small case on the desk.

"Anniversary of what?" she said, kind of guardedly, because this was just the sort of nonsense a Henry feeling more confident in himself might try, him ever so gently starting to suggest maybe they should try again when no, absolutely not—

He changed tack immediately. "Sorry. It's just a present." That hadn't been Henry. That had been the Skrull who'd worn his face, who realized in that second he'd chosen the wrong note to make this work. "Okay, let me frame that differently: it's something I've been working on."

222   "Oh no," she whispered now, "oh no!"

Opening the case, he revealed a hypodermic needle and an ampoule containing a green fluid. "It's a new growth formula," he said, "with it, if you want to be the Wasp, you can shrink down, but if the situation calls for a Giant-Woman, or whatever you want to call yourself, you'll be able to switch from one to the other *immediately*, without having to rest and prepare in between. It's fully tested. I mean, I could just about get this into pharmacies. I've used it for a whole series of trials with no problems. I figured this… it's me giving you even more freedom. Or that might be the wrong thing to say too. Anyway, whatever, it's useful, it's yours now." And he slid the case across the desk to her.

That evening, she flew herself off to some empty farmland to test it. She injected herself with the serum. She shrunk, then grew, back and forth, and laughed at what indeed felt like a new dimension of freedom, resolving to send Henry a thank you note that would somehow… well, maybe it could one day be a friendship, eventually, she had thought that evening. Really using this new power set would be something for the future, she thought that evening, because, of course, it would require new training.

She'd been such an idiot.

Henry knew she'd been tired of being small. That to be big at any given moment… it had been his dream, but it had also been hers, and the Skrull with his mind had trapped her with it.

She was swaying on her feet, lost in the pain, hiding in her memories.

And even as Cassie rushed toward her, she was growing again, bigger and bigger, faster and faster, and she could see that her hands, her arm, her whole skin was starting to blaze with some sort of all-consuming alien energy. Something was bursting from her every pore, some sort of chemical that was rushing out of her, and oh god, the agony!

Janet threw back her head screaming, and that scream was so big it resounded in every corner of the park.

FORTY-TWO

BALKAMAR

BALKAMAR STOOD in front of the monitor screens in Avengers Tower, where Jessica Jones had left him, awkwardly holding her human baby.

Well, this was quite the pickle.

His escape from the Helicarrier had been a close-run thing. He had grabbed a colleague who he knew to be able to teleport, relying on her to have her wits together enough to get them out of there, and, sure enough, she had. It took a few hops to get them back to New York, but as soon as they arrived in the city, she declared her duty lay in battle and disappeared once again, heading for Central Park. His own duty, following orders given in event of this contingency, lay elsewhere, and so he returned to Avengers Tower, placing himself in confinement, a situation that would be discovered by any of the Earth warriors who possessed sufficient technical or investigative skills. They would now know, after all, that there was a Skrull duplicate of Jarvis. It was up to him to convince them it was not he. Then he could spy upon the plans of any who reconvened here and offer a spot of misdirection here and there.

He had not expected Jessica Jones to be the one that found

him, and, he had to confess to himself now, the situation in Central Park had obviously progressed to a point where his duty here was somewhat meaningless. He wished desperately that he could go over there to lend a hand, and be able to say, in his declining years, that he had been present at the Battle of Central Park. And yet "they also served," old man, "they also served" and all that! The humans might still retreat here, and orders were orders. The baby did complicate things somewhat. Balkamar had no quarrel with the infants of Earth. Indeed, both his religious belief in prophecy, that the humans were to be a joyful underclass when this world was a Skrull one, and the memories he had taken from the original Jarvis, made him rather fond of them. To some extent, Ms. Jones had therefore been correct in the leap of faith that she had made entrusting the care of Danielle to him.

To some extent.

"I say," he said to the baby, patting its back, "do quieten a little, my dear, I am trying to think." Nicely, the baby did. "From what I see of the battle in Central Park, the words of the Prophets are coming true, albeit they are taking their jolly old time about it, and rather going the pretty way. What is happening with the Wasp there, Janet Van Dyne…"

He tapped one of the screens.

"She's releasing a nerve toxin especially created to target the power sets of super-powered humans—and certain other species, too. She's become rather a living factory of it, I'm afraid. And she is getting larger and more capable of production every moment, which is in some ways a great pity. I had become rather fond of her myself. The human warriors may all have been ignoring her of late, but they do all love her and look to her as a leader, and they will be absolutely unwilling to disintegrate her, which is what it would take to end this problem for them. So, I believe we may shortly see the end of the Central Park, and with it the end of the greater part of human resistance, though if Queen Veranke has given her life for the cause… well, it is how she'd have wanted to go. No, all in all, I do not now feel I am obliged to rush over there and join in the fray, as much as I would enjoy doing so. Let us see what is happening elsewhere. Perhaps I may be moved to lend a hand in other parts. In which case, young lady, you will be off around the world." He tapped a button and the screens began to cycle through news feeds from the rest of the Earth. "From the media in the United States, of course, you'd hardly know we'd invaded the rest of the planet too." He tutted. "That's the Yanks for you. Ah, here we are…"

He had found a broadcast from their forces stationed in Wakanda. It was Commander K'vvvr, who Balkamar knew well enough to pass the time of day with, making an announcement. He looked tired as always, but he was making a good show of displaying to the Wakandans that the Skrulls were in charge of the country now, standing on the bridge of his flagship, his hands grasped behind his back. "Citizens of Wakanda," he was saying, "your king, T'Challa, and queen, Ororo, have surrendered to us, and as we speak are being interrogated. Further resistance on your part will only make their suffering, and yours, worse. We respect the traditions of Wakanda. You have put up a noble fight. You cut us off from our technology and we disarmed yours in return. So, this battle was with the most traditional of weapons, something that perhaps you did not expect us to embrace as fully as you yourselves did. But we did in doing so, I hope we displayed to you our own nobility and martial prowess. We acknowledge that our invasion here has succeeded only at great cost. But make no mistake, succeed it has." He paused, as if distracted by something, and glanced over his shoulder, a puzzled look on his face.

Suddenly, with a blaze of static, the broadcast was interrupted, and the unmasked face of King T'Challa, their so-called Black Panther, appeared onscreen. Queen Ororo, the mutant weather-controller codenamed Storm, stood beside him, proud, determined looks upon their faces. Ororo nodded to the camera and moved aside as if needing to deal with something.

Balkamar cleared his throat nervously. What was going on here? Though the background was still that of the interior of a Skrull ship, T'Challa certainly did not look like someone undergoing interrogation.

226

"People of Wakanda," said the King, "it was not I who surrendered to the Skrulls. It was not my Queen. It was two Skrulls our people had captured, their forms fixed in our likeness, their voiceboxes controlled to say a few basic phrases of defiance. It is they who have been 'interrogated'—or rather, tortured—by the Skrull invaders. This stratagem has allowed the Queen and I the time to make a move or two of our own." He swung the camera to show a furious Commander K'vvvr, Ororo now beside him with a blade at his throat. They were alone on the bridge. Or rather they were now: Balkamar spotted a couple of Skrull officers slumped over controls. Nearby came a distant thumping. It seemed the bridge had been secured and those outside were trying desperately to get in. T'Challa stepped over to the Commander.

"The Panther God sees all, K'vvvr. You talk as if you are noble. And yet you have ordered butchery. I could give many examples of the innocents, the unarmed, who have died at the hands of your troops and by your own hand. You are in my land and subject to my laws—"

"God's will shall prevail! This world will belong to—"

"The sentence is death." And T'Challa sent his own sword quickly and neatly through K'vvvr's throat.

Balkamar placed a hand over Danielle's eyes as soon as he realized the way this was going. "Oh dear," he muttered to himself. "Oh, dear me."

"Wakandans!" bellowed T'Challa to the camera. "This is your signal! Rise up! Wakanda forever! Leave no Skrull alive!"

Balkamar quickly changed the channel. "Let us see," he said, "if we can find something a little more heartening, eh? Perhaps the BBC?"

He was indeed now looking at a BBC news channel broadcasting from London, the view from a helicopter flying over the moonlit Thames, just down from the Houses of Parliament by Balkamar's reckoning. The camera was looking down on Westminster Bridge, where some sort of battle was going on.

"It looks like one of their big guns, one of what we've been told are called Super-Skrulls, a magically empowered one," said the reporter, speaking loudly over the noise of the rotor blades. "It's got aspects of… I'm seeing something of the American magical hero Doctor Stephen Strange about that costume, and the creature is wearing some sort of chain. You can see he's got a flaming, horned head, making one assume there's some sort of demonic inspiration or dimension there. But what is incredible is who it's facing, who's been standing up to repeated assaults from this thing and just keeps fighting back, he's just not giving way. The costume may be different, and we've been hearing reports about how that came about, but I think we can feel confident that that is Captain Britain, and he's… oh!"

The figure on the bridge dressed in the colors of the flag staggered backward as the Super-Skrull brought down a flaming sword, but he'd countered with something. In his hand, Balkamar saw, he also carried a sword. "He's holding on there. He's carrying, from the markings, I think that is the legendary sword Excalibur. Now, if that is the case, the implications… well, I think we all knew this invasion was a matter of the utmost urgency, but this— Okay, I'm told we're going to be taking you now to where Natasha Khan is actually down there on the bridge."

The image switched to a reporter in a flak jacket, stepping carefully backward over rubble. She had one eye on the battle going on just past her, clearly terrified and yet getting on with her job. "I'm here with, I'd say a medical team, but it's just one medic, who's stayed to help another hero who may be familiar to you. I should warn you that this may be distressing." The camera turned to find on the ground, a figure with his ribcage exposed, but not as if he'd been wounded. It was more like it was being held open, his flesh floating in mid-air.

"Goodness," exclaimed Balkamar. "That isn't a power set we've seen before. Where did this come from?! Yes, do keep your eyes away, my dear, this is all still rather gruesome."

"Bit busy here," the young medic in question, who was wearing a hijab, was saying to the reporter while not looking at the camera but instead trying to concentrate, her hands in the air over the man on the ground, her fingers radiating power.

"What's your name and what exactly is it you're doing?"

"I'm Dr. Faiza Hussain. I just got super-powers tonight from some sort of exploding Skrull machine thing. This is Dane Whitman, the Black Knight, the former Avenger, who I'm trying to heal while not really knowing what I'm doing. I keep trying to knit him back together again, and, I guess, magic, which the Skrulls seem to be controlling now, keeps on wanting to pull him apart."

"You say the Skrulls are controlling magic?"

"I have no idea, but I keep working and something keeps trying to stop me."

"You know there's nobody else out here? You should really get to safety."

"*You* should get to safety, Natasha. I loved you on *The One Show*, but I've got a patient here."

"She's doing great," croaked Whitman.

"You know what would help?" Hussain looked up and called toward Captain Britain, who, the camera view swung to show, was once again parrying an enormous blow from that flaming sword. "Captain, break the magic! Or at least whatever's nearby that's using it to keep injuries open! I think it's probably that guy you're fighting!"

"Quite possibly!" shouted the Captain. "But at the moment it's all I can do to hold him back! Have you heard anything from Pete?!"

"Pete?" asked the reporter. "Now, who is Pete?"

"I don't know if I'm supposed to say, he's some sort of... secret agent. Or something. And he's off sorting—"

The Super-Skrull gave another roar, using the Captain's momentary distraction to nearly cut off his head, but the warrior ducked under the sword at the last second, grabbing his opponent by the throat. "I am not going to let you get any further!" he shouted.

"Your world is watching!" shouted the proud Skrull champion

in return. "Even a new Captain Britain, even with the last of British magic, even with Excalibur, against our holy destiny, you can only die!" With that, he grabbed the Captain's arms from around his throat, twisted the human aside and slammed him to the ground. The Captain yelled satisfyingly. The heroic Skrull raised his arm, doubtless aware that the human media were recording his actions, magical power building in his hand. "The last of Britain," he said, "one tired man wearing a flag."

His foe glared up at him. "You have no idea what this flag means," he whispered. "It isn't popular. It's not a gesture. It's about opposites just about managing to hold on together for the greater good—and it is worth so much more than anything you bring to the party."

"Captain!" shouted the young human medic. "You need to do something now!"

"No more speeches," said the warrior, and leapt up. To Balkamar's horror, the speed of his attack caught the Super-Skrull off-guard.

Excalibur caught the chain around the Super-Skrull's neck and with a shout Captain Britain heaved and shattered it.

Magical power suddenly, visibly, flashed out, roaring back into the world in a shockwave away from the bridge.

The Super-Skrull staggered back.

"Yes!" shouted the medic, and with one movement pulled her patient's chest together.

He stared up at her in amazement. "You saved me," he whispered.

"Mate," said Faiza Hussain, "you're with the NHS now."

"I'm getting told—" The reporter was clutching her earpiece. "Okay, we'll be taking you immediately to Northumberland National Park, to where our defense correspondent Mike Tooley and his camera crew have just been... magically teleported? Okay, over to Mike now."

A rather startled-looking reporter stumbled a little in a circle of light beside some prehistoric stones on a night-time hillside. "We were just brought here, Natasha, and I'm about to hand you over to a representative of the security services who won't give me his name."

"Mike," the voice of the previous human broke in, "I'm being told that's Pete Wisdom."

An annoyed-looking human in the remains of what Balkamar appreciatively noted was a finely tailored suit, his face covered in abrasions, adjusted his tie and pointed at the camera.

"All right, thanks to Captain Britain having brought the magic back, I have just done a literal deal with the… hopefully *a*… devil. I have had a very long night, and I have lost colleagues in battle trying to get magic back to Britain from Avalon, and I never got my supper. So—I want everyone to hear this, particularly the bloody Skrulls. I have been given the power of one wish, the results of which are just to cover the British Isles, and it is this—" Balkamar's mouth dropped open in horror. This was just the sort of hinge moment his commanders had always feared. "—no more Skrulls."

The sounds of cheering started to come distantly over the link. "Mike, we're cutting back here, you have to see this!"

The view cut back to the helicopter, and Balkamar found himself weeping as he saw the Super-Skrull staggering, energy pouring from him as he started to… disintegrate. And on the banks of the river, green explosions of flesh were peppering the city. "We're hearing that every one of the invaders is dead or dying!" shouted the human in the helicopter. "We've won, we've won, they came here and they did not pass, and, look, look!"

On the bridge, Captain Britain stepped forward, Excalibur in his hands, swinging a final blow. The head of that great Skrull hero went flying as his body combusted. With a final shout the human warrior took the sword in both hands and slammed it down into the body of the bridge itself.

Then, staggering, awkward somehow, he turned and hobbled away toward where the doctor and the knight were already getting up. "Oh no," said Balkamar, "oh no, we've lost a bridgehead in a whole county, Danielle, we can't have that, come on, there must be something…" Once again, he searched the channels.

He found a local affiliate in San Francisco, an anxious reporter at street level talking to camera, a large official building behind her. "The alien forces who have taken over the city have declared victory over all law enforcement and military agencies. The only exceptions to that are the mutant X-Men, who, for the last day or so, have been leading a guerrilla campaign in this city that's become the mutants' adopted home. But that may be over as I speak. The alien commander, H'Kurrek of the Skrull Imperium, has gathered what we've been told are over fifty thousand hostages in a large number of buildings in the heart of the city. His official announcement states that the spaceships hovering over the city are targeting those buildings. He has demanded the surrender of the X-Men within the next ten minutes, or he'll start firing on those buildings. The announcement included a number of provisions as to how carefully the Skrulls… I'm going to have to start to get used to calling them that… how carefully they've protected these buildings and their ships against the mutant powers of the X-Men. Now, the human population here… we're waiting to see if the mutants will give themselves up. Do we even want them to? We've seen them put their lives on the line to save, I'm sorry, I'm not sure what the correct term is, ordinary humans from the Skrulls. But now is surely the biggest test of that. I know I'm editorializing here. But if not now, when? Behind me is the Civic Center Courthouse, where we're pretty sure we've seen some of the hostages being taken. We're broadcasting here, I should say, at the sufferance of the Skrulls, who are basically using us to get their announcements across, so bear that in mind, okay, people?"

"And they're using telepathy," said a blue-skinned individual with a forked tail and a German accent, who'd just poked his head into the picture at the reporter's shoulder. "They sent us their message direct. Hello, viewers!" He waved a three-fingered hand in a big white glove.

The reporter, a little startled, turned on her heel. "Mr.… Nightcrawler?"

"Kurt." The mutant affected a bow. Balkamar knew from both

the exhaustive briefings he'd been privy to and from Jarvis's own formidable memory that Kurt Wagner was one of the more media-knowledgeable mutants, someone who'd spent their entire lives defusing the fact that they looked like a demon by coming over to the mainstream human populace as a fuzzy blue cartoon character who always enjoyed spending the time of day with those who might otherwise want to burn him at the stake. His power was teleportation, supplemented with formidable martial arts and quite some skill with edged weapons. All in all, Wagner was good at deflection, and thus his relatively happy tone, and the fact that the mutant leadership was nowhere to be seen, worried Balkamar not a little.

"Are you here to surrender?"

"Well, I'm here, aren't I? And here come my friends. We're not going to let them murder fifty thousand humans, any humans, not if we can help it, so…" And sure enough, the camera turned to show many mutants arriving and quickly assembling in front of the courthouse. From the main entrance of the building emerged Skrull forces, carrying shackles. Balkamar let out a long breath of relief. This was more like it. Perhaps he was just putting on a brave face.

"Are your leaders here with you?" asked the reporter. "Is Cyclops going to offer a formal surrender?"

"Well, here he is now." And there was Cyclops, Scott Summers, the mutant with optic blasts and tremendous tactical acumen, looking grim, so perhaps this was real, perhaps that clever Skrull commander had made certain this scenario wouldn't play out like the reversals in Wakanda and Britain.

"Angelique," nodded Cyclops to the reporter, clearly also having completed his media training, "thank you for your work in difficult circumstances."

"He is ever the charmer," noted Nightcrawler.

A Super-Skrull marched into frame and put a hand on Cyclops' shoulder. "That my eyes should see this moment! I thought you would all die in battle, like persons of faith!"

"That is rather the opposite of what persons in faith would

do, mein Freund," began Nightcrawler. "God tested Job's faith by making him suffer the loss of—"

Ah yes, this was also what Kurt Wagner was about. Fascinatingly, he had adopted one of the humans' many religious creeds and had proceeded to find many parallels between that path and the needs of mutants.

The Super-Skrull swatted him high into the air. Balkamar laughed to see it.

The camera swung to see the mutant hit the side of a building and crash to Earth, unconscious. "If suffering is a test of faith," cried the Super-Skrull, understandably frustrated that a captive should show such disrespect, "then you will thank me later!"

"X-Men, stand down!" shouted Cyclops, as all around him his people stepped forward, anger on the faces of those that had them. What awful, changeable people these mutants were. There might not be room for them, Balkamar felt, in the final settlement between Skrulls and their human charges. "No retaliation!"

The Super-Skrull laughed, turning to the warriors who'd arrived bearing the shackles. "Confine the teleporters and telepaths first. The restraints will neutralize their powers."

"Commander present!" called one of the warriors, and they all very properly stood to attention as H'Kurrek arrived.

"I greet you, X-Man," said H'Kurrek, raising his hand to Cyclops. "All across the city, my warriors have reported mutants arriving with their hands in the air. Many of them have already been taken back to our ships for processing. I congratulate you on the guerrilla war you waged. You held an overwhelmingly superior force off for far longer than should have been possible. You and I meet as brothers and equals." Oh, that was just excellent. Fair play to H'Kurrek for being so sporting.

"We do?" said Cyclops, looking at some data on a tablet of his own, then looking back to the commander in a most churlish manner. "Well, I *do* have a brother who's a murderous psychopath. And yet somehow," he cracked an insolent smile, "I still feel insulted."

Yet still H'Kurrek held up a hand to prevent his warriors from killing the mutant there and then. "You… disappoint me. I thought we could rise above our differences."

"Not when our differences include mass murder."

H'Kurrek looked suddenly very aware of the watching camera. He stood a little straighter. "I did my duty as a soldier."

"That's what you were when you started out. I think we both know what you are now."

H'Kurrek sighed. "I did you the honor of coming here to accept your surrender in person. I regret that courtesy now."

"I never said that we surrendered."

H'Kurrek looked around at the many mutants standing passively as the Skrulls were shackling them. "What? What are you—"

"Commander," shouted a nearby Skrull, "urgent message from the *Jora'Thrll*, coming in to pick up prisoners! They're in trouble, they—"

Everyone ducked as a Skrull shuttle hit the side of a nearby building. An enormous explosion rocked the structure and, captured in detail by the camera, the remains of the ship, bodies falling from it, fell to the ground.

"What happened?!" shouted H'Kurrek, he and the warriors and Super-Skrulls around him looking around for any sign that the X-Men were about to attack them. But no such sign came. Instead, a couple of Nightcrawler's friends were helping that mutant back toward the site of… well, Balkamar had thought it was the site of surrender, but he had no idea what was going on now.

"The pilot lost consciousness," said the Skrull with the communications earpiece, "and… Commander, I am feeling… unwell. Request permission to, to…" And she slowly sat down, staring in confusion and fear.

H'Kurrek looked around as, in every direction, Skrulls started to collapse. The Super-Skrulls were lasting the longest, but even they had started to succumb, dropping to the ground and falling unconscious. The commander himself put a hand to his brow and realized he was sweating. "What have you done?"

Balkamar's disgust and fury knew no bounds. That the mutants would use biological warfare against them!

Suddenly, Namor of Atlantis dropped into the frame, carried by those impossibly tiny wings on his ankles, or rather by the field they created. Not many humans knew or cared that the amphibian was one of the earliest mutants to appear on Earth, but that was indeed his nature. He bore significant characteristics not shared by any of the Atlantean race who, when they had a community, regarded him as its king. From time to time he had therefore opted to side with those who shared his heritage, as he was doing now. Presumably he had wished to continue being a big fish in a small pond, serving them, rather than join in the fight in New York. Or perhaps he was still uncertain, having been one of the targets of their forces' initial intelligence operation on Earth, who he could trust. It was possible that the equally surprising individual he was carrying now, Professor Charles Xavier, had powers of the mind enough to convince him that he knew who was a Skrull and who was not, but only when it came to their own people. All the briefings had said that Xavier was estranged from the X-Men now. The sight of these two great enemies of the Skrulls, suddenly on the battlefield in an unexpected position, with Skrulls reeling all around them now... it was almost too hard to watch.

"Scott," said Xavier, nodding to his former pupil.

Cyclops nodded grimly in return.

Xavier then looked to the Skrull commander. "We are united again to face your invasion. And the three of us together are ready to accept your surrender."

"What have you done?!" gasped the commander. Balkamar felt such anger and pity for how he looked in this moment. This was weakness and dishonor!

"We brought an infection with us. Sprayed on our skin and our clothes. It's airborne and highly contagious."

"Oh no," whispered Balkamar. "This is... this is..."

A blue-furred mutant, the Beast, who as well as being more

powerful and faster than humans also displayed extraordinary intellect in the field of biochemistry, stepped forward now, his expression stormy.

"Mutants, myself in particular, have had a great deal of experience lately in dealing with targeted viral attacks, designed to wipe out our species. And, of course, *all* humans share a common ancestor with you Skrulls. My instruments…" he looked to his watch, "tell me the contagion I have created is now present at every level of every one of those ships up there." He nodded to the warships floating above the city. "Everyone in your fleet will be showing symptoms within the next hour or so. A day after that they will all be dead."

Balkamar stared at this monster who would so casually admit his guilt in a war crime.

H'Kurrek grabbed Cyclops. "You upbraid me for murder and then use plague as a weapon?!"

"No," said the Beast. Oh, his codename was apt. "This is the condition I insisted upon before I set about this course of action. Not one of you has to die."

"Because," said Namor, swatting away the commander's hand, "though this would not be my choice, my adopted people have developed an antidote, and they are willing to share it with you. This, you do not deserve."

"We shall give you the antidote," said Xavier, more calmly, "once you have surrendered and are in custody, ready for eventual trial by the established authorities of San Francisco. We can make that happen within a day. All of you can live."

Balkamar knew in his heart that, whether he knew it or not, Xavier had just sentenced them all to death. If he had not, then these were not proper Skrulls on the holy mission they all shared.

H'Kurrek looked between the mutants, then strode to a nearby Skrull specialist, who was just about managing to stay on his feet. "Read their minds. Do they speak the truth?"

The telepath looked to the mutants then back to his superior. "It's all true, Commander."

H'Kurrek paused only for a moment. Balkamar tensed, worried

beyond all reason he was about to see a Skrull commander surrender in front of the watching human masses. But then H'Kurrek went to a Skrull comms officer who was still standing and put a hand on his shoulder. "Give me an open channel to the flagship. We will show these fools what we are."

The mutants exchanged worried looks. "Commander," said Cyclops, "for god's sake, end this."

"For god's sake?" replied H'Kurrek, proudly. "You'll see what I'm prepared to do for God's sake." He got a nod from the staggering Skrull and took from him the comms device. "All units, this is your commander. All of you that are mobile are to return to base ships immediately." There came a glimmer all around him as teleports activated. "The sacred struggle continues. But this battle is over. And we, all of us, are casualties. I have been proud to serve with you. To command you. This will be my last order, and it chokes me, yet it must be spoken, heard and obeyed. Turn all helms over to my control. And take comfort in His great love, as I do." He paused to check that all who were able to board had done so. The very Skrull from whom he'd taken the comms device had now gone. With an angry glance at the mutants, he hit his own teleport buckle and vanished.

Balkamar closed his eyes in relief. This commander was upholding the best traditions of his people. He wasn't letting the side down in any way. That was a small mercy, in the circumstances, but he found he could take comfort in it. The humans were, it seemed, forcing these relatively small reversals on them all over the world, and yet, here in New York, the humans' main force was losing. With that being the case, surely all would be well in the end. They must prevail. God had told them they would.

"Cyclops," began the reporter, "have they surrendered? What—"

"Wait," said Xavier.

The enormous sound of the Skrull fleet anthem blared from the ships high above the city, and with it came the voice of Commander H'Kurrek. "Command code is given. Self-immolation countdown is activated."

"No." The Beast looked at Cyclops' and Namor's cold expressions with horror. Xavier put a hand on his arm. "No."

Nightcrawler ran a hand back through his own hair. "This… this was not what we planned."

"Wasn't it?" said the Beast. "Cyclops, did you know?!"

Cyclops remained silent.

"I promise you, *I* did not," said Xavier. "Though perhaps I should have guessed."

"We should take it to New York," said Namor. "We should release it around the world."

"I do not have the supply to do that," said the Beast. "And I would not do it. Because, across the globe, it would not be possible to make an offer of surrender."

"And," yelled Wagner, furious with Namor, "we've now seen what it makes them do!"

Namor just raised an eyebrow, as if that would be fine with him. "I would be willing to let a handful of them live," he said, "if they told us where they're holding Black Bolt."

Balkamar had never hated the former King of Atlantis before this. He had seemed one of the more noble of their foes, even. But now he had seen him for what he truly was.

"Countdown complete," said the voice of Commander H'Kurrek. And with the enormous noise of spacetime being rended, a flash filled the skies above San Francisco, and the Skrull fleet vanished into the nothingness of the Destruct Dimension, the threat of the virus sealed off before it could spread further in the Skrull forces.

Balkamar found tears were streaming down his face, most unseemly. The… the humans would count that as a victory, but he had just seen the height of Skrull nobility in war, and the part of him that was Jarvis felt stirred at a heroic defeat. In some ways, the very English heart of this butler felt that such a noble loss was the best sort of victory. Balkamar shivered at the need for him to resist such a ridiculous notion.

Oh, the losses he had witnessed! This was just not cricket!

He had to find something, some broadcast, that would support his own soul in this moment of crisis, that he might show the same level of faith in God that the great Commander H'Kurrek had. He again flipped through the channels. Many of them were now reporting on these setbacks that the humans were claiming as great victories, their little voices gloating. "You really are a whiny lot," he said to Danielle, who just gurgled in reply. Finally, finally, he found one that had what his superior Skrull brain immediately understood to be Hindu scrolling underneath an image of a human child apparently floating helplessly through space, wreckage all around him.

Ah, this was more like it.

"This is Amadeus Cho," the boy said, evidently talking into the screen of his phone, the camera of which was providing this live feed. He spoke without the benefit of breathing apparatus, so obviously this void he spun in wasn't space in the conventional sense. And, oh yes, what was behind him suggested more an artistic conception of space than the real vacuum between worlds. "I think I've managed to hack the signal of this thing back to my own universe, to anyone with the right antenna on Earth. I just wanted to feel like I was talking to someone. If anyone's seeing this, get a message to any distant family I have left, to whoever knows me, because... I think I'm gonna die."

Balkamar let out a sigh of relief. This was much more the sort of thing that indicated the Prophets had been correct in interpreting the word of their God. Everything was on course to work out as it should.

"I did it, you see," Cho continued, "I did the hardest thing for me to do. So, okay, I'm kind of Hercules' assistant, mentor, sage, whatever you want to call it, and we've been on this quest. What you see as a sailing ship is actually a vessel for navigating the conceptual space where the gods live—" Balkamar felt a sudden wariness. Oh dear. Where the *what* lived? "I mean, Herc's used to this stuff, it's how he goes home from Earth to Olympus when he's had it with partying and helping the Avengers, and as soon as the

240

Skrulls invaded, he got this bunch of fellow human deities, you know, gods that humans, err, worship? He got them together, said he knew how to put an end to this invasion, and we all got on this ship and went off across... this place..."

Balkamar found his stomach in knots now. And not in the literal sense. This... this didn't sound good.

"Anyway... our 'God Squad' as I started to call it, because an awesome team needs an awesome name, right? We met Athena, the Greek goddess of wisdom and hunting, and she made this prophecy. Which in here is like writing code or something." Balkamar could hardly process the enormity of the blasphemy that he was hearing. "She said that when Herc was at his weakest I would save him by doing the hardest thing for me to do. A few seconds ago, Herc was fighting this Skrull deity, well, the leader of the Skrull gods, Kly'bn—"

"What?!" said Balkamar. "What?!" He put a hand to his mouth in awe, then quickly made the Signs of Appeasement with his free fingers. What he was hearing was beyond comprehension, was forbidden beyond all codes of law, but he had to keep listening. His duty, as perhaps the only Skrull who could hear this, was to pay attention. He felt both complicit and in the presence of the numinous, because perhaps he'd been meant to see this.

"—and you must understand, Herc was the last god standing, of all these representatives from most of Earth's major pantheons. Because that was the plan: our gods take out their god and his lesser gods."

"No," whispered Balkamar, "no."

"Anyway, right now, it's just him and Kly'bn, over there, on the remains of this shrine, floating in this extra-universal... mythic... nothing." He turned the camera so Balkamar could glimpse, in the distance, the human/Olympian crossbreed Hercules, who, along with all the other beings this child had mentioned, was not an actual god, just a very powerful alien/human hybrid—the Olympians and all the other ridiculously numerous "deities" humans worshipped being nothing more than races more powerful than they who had set up homes nearby. Well, mostly. Some of them didn't seem even to appear to humans in the flesh, or very rarely.

Honestly, humans would worship basically anything.

But then the picture zoomed in, and Balkamar felt his pulse start to thunder as he... saw God. There He was. This blasphemous creature Hercules was actually... *fighting* Him. "He loves us," he whispered. "He is allowing this fight. He could end it."

"Anyway, I was there with him when this fight started, and Kly'bn, the Skrull god, flung the remains of one of his fellow Skrull deities at us—"

What?! What?! Who?!

"—and I could have got out of the way, but I realized in that second that this was what Athena had been prophesizing. That I could save Hercules by doing the hardest thing, which for me is... nothing." His face filled the camera screen, the insufferable human whelp who thought his issues were more important than two gods, one of them the actual, real, God, in pitched battle. "Herc's too human, you see. He's always fighting for the person standing beside him, for *me*, quite often. He can't put aside the here and now for the big picture. And if ever we needed the big picture, it's now. So... I let myself be thrown off into space. He's focused now, fighting for revenge, and maybe my calculation there saved the world. I guess it's worth it. I guess."

"Good," said Balkamar. "Choose to follow a real god before you perish, there's a good chap."

Cho suddenly looked up and seemed to see something approaching. "Woah!"

"Oh no," said Balkamar.

Something impacted Cho, lifting him away, and suddenly the camera sped back toward the floating shrine. "Snowbird?!" Cho yelled delightedly. "But you died!"

"I've died before," said a dark, deep, female voice, "I know how to return."

From what Balkamar could see... oh, this was really too much. This "Snowbird" was actually another "demigod," one called Narya, whose existence was bound to the Earth country called Canada. Her credentials as to godhood were, like Hercules', slim enough to allow her to join a human super hero team, Alpha Flight. Even "gods" who weren't half-human, like Thor and Ares, did that on this world. Honestly, these people would accept just about anything when it came to both their deities and their heroes.

The view swept in toward the temple, and now Balkamar could hear what Hercules was saying, or rather shouting, at God. He was… laughing?! "Try harder, little god! Uncle Pluto is always happy to make room for the guests I send his way!" The horror of it. The vile infringement of all that was sacred. Balkamar found himself holding his breath with the size of this godling's presumption, afraid to let himself make a sound lest he bellow in fury and scare the baby.

"Still you take affront at our incalculable gift?!" That was actually the voice of God. No, he could not remain standing now. This was all surely meant to be. Balkamar placed Danielle carefully beside him and got down on his knees. The voice was everything he had expected it to be, calm and compassionate and yet also with the terrifying power of a warrior. Chancing upon this channel was indeed a miracle, an affirmation, right at the moment his faith was being tested. But now he was certain again, they must prevail, because it had been written. "I love you too, you know."

"A pity you're not my type," said the blasphemer.

"Without us, the people and gods of your Earth will destroy themselves in strife. Accepting our embrace is the only way you can survive. *We* will be *you* better than *you* could ever be!" It felt like a new scripture was being passed to Balkamar. To underline his point, Kly'bn released divine energy from his eyes, slamming the presumptuous man-god to the ground.

"Really, Kly'bn?" Hercules murmured, rising to prop himself on one arm. "You think you could replace my fallen comrades? My brothers and sisters like Amadeus Cho and Snowbird?"

Cho, insufferable, turned the camera on himself for a second so everyone could see his smug grin at Hercules' lack of awareness.

Then he turned it back to the scene. Balkamar found it hard to deal with the idea that his religious experience was going to be interrupted by such piffle.

"They were flawed, but their flaws meant their noble deeds and sacrifices shone all the greater. Their sacrifices brought us to this moment. Their sacrifices taught me more than your endless blather ever could." Slowly Hercules rose to his feet, brushing rubble out of his beard. "*Theirs* are the true names of myth. Aye, and one beside them too. One who is also flawed. Hercules, the Prince of Power." And suddenly he dared to grab God in his hands. "And your shallow *sameness* will never touch them again!"

Balkamar screamed as he saw God ripped in two.

His eyes and mind were full of the dizzying spectacle.

He had seen his God, the only thing of the Skrulls that was unchanging, or as the blasphemer had said, always the same...

He had seen Him changed. He had seen Him... ended.

He stared at the image for a moment, waiting for God to rise.

He did not, he could not. He could not change.

God was dead. *God was dead.*

He could feel it now, deep inside him, the way all Skrulls felt the wishes and words of God. There was, at the center of his changing self, a great... void.

He switched off the screens and fell to the ground. After a moment, he carefully placed Danielle beside him, because with how he was feeling right now, toward this pitiful place, and its... so-called "gods"... he might accidentally harm her in his collapse or... or worse.

He wanted to sob. He felt as if his insides were freezing, as if he might never change again; might never find his whole, real self again. He could feel the loss of God in the world, feel over and over and right to the heart of him the sudden, enormous absence.

The baby started to cry. He crouched again, then stood.

Slowly, he forced himself to come to his senses.

He dusted himself down, picked up the child and soothed it, pacing back and forth.

It was inappropriate to display such high emotion. Inappropriate to both his true self and his guise. He would not let himself or his people down. He didn't dare switch on the screens again, but... but...

Perhaps this was the biggest test of all?

Perhaps this had been foreseen also, the trauma of it told only to the Imperial Command? Perhaps the sacrifice of their God was *necessary* for them to gain a new home on this world?

The death of Janet Van Dyne would surely turn the tide of battle. It had to. How could it not? It would destroy all the heroes here, the majority of their forces. The Skrulls could then consolidate and plan for eventual assaults to regain San Francisco, Britain, Wakanda...

And yet... God was dead.

And what if the plan to use Janet Van Dyne as... as a biological weapon, but a justified one, one that their ethics allowed for, one that only targeted... no, no, he didn't want to let his mind get lost in the details of what was ethical and what was not... what if it didn't work?

He dared to allow himself to ponder that blasphemous idea, just for a moment... if it didn't, if the humans actually... won... what was he going to do then?

When God was dead?

He looked to the baby and decided that it wasn't blasphemy to plan for the worst. That was what his God would have wanted. He would serve his cause to the end.

Yes, if the worst happened, he knew what it was he had to do.

FORTY-THREE

JANET VAN DYNE

A FEW MINUTES BEFORE.

"JANET!" THOR was yelling. "What ails thee?!" He hovered beside her, swinging Mjolnir to create the magical vortex that kept him aloft.

She managed to reach out, a little wildly. She grabbed Thor and he let her draw him near. Stumbling, she was desperately trying not to hurt anyone on the ground. Through the haze of pain, she could see all her friends flying and running to her from all around, breaking off combat where they could. But as soon as they came close she could see them reeling, coughing, falling, until others grabbed them, dragging them back. Her presence appeared to even affect Thor himself, sweat breaking out on his skin, his muscles tightening in anguish. "I'm harming all of you," she managed to say.

"I care not," Thor called, "how can I help thee?"

"I'm... sending out waves of poison. Chemical... using me. I'm... I feel like I'm going to explode! I can't... do this... much longer. I am..."

"Let me away with you to Asgard! There our healers will—"

"No time. Seconds. Thor, you're… a warrior. Not a super hero. You know what you have to do."

Thor looked at her seriously, suddenly calm. "What would you have me do, brave lady?"

"You can use your hammer to send me… somewhere empty? Somewhere I can… let myself… go… die, without harming my friends?"

"There must be another—"

"Thor, I can't hold on! If I let this go everyone here will die, and the Skrulls will win! I will not let that be because of me! You have to do this! I am begging you!"

"Nay," said Thor, his eyes full of tears. "You are not. I would not deny such valor. I will do as you wish." She released him, and he started to spin his hammer.

"Janet, talk to me, are you okay?!" That was Simon, hovering nearby, looking perplexed that everyone else, everyone with a flesh and bone body, was staggering and crying out in pain. There were other calls too, from friends and sometime foes, all wanting to help her first, then themselves. That made it all the more important that she do this.

"Quickly!" she called.

"To outside this dimension with you," shouted Thor. "To a pocket universe where your sacrifice will not harm others. And thence to Valhalla!" His hammer was a blur. "To the land where the greatest warriors receive their reward! For I know not another with a heart as strong as thine!"

Janet turned to get one last look at her friends. Oh, she wished they could all have been together. Could have celebrated together. Could even have lost together. "Don't forget me," she whispered.

Thor brought down his hammer and something like a hand or a hurricane grabbed her and—

And the rest was silence.

FORTY-FOUR

THOR ODINSON

THOR, IN HIS FURY, turned from vanished Janet, fallen far and fast, dropped out of this dimension, whirlpooled away, and bellowed at the foes falling back, electricity arcing all around.

"Did you hear her, would-be warriors, half-clarted, cankered conquerors?! A warrior went from this world! Her death has killed defeat! And with her valor she brings *victory!*"

His comrades did not comprehend. They stared at his strength, as flummoxed as the foe. All were hying to their health, whole and heartening.

"Is… is she…" began Simon Williams.

"You mortals allowed this!" shouted Thor, hovering above his friends, now horrified. Around them the Skrulls were staggering back, aware that their weapon had vanished. "She was the best of you, yet where was she in your war of all against all?! Mere men! Mortals!" He spat the last word and then turned to face the foe now forming up. "She was the first Avenger. And now I shall avenge her!"

He ran at what remained of the Skrull ranks, his hammer swinging left and right, the berserker fighting free, forcing the fire.

And yet he did not yield to it. To discern friend from foe, to make mercy and care for quarter, these humans had heard that and hied instead to hate. Janet would not want it. So, he did not let himself loose.

Around him, friends old and acquaintances new whose names he'd heard in heat of battle, they all brought their stories to his side: Spider-Man and Fury and his young Howlers; Ares and this new Captain America, who carried himself with honor; Cassie Lang and her friends, Wiccan and Hulkling, Speed and Patriot, a team again, with losses of the flesh that would knit their hearts; the craven curs of Parker Robbins; the Wolverine, blasted and bloodied. Even he had retreated from rage, wracked by Janet's sacrifice. There was Reed Richards, his light illuminating. Luke Cage ran in from another quarter, throwing Skrulls sidelong, Jessica Jones, beside him, fighting fiercely. The Kree, Noh-Varr, walked fair beside them, his name always on his tongue, his weapon wasting the way before them. Above them flew Carol and Simon. Brand had found some guns to suit her, blowing all their foes asunder. Gauntlet grimly led those left from his few remaining followers. Taskmaster seemed to stumble, slippery. Danny and Natasha and Maya ran together, their enmity over, faces grim and skins abraded.

What fools these mortals be.

And in their foolishness, they had lost their leaders, their loves and had lowered themselves.

Ahead of them sprang an opening in the throng.

In it was the Skrull Queen, Veranke.

She stood again, incredibly, her form rebuilding, her life still unending, her faith forever. Though around her, Skrulls were running. Around her formed a guard Imperial, Super-Skrulls of the most grim visage, set to fight still further.

It would be a long, hard battle. Losses still would haunt the heroes, losses greater than those already.

But then, a cry, in the distance.

Thor felt it, in his heart unending, in his mind of myth and magic. It was the cry of godhood passing. It was the cry of alien wonder.

He looked into the eyes of his enemy. Veranke and those standing with her staggered, unbelieving, feeling, speared in the faith and in their bodies knowing what had passed in heaven.

"Their god is dead," said Thor, all quiet. He stepped forward, before another arrow from the bow of Barton could intervene to mar this moment. "Yield," he said. "All is lost. Do not fight with no cause remaining. Yield and ye will have our mercy. You have my word as—"

He never knew if he'd say "hero."

"He loves me!" yelled Veranke, empty. "We will not yield. We have been promised!"

Thor from the air an arrow swatted.

But now did Logan run in, screaming.

The Skrulls remaining roared with battle.

Thor's patience had hit the last of his limits. He had acted thus for Janet. His duty done, he had no care left. He swung his hammer at the field and sent the guards high in the air. Carol reached one aflying and punched him into high Earth orbit.

The Queen stood, alone, surrounded, human heroes now advancing.

Logan did his arm rise to her, the low sun glinting off the claw that would soon take her heart and kill her.

She closed her eyes, stood straight, defiant.

The field was silent for the ending.

"He loves me. But—"

Her head exploded.

Thor swung around, as did the others.

There stood Osborn, gun hand shaking, weapon still smoking.

A camera crew capturing the moment. He stood there, an ordinary mortal.

He looked briefly shocked, but then his expression became decisive. "Thunderbolts," he called, "pursue them. Kill all those who won't surrender."

And sure enough, from far behind them, now there came into the battle such shallow villains as Venom pursuing the forces in flight. Some they chased were fleeing, vanishing, teleporting to their transports.

Thor turned to look at Norman Osborn.

He turned instead to face the cameras. And his face was smiling.

FORTY-FIVE

TONY STARK

TONY ARRIVED back at Central Park just in time to glimpse Janet vanishing into one of Thor's vortices. The smart media interpreters that he'd bolted into this very old suit of armor he'd found back at the Tower—as part of an upgrade that had taken just two minutes, damn it—they had told him what had happened. The armor was a red and gold job that didn't connect to the Stark mainframe and thus hadn't been infected by the virus. It didn't have the systems to be infected from the viral load in his bloodstream. It had felt good to put it on. He was shedding a skin that had become contaminated in favor of something pure.

He found himself crying inside his armor.

He had loved her, many years ago. They had given it a shot. He'd thought that maybe that's why she'd sided with him. Though she had never really wholeheartedly sided with him.

He landed at the spot where she had vanished, moments after all the others had departed. He saw her enormous footprints, that she had somehow managed to avoid harming anyone else.

He stood there, mourning her. He felt alone in doing that. Even that.

From ahead, he heard cries of victory, and his suit informed him that Norman Osborn, of all people, had killed the Skrull Queen.

Oh well. As long as someone had.

He should do something.

No, he *had* to do something. There were still Skrull warships hanging in the sky above New York; any second their chain of command might right itself and the aliens might decide they didn't need *all* the world intact and start dropping missiles.

He took to the air again and set the suit to broadcast. "Avengers!" he shouted, meaning all the heroes he saw beneath him. "Those who can, take to the sky! We have to take out those ships!" Several on the ground immediately leapt into the air to meet him, though he saw Thor look up at him and hesitate. One group, however, scuttled away from the field of battle, and began vanishing into the trees. There went Parker Robbins and his criminals. Oh well. They had also served. It wouldn't be right to pursue them now.

Hey, maybe he *had* learned something.

Carol rose to hover beside him. "Tony, is that you in there?"

"Yep. Old school. Not a Skrull. And thanks to Reed you can know for sure if you need to."

"Are you okay?"

"I'm fine."

"Did you see what happened to—"

"Janet. Yeah. I saw." And he rocketed off into the sky toward the first of the Skrull ships. Carol followed a second later, and immediately following her was Simon Williams, Noh-Varr, Ares, and hey, the Blue Marvel, had he been down there? Then there was Thor, his expression—to coin a phrase—thunderous, grudgingly flying up behind them.

Well, they could have words later. They could talk about Janet. Over mead and… yeah, Perrier. Even though he could damn well do with some of that mead himself.

But no. No.

That wasn't what Janet would have wanted.

"I just heard," shouted Ares, by whatever power it was that allowed Olympians and Asgardians to just ignore the vacuum of space, "Hercules killed the Skrull god!"

"Really?" asked Tony. "Fill me in in a sec." They hit the air lock of the first ship like a missile, and broke straight into a big compartment of Skrulls in the act of materializing from all over the world. Skrulls in custody were weeping about their god deserting them. And there had been, his suit reported with joy, victories in Wakanda, the UK and San Francisco. Historians, he realized as he landed on the deck of the ship, would see this as a war of six battles: the Savage Land; the two in New York, and those three victories from very different communities of heroes. Plus, perhaps, whatever Hercules had done to kill their god. "So, what happened with that?" He had a moment to ask Ares again as they watched Skrulls both running away and grabbing for weapons. "How did their god die?"

"Pitifully!" laughed Ares. "At the hands of a half-human! Ah, you should be proud, Stark. This is what your whole life has led to. Your actions have resulted in the death of a god!"

Tony found a tiny part of him wanted to go along with that celebration, but the rest of him really wasn't on board. "This ship here, what can you do?"

Ares looked around at the Skrulls, some still appearing, some now vanishing again. "What *can't* I do? You leave this one to me, all of you, go on to the next!"

"You heard the man," Tony called, and they left Ares advancing on the remaining Skrulls, pulling his enormous ax from its sheath on his back.

As they emerged, a figure came flailing down toward them through space, falling from some higher orbit. He wasn't wearing a space suit, though he didn't seem to need one. He wore a cape and...

Oh, god, it was Bob, the Sentry!

Tony powered up, intercepting him at an angle that would break his fall. Bob grabbed him, looking desperately at him. Tony pulled a mic and earpiece set from his suit and forced it onto his head. "They fooled me," Bob shouted into the mic, "they made me think I was the problem! They made me turn tail. Away from Earth. Please, tell me, is it too late?"

"We've got them on the run," said Tony. "And we need you. Right now. Join in."

Bob beamed at him with a relief that almost made this whole thing worth it. Almost. "You need me? Really?"

"Really. But wait a sec, what changed your mind? Why did you come back?"

"Someone... someone came after me. They told me about their own experiences. That let me see what was... real."

A S.H.I.E.L.D. space shuttle slowly slid into orbit in the Sentry's wake. In its cabin Tony could see Maria Hill. "I thought the most help I could be was getting him back to you," she called over the comms link. "You're welcome."

BOB GOT into the fray immediately; an angry, pent-up look on his face as he ripped into the nearest Skrull battleship, pulling out a strip of its hull plating so Carol could fly in behind him and string power blasts all the way along its length.

They flew from ship to ship, homing in on power sources, Thor flying straight through cabins, sending Skrulls spinning out into space, Simon and Carol perfecting a technique where they'd hit both ends of a ship at the same moment and send a standing wave through it, a concussion of debris blasting out around them.

They turned at one point when Ares magically called their name across empty vacuum in that way the Olympians could, seeing that fearsome god at the prow of the ship they'd left him inside, gripping it with both hands and impossibly flinging the ship in a great circle around himself.

Until he let it go.

Tony tracked the Skrull carrier as it hit escape velocity, tumbled toward another Skrull ship and—

The explosion must have lit up the entire hemisphere.

"I hit one of them with another!" yelled Ares. "And there are still lots up here!"

Tony turned to see that the last few Skrull ships were turning. They seemed to have made some sort of collective decision to abandon Earth. "Then that's where we're going," he said.

Suddenly Thor was beside him. "You would attack an enemy in retreat?!" he yelled.

And Tony felt something break inside him. "I would not attack an enemy *that had surrendered*!" he bellowed back, with all the amplification his armor allowed, hoping gods could hear in space as well as talk. "But that's not what's happening here. The Skrulls will head back to deep space, regroup, and given their religious fanaticism might well try to sneak back down here and have another try. So I want them to be hurting so much that they won't think about doing this, about killing thousands of us puny mortals, ever again! Is that all right with you?!"

Thor, to give him credit, seemed to realize he'd spoken in anger. He nodded, and together he, Tony and the others headed to orbit.

Ares, who seemed very into this, headed straight for the first Skrull ship they caught up with and proceeded to gut it stem to stern. With entirely less glee, Thor joined in with the feats of the impossible, bringing lightning to the vacuum, flashing it from ship to ship, shorting out alarm systems and drives. Simon, Carol, Bob and the others waded in to do the rest. He had long since sent Hill back to Earth.

Tony sped up to come alongside Bob. "You've done great. We're nearly finished here, so, new orders. You go back to Central Park—"

"Are there still Skrulls there?"

"Only surrendering ones. I want you to go back there and make contact with our friends. Make sure you sit down, and get some support and a hot drink, and maybe a foil blanket, okay?"

"But... I'm not hurt."

256   "That's an order, Bob. You're a team player, right?"

Bob finally nodded, still looked confused and anxious, and flew Earthward.

Noh-Varr approached, the enormous grin on his face visible through his art deco space helmet. "I will remain free now, yes?!"

"That'll have to go through due process, but you've done great work today. I mean, I'm going to speak up for you, whatever comes next."

The grin faded slightly. "I just want to kill Skrulls, man. That's what Marvel Boy is for. It's what Mar-Vell would have wanted." And before Tony could raise an eyebrow at the idea of Mar-Vell "just wanting to kill Skrulls" when the former Captain Marvel had spent all his life seeking peace, he sped off to continue doing that.

As the rout continued, Tony found himself hovering at a distance from it. He wanted to land some sort of coup de grâce, but what would be the point? Janet stuck in his thoughts. As she should. Of course. What was he going to do after all this? Were things just going to go back to how they had been?

No. Of course not. There would have to be a general amnesty of some kind. Peace talks. Something to sort out the situation of people like Noh-Varr. Him and Luke should get together to have a beer... or in his case a Perrier, get ahold of yourself, Tony... a meeting where, sure, he'd let himself be shouted at a little, but the other side would come to realize what Janet had—that law, in the end, was what they were about. "Keep the casualties as light as you can, everyone," he called over his comms. "Let them surrender if they want to. We should take prisoners. We need to be seen to do that, and we need the intel, and, you know, it's the right thing to do."

He realized his suit was trying to tell him something.

There was one Skrull ship ahead, a transport, quite small, almost deliberately unobtrusive, that was showing some unusual bio-signatures. "Oh my god," he whispered when he saw the detail.

From that moment, nothing could stop him. He blasted his way into that ship, Skrulls flying into space from where he'd breached their hull. He got to the control deck, blasted every remaining

Skrull, found his way into the control systems, saw what was meant to be in the aft section and set course for New York immediately, a message that this ship was under his control broadcasting on repeat. He got in touch with the others who were with him in orbit, just to be sure. They asked him what he was doing. He told them he didn't want to raise false hopes, but here was a win, a real win, a win that would signal the end of this war.

Then he went back into the main body of the ship, to see what he would find there.

FORTY-SIX

JESSICA JONES

JESSICA LEANED against Luke, watching as the Thunderbolts finished what was being called "mopping up." That largely seemed to involve them mocking dying or injured Skrulls, then shooting them through the head. She'd tried calling for them to stop, couple of times. But they simply ignored her. And in the end Luke had asked her if she really wanted to fight that battle right now—adding he was glad she did, though. The two of them rallied guards from The Raft and Stark's other prisons, who'd gamely showed up in the hope they could help, to start taking living Skrulls from the field in power shackles. A couple of the Thunderbolts looked over, but Luke glared at them. Osborn was over there talking to TV, and they decided not to make a thing of it. Reed approached, his face ashen, and flared his blue light over all of them. It was definitely humans taking the Skrulls away. Reed leaned against a tree, shaking, as the vans drove off. "How many did we lose?" asked Jess.

"Janet," said Luke. "Three of the Howlers in Times Square. Sixteen of the Initiative."

"Damn," whispered Jess.

"And all the ones who turned out to be Skrulls."

"Yeah."

"I've heard the Sentry's on his way back. We don't know how Kate Bishop's doing. From what I'm hearing, we won today because of Janet's sacrifice, what other heroes did around the world, and because of something Hercules did on some higher plane."

"At least our people saved a lot of everyday folk today."

"Yeah. There's that. But several million everyday folk across the world are dead."

Jess looked over to where Clint Barton was lying on the ground, his bow in his hands, staring up, lost. "As soon as I get somewhere private," she said, "I'm taking off this damn costume and it's never going back on."

"Fine by me."

"We got incoming," said Fury looking grim as he strode up. There was nothing celebratory about him. He just looked tired. His Howling Commandos gradually approached. Those that had made it as far as this battle had all, it seemed, survived this experience. None of them were celebrating either. "It's a Skrull ship that's meant to be under Stark's control, but hey—"

"Yeah," said Jess, looking up. And there it was. A single, small transport ship, a dot becoming larger in the otherwise miraculously empty sky.

Reed reflexively swung his scanner up and looked at the display. "It's okay," he said, "it's full of… humans."

Jess would remember that moment afterward. That it had taken even Mr. Fantastic a moment to realize the full import of what he was saying.

"Oh," said Luke. "Oh, sweet mother of—" Only that wasn't exactly how he'd said it.

The news spread quickly, and suddenly everyone was running toward the descending ship. Osborn, surprised, looked around, but seemed to decide that his moment in the spotlight was more important than a captured ship.

260   The ship dropped to the ground with an enormous thump.

Jessica and Luke pushed their way to the front of the crowd, right beside that new Cap, who held up his shield, ready for anything. Maya, beside him, was shaking off the tension of the fight, poised in case another was about to begin. The crowd parted, allowing Reed through. He was shaking his head, as if he didn't want to think about what was inside this thing. He raised his detector and again shook his head. "No Skrulls in there," he said.

The big hatch at the side of the ship broke open. "Just like the one in the Savage Land," said Luke. "Same kind of…" And then he trailed off, because he could see what Jessica was seeing.

Inside the ship's main bay, with Stark standing proudly behind them, his helmet off, a slight, hopeful smile on his face…

There stood their friends.

Among a handful of S.H.I.E.L.D. guys, there was Dum Dum Dugan.

Black Bolt of the Inhumans stood beside Elektra.

Henry Pym, incredibly, was in there, looking as anxious as any of those standing outside this thing were.

Oh, god, there was Sue Storm, becoming visible, an equally uncertain look on her face.

And at the front of it all, looking not at all anxious, but affecting the most nonchalant expression, was Jess' own closest friend, Jessica Drew, the real, the actual!

"It's them," whispered Reed, looking up from his device. "It's actually—"

And he was suddenly a squiggle in the air, rushing to grab hold of Sue, who fell into his arms, both of them yelling in relief and amazement.

"And I had a line all ready," said Jessica Drew.

But the dam had broken. Those inside came out, those outside rushed in, and there was crying and embracing. Jess found Jessica and held her. Then Carol landed right behind them and rushed in to hold her too. "Oh my god," she said, "are you okay?"

"No!" said Jessica. "I am not even a little okay. I've been fearing for my life for months now, in a Skrull prison camp and then in this transport ship, and we kind of guessed there was some sort of invasion going on, and I… wait. Why are they all looking at me like that?"

Jess looked over to see Logan, Fury, and even Luke had complicated expressions on their faces at the sight of Jessica. "Oh, knock it the hell off," she said, only she didn't say hell. And, to their credit, they did.

"What did I do?" Jessica said. Then she realized. "Oh god."

"It's okay," said Carol, putting her arm through hers. "*You've done nothing wrong.*" Outside the ship, their friends who'd gone to attack the fleet in orbit had started to land and join in the astonished celebrations.

Henry Pym held the hands of Stark. "Do I even want to know what year it is?" he said. "I guess you… you won, right? They kept telling us they were going to come here and… you guys kicked them out?! Damn, I wish that… hey, was Janet not with you?"

Stark looked desperately sad at him.

Jess watched as Pym got the idea. "Oh no," he said. "No."

"She died a hero," said Stark.

"I don't care," said Henry, his voice utterly empty. "I… never got to fix it."

Stark led the man away out of earshot. He would already be saying, Jess was sure, how awful it was when men didn't get to fix things. She turned around to see Elektra and Daredevil regarding each other calmly. After all that, all the great assassin managed in terms of high emotion was a single nod. Then she turned and walked away. To his credit, Daredevil managed to nod back, and even crack a smile.

Jess looked upward to see Black Bolt, the King of the Inhumans, already in mid-air, heeding some call from his people and caring, of course, not a whit for any of this human stuff going on down here.

Fury handed Dugan a hip flask. "Hey, you old walrus."

"I got in a little trouble," said Dugan. "It worked out."

And now there were a few more people slowly making their way out of the ship, a little more reluctantly than the others. There

262

were a couple more S.H.I.E.L.D. guys she didn't recognize, and wow, the Skrulls had really picked some minor villains to swap out, and there was—

She suddenly felt sick with terror.

"I am so sorry, sir," said Edwin Jarvis, still wearing his butler's formal wear and bow tie, as he made his way toward Stark.

"Well," said Stark, "that explains a lot, and you have nothing to apologize for, Jarvis—"

"Oh god," shouted Jess, horror bursting into her head, "no!"

Luke ran beside her, but she couldn't explain to him, she had to get out of there. A second later she was in the air, screaming Danielle's name as she went, heading for Avengers Tower like a rocket.

She didn't bother with the hatch on the roof. She went straight in through the window, glass bursting around her. She ignored it.

She sped from room to room, from the nursery to the lounge with the big screens where she'd left him, damn it, where she'd left him with her baby! He'd been standing right there. He'd been himself, so utterly himself, and she was a detective, why hadn't she realized, why had she been so stupid?!

She covered the whole building's interior in less than a minute, shouting Danielle's name, hoping against hope that she'd suddenly hear some gurgle in reply, the sound of her crying, anything. "Oh no, oh no, please, no…"

When Carol and Luke found her, she had collapsed against a wall, adrenaline and exhaustion fighting inside her. She wanted to throw up, she wanted to attack something. "Jess—" Carol began.

"They took the baby!" she screamed. "They *took our baby!*"

FORTY-SEVEN

CLINT BARTON

CLINT SAT on a park bench, hanging back from the celebrations. He didn't feel like joining in. He'd been reflexively dialing the Vision on the Young Avengers' number that Kate had given him, but he wasn't picking up. He needed to know where she'd been taken, how she was doing. He'd seen the transport ship land, and had understood who was inside, but couldn't bring himself to go over there and join in. He'd been glad to see some familiar faces, in the distance. But it wasn't like Cap was going to be in there, was it? He hadn't been taken by the Skrulls, he'd been killed by their culture's own idiocy.

And she wouldn't be there. He hadn't let himself hope for it. Not this time. He'd pulled his mask back down over his face, because he didn't quite want anyone to see how he was looking right now. Kate's bow was still in his hand, her quiver strapped to his back. They felt good. Better than they should. They were hers, damn it, and he would give them back to her when he saw her alive and well.

Fury and Dugan walked over, and with them, from out of that ship, was… Clint managed to remember her name, that other

S.H.I.E.L.D. bigwig, an actual Contessa, Valentina Allegra de Fontaine. An old-time Fury loyalist, someone who'd been beside him through thick and thin. Wow, the Skrulls had really got into the higher ranks of that organization. Val was grinning, and Dugan echoed the expression. But Fury had a distant look to him. He put a hand on Dugan's shoulder, then gave the Contessa a single look, and then he stepped away, to where, nearby, the survivors from his Howling Commandos had gathered, a teleport spell forming around them. "But…" began the Contessa. "Nicholas—"

Fury raised a hand, to call for silence. He shook his head and a moment later he was gone.

"He don't trust nothin' no more," said Dugan, watching his oldest friend depart. "And who can blame him?"

"Hey," called a voice from nearby, "was that Nick Fury?!"

Clint jumped to his feet and turned to look, feeling suddenly sick with fear and hope.

It couldn't be. Oh god. After all this, he couldn't let himself hope.

She came running up to them, not even looking at him.

"It *was*," said the Contessa. "You'd think he'd stick around to see *all* his agents, right?"

"Bobbi," said Clint, stumbling over. "Bobbi?" He pulled down his mask.

It was her. She was staring at him, and it was her. "Oh my god, Clint?!"

"Hey," said Dugan, "she's been through that doohickey of Reed Richards'. We all have."

He ignored that. He couldn't let himself trust that. "Is it you?" he said to her. He stared right into her eyes. They were her eyes. But he'd thought that last time.

"What the hell are you wearing?" she said. "You look terrible."

Clint burst out laughing. He couldn't help it. He gathered her up into his arms and she kissed him before he could kiss her, and it was her.

It was her. The real her. "Of all people," he said, "of all people!"

"What?" She was laughing too amongst their tears.

"It's *you and me* who get a happy ending?! Like this?!"

"Hey," she said, "don't jinx it."

In the corner of his eye, Clint saw a small movement. He spun, still ready for battle, and there was Maya.

Maya regarded the two of them together and Clint felt his heart sink. "I'm sorry," he said.

Bobbi realized what this must be and looked anguished. "Okay, so, if you two need to talk, I mean, if Clint thought I was dead, I can't claim—"

"No," said Maya. She looked devastated, but she also looked just as heroic as when she'd been fighting the Skrulls. "This is the life we lead, right? We have to deal with emotional situations nobody else does. Life and death and life again. Damn it. But it means I got a preview. So, I get it. I've seen how it goes with you two. Good luck to you."

And she turned and walked away.

"Oh god," said Bobbi. "I guess I jinxed it after all."

FORTY-EIGHT

REED RICHARDS

REED HAD theorized that the Skrulls would probably be keeping the originals of those they'd copied somewhere reasonably close at hand. They would have needed, from time to time, to replenish the DNA samples upon which they'd based their power duplication process, especially if some power-draining accident befell one of their duplicates. And so, in the back of his mind, he'd allowed himself some hope that Susan might be alive somewhere. He had seen, on security footage transmitted to him from the Baxter Building, her duplicate arrive and breach the Negative Zone containment fields. He had seen, in the Savage Land, another such duplicate, and been attacked by many of them, with that sick Skrull irony, on the field of battle.

But now here was the real Susan, the best part of their family back in his arms, in his life once again. They swiftly established where and when she'd been taken: after giving a talk in Vancouver, when she'd taken a cab back to the hotel on her own. That had been less than six weeks ago. So, the Susan who had grown so frustrated and angry with him during the Civil War, who had left him for a while… "No such luck," she said. "That was all me."

"I think my luck is doing fine," he said, holding onto her with every fiber of his being. "And only you would think like that when you've spent weeks as a prisoner of aliens!"

"Now I can say I did it too."

"I did it twice, though."

"So, these various other Sues—"

"The most intimate I got with any of them was their invisible fists in my face."

"In *six weeks?*"

He looked awkward. "You were away a lot. And I was busy."

"Wow. *Wow.*"

"But listen, there is a situation I had put aside because there was nothing I could do to change it, and this battle was, horribly, more important, *but*—" He strained his muscles upward to become tall and thin enough to let her see over the trees to the Baxter Building, Susan using her forcefield immediately, and intimately, to stabilize the effort.

"The children," she said, when she saw the effect still flickering around the top floors, a globe of energy that was showing no signs of dissipating. "Oh my god!"

"Johnny and Ben were with them," he said. "And my sensors tell me the situation there isn't changing, moment by moment, though that's just about the only data they *are* providing, but now we need—"

Before he could finish his sentence, she wrapped him around her like a backpack and used her forcefields to step them through the air, over the trees, and at speed through the city. "You're starting to worry I'll hate you because you prioritized the battle over the children," she shouted over the rush of air. "And you needn't. Because I know you'll have made sure there was nothing you could do."

Reed looked to the NYPD in the streets below, beginning to emerge and trying desperately to manage the aftermath. It looked like they had kept up a barrier around the Baxter Building even during the fighting. Now, as the two of them approached the building, that crowd started to cheer. He felt rather ashamed, though he extended a long arm to acknowledge them. "The general public," he said, "don't get the two of us at all. You're the most logical one. I have been… in recent months I have made some bad decisions."

"Damn right you have." The Baxter Building's midsection doors swung open to meet them and within a moment they were striding through the familiar corridors of home. "So. What can we do?"

"There's a secure line backup procedure in sub-basement nine, for use if the Negative Zone portal was ever breached."

"Because of course you had a contingency plan."

They got into an elevator and Reed sent them swiftly downwards. "But it needs two of us to activate it, in case something from out of the Zone got hold of one of us. That was why I couldn't rescue them before."

"I believe you. This guilt isn't helping anyone."

"And it can be activated from the other side, if you know the right codes…" They stepped out and found the right doorway. "So, if Ben and Johnny had somehow been able to find their way back, the door would have been open for them to—"

They stopped at the door and looked at each other. From inside the sub-basement, they could hear familiar voices arguing. "The blue button! You hit the blue button first! Why didn't Reed leave a manual?!" Reed raised a finger to say wait and checked the readings on his Skrull monitor. Then, feeling himself begin to shake with emotion, he burst into the room.

There stood Ben and Johnny, the room illuminated by Johnny's flaming finger, trying to work the console that would re-seal the Negative Zone. But Reed registered them only for a second, because at their feet, with a big sheet of coloring and some crayons, were Franklin and Valeria!

Reed and Sue leapt at their children and gathered them, laughing, into their arms. "Mommy," said Valeria, looking calm and slightly annoyed to be taken away from her red dinosaur, "you're better."

"Was I… not well before?" Sue asked, carefully.

"Well," said Franklin, objecting to Reed smelling his hair. "Turns out you'd been replaced by a Skrull."

"A Skrull who blew up the house," said Valeria, sounding even more annoyed.

"We kind of took care of it ourselves," said Franklin, "just so you know."

Reed turned to look seriously at Ben and Johnny. Ben had that tough look on his face that said he was trying not to get too emotional. "Thank you for saving them," he said.

"Yeah, well, we thought about leaving 'em out there," said Ben, "but then we thought—"

"Sis would kill us," finished Johnny.

"So, what happened to you?" asked Sue. "After you got sucked into the Negative Zone?"

"Well," said Johnny, rubbing the back of his neck, "funny story, that Skrull who was pretending to be you—"

"—turned out to be Johnny's ex-wife!" said Ben, grinning.

"Lyja?!" said Sue. "Lyja, who you married thinking she was a human?! *Lyja?!*"

"Yeaaahh… She tried to persuade us that she was the real you and you'd taken the Baxter Building into the Zone to save us, but that lasted about two minutes."

"There were monsters," said Valeria. "They came at us. I found a battle mech suit. Franklin helped."

"I had armor too!" yelled Franklin.

"Then *I* had the idea of us all going to Tony Stark's Negative Zone prison where the super villains are."

"And Johnny kissed Lyja," noted Franklin gleefully.

"Seriously?" said Sue. "After all she did to you? And, hey, she wasn't looking like me at this point, right?!"

"Ick! Of course not!" Johnny looked appalled.

"Just saying."

"Ick!"

"But she was still, like, a fascist invader who'd abducted us all," said Ben.

"Except she'd been under orders to just kill us all, the kids too," said Johnny, "and she changed those orders to 'take us out of the picture,' and I think that's worth a certain amount of consideration."

"And kissing," said Sue. "At least this time round you *knew* she was a Skrull."

"*Anyway*," said Johnny, "at the prison we found the Tinkerer, and he was pissed that Tony Stark had had him arrested even after he'd retired—"

"—but he didn't want Earth to be invaded any more than we did," said Ben. "He's got grandchildren. So, he did what he could have done all along, 'cept he was serving his sentence, tinkered a device to return us to Earth. And still he stayed put."

"Lyja stayed in the Negative Zone too," said Johnny. "She didn't want to rejoin the Skrull army. You know, after all the kissing."

"Reed," Ben cut in, "you didn't lissen to me about this before, but now yer gonna—"

"Yes," Reed closed his eyes, "I am."

Ben placed a big hand on his shoulder. "I know you did the right thing in the end. You always do. But you were on the wrong side of this thing. Guys like the Tinkerer shouldn't be in some other dimension. Tony Stark used a hammer to fix a... jigsaw puzzle or somethin', I don't know. After we've kicked the Skrulls'... behinds—"

"Reed did that before we got here," said Sue.

"Not me," said Reed, "no."

"Now that's done, then," finished Ben, "you need to make better choices. All of us do. And that's all I gotta say about that."

Reed took a long breath, very aware that his children were looking at him. "Starting today," he said. "I give you my word."

Ben pulled him into what quickly turned into a group huddle. After a minute or so of sheer relief, Reed stretched out a hand and tapped out the codes that would seal the Negative Zone once more. A schematic of the building appeared on a screen above the console that Ben and Johnny had been fighting over. On it, they watched the energy bubble around the complex vanish. But then so did the top floors. And then, very fast, on the schematic and above them in real life, the building started to reconstruct itself from what remained. Even from down here, they could hear the crowds outside cheering.

"But our stuff!" said Valeria. "It's all gone!"

"It's just stuff," said Reed. "We've still got everything important."

FORTY-NINE

TONY STARK

TONY HAD been trying to reach Carol, to ask about the situation with Jessica Jones and Cage's kid. Didn't they realize that he'd be able to put... well, what little remained of S.H.I.E.L.D. at their disposal, that they could work together to sort out whatever was going on there? He didn't expect Luke to trust him, but he thought Carol would. After a few minutes, he gave up trying and wandered over to where Thor had just left off giving his congratulations to Barton and Bobbi Morse. Paramedics and Damage Control teams were arriving in the park now, along with the media. Even Osborn seemed to have moved his many interviews off to another location. Now was traditionally the time when super heroes ran off back to secrecy, and he wanted to make sure enough of them stuck around to reassure the population that order was being fully restored here, and the heroes were here for that process. And hey, they had just saved the world!

Besides, he wanted to have a serious conversation with Thor, and with that new Captain America to whom the Odinson had just offered his hand, which this new guy had immediately taken. Cap Two had certainly proved himself in battle, but if he was going to take that identity forward... okay, Tony didn't want to think about the business of super human registration right now, but the public were going to want to know who their Captain America was, right?

"I can vouch for him," said Natasha, suddenly appearing at his side. She looked wonderfully tousled, bruised and cut; as though she'd got the best of a dozen battles.

"Everyone seems to be reading my mind today. I mean, without actually reading it."

"Well, you're pretty easy to read."

"So, who is he?"

"That's his secret to tell."

"Natasha, come on!" But he turned his head away for a second to acknowledge someone giving him a thumbs-up: when he looked back, she had gone.

Thus, kind of awkwardly, he approached Thor and New Cap. "So..." he said. "Hey. Guys. Thank you for all you did today. You were amazing. We have so much to do now. I'm... I'm just really glad you're back with us, Thor. And I'm glad there's a worthy inheritor of that shield... Cap." He hoped using the name would have a good effect there, but this guy behind the mask looked pretty damn stoic still. "I'm glad we can all finally—"

"Knave!" shouted Thor, turning on him. "Do not presume anything has changed between us, Stark! I came here today because the mortals needed me. I told you I would never fight alongside you again. I told you I would never join thy ranks again. Such promises may be broken for a better cause, but do not act as if I would continue to infringe them. I abhor what thou hast become. If you dare look for the cause of all this—" He gestured around him. "Then look first to yourself. The blame falls on your shoulders. Others will feel the same way. If you wish to ever share my company again, you must first acknowledge that. Then you must make amends. I judge you capable of neither."

And with that, in a flurry of cape, he threw himself upward into the sky.

274

Tony watched him go, his heart sinking. He closed his eyes and when he opened them again the sky was empty. He looked back to the new Cap to find a look in those eyes that matched Thor's.

The man with the shield just turned and walked away.

FIFTY

TEDDY ALTMAN

TEDDY, THE rest of the Young Avengers beside him, found Kate Bishop in a room at Mount Sinai Hospital. The bill, the attending doctor told him, was being met—as it was for Diamondback in the next room and for all those who'd been injured in battle—by Tony Stark. When they entered they found the Vision, his face still a mess, trying to persuade a woozy Kate not to take the I.V. drip out of her arm, that she had to stay in bed. "No, they'll arrest me," she was saying. She looked up at them and blinked. "They'll arrest all of us. So what the hell are you all doing here?!"

Teddy gave her a big hug, told her the invasion was over and she could stand down. For at least a while, everything was going to be okay.

Billy, beside him, added that Clint Barton had her bow and quiver and had been using them well. Which was the cue for Clint to enter behind them, Bobbi Morse at his side. "Hawkeye is back in town!" he'd said.

"Yeah," Kate had said, staring in amazement at Bobbi. "In that *I'm* still alive. And it looks like I'm not the only one."

A lot of explanations and hugging followed. Clint held Kate

for the longest time, Bobbi wearing a smile that said she'd like to be briefed a little more thoroughly on this subject but knew a found family when she saw one. They finally headed off, Clint signing to Kate that she should text him as they left.

"Okay," Elijah finally said, "I think, long term, Kate might be right. I don't trust this peace. We should get out of here."

And so, Kate, having let the Vision do another check of her internal organs using his sensors, was helped out of bed. Elijah asked if he was correct in thinking that while she was injured, he should resume leadership, and she nodded. "So, we should find someplace new to hide," he said.

"Err." Teddy had felt awkward about asking. "There's something I'd kind of like to check on first, if it's okay, in the park."

"What's that?"

"I'm... kind of worried about the Skrulls. I mean... about what's going to happen to them now."

So that was how, after only a little incredulity from the others, they ended up stealthily approaching the fringes of Central Park once again, evading police to get through the cordon. They found a group of Skrulls being led off by guardsmen from one of Stark's prisons, arms shackled by power-draining equipment. And there was Noh-Varr, looking angry at them. "Don't shape-shift one molecule," he said to one of them, cocking that huge gun of his and pointing it at them, "or I'll shift your head off your body."

"Are you okay, Teddy?" asked Kate, noting his expression.

"He looks like a Kree fascist," said Teddy. "He speaks like a Kree fascist."

"So, he probably is a Kree fascist," said Billy.

"I don't trust Stark not to let him interrogate the prisoners. I don't trust Stark not to torture them, period. Even with the little I know about my heritage, I know this isn't what the Skrull Empire has always been about. This was extremism. Terrorism."

"I don't understand why they want the Earth so badly," said the Vision. "Did you not once tell us they were masters of twelve planets?"

"I did," said Teddy. "They are." He let his features shift into their natural Skrull-like shape. The codename "Hulkling," which he'd adopted before he'd known about his true heritage, was going to spare him a lot of grief in the near future, he was pretty sure. He was also pretty sure it was grief he didn't want to be spared. He found he couldn't help it. He marched over there, and the others followed.

The officials reacted to his arrival, immediately on guard when they saw his face, but the presence of those they'd recognized from the battle, and a quick flash from one of Reed's devices, calmed them. "Hey, comrades in arms!" called Noh-Varr. "Well fought, fellow kids!"

Teddy ignored him, approaching the nearest captive and speaking to him in one of the more widely used Skrull dialects. "Why did you do this? Aren't all the worlds in the Empire enough for you?"

The Skrull looked surprised to be spoken to in such relatively gentle language. "Tragedy," they said, "has decimated our people. None of those worlds now exist. We are without a home. What was written in the book of our faith long ago, and had for so long been ignored, it seemed to offer us a last chance." They lowered their head. "*This* was our last chance."

"Hah!" said Noh-Varr, gleefully. "And you blew it!"

Teddy felt Billy place a hand on his arm. He realized that what he did in this moment might re-ignite the Civil War. If it had ever ended.

He showed restraint. He walked away, and his friends, human and otherwise, walked with him. But he was a hero, and he would do what was right, and he would pay close attention to what happened to the Skrulls in custody. "This isn't over," he said.

"Is it ever?" said Billy.

FIFTY-ONE

TONY STARK

ONE WEEK LATER.

TONY STARED at the news in astonishment. A few minutes ago, an awkward phone call came in from a friend at the Capitol, who'd indicated something bad was about to happen. He'd been so busy in the last week, managing the clean-up after the Battle of Central Park and bringing together what little was left of S.H.I.E.L.D., that he hadn't realized there'd been radio silence from Washington. Now he was paying the price for taking his eye off that ball.

"Tony Stark," the President was saying from the podium, "was the guy who stood on the mountaintop and decided he was in charge of the world. He said he could protect us all, but guess what? He couldn't. These super heroes, they spent all their time fighting each other, and they missed the fact that aliens were about to *invade the planet*! So Tony Stark is out. S.H.I.E.L.D. is out."

"What?" said Tony, shaking his head in disbelief as he paced back and forth. "What?"

"That organization has been compromised beyond recovery.

We're going to shut it down, and replace it with something superior, something modern. I mean, no more of the superspy tuxedo stuff. The new agency's goals will be to keep the Earth safe, particularly the USA, from those who would attack it from within *and* without." He looked over his shoulder and the curtain behind him dropped, to reveal the same Avengers "A" logo that adorned the very tower that Tony was currently standing in. He really should have copyrighted that, damn it. But back in the day, when he'd floated that idea, Cap—the real Cap, Steve Rogers—had said that image belonged to everyone, and so he'd backed down.

He'd compromised so much. And it had led to this: him being out of office, replaced by some faceless bureaucrat, probably, who'd be flying an Avengers flag! "I am going to sue for that," he said, pointing at the screen. "My lawyers will be able to make something of that." He'd been talking to himself a lot lately. Too much.

"If this invasion has proved anything at all, it's that we need a certain type of man at the head of the table," the President continued. "We've all seen the footage. We've seen a true hero at work, being decisive, getting things done, like real heroes do. We know what type of hero we need watching our skies, our borders. That hero is…" He gestured sidelong, and onto the stage beside him walked—

"*Norman Osborn!*" Tony actually yelled it out loud, drowning out the President saying exactly the same words.

Osborn strode onto the stage, waving to the crowd like he was at the damn Oscars.

The President put a hand on his shoulder as he continued. "All that fell under the purview of S.H.I.E.L.D. including the Avengers, the special prisons, the Fifty State Initiative of training schemes and local super heroes, that's now all part of the Thunderbolts project."

"Oh, Norman, you have been busy," said Tony.

The President stepped back and Osborn took the podium. "Thank you, Mr. President. First off, I want to make something perfectly clear. Stark technology will no longer be used by any government department, in any defense capacity, anywhere. The entirety of Stark Enterprises has been compromised by the aliens, to the point where none of its products can be trusted."

"And that just happens to suit your own business, as my competitor!" Tony shouted.

"A full-scale investigation into what led to the invasion will be conducted, by a committee with subpoena powers. Those deemed negligent or complicit will answer for their actions. I am not ruling out indictments, including for Tony Stark himself. And now I'd like to introduce the first two of those true heroes who are going to be at the heart of my Avengers, two you'll recognize as having performed mighty feats against the Skrulls." He raised a hand and onstage walked… Bob and Noh-Varr?!

"The world needs order," began Bob, "so do I. As the Sentry. So…"

Noh-Varr swiftly took the mic off him. "I am Marvel Boy! I have been charged to continue the legacy of a great warrior! And I promise you this: no Skrull will set foot on Earth and live!"

And the crowd went wild.

"And you got a full pardon in return, right?" Tony couldn't take it any longer. He switched it off, because he was about to throw something at the screen. He sat down, feeling empty. "I've wasted my life," he said. He had tried so hard to change the way they'd all done things. But all he'd provided was the illusion of change.

He'd never wanted a drink so much in his life.

But then he saw his desire to have a drink with the futurist part of his mind. He saw that here, right now, was a turning point. Much the same as when he and the rest of those big-time heroes who'd set themselves up as representing Earth had gone to visit the Skrulls. As much as the moment when Henry Pym had slapped Jan.

That small organization: him, Xavier, Strange, Reed, Black Bolt, Namor… it was gone now, scattered, all of them back to what they valued the most. Except Strange. Who knew what the hell had happened to him?

Maybe he had paid the price for… for what Tony had done. This was all his fault.

The death of Janet. The falling line of dominoes that had led to all this. It was always the women in their community that suffered the most. And it was all down to him.

He could either feel the guilt of that and have a drink, maybe then he'd end up the super villain several of his former friends already seemed to regard him as, as the media were surely about to portray him as; or he could take the guilt...

And damn well do something about it.

He had taken his version of how the world should be run as far as he could take it. And it had failed. But that was the nature of experiment, right? Time to step aside and let someone else take a turn with their version. Time to give up trying to lead and instead support that. To see if someone else could provide *real* change. And he knew just where to begin.

Tony Stark stood up and went to get a Perrier.

He had never felt more alone. But that wasn't a bad place from which to make a new start.

FIFTY-TWO

PETER PARKER

AFTER THE battle, while they had all still been hanging around in Central Park, the new Captain America, whoever it was, had rallied everyone—Peter included—making arrangements to meet up later. And so, once Peter Parker had gone home and had a bath, and fallen asleep in that bath, and had dreamed about all that had just happened and had woken up with a yell and a splash... he'd swung off again to an address on the Lower East Side. He'd been told what to expect, and that he had to enter quickly, so, err, this was going to require kind of a leap of faith.

"There is no spoon! There is no spoon!" he yelled as he swung on his webline straight at the brick wall.

He went straight through the wall. Breathing a sigh of relief, he landed in what looked like an old warehouse, zussed up by someone with a sofa here, a house plant there. There was a widescreen TV and a floor thick with dust. Yep. This was a super hero hideout all right. Like a frat house with a budget. "Hey," he said to Logan, Clint Barton and Bobbi Morse. "That was pretty cool. I mean, you thought that was cool, right? I swung in *through the wall*."

Logan looked for a moment like he was going to reply, then visibly decided not to.

"Hey, Spidey," said Clint. "I don't know why I came here. I am beyond tired."

"Try a beer," said Logan, reaching into a rucksack of them he'd brought along.

Clint shook his head. "My body is a temple."

"So put a beer in your temple."

Bobbi took the can instead. "So, whose place is this? I mean, Clint explained all that's happened while I've been away, and hoo boy, but if this is going to be the new Avengers Mansion, I have notes."

"I'm guessing it's Cap's place," said Logan. "He invited us."

"Do we know who he is?" asked Peter.

"Nope."

"And we think he's not a Skrull because?"

"Because we're done with them," said Clint. "And Reed shone that light of his all over on the battlefield, so if he is now…"

"Okay," said Peter. He looked to Bobbi. "How's not being dead?"

"Pretty good. But… I lost years of my life. I can't be cute about it."

"Sorry."

"No, not you. I don't know what I'm supposed to be doing now. I don't know where I belong."

"We'll figure it out," said Clint, managing a smile. He just seemed delighted by her every moment.

"I don't know how you can be so zen about this."

"You deserve to be angry, and you're going to be. About Maya and about so much else. But right now, I'm just going to enjoy the fact that you are back in the world. Okay?"

"Okay." She looked at Clint now with that same delighted expression.

"But… I'm also going to be angry and sad and yell at people for no good reason because…"

284   "We lost Jan," said Peter.

"Yeah."

A silence descended.

Peter finally decided to speak up. "While we're waiting for whoever else New Cap has invited, can we just… can we just take a minute to freak out about all that happened to us? We almost lost the planet. We almost lost it."

"But we didn't," said Logan, and finished his beer.

"Thor's back! Nick Fury! And then they went again! I take one look at my phone, and Norman Osborn, the actual fricking *Green Goblin* has been put in charge of everything!" Peter shook his head in incredulity. "I mean, anyone else here have their archenemy made literally the boss of them today?! I didn't think so!"

Whatever the others might have said in response was cut off by the entrance of Danny Rand, walking through the wall like he did that kind of thing every day. Which he kind of did, only usually the wall wasn't so cooperative. "Hey, you guys hear from Luke and Jessica?" He took a beer from Logan. No temples for that guy.

"No," said everyone.

"Huh. I saw Jess take off after the battle, and then Carol and Luke went after her. And now none of them are answering their phones."

"I saw them," said a voice from the entrance.

Peter turned to find Jessica Drew standing there, in her Spider-Woman costume under a S.H.I.E.L.D. flight jacket, looking the most vulnerable Peter had ever seen her.

"Who invited you?" asked Clint, looking as though he knew it was wrong to say it even as he let it out, which wasn't anything new for him.

"I did," said Logan, calmly. "Because she didn't do anything wrong."

Peter found himself nodding adamantly. He went over to Jessica and led her into the center of the room. Incredibly, Clint looked away. "Clint—"

"It wasn't her," said Logan. "Skrulls took her and replaced her, just like with Bobbi. She got it the worst of all of us."

"I'll go—" began Jessica.

"No," said Peter, grabbing her hands. "Please."

"I only came," said Jessica, "because… I don't know where else to go. I mean, I have this face, this is my face. Am I going to be on the run, because there I am on TV apparently being shot in the head by Norman Osborn, over and over? I'm going to have sickos coming at me in the street, wanting to give that a turn themselves."

"And not-so-sickos," said Clint.

"Clint," said Bobbi, "you are definitely not a Skrull, and I love you, but it is time for you to shut the hell up." She went over to Jessica and shook her hand. "Bobbi Morse, Mockingbird. My husband is an idiot."

"No. No, I'm sorry." Clint stepped forward. "All I meant was that people who've lost someone will also be angry at you. And that's wrong. I'm just having a big reaction to… to your face, and… sorry. We were Avengers together. You are an Avenger. Sorry."

"I get it," said Jessica. "Really. Thank you."

"Have a beer," said Logan, handing her one.

"So apart from Luke, Jess and Carol," said Peter, "is this everyone?"

"I was hoping for Maya," said Bobbi.

"I was told she was invited," said Clint, "but I don't think we'll be seeing her. Sorry. Again."

"Carol's with Stark," said Danny.

"I'm hopin' nobody's with anybody now," said Logan, "especially now Stark's out of the loop."

"Are we saying Norman Osborn might be better?" said Peter. "Because no."

"I think Osborn is another consequence of Stark, and I think his rise means the world needs the Avengers more than ever," said a new voice. The new Captain America, strode into the room. Peter saw that he'd cleaned himself up after the battle, both abrasions on his face and on his uniform. So, this Cap cared about what people thought of the costume. He couldn't decide if that was a good sign or not. "I know at the start of the Civil War, Cap put this team, most of you folks I see in front of me, together. He would have been proud of what you all did today. You won a war. I should know." He pulled off his mask and revealed a young face with old eyes, a mop of dark hair. "My name is James Barnes. I used to be Cap's partner, during World War II. He called me Bucky."

"You're the Winter Soldier," said Clint, not sounding entirely pleased at this revelation. "The Russians froze you after the war and decanted you, and you went after Cap and a bunch of our people. You going to keep *that* crap going?"

"Geez, you're on a roll today," said Bobbi.

"He fought well," said Clint, standing his ground, "but that… you don't just get to do all that and then put that costume on. That costume means something."

"And it's a Stark costume," said Logan. He seemed to realize people were puzzled as to how he knew. "Got a smell to it," he said.

"And that's a holster for a gun," said Peter.

Barnes looked around the room. It looked like he'd been prepared for this to be difficult, hence the tidying up. "Yeah, that's all true, but I was never in Stark's employ or his faction, and I broke the Russian control over me and made amends. And as to the gun… Cap, Steve, sometimes carried one during the war, when he had to. I'm only going to use it when I'm facing arms bearers. But it's part of my skill set, and if I'm going to do this, I need all the help I can get. I'm not planning on being Steve. But what you won't see is me doing anything that diminishes this," he pointed to the star on his chest. "I care about Steve's legacy as much as you do. I'm a different guy, but if I don't turn out to be a Captain America who honors what Steve established, then I'll stop. You have my word."

"Good enough," said Logan.

"All right," said Peter. He hoped it hadn't sounded as guarded as he felt.

Everyone looked at Clint. He raised his hands. "Hey," he said, "if you'd been frozen in time alongside Steve after the war—"

"Actually—" began Barnes.

"—okay, if you'd been frozen for as long as Steve was, I'd be saying you were the *only* person who could take over. So… okay." He lowered his hands. "But there's only one Cap."

"No argument here," said Barnes.

"So, you gonna tell them the plan?" said Logan. "You brought us here because you got one, right?"

Barnes looked around the room, sizing them all up. "You're Captain America's Avengers, by which I mean Steve's Avengers. So, if I'm Captain America now, this base is your home as much as mine. It has everything a base for our sort of people needs. And it's completely off the books. So, at least while Osborn is in charge, this is Avengers headquarters. Because that name is yours, not his."

"And, so, what, you think you're going to be leading us, wing-head?" said Clint, but there was now a little bit of a wink to it.

"I think we elect a Chair, same as you always did."

Peter felt the room had come around to what Barnes was saying, and, yeah, okay, he was on board with it, at least for now. Because was he ever going to need help once Osborn had the ability to send the resources of a whole nation after him. They might have, as a community, saved the world, but it felt like what awaited them in the aftermath of that was… more of the same spiraling crap they'd just been through. He just needed a win that felt like a win. One that he could keep in his heart when he was going through stuff like this, one where he could say "that's what we do." But still, in the meantime, under the circumstances, this sort of Avengers was as good as any other sort of Avengers. However, as he was about to voice his agreement, he realized that everyone was looking past him toward the entrance.

He turned and saw Jessica Jones, Luke and Carol stumbling into the room.

"They got the baby!" shouted Luke. "They got Danielle!"

288

FIFTY-THREE

JESSICA JONES

HORROR. EVERY parent's nightmare, come true. Desperate, clawing, helpless anger and fear. Fear like nothing she'd ever known, even more than with Killgrave.

But inside that fear, fury and certainty and speed. She was not going to let her child down by not doing everything she could at every damn moment. They searched everywhere in the Tower, they used all its systems—even as government employees and law enforcement began arriving, with Carol fronting for them—to see if anything had registered on the security cameras, but the records had been erased. Finally someone arrived saying there was a warrant out on Luke, and Carol had flown them out through a wall. They tried a few of the more obvious places for a Jarvis to go, such as his former lodgings, where, horribly, the real Jarvis had answered the door and had to deal with Jess grabbing him. He had been so compassionate but no damn use at all. Then, they stormed places they thought Skrulls might be trying to gather. But no, no, nothing. She was a detective, and she couldn't find a single lead to pursue. Finally, they'd decided that maybe their desperation, the fact that they couldn't be dispassionate about this case, that their professionalism had fled, was getting in the way. So, they came to find the others.

Now she walked back and forth, back and forth, as Luke told them what had happened. "He could be any shape or size," he was saying, "he could be anyone. Our baby could be dead, we…" And he stopped, his face completely still for a moment.

"She's alive," said Logan. "If he'd wanted to kill her, he could have done it there and then. He's taken her as a hostage to barter with, to get off this planet alive. You got somethin' of hers?" Jess had already thought of that. She'd brought with her Danielle's Sally Seahorse, that was woolen and smelled comfortingly, awfully, of her. Logan took it from her, very gently, and sniffed it deeply. Then he looked at her and just nodded. "He's mine," he said. And she had never felt so supported.

"Okay," said that new Cap, who, oh, was Bucky Barnes, she'd kind of already worked that out, she realized. "How about just for right now Luke is Chair in the field—"

"No," said Luke.

"I'll do it," said Carol.

"—okay, and I think I know who we should go see."

AS QUICKLY and stealthily as they could, they made their way over to the Baxter Building. Everyone, apart from Luke and herself, felt the need to go in costume, to be the Avengers again, off on a mission. And honestly that felt good. She'd pulled hers off in a second as soon as she'd found her own clothes back in the Tower, and she was never going to wear that thing again, but to have these people around them when they needed their friends the most… it was some small comfort against the horror that felt part of her now, that would only be healed by having Danielle back in her arms again.

Spider-Man, using a codeword, got them through the automated security. So that never changed, she noted distantly, even when Spidey and Reed were on different sides. Even given Reed's amazing attention to detail. That was a small, lovely thing that was… not important now. They found the top floors of the building almost entirely a shell, a forcefield of some kind for a roof and walls in which a few small tents had been pitched, a camping stove between them. The tents were, of course, blue and had a 4 logo on them. Beside the tents there were already a bathroom and a kitchen, walls without a roof, making the whole place look like a film set. And at the sink in the kitchen, in her robe, getting herself a glass of water, there, thank god, was Susan Storm. "Sue," shouted Jess as she ran in. "We need the Skrull detector!"

"Oh," said Sue, clearly thinking this was normal super hero crap going on, "Reed's asleep, how urgent is—"

"A Skrull has our baby," said Jess.

Sue turned and bellowed to the tents. "Everyone up!"

WITHIN MINUTES, Reed Richards, in his blue pajamas, was using his long fingers at eight keyboards at the same time, his eyes literally on stalks as he checked out multiple screens in what was already an impressive scratch-built computer lab. "The good news is," he said, "we're still at a Code Red alert all over the country. That means airports are closed, and the bridges, tunnels and ferries in and out of New York are secured by the military. Fliers are being tracked and intercepted, so it's a good thing you all came here on foot. That situation will remain the same as long as there's a possibility of any Skrulls being out there. There have been no Skrull sightings since the clear-up after the battle. I hesitate to make assumptions, but I think one avenue we could usefully pursue is the theory that this Skrull Jarvis is still in the city with no way out. I've hacked some surveillance satellites and routed my Skrull scanner through them, and I haven't yet seen any unidentified powered persons. We'll get an alert of any shape-shift within the boundaries of the city. I've made sure the authorities know to be on the lookout."

Jess still found that she needed to pace. "Okay. Great. That's the safety net in place. Now what do we do in terms of active pursuit?"

"Let's get out there," said Carol, "all of us in our own specialties, shake some trees."

o————o

THEY HAD maybe a day before Osborn got his dominoes in line and started getting in the way of super heroes going about their business, and they couldn't waste a single moment. So Jess was there when Jessica Drew and Danny Rand took out a Hydra cell who were experimenting on what turned out to be a captured Skrull—not theirs—in a Brooklyn cellar. They left Hydra tied up for the NYPD and took the Skrull. She helped Clint and Bobbi break into Advanced Idea Mechanics and give Reed access to run the search using their version of tech, which went weirdly counter to his. Nothing new was revealed. She went down into the sewers with the rest of the FF, who negotiated with the underground communities of small, big-eyed Moloids. There were, she knew all too well, little corners of hell all over this city, people who'd hide anyone, for the right price.

And then they actually, incredibly, found something.

In the Baxter Building infirmary, the Skrull who'd been held by Hydra woke from his coma and, grateful and reconciled to the idea of surrender, told them he knew of one other Skrull on the run who he'd spent a few hours with after fleeing Central Park. That one had said he had a "vital bargaining tool" stowed safely nearby. Jess agreed to be called into the room only after Reed and Sue had explained the situation. She hadn't had to do any acting to show the Skrull her desperation. The Skrull told them what new role his comrade was planning to pursue.

And so, in the early hours, she, Luke and Logan marched into the Classic, a midtown bar that kept odd hours and had a flying car in neon in its window, an old S.H.I.E.L.D. hangout.

It was full of S.H.I.E.L.D. officers, all of them still in uniform, the sort of party where they'd sent out invites saying, "last chance to wear the old gear." There were trays of shots on the bar, and most of these guys looked blind drunk, while still having those big space-age weapons on their many belts and pouches. Someone had written something rude about Osborn on one of the chalk menus. The barkeep stared at Logan in his full X-Men costume, as he marched in, and a jukebox played some old country song. Within thirty seconds the place was completely silent apart from the music. Everyone in the place turned to look at them.

Except one woman sitting at the bar. She still had her back to them.

"You!" roared Logan, pointing at her. "Get up!"

"Crap," said the small woman. She got off her stool and faced them. As her fellow agents started forward to get between her and the newcomers, she seemed to decide *the hell with it* and let her face shift into its Skrull form. The agents around her stepped back and drunkenly started drawing their weapons. "Please," she said, "I don't want this. I just want to live. I want to be one of you."

Jess' heart sank. Sure, you never knew where you were with a shape-shifter, in terms of gender or even apparent mass, but this did not feel like Jarvis to her.

"Guns down," said Luke. "We need to talk to her."

"Well excuse me, fugitive," said one of the S.H.I.E.L.D. guys, we'll take this from here. She's killed and duplicated one of ours—"

"No," the Skrull was shaking her head, "no, I made her up. I mean, this is the face of an actor. Who's still alive. I just thought I could hide in plain sight, I've... I was a Skrull comms operator, I still have some of their tech, their codes, I was going to use it as a bargaining tool, if I could get to someone of rank—"

Oh god. There it was. Jess stepped quickly forward to where Logan sniffed the air around the Skrull, shaking his head. "It's our baby," she said, "do you know any other Skrull in hiding, one with a human baby?"

"I... wait a sec, I can't think—"

Jess saw something in that expression, recognition. The sudden hope made her realize too late that this was a feint.

Suddenly, the Skrull transformed into some kind of propulsive bat/gazelle thing, a blur of fleshy wing and thrusting limbs. She leapt for the door.

Luke grabbed her on the way and threw her through a wall.

Within seconds, all three of them were on the Skrull in the parking lot. Luke grabbed her from where she had fallen, slamming her back into the ground and holding her there. "Jarvis!" he yelled. "You've seen him!"

Jess pushed past him to get hold of her. "Where did he go?!"

"I can't say!"

"I just want to find my baby! Do you understand?! You lead us to him, and we will let you go! Okay?! We will let you get away!"

"Okay…" She started to get to her feet and this time she looked like she meant it. "Okay. He's—"

The shot sent the Skrull's head flying back. She was dead by the time she hit the ground.

Jess leapt up to see the S.H.I.E.L.D. guys standing there, exchanging high fives. Logan had to grab her and hold her back. "My baby," was all she could say as Logan rushed them away, looking into Luke's equally traumatized face. "That's all we had. What else can we do?"

Luke suddenly looked away. "I… have an idea," he said.

ALL IT took was a couple of phone calls.

By five o'clock in the morning they were sitting in an office, staring at the person Jess had ridiculously thought it would be hard for them to get an appointment with.

"Do you have kids?" said Luke. It was hot in the office, too hot. It was five in the morning and there was no light coming through the only window and it was already too hot.

"Yes," said that calm, official voice. He wasn't allowing himself an ounce of smugness. He must have known how much on a knife edge this was, that any hint of triumphalism on his part might end this. This weasel was good with people.

"Then you might understand how we feel here," said Jess.

"Of course."

"So. We've done everything I can think of, and now we're coming to you for help."

"I know how big a deal this must be for you both."

"I'd appreciate it if you just… did this for us, just human being to human being," said Luke.

"But…" said Jess, because there had been absolutely no change in the expression of the man across the table from them, and now she had crossed over that little gap of hope herself, damn it, there was no going back. "We understand if you won't. We know you will probably want something from us in return."

"Or perhaps just from me," said Luke.

"Because I still don't plan on returning to the business."

"I wouldn't need you to," he said. "I'd settle for Mr. Cage leading this new team I'm putting together. Would you be willing to do that, Luke?"

"Yes," said Luke quickly. "You have my word."

"Then we have a deal." Norman Osborn smiled at the other two inhabitants of the room, the professional assassin Bullseye and the alien monster symbiote called Venom, who, last Jess had heard, was bonded, sticky black goo surrounding human flesh, to the career criminal Mac Gargan. The last time Jess had heard about what Mac was up to, he'd been trying to murder the nearest and dearest of a news photographer. "Gentlemen," said Osborn to the two horrors, "you may soon be working for this great man as Avengers, though not in your current guises, of course. Let's go find his missing child."

BY THE time they got to The Raft, the sun was over the horizon. Jess noted that Osborn's officers in the helicopter already wore jumpsuits bearing what must be the chosen logo of whatever new organization Osborn was creating. A hammer. Bullseye and Venom were with them. "All the captured Skrulls were sent here,"

said Osborn as they stepped from the helicopter onto the island. "We've only just begun processing them. We've identified a few from the higher ranks. We'll start with two of those."

"Why two?" said Luke, warily.

"Just the way I work," said Osborn.

They were taken to an "interview room" that looked more like a storage cellar. In it sat two Skrulls in power-draining collars. Both had stoic expressions on their faces. "They won't tell us anything," said the guard at the door.

Osborn sat down in front of one of them, quite calmly. "What's your name and rank? An honorable Skrull officer should be able to offer his captors that, surely?"

The Skrull didn't say a word.

"Okay," said Jess, "let me tell you why we're—"

"Mac," said Osborn.

Venom walked over, looked down at the other Skrull sitting in a chair, and in one move bit his head off. He flung it up into the air, caught it in his mouth and swallowed it. Green blood gushed everywhere from what remained of the corpse. Venom licked his lips with that enormous tongue of his.

Jess made eye contact with Luke, who was very visibly keeping himself under control. She grabbed his hand. They'd known that this was going to be. They were complicit in this now. And they would allow themselves to be. They'd learn from it. If it meant getting Danielle back.

"There's a Skrull who was posing as Jarvis," said Osborn. "Where is he?"

"We... we don't all know each other."

Osborn paused for a moment, obviously pleased that the Skrull was talking now. "We have seventy-four more Skrulls of similar rank in custody. Tell us something of value or we'll get the next two in here."

The Skrull paused for a long moment. There might, Jess thought, be something in their background that made the idea of being *eaten*, of their ever-changing bodies being consumed and changed against their will into part of another being, especially repugnant. She thought it was entirely possible Osborn had worked that out too. "There was... there was a meeting place," it said finally, "where the advance team met and planned their operations."

"Where?" said she and Luke together.

Osborn smiled.

JESS AND Luke hadn't brought their phones along with them on this treacherous journey. They had made sure there had been nothing on them that might give away the location of their friends. Now they had a location and some surveillance intel, Jess, in her hotel room, still pacing, felt incredibly tempted to give this to the others, to have people she trusted follow this up. But no, no, this was the play. Luke was still asleep, or the half-sleep both of them were getting, the result of sheer exhaustion. She'd been beside him up to a minute ago, but now she had got up to stare out into the night. She checked the phone Osborn had given her, to make sure there wasn't some new message from him. Nothing.

The warehouse the Skrull had identified as the meeting place turned out to be an old base of the criminal known as the Owl. Osborn had done well in setting up entirely covert eyes on the place, using some of the super-powered goons at his disposal. He'd found out, from the other Skrulls he'd "interviewed," that there was a powerful teleportation device at that place: not just the short-range kind that they'd seen Skrulls use to hop around the country, but one that could take them back to, well, whatever extra-solar planet they were using for a base now they didn't have a homeworld, or some ship way out of Earth orbit.

Hearing that scared the crap out of Jess and Luke, but Osborn clarified that this was good news because it took one Skrull to operate the device while the other made the jump. That meant there was a chance that "Jarvis" kept returning to the warehouse, or at least kept observing it, in case he saw another of his people arrive there. Now there was round-the-clock invisible surveillance in place. It was such a tiny chance, but—

Suddenly, the phone lit up with an alert of an incoming call. Jess yelled, nearly dropped it, fumbled it, but didn't. "It's on," Osborn said. "You want in?"

○———————○

WHICH WAS how Jess and Luke came to be sitting in the shadows inside a warehouse in Queens in the early hours of the morning as a door slowly creaked open.

Silhouetted against the night stood a small figure.

He was carrying something.

They'd talked about how this would go. They had laid down the law to Osborn. He had agreed to everything, way too easily. He had people in place to stop the Skrull if he ran. They waited until he'd closed the door behind him. Then Jess switched on the light.

There was "Jarvis," a bundle in his arms. He looked more resigned than shocked to see them.

"Give me the baby," said Luke, getting to his feet.

Jessica wanted to run over there and grab for it, but they'd agreed they didn't want to scare him, didn't want to make him run, not with Osborn's collateral-damage-happy goons waiting outside. "She is entirely unharmed, I promise you," said the Skrull, very gently. "She's sleeping."

"Why did you take her?" asked Jess.

"Madam, I did not. You left her with me, and when I had to leave the Tower, with no indication of when it would next be occupied, I hardly felt I could leave—"

Jess swore at him. "You could have dropped her with any of our people and still got away. You wanted a hostage."

"Jarvis" sighed. "Indeed. For all the good it has done me. I am, you see, having something of a crisis of faith. I don't like to talk about such things, obviously, but it seems to me that God is... dead. To have this small person to take care of, someone who

298

should be my enemy... I have held far too closely to the personality of this human I am impersonating. To be him, to be as kind as him... it has been an enormous comfort—"

"Stop talking and give her to me," said Luke.

"I'm very much afraid that if I do that, you'll kill me."

"I will if you don't. But... on my honor, if you make this right, I won't. Neither will Jess. We're not playing word games here."

"Right," said Jess.

"We'll take our baby and walk out of here. You can wait until another Skrull shows up, beam yourself up, or just walk away, whatever you need to do."

"You... you cannot have come here alone."

"That's true," said Jess, "but those working with us have made the same promise. If you stay here alone, they will leave. If you walk out of here alone, you will be allowed to keep walking." She did not believe Osborn would keep to these agreements, not for one moment, but she had heard those words from him, and she was being as honest as she could be.

"I do believe you are telling the truth. But surely you must realize you have been lied to?"

"It's entirely possible," said Luke. "But this is all we got."

The Skrull looked desperate. "If his forces are here... all right, you must tell Osborn to release the prisoners! Yes! If he releases my comrades, you get the baby. That is my decision! We'll leave. All of us. We shall not trouble you again. My friends are in there, being tortured!"

Luke took a single step toward him. "This ain't a swap meet. You know none of that's gonna happen. Give me the baby."

"My people have been destroyed!"

"That," said Jess, joining Luke, "has nothing to do with that little girl."

"We just want our kid," said Luke.

The Skrull closed his eyes. He looked desperately sad. "I came to understand this man. So deeply. He just wanted everything to be right. I gather he has now returned to a life of making sure that it is so. I wish I might join him in that. But… it seems that is not to be." He took a deep breath and handed Luke the bundle.

Very slowly, Luke took it and unwrapped the blanket.

Jess was seized by a fear so deep. Had she imagined she'd seen the face of her child move, heard the smallest of breaths?

Danielle opened her eyes, looking grumpily at them.

"She's really okay?" said Luke, kissing Danielle's head at the same moment Jess did. His eyes and voice were full of tears.

"Please, sir," said the Skrull, "I'm not a monster. I regret that I made a decision in the moment which in retrospect was—"

A single bullet hole appeared in the middle of his forehead and he collapsed to the ground, dead.

Luke and Jess turned to the window, which now featured a single perfect bullet hole.

The mark of Bullseye.

Luke closed his eyes. "Osborn didn't keep his word," he said. "Of course he didn't."

"Good," said Jess, taking Danielle from him and holding her to her body, feeling her breathing. "That'll make the next part so much easier."

THEY HAD brunch with Osborn next morning at Avengers Tower. He inquired, over his pastries, as to Danielle's health. Jess, having hardly managed to let go of her since they'd been reunited, said the doctor Osborn provided had given her a clean bill of health. The Skrull had taken good care of her—fussily good care, even.

Osborn raised an eyebrow at that little detail. Venom and Bullseye were at the meeting too, eating raw meat and children's cereal respectively. Bullseye kept glancing over to them, grinning, as if he expected their thanks or annoyance. They'd given him nothing in the way of either.

"So," began Osborn after the third cup of coffee, "let's get into the detail of you leading my new team of Avengers. Mac here is going to be the new Spider-Man, Bullseye will be the new Hawkeye.

We have various other reassuring legacy costumes set up, but I'm looking for more original heroes who might want to come onside alongside the Sentry and Marvel Boy. What are your thoughts?"

"Well," said Luke, "first I want to show you this." He reached into the bag he'd brought to the meeting and pulled out what looked like an ordinary crowbar. "Check it out. This is something I took off the Wrecker. It's made of the same stuff as Thor's hammer, infused with the power of Odin."

"That could indeed be useful," said Osborn.

"It's got powers?" said Bullseye, through a mouthful of sugared shapes.

"Oh yeah," said Luke, and smashed in the side of the assassin's jaw with it.

Then he threw the crowbar to Jess who leapt at Venom, the baby still in her arms.

Before he could even begin to react, one blow from the magic crowbar flattened the alien symbiote into a puddle that splattered back into its seat, twitching.

Luke and Jess turned to face Osborn. Bullseye had fallen from his chair, screaming.

"Is... is this an assassination attempt?!" yelled Osborn. "A coup?! How far do you think you'll get?! So much for your word of honor!"

"Oh, it still holds," said Luke, "even if you broke *your* promise to *us*. That little demonstration with the crowbar was just my reaction to the idea that *these* two," he gestured to Bullseye and Venom, "could ever be Avengers. I'll still lead a team of Avengers for you. As promised. But if I do, they'll damn well be super heroes. Who don't kill. Who always try to do the right thing. And who, when they don't do that, like when we let you make us complicit in the death of that Skrull, like when any of us act like Stark acted... when they don't act like heroes, they know it. They own it, and they try to do better. Do you want that? Because you can still have it. If that's what you really want."

Osborn looked long and hard at them for a moment, as if he

was considering whether he was up for the long process of wearing Luke down, tricking him, compromising him. Or if that process would ever actually work on Luke Cage. "You're under arrest," he said finally.

"Get used to those words," said Jessica. "You'll be hearing them again. Avengers Assemble."

And Carol Danvers burst through the roof, grabbed them and they were out of there, Danielle in hand, up, up into the sky.

And away.

EPILOGUE ONE

ABIGAIL BRAND

BRAND SAT in a cocktail bar in Tahiti, across the table from Maria Hill. Neither of them had taken up parallel offers to work in the new administration. Both were considering their options. Which very much included, Brand felt, the option to never again be put in a position where it was just her looking out for planet-wide security threats. They had messaged each other and arranged to meet here. But now that they'd actually got here, they'd just sat in silence. Brand's cocktail was a "Great Responsibility," the ingredients of which suggested that it had been named somewhat wryly. Hill had carried over an "Innocent Bystanders." That looked equally sarcastic. Neither cocktail had anything green in it.

Now they both let out a single, long, relieved breath.

"So," said Brand finally, "what's with the t-shirt?"

EPILOGUE TWO

ALICE CREASY

SO MANY of Alice Creasy's friends were dead. The world death toll, of ordinary human beings, was somewhere close to twenty million, and it was quickly rising. Many of those who'd been badly injured by technology doctors didn't understand… well, a lot of them weren't going to make it. And sure, some of Alice's friends online were saying the numbers were inflated, that history was being rewritten by the winning side, that of course there would be accidental casualties in war… but she found herself not connecting with those guys so much now. Because she'd walked around what was left of New York, as soon as she'd had the chance, and it had turned out she knew so many people who'd lost someone. Some of their stories too, were stories of actual fascist cruelty by the Skrulls, and… she kind of hoped nobody in her work life would remember that she'd started to talk about the possibility that what the Skrulls had been saying was true. Because that was far as she'd taken that, right? She'd gone along to see for herself on that day with the placards, and had merely entertained the possibility, and had just been asking questions. A lot of people had been in that same situation.

And yet, there was Norman Osborn on TV, in his new power armor, declaring himself the Iron Patriot, and announcing his new team of Avengers in front of the Stars and Stripes, and behind him, sure, there had been some of the heroes who'd fought the Skrulls, and who therefore, she now grudgingly admitted, might have been on the right side, but who were these other guys? It was like they were all being told to skip over the fact that some of these Avengers were meant to be the people they'd been before, but clearly… weren't? She quickly agreed with her friends online that no, nothing had been learned, here was all that fascist super-powered crap again, only more so. *This* time they were *definitely* lying to them.

Now here she was, standing on the roof of the apartment block where she was sneaking some floor space, her new home in the city, because rents had dropped, just a little, because, you know, nobody wanted to live here anymore, and here was, incredibly, Spider-Man, squatting in that creepy way of his on one of the air-con stacks, doing something with her cat, and looking at her like she'd just caught him out when she'd stepped out of the door. "Oh," he said. "Hi."

"What are you doing to my cat?"

"He… is it a he? He just looked like he might be trapped, and I was swinging by, and… and it looks like he didn't actually need my help." Because the cat had indeed just nonchalantly leapt down and was wandering off.

Alice folded her arms. "I'm surprised you're not off silencing student protests, with the rest of the Avengers."

Spider-Man's body slumped. "Those guys," he said, "are *not* the Avengers. And that's not me. I mean, I'm not that Spider-Man. I am *a* Spider-Man. *The* Spider-Man. The original! He is not. I'm with the real Avengers. He isn't. Though those guys say they're the real Avengers and have official clearance and… Did I just actually make any of that any clearer?"

"So…" Alice had heard something about this, that there was still a team of Avengers who'd been forced into hiding, like during the Civil War. "You're one of the rebel guys? The Spider-Man on that team is a different guy?"

"Exactly. It's someone pretending to be me. There, that's it in one. I should have said that before."

"Well, that's huge."

"Yeah, it is! Tell everybody! Please!"

"I heard you rebel guys had some sort of secret memorial ceremony for the Wasp? And then those Osborn's Avengers came and—"

"Used it as a chance to try to arrest us, yeah." Spider-Man rubbed the back of his neck. "Which was a shame, because even Tony Stark had come along, you know? He said he'd come to start listening. That he was willing to be *led*. Can you imagine?"

"No!"

"Oh, and Doctor Strange was there. He'd only just fought his way out of some other dimension the Skrulls had trapped him in, back when this all started. As soon as he got the goo off him, he was devastated. He felt personally responsible. Like a lot of us do."

"I'll bet. And some of you really were responsible."

"Yeah." Spider-Man sounded like he meant it. "Me, for a start."

"Not you!"

"That's kind of you, but let me have my thing, okay?"

Alice found herself smiling at his voice. "I think I like you rebel guys better than I did the real Avengers back in the day."

"But… if we win, we won't be the rebels anymore, and then—"

"Deal with it, dude. Human nature. So, what happened with Osborn's Avengers attacking you?"

"Henry Pym had just finished speaking… and not all of us were into the idea of him getting to do that—"

"Yeah, I wouldn't have been."

"Well, me neither, honestly, but… I'm probably wrong about that. He's trying to do better, you know? He's walking the walk. He'd just said that the Skrulls had probably played him as a better human being than he actually had been."

306   That struck a chord with Alice, that way the Skrulls had

seemed to spotlight a goodness about humanity that was surely genuinely present in humanity somewhere, but that you never seemed to see much of, ever. "So, he's switched sides?"

"There aren't any sides, really. Not anymore. Just, you know, like always, good and evil." Spider-Man straightened up. "You know what? No matter where we are right now, to get back to knowing who the good folk are, to me that's kind of… a win that feels like a win?" He aimed at a nearby building with his wrist, fired off one of those webs of his, and was suddenly swinging away.

"Take care," he shouted, "we'll be around if you need us."

Alice Creasy watched him go until he was lost in the distance, a speck in the tall buildings of New York as it was being rebuilt. And she thought about what he'd said for quite a while.

THE END

ABOUT THE AUTHOR

PAUL CORNELL has written episodes of *Elementary*, *Doctor Who* ('Father's Day' and 'Human Nature'), *Primeval*, *Robin Hood* and many other TV series, including his own children's show, *Wavelength*. He's worked for every major comics company, including his creator-owned series *I Walk With Monsters* for The Vault, *The Modern Frankenstein* for Magma, *Saucer Country* for Vertigo and *This Damned Band* for Dark Horse, and runs for Marvel and DC on *Batman and Robin*, *Wolverine* and *Young Avengers*. He's the writer of the Lychford rural fantasy novellas from Tor.com Publishing. He's won the BSFA Award for his short fiction, an Eagle Award for his comics, a Hugo Award for his podcast and shares in a Writer's Guild Award for his *Doctor Who*. He's the co-host of Hammer House of Podcast. His latest book is the SF novella *Rosebud*, his latest graphic novel is *The Witches of World War II* for TKO and his latest comic series is *Con and On* for Ahoy.

For more fantastic fiction, author events,
exclusive excerpts, competitions, limited editions and more

VISIT OUR WEBSITE
titanbooks.com

LIKE US ON FACEBOOK
facebook.com/titanbooks

FOLLOW US ON TWITTER AND INSTAGRAM
@TitanBooks

EMAIL US
readerfeedback@titanemail.com

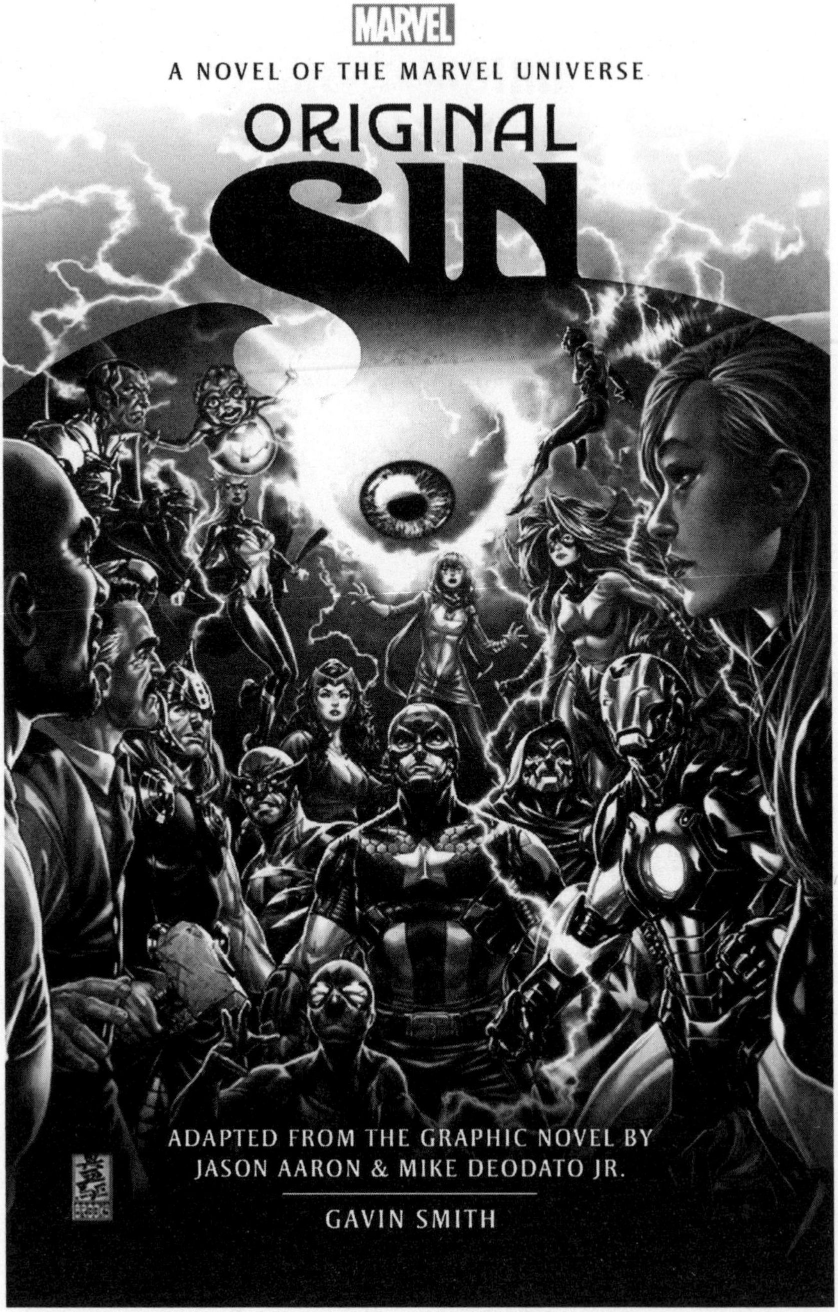
MARVEL
A NOVEL OF THE MARVEL UNIVERSE
ORIGINAL
SIN
ADAPTED FROM THE GRAPHIC NOVEL BY
JASON AARON & MIKE DEODATO JR.
GAVIN SMITH

ORIGINAL SIN

GAVIN G. SMITH

Uatu the Watcher, a mysterious being who observes mankind from the Moon, is dead. Nick Fury leads a cosmos-spanning investigation into the murder, forging unlikely alliances and sending Marvel's mightiest heroes to the farthest corners of the universe.

To uncover the truth, Doctor Strange and the Punisher must cross deadly dimensions, the Guardians of the Galaxy, Moon Knight and the Winter Soldier head into deep space, and Emma Frost, Ant-Man and Black Panther journey to the center of the Earth. All the while, Unseen forces gather, and just when the Avengers think they've cornered their murderer, everything explodes—unleashing the Marvel Universe's greatest secrets and rocking the heroes to their core!

In this novelization of the epic storyline by Jason Aaron and Mike Deodato Jr., truths will come tumbling into the light and the original sins of our heroes will be exposed for all to see.

MARVEL

A NOVEL OF THE MARVEL UNIVERSE

GUARDIANS OF THE GALAXY

ANNIHILATION:
CONQUEST

BRENDAN DENEEN

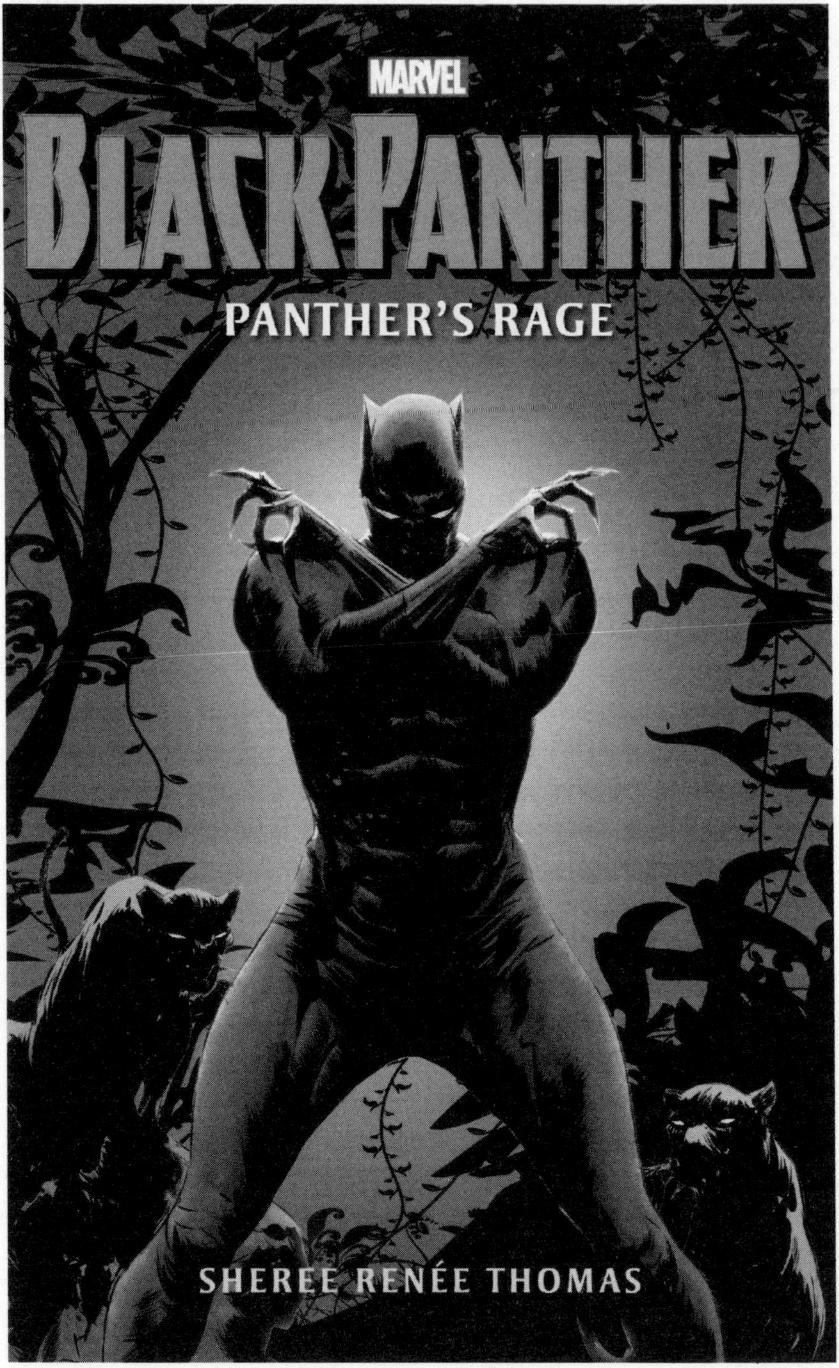
MARVEL
BLACK PANTHER
PANTHER'S RAGE
SHEREE RENÉE THOMAS

MARVEL
A NOVEL OF THE MARVEL UNIVERSE
CIVIL WAR
MICHAEL TURNER
STUART MOORE

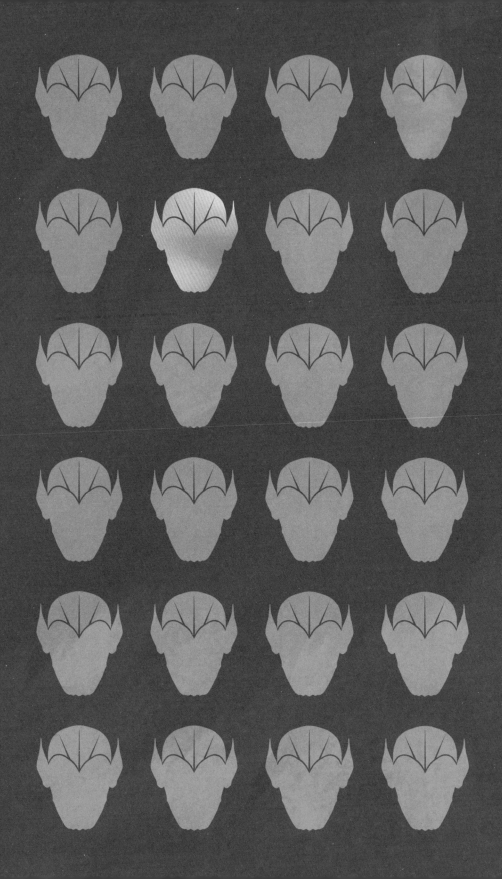